WHAT I NEVER TOLD YOU

ALSO BY DAWN GOODWIN

The Accident
The Pupil
Best Friends Forever
The Pact

WHAT I NEVER TOLD YOU

Dawn Goodwin

An Aries Book

First published in the UK in 2021 by Head of Zeus Ltd
This paperback edition first published in the UK in 2022 by Head of Zeus Ltd,
a part of Bloomsbury Publishing Plc

9 7 5 3 1 2 4 6 8

A CIP catalogue record for this book is available
from the British Library.

ISBN (PB): 9781800246171
ISBN (E): 9781800242180

Typeset by Siliconchips Services Ltd UK

Printed and bound in Great Britain by
CPI Group (UK) Ltd, Croydon CR0 4YY

Head of Zeus
5–8 Hardwick Street
London
EC1R 4RG

www.headofzeus.com

For my family

Prologue

"*Tell your mother I saved your life.*"

The words are like hailstones. Cold. Hard. Biting.

Hands shove against a zipped-up coat, quick as a flash. Feet slide in the dirt and sand, the soles of the worn trainers, smoothed by time, providing no traction.

Eyes widen as gravity pulls and awareness of what is happening taps on their shoulders.

Hands reach out again to grab onto something, anything. The coat, the zip, a sleeve. But the hands find only air. The coat is already out of reach, the body inside pulling it backwards over the cliff edge, gravity doing what it does best.

Mouths gape, but no sounds escape. Eyes plead. Seconds feel like hours.

Just the sounds of the sea far below and the raucous calling of the seagulls, like hysterical laughter. Then a guttural scream cuts through the bird call, raw and coarse, rising in urgency from below, followed by a thump, weighted, nauseating.

Silence.

There's no need to lean over to see what is painfully true. A twisted shape on the rocks below. Limbs at unnatural angles. A spreading pool of darkness, like spilled wine. Then the waves washing it clean, pulling at the splayed fingers, coaxing into the depths.

Two thin drag marks remain in the dirt where those feet lost their battle for grip.

A newer trainer, branded, the latest design, smooths over the dirt before walking away.

Nothing to see here.

I

NOW

The house was winking at her.

She knew it was just the sun casting a shadow over the glass, but even so, those windows had always looked like heavily lidded eyes to her. Below them a solid wooden door like a mouth, ready to breathe her in.

Helen Whitmore stood at the end of the gravel driveway and stared at the house. She shuddered, even though this had been her home for most of her life. The root of many an urban legend in the village, causing small children to shiver as they walked past the end of the driveway, their eyes looking anywhere but at the house.

Tall tales whispered into little ears.

This eccentric, unusually tall house, unimaginatively named "Cliffside", was Helen's childhood home and before her, that of her mother, grandmother and great-grandmother. Cliffside had belonged to the women in her family for generations, each one compelled to return to it with their husbands and raise their children there. Every generation that had lived there had added on another bit – an extension here, another floor there – until it stood in the present day, lopsided and gangly, but still with those eyes of glass, all seeing and yet revealing nothing. That gaping mouth.

It had always felt like a living, breathing entity. Helen had never wanted to come back here, but it had a way of pulling at you, tugging until you succumbed. The longer you spent here, the more you could feel its malevolence creeping into your bloodstream.

Nothing good had ever happened to her here. And yet, she couldn't pull herself away. It was her home. As simple and as complicated as that.

She reached into the letterbox by the gate post and grabbed the handful of envelopes inside, picked up the shopping bags and headed up the gravel driveway, feet crunching, teeth grinding.

Arthur, the caretaker of the property, waved at her from where he was pruning the roses along the driveway, his grey hair tucked into a flat cap against the breeze, his gnarled hands in thick gardening gloves. Helen couldn't fathom how old he was, but he had worked for her family for as long as she could remember, all the way back to when her parents had employed him. She waved back, swapping the bags of shopping into her other hand, but feeling like the weight of returning home from work was straining her shoulders more.

Helen owned a small, independent bookshop in Hamblemere, a little village on the Cornish coast not far from the more popular tourist area of Padstow. The house was situated on the cliff above the sea, as though it was looking down in judgement on the vast expanse of agitated water. In return, the waves inched closer to the cliff walls with every passing year, the sea reminding the house that it was there and that it could swallow it whole at any point. The coastal path weaved along the far edge of the property, acting as an ineffective mediator.

The bookshop was a picturesque fifteen-minute walk from the house. Located in the village square, it was tucked between a deli that smelled strongly of ripe Stilton cheese on a warm day and a bakery selling loaves of sourdough and goat's cheese paninis. It was a pretty village, with brightly coloured hanging baskets adorning shop fronts, cobblestoned streets and not a McDonalds as far as the eye could see, which you would think would mean the shop was guaranteed footfall, but the village was slowly being suffocated by the bigger towns around it with their superstores and branded retailers. Once an area full of huge homes owned by the wealthy, the village and its surrounds were now characterised predominantly by holiday homes for those who could afford such luxury, summer rentals, and pensioners seeking a quieter way of life and a library card. Pastel-coloured bungalows with ramps and stair lifts juxtaposed with modern behemoths of glass and sharp edges.

As a result, the bookshop was always teetering on the edge of insolvency, but that didn't matter to Helen. It had never been about earning money. She loved books. Reading them, writing them, inhaling them. She always had. It had been the one constant she could fully engage with when she was younger and it became her saving grace as a teenager. A way to shut everything out with the turn of a page or the click and clack of her typewriter. It was still her therapy now, even as a married woman with a daughter, two stepchildren, a husband of seven years and a geriatric rescue dog.

So when the bookshop was in the midst of one of its usual downturns, she supplemented the shop's coffers with the meagre income generated from renting the tiny flat above the shop and the even more meagre royalties from the books she wrote under a pseudonym.

At the end of the day, she would lock up the shop and head home, back to the weirdly gothic house at the top of the hill overlooking the Cornish sea, that wild, rugged narrator of many a tale of stolen treasure and scandalous adventures.

The keeper of many secrets.

She opened the heavy, wooden front door, her hands hurting from the handles of the shopping bags. Clive, her ageing British bulldog, shuffled over to greet her, his eyes alight and his bum dancing. Some days she took him with her to work where he loved to chat to the customers, greeting them eagerly with enthusiastic wiggles of his ample bottom, his presence as much a part of the fabric of the village now as the bookshop was, but today it had been drizzling when she left and he wasn't one for outdoor excursions in inclement weather. He had looked at her witheringly when she'd brought out his lead this morning, before sloping back to bed without a second glance.

Helen headed straight for the kitchen and dumped the heavy bags on the kitchen table. A vase of freshly cut roses on the table caught her eye and she smiled. Arthur was the only man to bring her flowers these days.

She unpacked the shopping, most of it requests from

the family. The sourdough that her husband liked from the bakery and some of his favourite cheese from the deli; her stepson's protein powder as he pursued bigger muscles with the free weights he'd stashed in the garage; her stepdaughter's tampons. The only thing she had bought for herself was a packet of extremely indulgent chocolate biscuits from the little M&S around the corner from the bookshop.

She hummed as she filled the kettle and sat at the table while it boiled, absently flicking through the mail. Her phone vibrated next to her and she smiled as she read a text from her friend Julie, thanking her for the birthday flowers. Thank goodness for online reminders and deliveries. She read through a letter from the local business association about a meeting to discuss the new retail park being constructed on the outskirts of the village. She made a mental note to put the date in her diary. She may not voice many opinions at such meetings, but it was important that her face was seen. The gas bill was an unnecessary reminder that this ageing house consumed energy greedily and that perhaps it was time to replace the noisy boiler in the basement.

At the bottom of the pile of post was a white envelope, addressed simply to *HELEN*, her name handwritten in blue capital letters. No address or stamp. She opened it while still humming the old Carpenters song that had been stuck in her head all day. She expected an invitation to a school function or a celebration of some sort. Her husband, Hugh, was now in the age bracket where such invitations were not to weddings and christenings any longer. Instead, they were thinly disguised attempts to make divorce and retirement parties look like joyous achievements rather than the depressing signposts of failure they actually were.

The kettle clicked off loudly.

The hum died in her throat.

Inside the envelope was a Polaroid photograph.

Two girls, smiling into the camera.

One of those girls was Helen.

The other was dead.

2

THEN

"Have you seen the new girl?" Eloise says as she sits down next to me in the canteen. "Oh my god, I wouldn't be caught dead in those shoes."

The first day back at school is dragging on, but at least I'm not at home. I've had enough of my own company almost as much as listening to the constant bickering through the walls. There is only so much catalogue clothes shopping you can do before even spending money gets tedious.

I look over to where the new girl is standing, tray in hand, eyes wide.

"And the hair is a disaster." Eloise is not making any effort to keep her voice down. "No one wears low ponytails. Although with hair like that, what else can she do, I suppose. Oh! Hi, Brian. Don't think I haven't noticed you checking me out all day." Mouth pouting, eyelashes fluttering. I look away.

"Ah, El, I can't take my eyes off you," Brian Firth says as he saunters past. He jerks his fringe from his eyes like he has a twitch. Eloise giggles. I stir the plastic spoon through my yoghurt pot in slow, aimless circles.

"He is *so* into you, El," Steph says, leaning forward excitedly. The end of her long plait drops into her own yoghurt.

"Steph, are you going to paint with that hair later or just use your fingers? Maybe Mummy will put it on the fridge for you," I say, nodding at her hair.

She blushes, puts the end of her hair in her mouth and sucks on it. I look away, disgusted, and she blushes an even deeper shade.

"And who starts at a new school at the beginning of their last year anyway? Talk about making it hard for yourself," El continues. "Unless she's super bright or something. Although I can't imagine she is."

"I heard she lives on the farm on the outskirts of the village. You know, that one just past your house, Hels," Emily says. "It looks like a right dump."

I shrug. "I didn't see her around over the summer."

"If that's so, how can they afford to send her here?" Eloise's nose is elevated, making her neck look scrawny, her head like a lollipop on a stick. "Probably one of those scholarship kids."

Eloise has a point. Seahaven School is elitist. Those that come here have bankers and lawyers and landed gentry for parents. The air is pungent with old money and entitlement. Many of the kids are dropped at school each day either by the hired help or by surgically enhanced mothers in pristine walking boots and shoulder pads, driving Range Rovers that never see a dirt road unless it's the long, sweeping driveway up to their large houses. Even the bus that ferries around some of the more local kids like me is more fitting for a professional sports team than transporting a bunch of spoilt kids a few miles to school. Miles that could easily be walked.

I've attended the school since I was four years old, along with Eloise. Steph and Emily recently wormed their way into our social group, but we made it suitably hard for them. Nothing comes easy, certainly not our attention. You must earn your place. We are The Originals. The Queen Bees of our year. Eloise in particular works hard to maintain our reputation as such.

I look over at the new girl again. She has found a seat at an empty table and is reading a book while absent-mindedly eating fish fingers. I can't make out what book it is, but she's engrossed – or pretending to be.

I push my tray away. "Maybe standards at Seahaven are slipping."

"I bloody hope not! My father will be furious. He is on the board of governors, after all. I should ask him – if I see him this week," Steph says indignantly.

"She's reading a book." Emily is horrified at the idea.

"It's ok to read books, Em. It might actually help you pass your exams," I say. "You do know how to read, don't you? I mean books without pictures?"

Eloise laughs loudly. I turn away from the hurt look that passes over Emily's face.

"Come on, let's go," Eloise says abruptly and glides to her feet.

We follow like sheep, discarding our trays and trailing after our leader. Instead of taking the direct route from the canteen, she weaves towards the back, past the table where the new girl is sitting. Brian's group is chatting loudly at the next table over. As we approach, the new girl keeps her eyes firmly on the page in front of her. I see the flash of annoyance on El's face at being ignored, before she says loudly, "Hels, something stinks around here." She sniffs the air. "Can you smell that?"

"Yeah, I can," I say, wrinkling my nose.

"Ugh, smells like fish." El looks pointedly at the new girl, sniffs again and says, "Yes, definitely fishy."

The girl keeps her eyes low, but her skin flushes a darker shade.

"Ugh, disgusting!" Emily says, while Steph holds her nose dramatically.

"Brian, how can you stand sitting so close to *it*?" El says, fluttering her fake eyelashes.

He whistles at her and El sashays away with a flick of a smile over her shoulder.

When I look back as we leave the canteen, the girl is rigid, expressionless, still staring into her book, but I can guarantee she isn't seeing the words on the page anymore.

3

NOW

Helen hated this room. The dark wood panelling, dim lighting and weighty maroon velvet curtains made it feel heavy and stifling. Hugh enjoyed the oppressive opulence of it, but she had always disliked it. It might appeal to Hugh's delusions of grandeur, but reminded Helen of being banished from her parents' endless dinner parties as a child, the air pungent with cigarette smoke and brandy fumes. Hugh insisted that they eat all their family meals here in the dining room, even though the long oak table in the kitchen, with its knobbled and dented wood, was much more of a welcoming, warming place to eat in Helen's opinion.

Not that there was that much sharing going on.

Tonight she sat in this room, taking her usual place at one head of the table, her husband at the other, looking at the faces around her.

Her family.

She found herself wondering what they actually thought

of her, once the obligations of blood and marriage were stripped away.

Whether they actually liked her.

And did she like them?

These were the kinds of thoughts that had been twisting around her brain since she had opened that envelope. A Pandora's box of paranoia and anxiety.

She tracked a green bean through the gravy on her plate and looked at each of them in turn, their heads bowed to their plates, their mouths chewing silently. These were the people who should know her best. Her daughter, her stepchildren, her husband. But of course they only knew what she had chosen to let them see.

And Helen was not a huge fan of the truth.

She sipped at a glass of water, cold against her teeth.

Do we ever really know what people think of us, she wondered? Do we want to? Not the platitudes of *you're so lovely* after they've opened your thoughtful gift or *your hair looks amazing* as you arrive at the party, the words said loud enough to be heard by those in close proximity and carrying enough weight to make the person vocalising them feel self-righteously proud of themselves in that moment, while on the inside they are judging you, hating you.

What about what they actually think of you when they spy you walk past the coffee shop window as they sip on a skinny latte, their eyes narrowed as they track your footsteps, inwardly smirking when you trip over that loose paving stone? Or when you bump into them in the supermarket and their eyes dip towards your trolley, taking in the organic vegetables, thick-cut fillet steaks and bottle of Tanqueray that they wish they could afford? When they say *you look amazing in those jeans* while running their eyes over the roll of fat bulging over your waistband, inwardly salivating at any visible sign of your weaknesses?

It's all based on their perception of your reality. Assumptions about your level of happiness, self-image, financial standing. But they don't let you see that. They just quietly judge, seething inside while smiling at you with tight lips. And you do your best to keep up appearances and play to your audience.

But being thin, pretty or rich won't make you happy – and the only friend you can really count on is yourself. In Helen's experience anyway.

She pushed the food around her plate half-heartedly, wondering what her family would say if they were allowed to be honest about her, what things they were quietly seething over as they sat around the table, pretending to play happy families.

"Helen, could you pass the gravy jug please?" Hugh said into the silence.

Hugh was the most mild-mannered man Helen had ever meet. Beloved history teacher by day and ancestry investigator by night, everyone who knew Hugh described him as *nice* and *lovely*. And that was true.

What they didn't see was that he was also inconsiderate, lazy and occasionally extremely patronising. There, how's that for honesty?

He could've asked one of the children sitting closer to him to pass the bloody gravy. Or could've got up himself.

Helen stood up and walked around to his end of the table to pass him the porcelain gravy jug, barely resisting the childish urge to snatch it back as he reached for it.

She returned to her seat and pulled in the heavy chair. The chair legs scraped, loud in the leaden room.

"Helen, what did you used to be like?"

At fourteen years old, Lydia was petite with blonde hair that would likely darken into mousey brown and blue eyes that always seemed to be cast down to the floor. She was Hugh's daughter from his previous marriage to Francesca, a rotund HR executive who discovered more than just her love of almond milk when she signed up with personal trainer Todd. She left Hugh and ran away to Brighton with Todd to run a vegan café. Rumour had it she'd never looked or felt so good in her life, but the kids usually came home from their visits to Brighton begging for bacon sandwiches.

Helen paused, her fork hovering in front of her lips, chicken drooping from the end.

"When?" she replied.

"When you were our age?" Lydia said.

White envelopes and Polaroid snaps of moments in time flashed into her head once more. The heavy wooden panels took a step closer into the room.

Matt snorted in between shovelling food like he hadn't eaten in weeks. Only a teenage boy could eat with such gluttony, as though his very survival depended on him getting through his meal as quickly as possible. "She can't remember that far back," he sneered without humour.

Matt was Lydia's brother. Nineteen, boy-band handsome, with dark hair that reached down to the chip on his shoulder. He had inherited Francesca's Italian genes. Lydia was more like her father – pale, uninteresting.

Helen glared at the top of Matt's head. Sometimes her stepson could be a right prick.

Actually, most of the time. Who was she kidding?

Helen put down her fork and looked across at Lydia as she waited patiently for an answer. "What do you think I was like?"

Lydia shrugged. "I've heard you were a bit wild." Her voice was timid. Helen couldn't recall ever hearing her raise it above a whisper. Even when she was squabbling with her brother, it was done on mute. Helen often found herself asking Lydia to repeat things, knowing she had spoken but not registering what she had said. She was white noise. Helen wished she would burst out with a stream of screamed expletives, just so that she knew there was a personality in there somewhere. Lydia could be beautiful one day, but as a fourteen-year-old she was still very much an awkward child, her head full of Disney naivety and unicorns.

"Heard from who?"

Matt's knife scraped across the plate, the noise making Helen's teeth clench.

Lydia didn't answer. Her fork weaved through the gravy, leaving track lines.

"Ah, well, that's where I came in," Hugh said from the other end of the ridiculously long table. "She may have been a little *rambunctious*, let's say, but then I caught her in my trap and tamed her."

Matt made a low gagging noise. "I'm done," he said and pushed back in his chair. Another high-pitched squeal across the parquet floor, sending Helen's teeth on edge again.

"Matt, you'll wait until we're all finished, thank you very much," Hugh said with practised patience. He pushed his glasses further up his nose.

Matt sighed dramatically, but remained seated, arms

folded, and began to rock back in his chair. Helen found herself hoping the legs would flip out from underneath him. She hid a small smile in her napkin and picked up her fork again, but her appetite for the dinner in front of her had vanished. She pushed some broccoli around the plate, then put her cutlery together and nudged her plate away.

"Not hungry, darling?" Hugh said. "I guess it does need a bit more seasoning, doesn't it? And the Yorkshire puddings were a bit flat."

Her hand twitched in readiness to throw her plate of roast dinner at him. She smiled thinly. "Just tired tonight, a bit of a headache. Early night for me, I think."

"Yeah, she was a real party animal," Amelia said with a smirk across the table.

Amelia was Helen's biological daughter, although she preferred to be called Mills. Fiercely independent and intimidatingly intelligent, a firecracker of a seventeen-year-old. The result of Helen's former life. For many years it was just the two of them.

"Hey you, you're supposed to be on my side," Helen said.

"Now, now, there are no sides in this family. We're all on the same team," Hugh said and Helen could see how much it strained Mills not to roll her eyes.

It took self-restraint for Helen, too.

Lydia watched Helen at the head of the table, sitting with her back straight, picking at her food like she was Victoria Beckham, when Lydia knew she liked to stuff her face with anything she could find when she thought no one was looking. Lydia had seen the wrappers in the bin, the crumbs on her shirt.

Most of the time Helen didn't notice Lydia was there.

None of them did.

That's the thing with being the quiet one. They all looked through her, like she was clingfilm. And if they couldn't see her, then they mistakenly thought she couldn't see them, so Lydia became insignificant. Out of sight, out of mind.

Except that Lydia did see and hear everything.

She saw them all very clearly. What they were hiding. The parts of themselves they were desperate to conceal or deny. Like the fact that Mills had bottles of vodka stashed under her bed and liked to lean out of her bedroom window and exhale cigarette smoke into the night air. Sometimes Lydia sneaked into Mills' room and poured some of the vodka down the sink, replacing it with water. Yesterday she had stolen a cigarette from the pack in Mills' bedside table, and had coughed and puffed at it until she felt dizzy and sick. Mills never noticed. Because Lydia was invisible.

Even Matt, her own brother, who spent hours online practically stalking one of the girls at his art college, greedily consuming every tiny movement of her social media feeds, following her on Snap Map, salivating over her Insta stories. It was beyond creepy.

And Helen – well, Helen had quite a few things hidden away. Secrets that she didn't want exposed.

The only one who seemed to be transparent and true to himself was her father.

Lydia wished they would all see her.

But then she would remind herself that part of the fun of being invisible was that you tended to be underestimated. And that was a powerful position to hold.

4

THEN

Shouting, shoving, banter around us as we stand in the bus queue outside the front of the school, the relief of being released from the classroom tangible as we wait. The sun is still warm on my face, September being kind, and I can smell the sea on the breeze, but the chill is lurking in the background now that summer is over. My last year in school ahead of me. Decisions to be made, exams to be written, a life to be mapped out.

Father wants answers – where have I applied? Am I working hard enough? *You won't embarrass me with your failure, will you, Helen?* There is no question that I will fail in some way. His attention comes in short, sharp bursts, usually at the Sunday lunch table before he disappears back to London, my mother nibbling silently on the olive in her martini, a cigarette burning to ash between her thin fingers. I'm usually pleased to hear the door slam as he leaves for the week, a break in the atmosphere for a few days. I preferred it last year when he was oblivious to my presence in the house.

I don't have any answers for him. Well, not the ones he wants to hear. A corporate life fills me with dread. I want to get away from Hamblemere and the confines of Seahaven School, the faces I have known for most of my life, maybe see the world, live a life most ordinary. But that won't do for our family. We have standards to maintain, a reputation to honour, an inheritance to protect.

The bus rumbles up the sweeping driveway. Bags are grabbed; bodies wrestle into position. Eloise pushes past a group of Year 7s, cuts off their mumbled complaints with one withering glare. We follow, her underlings in tow, as she weaves to the back of the bus and takes up residence in the last row. Steph goes to sit next to her, but she puts a hand on the seat and says, "I don't think so, Steph. Hels, sit here."

Steph looks like her feet have been swept out from under her, but moves along as instructed. I sit heavily, already thinking about the revision I have planned for the evening. I have that new Stephen King book waiting for me too.

"What are you doing tonight, Hels?" Eloise asks, pulling a pack of gum from her bag.

Sometimes I think there is witch blood in her, the way she can tell that I'm thinking about something that she would find easy to diminish with the casual toss of a snide comment. Her eyes are piercing blue and she has made an art form out of seeing straight into you and finding that one weak spot that would unravel you like a tangled piece of string if she pulls hard enough.

"Nothing. We have that geography test next week, but I can't be bothered to revise. Easing myself in gently. Maybe

I'll just watch TV, run a bath and use that new face mask." I look over my shoulder, out of the window, away from her eyes.

"Ugh, I know what you mean. I'm thinking a face mask tonight too. I can feel a pimple coming and it will be a disaster if it flares up tomorrow," she says, chewing like a cow.

"There's that girl, look," Steph says.

We swivel in our seats. El is sitting sideways, her long legs, still tanned from her family trip to Italy in the summer, draped over mine.

"Is she walking home?" El sounds horrified. "Why would you?"

"It's not far – maybe she likes the fresh air," I say, then notice the look of disbelief on El's face. "But yeah, stupid, right?"

The bus has pulled alongside her. El starts to bang on the window. The girl looks up to see El flicking her middle finger at her while Emily and Steph snigger.

El stands on the seat, steps over Steph and Emily, and reaches up to open the top window. She leans her head through and spits her gum straight at the girl as the bus passes her.

The gum lands at the girl's feet.

The girl stops, looks down, then carries on walking as the bus pulls further away.

5

NOW

Helen loaded the dishwasher in silence. Scraping plates, rinsing, stacking gave her a quiet sense of purpose, a moment of calm. She could hear the television filtering through from the family room across the hall. Canned audience laughter as Mills watched reruns of old *Friends* episodes on Netflix, never tiring of the same stories playing out again and again. Lydia and Matt had disappeared upstairs to their rooms straight after dinner and Hugh was in his study across the hall, his eyes itching from the laptop glare as he continued on his DNA quest to discover whether he came from noble stock. He would love to discover that. So far, his results told him nothing he didn't already know, so that was money well spent.

No need to tell him that Helen's background was a bit more 'old money'. The size of the house they were living in was evidence of her inherited social standing. Helen's mother may have disowned her in life, but had kept her well cared for in death by leaving her this house. As always, passed from mother to daughter through the generations. Helen tried really hard to make sure that was all that her mother passed on to her.

Helen watched as congealed gravy slid from the plate into the sink, like a glob of snot, viscous and cloying. She thought about what Lydia had asked in her quiet, innocent voice earlier.

Why had she asked that particular question tonight, out of the blue, in between a roast chicken dinner and a bowl of ice cream in front of the *Strictly Come Dancing* results?

What had she heard? Who had she been talking to?

The truth was that Matt wasn't too far wrong, much as it – he – annoyed Helen. But it wasn't that she didn't remember that far back.

It's that it was best if she tried not to.

"Hugh will say you're wasting water," Mills said, coming up behind her. Helen turned off the tap and smiled as Mills held out her arms. "Can I have a hug?" Mills asked.

"Sure," Helen replied. Mills leaned in and Helen softened, feeling some of the tightness loosen in her shoulders. It was rare for Mills to ask for hugs these days. She could be prickly sometimes and often seemed to be only half there, the other half distracted by Snapchat, Instagram and a whole teenage world that Helen found alien.

Mills pulled away and went to rummage in the fridge. Helen watched her, her heart quietly full and longing at the same time, longing for those days when it was just her and Mills hanging out in this huge house, playing hide and seek in the countless rooms and having sleepovers in front of the stone fireplace in the lounge, the couch pushed back, a mattress on the floor and custard eaten straight from the tub. Mills pulled out a can of Diet Coke and slammed the door shut. A fridge magnet slid from the door and fell with a clatter onto the tiles.

"You ok, Mum?" She was watching Helen closely with her jade green eyes. Helen could only assume she'd inherited those from her father.

"Yeah, like I say, headache, that's all." Helen paused. "You ok?"

Mills just smiled cryptically and left.

Helen wandered over to the fridge and picked up the magnet. A photo of Hugh and her on their wedding day, seven years ago now, the age gap between them apparent even then.

Two families, coming together later in life. All of them so different, like pieces of a jigsaw twisting and turning to fit together in the hope that they would mould into the picture of a happy, blended family.

There were still some pieces missing.

Helen put the magnet back in its place, then straightened it ever so slightly. Hugh liked straight lines and neat corners.

She moved back towards the sink, then hesitated, turned back and nudged the magnet out of alignment again.

Helen curled her feet underneath her on the couch, enjoying the glass of red wine she had poured herself. She had had one with dinner, so this would be her last before bed. Never more than two glasses these days. She had become one of those women whose hand hovered over her glass when the host came around with the bottle. The one who said, "No, really, I mustn't." Hugh didn't like displays of overindulgence.

Clive sat at her feet, his head propped up on the couch cushion. She stroked his soft ears until he flopped down onto the rug and fell asleep, snores making his lips tremble.

Mills had disappeared upstairs and Helen hadn't seen anything more of Lydia or Matt since dinner, but that wasn't unusual. She knew she should reach out to them more, but some days it was just too damn hard. Their mother was a hugger, tactile to the extreme by most accounts, whereas Helen preferred to express her affection by keeping the cupboards full and waiting on them all hand and foot. She was no Francesca, not that she would want to be. Tofu tended to give her wind and it was difficult to make Lycra look fetching on her thighs.

Lydia in particular should demand more of Helen's attention. She was a closed book, so quiet and unassuming that Helen often forgot she was in the room. Helen knew what that felt like and it was a lonely place to inhabit. But Lydia was so different to what Mills was like at her age, making it tricky for Helen to bond with her. Mills was curious and feisty, questioning everything, challenging everyone, determined to make her own mind up. Lydia was a people pleaser, happy to accept whatever you told her without forming her own opinion. That's why she melded into the background so much. She never stepped out of the shadows cast by other people. Even her brother looked through her like she was translucent.

Helen swirled the merlot, watching the liquid swill around the glass, coming dangerously close to the top before retreating. The news was starting on the television, stories of sadness and gloom. It was early October and Helen fully expected the Christmas marketing to kick up a notch very soon. 2019 had been a quiet year for them. Helen hoped 2020 would be a little livelier. A holiday would be nice. A beach, a view, a good book. But Hugh didn't like to travel. He liked his home comforts, nothing too exotic. He was a korma man, nothing too spicy, and liked knowing that a good cup of tea was within reach at all times.

Christmas felt like it arrived earlier and earlier every year. Helen needed to think about plans for the bookshop and what festive preparations were needed there. It was her favourite time of the year, all that sparkle and colour. Knowing there was glitter at the end of it made the beige hue of the rest of the year bearable. Maybe she should see if Lydia wanted to help out at the bookshop, a few hours after school perhaps or helping to plan the festive displays.

An open book sat on the couch beside her, a new novel by a familiar author, but her mind kept running away with her tonight. Hugh was still in his study, but the draw of the news headlines would be too much for him to ignore. True to form, she heard the study door open across the hall and his slippered feet shuffle across the hard wood floor.

"I thought you were going for an early night?" he said as he came up behind her, leaned over and kissed her forehead.

"I took some headache pills and I'm feeling better now."

"The wine won't help." Disapproval knotted his brow.

"You're probably right." She took a large sip and looked back at the television.

The springs groaned with age as Hugh sank onto the couch next to her and lifted her legs into his lap. Her hip was now angled uncomfortably and she shifted a little, trying to straighten out, but he pulled her legs closer in, oblivious to her discomfort.

"Your feet are as cold as ice," he said, making it sound like an accusation, and took one in his hands to rub it. Helen wanted to pull away, but forced herself to endure the affection. "Are we still on for dinner on Friday evening? I'll book." He said this as though either of them might have alternative plans, but every Friday evening for the last seven years they had gone out for dinner. A date night, if you will, but always to the same Italian restaurant in the village where he ordered the same dishes off the menu for them both and they were usually home by 10 p.m.

"Sure, go ahead and book," Helen replied, trying to sound more enthusiastic than she felt.

"Actually, I might have some of that cheese in the fridge. Are there any crackers?" he said.

"Yes, in the cupboard."

Helen washed down the sigh in her throat with more wine as he left the room. He hadn't offered her any cheese and crackers. Not that she wanted any, but the offer would be nice. Outside, beyond the window, Helen could hear the sea in the near distance, crashing and churning against the rocks. She wanted to head out there, take a long walk on the beach in the pitch black. Nothing but the biting wind and the stinging sea spray reminding her that she was actually alive.

Hugh returned with his plate of cheese and crackers in one hand and a glass of the merlot in the other.

"I thought I'd join you," he said proudly, as though he was doing her a favour by saving her from drinking alone. "You're leading me astray."

Helen smiled, her lips pressed tight to her teeth.

It wasn't long before his head was lolling in time to the snores rumbling from his throat, his plate of crumbs abandoned on the coffee table next to the glass of wine he hadn't finished.

In all the years they had been married, Helen could count on one hand how many times he had managed to stay awake past 11 p.m.

The urge to head out to the beach, to walk through the wet sand and scream into the night had passed. She stood up gently, careful not to shift her weight too much in case it woke him. Grabbing his wine glass, she drained it, returned the glass to the coffee table and headed upstairs to bed.

Mills heard her mother walk past her closed door and on up to her own bedroom on the third floor of the house. Hugh would still be asleep on the couch downstairs. She often saw him there when she was getting a glass of water on her way to bed.

They had a strange marriage, but Hugh was harmless. Mills didn't mind him as far as father figures went. And it wasn't like she had many other options. She had no idea who her own father was.

She walked over to her bedroom window and opened it wide, then perched on the ledge and leaned back against the window frame. Her bedroom light was off and she felt like she was hovering above the ground, everything dark and still around her. The air was fresh but not too cold, tangy with sea spray. She could see the flat expanse of water in the distance, the moon reflecting off the water.

She loved it here. The sounds and smells that only came with being next to the water. The people that she had known all her life, saying hello as she walked past. The sense of belonging.

Even this house. She knew a lot of people would find it ugly, misshapen, grotesque even, with its angles and additions like growths, but she liked the eccentricity of it, the way it didn't conform with its surroundings.

She knew it wasn't cool to admit that you liked it at home, but she didn't want to be anywhere else.

She lit a cigarette and inhaled, the nicotine hit making her momentarily giddy. She was working on practising perfect smoke rings. They weren't quite perfect yet.

She sat, smoking quietly until the cigarette had burned away, then stubbed it out on the underneath of the window ledge. Movement deep in the darkened garden caught her eye. A fox maybe. She narrowed her eyes. Not a fox – too big.

She recoiled. It was a person.

Dressed in dark clothes, camouflaged against the night, only their steady progress up the garden discernible as they kept to the shadows.

They stopped halfway and stood, staring up at the house.

Then Mills felt more than saw the eyes come to rest on her.

She stared back, more curious than afraid.

This wasn't the first time this person had come into their garden. Mills knew there was a gate tucked into the stone wall that separated the house from the public coastal path. It was supposed to be kept locked. Her mother was insistent about that.

The shape moved again, retreating back down the garden, back to where they had come from.

Mills exhaled her held breath, but sat for a moment longer, making sure she was alone again.

6

THEN

I get off the bus and walk the short distance down the road towards the coastal path and my house. Mine is one of the first stops. I live on the edge of the village, overlooking the sea. There was a time when people used to go on and on about how weird the house was, saying it was haunted, twisted and sombre as it perched above the sea. It isn't modern like some of my friends' houses. Over the years my mother has tried to lighten it, painting the outside white, adding glass doors and larger windows, even installing a long, stained glass window above the stairs, but the house seems to hang onto the gloom, determined to remain in the shadows.

I don't mind it though. It is the kind of house that Stephen King would write a novel about and I think the place has character, a personality, unlike the blank canvasses of the houses around us. Many of the other houses nearby are empty for much of the year, holiday homes locked up as the summer draws to a close, dust sheets thrown over furniture and shutters closed to the shortening days. They may open them for a flurry of activity at Christmas, but for the most part they remain dark and uninhabited until the warmth reappears. Sometimes I imagine my house feeding off the others, slowly sucking the life from them over the summer until it is sated and they are depleted, needing hibernation to recuperate before opening themselves up again.

I should write a story about it. The house that feeds on the souls of those around it. Or in it. There's a few lost souls in mine.

Not a story for anyone to actually read, of course. El would have a field day if she knew I wrote in my spare time, let alone read books that didn't have photos of celebrities in them.

I reach up to let myself in the back gate. The sea is noisy over my shoulder, the salt spray strong and tangy on my lips. I turn, one hand holding the gate, and look out at the rolling white horses and scavenging birds dipping, diving, shouting. The sea seems angry today. Most days. I stand for a moment, enjoying the spit of salt as it peppers my face, seeing the clouds build in the distance. Rain coming later.

I stay there for some time, not wanting to go inside just yet.

I only turn to go when my shoulder begins to ache from the weight of my school bag. Only then do I notice I am not alone. Further along the coastal path stands a solitary figure, face pointed to the sea, hands rooted at their sides, shoulders slumped. It is a girl with a cloud of tight, ink-black curls pulled into a low ponytail.

She turns slowly to face me, then stoops to pick up the bag at her feet. She doesn't look back as she walks away.

I lumber up to the house. At the far end of the garden, our caretaker, Arthur, is cutting the grass, releasing the smell of late summer into the air. I look up at the house and see the housekeeper in the kitchen prepping dinner and one of the cleaners at the back door, shaking out the doormat. And on the third floor, my mother stands in the window, staring down at me. She doesn't raise her hand in greeting or move to come and meet me.

I say hello to Teresa, the cleaner, and step past her into the kitchen. Martha, the housekeeper, is filling the kettle at the sink.

"Good day, Helen? Nice to be back at school?" she asks me with a warm smile.

"Yeah, it was ok, thanks," I reply and shrug.

"Can I get you something to eat? I've baked oat and chocolate chip cookies."

"No, thanks, I had a big lunch."

I dump my schoolbag in my bedroom and pause at the bottom of the stairs leading up to the next floor, tilting my head at the audible sounds of sniffing.

Sighing, I climb the stairs. Mother is still in the window, staring out at the sea in a haze of cigarette fug, a tissue clamped in her fist.

"Hi, Mother," I say quietly from the doorway.

She sniffs in response.

"Are you ok?" I almost don't want to ask. I step further into the room.

There have been a few episodes in the last few weeks, her moods becoming more intolerable and harder to anticipate. Sometimes she is flung on the bed, her face pressed into the pillows, moaning; other times she is pacing across the carpet, wringing her hands. I suspect she has been relying too much on her little daily doses of pharmaceutical happiness lately.

"Do you want to talk about it?"

At that, she spins around and throws herself on the bed, pulling her legs up as she sighs. "He's having an affair, Helen. I know he is!"

"Mother, we've talked about this before. I'm sure he's not. You have no evidence of that."

"I can feel it!" She buries her face in the pillow and heaves a shuddering sigh.

There was a very heated discussion last weekend when she accused him once again. I could hear the finger-pointing through the walls. This is quite normal though. I've never known anything different.

My parents are the epitome of a tragic love story. And I am just a spectator, watching from the stalls. They bicker, then argue, throwing allegations like grenades while I cower in my room, trying to avoid the flying shrapnel. I have often wondered why they are still married. They don't seem to like each other very much – and yet there is an underlying sense that they wouldn't be able to exist without each other.

There is still beauty in my mother beneath the skeletal limbs and sunken cheeks, as well as a wit that occasionally bubbles to the surface when he manages to make her laugh. But those moments are becoming a rarity. When he is in London through the week, she wanders through this massive house like a phantom, using cigarettes and alcohol to quell her appetite, which feed her paranoia in return... but there is never a question of her going to the city to be with him. I suspect he needs the space away from her to fortify himself for their weekends together. She can't bring herself to leave him though, which she should because she is probably right about him, but she has gone way past being able to function independently. She can plan and host a fantastic dinner party for prospective investors, turning on her glamour and charm as necessary, but she can't manage a cheque book or even find her way to a supermarket for bread and milk. That's the female role model you want in your life, isn't it?

"If that's true, why don't you just divorce him?" I say.

She moves quick as lightning and strikes out at me, catching me on the cheek with her ring. "Get out! Get out!"

Later, as I sit on my bed working on a short story idea, I can hear her shouting into the telephone in her bedroom, her voice nasal and slurred from the martinis she washed down her non-existent dinner with. Soon after, she bounds into my bedroom, her face light and happy, the shadows flushed away for the time being. She flounces onto the edge of my bed.

"He's taking me on holiday."

"Who?"

"Your father, of course! He's taking me with him when he goes to New York later this month and we're going to take some time afterwards to travel around together. We'll be gone at least six weeks, he says!" She is beaming. She doesn't mention the lurid red cut on my cheek that I will take great care to cover up with make-up tomorrow.

"That's great, Mother."

"You'll be ok on your own."

It's not a question.

"You're seventeen now and Martha is here. You'll be fine."

I want to think they'll miss me, but I know they won't. That's not how we do things. "Sure, I'll be fine – and you'll have a great time."

She squeals like a little girl and throws her arms around me. I flinch and stiffen, but just as I'm about to return the affection, she launches off the bed and I'm left feeling like a hung sentence.

"I must start planning," I hear her say as she dances from the room.

7

NOW

Monday morning, 06.15. Helen sat at her dressing table and sipped on a glass of tepid lemon water, cursing herself for draining Hugh's wine last night. It had left her dehydrated enough to sleep restlessly and meant there was now a tiny hammer tapping at her temples. The swirling wallpaper behind the mirror hurt her eyes, so she looked at her reflection instead. She'd fared relatively well for her age, but her skin was slackening and the lines on her brow were deepening the further into her forties she went. She looked away from the reflection of a face she struggled to recognise some days.

She pulled on her swimsuit, feeling the Lycra catch momentarily on her loose belly, then smothered herself in a thick bathrobe before slipping her feet into slippers and creeping downstairs.

The cold air blasted her as she opened the French doors in the kitchen and headed out into the garden. The trees and shrubs were fighting against each other for air, like grappling hands and scratching fingers. She rushed down the garden, the cold chasing her the whole way, and let herself into the glass pool house. It was much warmer inside, the air humid and thick, but dark because ivy covered most of the windows. Helen liked it like that though, secretive, isolated, keeping the darkness in. She didn't even bother to turn on the overhead lights. Instead, she dropped her gown, kicked off the slippers and slid into the warm water. Extravagantly, the pool was kept heated all year round so that it was always the perfect temperature for her daily swim. That was one indulgence battle Hugh hadn't won.

She emptied her mind as she pulled herself through the water, gliding and reaching, the minutes melting away. After half an hour, she climbed out, feeling more energised, her mind calm for now.

She passed Clive in his bed in the kitchen on her way back into the house. He opened one eye, let out a half-snort, half-sigh and went back to sleep. The middle of the house was dominated by two extravagant sweeping staircases that curled from the middle of the ground floor hallway all the way up to the main bedroom on the third floor. They lead nowhere but back to each other on each floor, as though they couldn't bear to be apart from each other. If you looked up, the house had a semblance of symmetry, but in reality each floor had random corridors that only brought you back to where you started, as though someone had lost interest in planning the layout properly.

The one focal point dominating it all was the huge stained glass window on the back wall of the house between the staircases. This morning it framed the dawn breaking in pinks and oranges, the light cutting the carpet into shards of colour. From the back garden, the window looked like a Picasso painting, with its garish colours and sharp-edged shapes. Her mother had commissioned it back in the 1960s and, although Hugh disliked it immensely, Helen loved it for its irregularity, vibrancy and determination to be noticed.

By the time she had climbed the many stairs to her bedroom on the third floor, she was a little out of puff. Hugh's alarm ripped through the silence. She knew from habit that it would be the third time it had gone off. Helen always woke on the first alarm, but Hugh never did. It used to annoy her. Now she just accepted it and got up to swim. She heard him snort, fart, roll over and hit snooze one more time. He was becoming more like Clive every day.

Dressing quickly, she was back downstairs by 7 a.m., her first cup of coffee in hand, making breakfast for the masses. She could hear the house awakening, the floorboards moaning above her as bodies roused, pipes complaining loudly as showers were turned on, radio alarms blaring into life. Clive was up and eating loudly from his bowl in the corner, his name tag clattering against the metal as he bolted down his breakfast. The sun was reluctant, still just peeking out, like the teenagers in the house.

As always, Lydia was first to appear, her tie knotted neatly and long blonde hair plaited into a perfect French braid. She barely looked at Helen as she mumbled her thanks for the plate of scrambled eggs on toast that Helen held out to her.

Helen sat at the head of the kitchen table, her coffee mug cradled in front of her as Lydia ate in silence. Lydia was distracted, preoccupied with her phone. Helen ran her finger over a dent in the table top, smoothed by time, then started to say, "So, what's—", but Hugh interrupted her as he bustled in, his tie sitting haphazardly, his hair sticking up on one side.

"My glasses. Where are my glasses, Helen?"

"On your head," she replied.

He reached up, plucked them from his hair and chuckled as he settled them on his nose.

Helen stood up and corrected his Windsor knot, smoothed down a tuft of his white hair.

He kissed her lightly on the cheek, patted her bottom and sat down next to Lydia before pulling the newspaper towards him. Lydia had a smile for him. Helen placed a bowl of steaming porridge in front of him, blueberries bobbing in the milk like men overboard, alongside a mug of overly sweet tea, just the way he liked it.

"Thank you, darling," he said. "You ok?" But his attention was already on his newspaper. "Nice swim?"

"Yes," Helen muttered, quelling the urge to say what she really felt.

There was a moment of quiet then, only the rustle of the newspaper and the slurp of tea before the air shifted as Matt sloped in, yawning widely, rings under his eyes. Helen suspected it was another late night of gaming for him. At least that's what Hugh said he was doing every night when Helen walked past his closed bedroom door and could see the shifting blue light of a computer screen illuminated in the gap beneath it. Helen had her own private suspicions that he was up to something less wholesome.

"Morning son," Hugh said as Matt flung himself into a chair at the table.

She put toast and peanut butter in front of him, with a banana on the side, but he scowled and said, "Not hungry."

"Is everything ok?" she asked. He ignored her and pushed the plate away.

There was a stain on the front of his pale grey t-shirt, visible just below the expensive brand name. Hugh gave him a sideways glance and said, "Don't you have a cleaner shirt for today?"

Matt looked down at the stain and said with a nudge of his head in Helen's direction, "No, she hasn't done my washing."

"Darling, can you sort that out for him today please?" Hugh had barely looked at Helen so far, but he could see a stain a mile away.

She clenched her teeth, knowing full well that the laundry had been done, but cursing herself for not checking Matt's bedroom floor for the pile of dirty clothes that wouldn't have made it into the hamper in his bathroom a few steps away.

"Of course, sorry, I must've missed some things," she said.

Hugh pushed to his feet, folded his newspaper neatly and said, "Lydia, the Dad Taxi is leaving in five minutes sharp." He turned to Helen then and said, "Millie will need to hurry or she'll have to walk."

She hated being called Millie.

And there she was, her eyes made up in dark flicks of eyeliner, her hair pulled into a high ponytail, the ends dyed purple, and the waistband of her school skirt rolled up one too many times. Mills sauntered into the kitchen, ponytail swinging, kissed Helen lightly on the cheek and leaned over

Matt to grab a banana from the bowl in the centre of the table. Her skirt rode up dangerously high, revealing a flash of pure white knickers.

"Ah, there you are. We're leaving in five if you would like a lift?" Hugh said. "And unroll the skirt, please."

"Hugh, tut tut. You shouldn't be looking," she said with a sly smile.

Hugh blushed around his collar.

"Mills, roll down the skirt," Helen said.

She looked at her mother for a second before shrugging and unrolling the waistband until the hem sat at a slightly more appropriate length.

Helen hid a small smile. The apple didn't fall far from the tree.

"Right, wagons roll!" Hugh announced.

Bags were thrown over shoulders, mugs were drained and goodbyes were tossed about in a flurry of activity.

Then the front door closed and Helen was alone again.

She exhaled.

The table was littered with breakfast debris, with only Lydia managing to get her plate to the sink. Matt's toast sat untouched, so she fed it to Clive, the peanut butter making his tongue smack against the roof of his mouth. Matt had taken the banana with him at least. Helen took that as a win.

She walked through to the lounge and stared out of the picture window. Matt was still in the driveway trying to get his car to start. He hated that car, but Hugh was big on getting the kids to learn the value of money, so he made sure Matt had worked in order to save up for most of it. Helen could see him now, scowling as he banged on the dashboard.

One more turn of the key and the engine coughed into life. He reversed quickly in a cloud of gravel dust and tore off down the driveway, grinding the gears.

They could afford to buy him a new car. The house was mortgage-free, Helen had some of her parents' inheritance left, although she was saving much of it for Mills' future, and Hugh had a good income as a head of year and history teacher. They didn't live extravagantly. No expensive annual holidays or fancy toys. Their family car was a Skoda, for god's sake. But Hugh was adamant that it would be giving in, spoiling Matt, and *what we do for one, we have to do for the others*.

Helen would've bought him the damn car.

She headed back into the kitchen to tidy up. She turned on the radio, letting the music fill the space, and made another cup of coffee and finally some porridge for herself. Opening the notebook stashed in the kitchen drawer under the takeaway menus they rarely used, she logged her planned food for the day, making sure she kept within a miniscule calorie limit. Long gone were the days when she would survive on nothing but coffee, cigarettes and pills. These days every mouthful was planned, every indulgence recorded, new promises made to herself every morning and broken by lunchtime, with disappointment in herself weighing her down by bedtime – and the waistband grew tighter and the butt wobblier as she let herself down again and again. The pages of this notebook were filled with yet more lies. She sighed, pushed it away and stared at the uninspiring breakfast in front of her. Some days she wondered what the point of it all was.

Would any of them notice if she disappeared?

She pushed her feet into her dirty trainers by the front door, shrugged into a big coat and grabbed Clive's lead from the back of the kitchen door.

Matt found he could breathe a little easier as he drove away from the house. It wasn't her, as such. As far as stepmothers went, she was alright. She didn't get in his face, never asked too many questions, made a good dinner.

And she was loaded, so the house was massive and he could have his own space.

But he felt unsettled there, in those walls. Like the house itself was watching him, judging him, getting under his skin, consuming him from the inside, waiting to spit him out.

The gears scraped as he pulled away and he cringed. It was now a grey day and he hoped it wouldn't rain too hard because the windscreen wipers on this heap of shit he was driving didn't work very well. And he had promised he would pick her up in the village on the way to college.

Maybe that's what it was. Maybe the fact that Helen was loaded and they were living in her weird mansion of a house, and yet he still had to drive this crap car, get a job to pay for his own petrol, buy his own stuff. It seemed old-fashioned of them to expect that. Francesca, his own mother, was no help with money either. That stupid café she ran with Todd was not exactly a thriving business. And these days Todd had all of her attention, as though she'd washed her hands of him and Lydia once they'd moved in with Helen.

Still, his mother looked happy and certainly sounded happier than she had been with his dad. So that was something. Or maybe it was all the yoga she was doing.

Matt looked at the time and accelerated into the corner, then braked hard as the road narrowed to a single lane again. He hated this village. It was claustrophobic. He wanted the excitement of a city, the vibe of a normal teenage social life. What he wouldn't give to live in Brighton with its thriving local art scene. He could move in with his mother, ditch college and start living his life. But his father wouldn't have it.

The art college he attended was a half-hour drive inland from the village and the only good thing about it was that *she* went there too. He had to force himself to slow down though as his foot itched to press harder on the accelerator and get him there as quickly as possible.

So that he could see her.

Diana.

He didn't want to be late. This was the first time she had accepted his offer of a lift.

She was all he could think about. At school a few years back she was just someone he had watched from afar. She had been way too cool to even acknowledge someone like him, the typical sporty one, rugby team captain, hiding behind testosterone and arrogance. But now that she had turned up at his art college, they were in class together every day. A few days ago she had actually started a conversation with him.

Her voice was throaty and almost masculine, like she had smoked too many cigarettes, and her hair smelled like cherries from her vape. She was tall, so that they stood eye to eye, and Matt found himself wanting to reach out and stroke her auburn hair. He imagined it felt like a length of silk under his fingers.

What the fuck was the matter with him?

He opened the car window and let a blast of cold air hit his face and cool his flaring cheeks. Until now she had been polite, interested, happy to engage in long conversations about art, books, music. But she still had Matt firmly in the friend zone.

He needed to change that.

8

THEN

I cross my ankles underneath the desk and sigh. Mrs Aldridge is droning on and on about chemical formulae. I revised all of this last night and could probably recite what she is saying in my sleep. I look across at Eloise, who is chewing on her pencil and trying to catch Brian's attention. She is crossing and uncrossing her legs, aiming for seductive but looking more like she needs the toilet. Oblivious, Brian is staring at the teacher, confusion written all over his face. He's not the brightest, but he can kick a ball, so I suppose that's something.

I look across to my left where the new girl is sitting next to the window. She looks like she is actually listening to the teacher. She scribbles something in her book, then chews on the skin around her nail while she reads it over.

"Ok, we are going to split into partners today. I have a little project for you to get your teeth stuck into. It will be fun," Mrs Aldridge says, her face alight. She clearly has a different idea of fun to us, going off the loud groan that fills the room.

"And because I think it would do you all good to be partnered with someone you wouldn't normally pair up with, I will ask half of you to draw a name from my hat here. Whoever you pick is the person you are working with. The project is due in at the end of the week. Let's draw names, then we'll talk about what is required. Right, this side of the room, are you feeling lucky?" There is no answer.

She passes a manky looking fedora along the front row of desks. Hands duck in and out; small pieces of paper are unfolded. By the time the hat reaches Eloise, more than half of the names have been drawn already. Mrs Aldridge has her back to us, handing out pages of notes to the front row. El reaches in, rummages around, picks one and opens it, then wrinkles her nose in disgust and drops it back in. She picks again, opening a few, tossing them back before finally settling on one she is happy with. She passes the hat to me with a wink. I take whatever piece of paper my fingers touch, then pass the hat on to Steph. I open the scrap of paper.

Tracey Deane.

The new girl.

Eloise whispers, "I got Brian! Who did you get?"

"Tracey," I say.

"Oh god, I got her first. Why didn't you check and swap it? You don't want to be stuck with the likes of her all week."

I shrug. "It's fine. It's a project. It's not like we're hanging out. I'll make her do all the work."

I look over at her again. She has twisted in her seat and is staring out of the window with her back to the room.

Her hair is still held back in a low ponytail, thick and curly across her shoulders. Her feet are crossed, her simple black slip-on shoes worn at the heel and dirty with old mud on the soles. She twists around and turns to look at me. I look away.

Mrs Aldridge tells us to pair up with our new partners. I feel awkward as I get to my feet. "Good luck with that," El hisses in my ear.

I notice that Steph and Emily have manufactured it so that they are partnered with each other. So much for finding new partners. Eloise flounces over to Brian's desk and loudly declares, "You're all mine now, Brian."

I hover behind Tracey's chair. "Um, Tracey, right?"

She turns and looks me up and down, dislike obvious.

"Where do you want to sit?" I say.

She shrugs, so I point to two desks that are free at the back of the room and make my way towards them before she can object. My shoulders are so stiff, it feels like they are brushing my earlobes.

I sit and wait for Mrs Aldridge to come over with the project papers.

Tracey sits silently in the desk next to me.

"Wonderful, I think you two will work really well together," Mrs Aldridge says with too much enthusiasm.

I look at the instructions, reading the words but conscious of the ugly awkwardness.

"Ok, so it looks like we have to analyse these elements and there's a few experiments to do and stuff." If I stick to talking just about the project, it might make the time pass quicker.

We discuss what we need to do in short, sharp sentences.

She is clever, knows her way around an elemental chart. She's throwing her words at me, like she's trying to outsmart me, but I match her each time. Her Midlands accent is strong, which sets her apart from the rest of us immediately, but that's not the only thing. One glance around the lily-white faces in this classroom tells you what else does.

After half an hour we have a solid plan of what we are going to do and some good ideas are bouncing between us, the sentences becoming less staccato, the atmosphere a little less brittle. She even cracks a smile at one point when I forget myself and make a rubbish elemental joke.

At the end of the lesson, she packs up and goes to leave without another word. As she walks away, I say, "That's a good book," and nod at what she is holding in her hand.

She frowns, then looks at the copy of *Return of the Native* sticking out of her bag.

"Yeah, it is. You like Victorian literature then?"

"Yeah, I'm rereading—"

"Ugh, Hels, step away from her or you'll never get the smell of monkey shit from your hair," El says loudly from over Tracey's shoulder.

Tracey turns and walks away without another word.

"So is she as lame as she looks?"

"Totally," I say, watching her go.

Later we are paired up again, this time for French. It's like I can't get away from her, fate pushing her into my direct path – or the teachers manufacturing it that way. Eloise, Steph and Emily don't take French, but their judgemental shadows hang over me as Tracey takes the free desk next to me. The teacher has paired us up for dialogue practice and I'm not sure what to say initially.

She says, "How's your French?"

"Not bad, I guess. My accent sounds a bit dodgy, a cross between Inspector Clouseau and the old guy from 'Allo 'Allo, but passable, I guess."

She laughs and we start going through the dialogue.

Her French is good. Better than good. She's clearly very smart and now I'm feeling a little intimidated. I could keep up if I tried, but I'm used to dumbing down for the company I keep. No one is allowed to be smarter than Eloise. This is unnatural ground for me.

When the bell rings for the end of the lesson, this time Tracey starts chatting to me as we pack up.

"So I guess you've been at this school a long time then?"

"Yeah, from the start. I live in Hamblemere, always have done. What about you?"

"We've just moved here from Nottingham. My grandad owned a dairy farm down here and he passed away, so my parents sold up to come and take over the farm."

"Was that Mr Deane?" I remember him from the village, always in wellies and a flat cap, raising a hand in greeting whenever anyone walked past, often seen sitting on some form of farm equipment. I hadn't made the connection until now.

"Yeah. We've scaled the farm back a little, but my dad didn't want to sell it completely, so I help out a bit when I can."

She makes it sound like it's nothing. I don't even make myself a cup of tea most days.

"I'm sorry – about your grandad. He seemed nice."

She shrugs. "I didn't really know him that well."

We're at the classroom door and I can see the top of Emily's head as she bops behind Eloise, weaving through the masses heading to lunch.

Tracey sees them too. She smiles at me almost sadly, then disappears.

El waves me over. "Brian is *so* into me," she says.

"Is he?" I reply flatly.

"He *so* is," Steph agrees, as she does with everything Eloise says. Anything to be awarded the honour of walking in her shadow. I look at the three of them, clustered together with their identical hairstyles and matching clothes, and it hits me. What we must look like, sound like. Clones. Barbie dolls with no substance. Is that what I want? What I'm aiming for? What I will look like years from now? A vague shadow of a woman with a mid-afternoon alcoholic beverage in one hand, a cigarette burning down to the filter in the other and an empty brain rattling in my head like the last pill in the bottle? They stand in front of me, their eyes alight because a boy with a spotty forehead and a posh voice has winked at them.

I want to push through them and run screaming from the building.

But these are my oldest friends. El and I have been friends since the first day of school. It's not their fault that I'm now feeling restless, itchy to get away from them, my parents, this village. Part of me wants to blame Tracey. A couple of hours in her company and it's like she has come up to me with a mirror in her hand and made me look at myself for the first time.

And I don't like what I see.

My teeth pull at the skin on my lip as I follow the three of them into the canteen. We line up, plastic trays in hand, El at the front as always. She grabs a drink, a yoghurt and an apple. Steph and Emily watch her, seeking silent permission for their own choices, pick up the same flavour yoghurt, the same sugar-free drink.

I look at the plates on offer, at the toasted cheese sandwiches and chips, my mouth watering, and I pick up a plate. I trail behind them to the same table we always sit at, right in the middle of the canteen, like we are the sun around which everyone else must rotate.

Eloise looks pointedly at my plate. "You're not going to eat that, are you?"

"Well, I'm not planning to wear it."

She glares at me. Steph and Emily sit open-mouthed.

"I've got my period, ok? I need something greasy," I reply hastily.

El shrugs in response, but I can see her nose twitching and I bet her fingers are too, desperate to reach out and shove a handful of chips into her mouth.

The funny thing is I wouldn't bat an eyelid if she did. I'd probably like her more.

Out of the corner of my eye, I notice Tracey walking around, her tray held in front of her like a shield.

Without thinking, I stand up and wave at her. "Tracey, sit here."

El looks horrified, while Steph and Emily merely gape. "What the fuck are you doing?" El hisses at me.

I ignore her and move over to make space.

Tracey hesitates, then comes over.

"Have you met everyone? This is Eloise, Steph and Emily," I say, indicating each pinched face.

"Hi, I'm Tracey." She smiles nervously. I notice she has opted for the toasted cheese too. I smile back and take a big bite of my sandwich. God, it's good.

"So, settling in ok? Finding where everything is?" I say to fill the awkward silence. El is staring resolutely in the opposite direction, her legs crossed so that anyone wanting to pass must step over her dangling foot.

"Yeah, I guess. It's not that much different to my old school, except it's smaller and everyone seems... posher, I guess. I hope you don't mind me saying that."

"Not at all – and you're right! Wall-to-wall privilege here, me included, I'm afraid." I laugh shrilly.

"So what are *you* doing here then?" El's voice is frigid.

"Um, well, my parents inherited a dairy farm and this is the closest school, so here I am."

"I guess they'll let anyone in these days," El replies.

Steph and Emily titter.

"Where are you from originally then?" El persists.

"From Nottingham," she says.

"No, I mean *originally*."

"Nottingham," she says pointedly.

"Oh god, school photos later this afternoon. I almost forgot." I say loudly and grimace. I'm going for change-the-subject chic, but my voice is loud. It slips and slides across the ice that has formed in the air.

El points at Tracey's hair and says, "You obviously didn't know it was photographs today. But there's probably not much you can do with your kind of hair. How do you even brush that?"

Brian wanders over with a posse of boys behind him. "Ladies," he says. I want to shudder at how creepy he sounds.

Eloise swivels towards him, uncrosses, then recrosses her legs so that her skirt rides up a little higher. "Brian."

"Are you going to introduce us to your new friend?" He reaches out and takes Tracey's hand in his, pretending to kiss the back of it.

El freezes.

"Leave her alone, Brian," I say.

"Oh, come now, I'm only being polite to the pretty lady. Where are you from?"

"Nottingham," Tracey and I both say at the same time and I smile at her, embarrassed by my friends' ignorance.

Eloise's eyes have narrowed. She reaches over and grabs the tomato ketchup sachet from my plate.

"Can I have one of your chips please, Hels? But with ketchup?" she says and angles the sachet at Tracey.

She tears into it and the ketchup squirts out of the sachet, all over Tracey's white shirt. Tracey jumps back. Her knee connects with the table, overturning the drink on her tray. She is left with ketchup dripping down her front and a wet lap.

Brian and his friends start laughing uproariously, followed very quickly by Steph and Emily.

"Oops, what have I done?" El says, before starting to laugh herself.

Tracey staggers to her feet, looking aghast, then grabs her bag and flees from the hall as the laughter spreads like a virus from table to table. It feels like the only one not laughing is me.

I want to follow Tracey and make sure she is ok, but El catches my eye and gives me a withering glare, so I stay where I am. The laughter dies down, El begins flirting with Brian, and his friends pull up chairs.

I look at the plate in front of me, suddenly not hungry anymore.

"Aren't you going to eat those after all?" El says, before Brian's hand reaches in and starts wading through my chips.

9

Helen stood alone on the sand, staring out at the blue expanse in front of her as Clive snuffled in pools of water and climbed on the less scary looking rocks. With the tide out, the beach was exposed, but the tide was notoriously fickle and the sea quick to engulf this little patch of sand in favour of clattering and clashing against the rocks with lethal force.

The steps back up to the coastal path were narrow and treacherous when wet, especially for Clive's chunky turkey legs, but Helen had needed to get out into the spray and chill this morning, to breathe deeply and have a moment. For that, she needed his company. Someone who would just be with her unconditionally.

She usually had this beach to herself as very few would dare to wander on it and run the risk of getting caught in the tide. After all these years though, she knew they had another ten minutes or so before they had to make their way back up, before the water started to encroach on their liberty. She turned away from the sea and stared up at the house peering down on her from the cliff. She could just make out the top of the ivy-clad pool house in the near distance and the top windows of the house further back. It felt like the house was keeping an eye out, peeping over the cliff, checking up on her. Always in her peripheral vision.

Always watching.

She needed to gather up Matt's dirty laundry, put a load on to wash and then head to work, but was lacking motivation to even begin today. One of those days when slipping back under the covers seemed a better idea.

The only idea.

It had been a while since she had felt like this. Suffocated. Like the walls were closing in.

And that house. Always watching. Judging.

She checked on Clive, who was tentatively dipping his paw into a rock pool, and turned back to gaze out at the water. There was nothing to see apart from the constantly moving water, slowly building waves and screeching seagulls overhead. It was hypnotic to watch everything sway and adapt. Never still. She felt all too often lately that she had stopped moving.

The hairs on her arms stood up. She was not alone.

Clive plodded over, seemingly unaware, and gazed up at her, as though asking if they were done yet. Helen spun around, looked up and down the sand, but could see no one nearby. She looked up at the house again and along the edge of the cliff where the coastal path ran dangerously close to the edge. The occasional dog walker and jogger, tiny little moving shapes, but otherwise nothing out of the ordinary.

And the house. Always the house.

She shivered despite her coat, stroked Clive on his head and said, "Come on, enough for today."

She started back towards the stone steps, Clive at her heels, ice still running up her spine. Her eyes scanned the edge of the water, keeping a check on how quickly it would start to engulf the rocks. A glint of light caught her eye. There was something shiny on one of the rocks set back against the cliff wall. She was drawn to it like a magpie. She picked her way over the slippery rocks and around the pools. Clive stayed by the steps, waiting patiently, preserving his energy for the climb back up to the top.

A little silver bicycle bell sat on a rock.

It didn't look like it had fallen or been washed up. It was clean, sparkly, posed, like it had been placed there.

A cold realisation swept up and out of her stomach. She reached out to pick it up, then withdrew her hand quickly.

She looked around, behind, above her, but she was alone.

A coincidence. Nothing more. A child dropped it when playing in the rock pools maybe.

Nothing to connect it to the photo of the dead girl.

Nothing to connect it to the bicycle that girl was riding the day she died.

Clive was panting hard by the time they reached the kitchen door. Helen had practically run back to the house and he was in need of an extended lie down when she let him into the house. He went straight over to his bed and flung himself down in exhaustion.

Helen closed the door behind her, hesitated, then locked it. She stared out at the grey October sky, all signs of the earlier sunshine now dissolved into cloud and impending drizzle.

The silver bicycle bell was heavy in her coat pocket. She should've left it where it was. She pulled it out and tossed it onto the table where it rolled and clattered against the fruit bowl.

She felt restless despite the walk, like she had an itch she couldn't reach. It had been there ever since she received the photograph. An urge to run away and not look back. But she'd done that once before and had returned in the end, this place always pulling her back, like she was attached to it with a long piece of elastic that refused to snap.

She swore back then that she would never come back, but here she was.

Her home, but not a home she had ever wanted.

The photograph was tucked into her writing notebook in her handbag, between the pages containing new book ideas and character sketches, hidden out of reach of prying eyes. She kept the notebook on her at all times since ideas could come to her at any moment.

Hidden in plain sight.

Helen hadn't worked out where the photo had come from yet. A plain white envelope, her first name in block capitals, nothing out of the ordinary. She had been alone when she opened it, no witnesses to her reaction when she dropped the Polaroid, her fingers burning like it had scalded her.

It had landed face up on the carpet, the girl smiling back.

A face that haunted Helen.

The envelope was empty apart from the Polaroid. No note or letter; no indication of who had sent it – or why.

Why now? All of that happened thirty years ago.

Was she reading too much into the bicycle bell? Was that just a coincidence? Or placed there by whoever sent the photo? Did they know she walked on that beach?

Helen needed to put it out of her head before she drove herself crazy. She needed to focus on the bookshop and her next writing project, try to distract herself, forget about all of it. No good could come of any of it.

She heard a key in the front door and kicked off her sandy shoes, before walking in her socks to the front door. Her cleaner, Pauline, had just arrived, ready to bleach away the family's dirt.

There was some dirt that could never be cleaned though, no matter how much bleach they poured on it.

"Hi, Pauline, how's things?"

"Hey, Mrs Whitmore, can't complain. Clive! Hi!"

She saw him twice a week when she cleaned for them and she always treated him like she hadn't seen him in aeons. He snuffled and snorted at her in greeting. The front door was still standing open and Helen could see the postman at the bottom of the driveway. She didn't want to walk down to see what little surprise was in the letterbox today. She could leave it, let Hugh collect whatever was in there when he got home, but then he would see if there was another white envelope addressed to her. He'd want to know what it was all about. Like ripping off a plaster, she slipped her feet into Hugh's Crocs sitting by the door and stepped outside. Clive let out a half-hearted bark, but the postman held no exciting thrill for him anymore. The postman looked up and waved, his hand a blur at the bottom of the lengthy driveway.

Helen waved back, but he had already turned away.

There was another white envelope in the postbox. Helen's hand shook as she ripped it open on the spot, not even waiting until she was back inside.

It was just the phone bill.

Nothing more sinister than that.

Matt's bedroom door was closed. Helen stood outside it, feeling ridiculously invasive.

This is my house, she reminded herself. She pushed open the door.

It smelled musty inside, as though the windows hadn't been opened in weeks, and there was an undertone of sweat and testosterone, like the smell of a brewery on a hot day.

His bed was unmade, the curtains still closed. She picked her way across the floor and pulled them open. The sea stared back at her from behind a large tree in the garden, the white horses visible on the swell, the tide rumbling in quickly now.

The carpet was completely obscured by discarded clothes, magazines and textbooks. Helen began the process of picking through the debris for dirty pants, stray socks and stained shirts. It was a thankless task, wading through someone else's dirty underwear, and she could feel resentment bubbling in her throat at Matt's laziness. She couldn't understand how Pauline could clean other people's filth for a living. A thankless, never-ending job.

I don't have time for this. I'll be late opening up at this rate.

Her frustration was building. After ten minutes the laundry basket on her hip was full. She put it in the doorway and began to tidy everything else. Pauline was instructed to leave the kids' bedrooms and only clean their en suite bathrooms. They were supposed to tidy their own rooms. They never did though.

Matt's desk was also covered in paper and books that Helen had never seen him read. She pushed aside a pile of papers and picked up a couple of paperbacks sitting partially hidden underneath. The top book she recognised with a jolt. It was one of her earlier novels. She had no idea he had read it. He never mentioned her other career as a writer. The second paperback was a gothic horror story that Helen knew well, Bram Stoker's *Dracula*, and she was almost more surprised at that. She didn't think he would be interested in something so classic. A torn piece of paper was wedged between the pages like a bookmark. On it was a handwritten message in a curly, feminine script.

I think you'll like this one. D x

Helen closed the book and put it on top of the papers she had shuffled together, feeling a little piqued that he had never asked her for book recommendations or opened a discussion with her about anything bookish. She was a published writer and owner of a bookshop, after all, not to mention his stepmother.

From the corner of her eye she noticed the top drawer of his desk was open slightly, a magazine trapped in it. She slid the drawer open. Resting on the top of the magazine was a small metal tin. She opened the lid and the faint scent of weed was released. She rolled her eyes. How stereotypical of him. She moved the magazine aside and felt the hairs on her arms rise as cold washed over her.

It was a pile of white envelopes, just like the one that had contained the photograph.

Surely not.

No, there were plenty of other explanations, not least the fact that these envelopes could be bought in any newsagents or stationers.

She scanned the desk again. Was there anything on it with his handwriting? Something she could compare the capital letters on the envelope to?

No. Stop it, Helen.

It was just a coincidence. Just like the bicycle bell. A paranoid mind connecting dots that weren't there. The truth was that what happened all those years ago had never really gone away. It had just been nipping at her heels for the last thirty years and Helen's brain was now making connections that didn't belong together.

She pushed the drawer shut and exhaled, trying to shake it off. She began to strip the duvet cover and sheet from his bed. She would leave clean sheets out and ask Pauline to change them for her. Something under his pillow was weighing down the sheet. She lifted the pillow. Matt's laptop was pushed underneath it.

She opened the lid. A password request popped up, so she slammed it shut and placed it on the desk before carrying on with the sheets. But her eyes keep straying over to the laptop.

What was on it? And why tuck it under his pillow? Or was it just another symptom of a lazy teenager? If she could just figure out his password, she could see…

No. He was her stepson and she should trust him.

*

The shop was quiet as usual. The tourist foot traffic of the summer months had dissolved away. The shop always experienced a downturn over the winter, but Helen was reluctant to sell up. Apart from her writing attic at the top of the house, this space was her sanctuary. She had opened it when she returned to the village as a single mum after her parents' death, using some of her inheritance to buy the property because she had needed something to fill her days, something she could do with a small baby in tow, and the shop provided that. It was somewhere quiet that didn't need too much thought, where Mills could toddle between the bookshelves and play in the corner. Now Mills was as much a lover of books as Helen was. She was never without either a book or her phone in her hand.

On the table by the window was a display of Helen's own books, although only a few people knew about that side of her because she wrote under a pseudonym. Anonymity suited her.

A scented candle burned on the desk by the register, filling the air with vanilla and coconut, reminding her of Bounty chocolate bars, pina coladas and summer holidays. Her stomach felt empty. She pulled the bottom drawer of the desk open with the toe of her shoe, exposing her stash of biscuits, crisps, pretzels and chocolate, ready to fill the void, to push back the emptiness that sometimes made her feel so hollow and cavernous. There were two customers in the shop though, so now was not the time for snacking. She nudged the drawer closed again reluctantly.

A woman of about Helen's age was poring over the shelves

while nudging a toddler in a pushchair, occasionally bumping into tables and muttering apologies as books toppled. Helen recognised her as the woman who rented one of the cottages further up the coastal path. Helen would often bump into her walking her dog with her toddler in tow. She was also heavily pregnant, but Helen had never seen a partner around. Ambitious for a woman in her forties, but then Helen wasn't one to judge other people's choices when it came to parenting. Today the woman was looking at birthing books while feeding raisins to the toddler. Helen couldn't remember her name, but thought she remembered there being a story there, something she had overheard at the book club she hosted in the shop about how the woman had moved here on her own not too long ago. Rumours of a dead husband maybe and something to do with the child not being hers.

None of Helen's business though. Everyone had a right to their secrets.

The other customer was an elderly woman who was browsing through the books on the tables. She picked up Helen's latest book and read the synopsis on the back, then put it back down before choosing the one next to it.

"Those ones are signed by the author," Helen said into the quiet. The pregnant woman simultaneously jumped and flinched.

"Oh, how lovely," the older lady said. "They're not too… saucy, are they?"

Helen smiled and said with a wink. "I guess you could say they are a good romp, but nothing too *indelicate*."

The elderly lady smiled cheekily, put the book under her arm and moved over to the recipe books on the next table over.

Helen looked back down at the laptop in front of her as she went over last month's sales. Not a pretty picture. Hugh wondered why she persevered with both the shop and the writing. God knows she didn't need to do either. Her thoughts were interrupted by the pregnant woman pushing her toddler past the desk and bumping the wheels against a stand of bookmarks, sending them cascading to the floor.

"Oh!" she said, her hand shooting up to her mouth. The toddler giggled and dropped a raisin.

"Don't worry," Helen hid her annoyance behind a benevolent smile. "I'll get those tidied up."

The woman's wan smile made Helen feel exhausted for her.

The old-fashioned bell above the door jangled as Helen bent down to pick up the bookmarks. Whoever it was stood aside and said in a throaty voice, "After you," and held the door open for the pregnant woman and her toddler to leave.

Helen stood up with a handful of bookmarks and turned to see a strikingly beautiful young girl walk into the store. She was looking around with a small smile. Helen watched as she wandered over to the fiction shelves and began to browse the latest bestsellers. She was wearing skin-tight jeans that had been painted onto her long legs, and heavy black Doc Martin boots with neon green laces. Her hair was auburn, the colour of autumn leaves, and it moved effortlessly across the shoulders of her fluffy pale pink coat in a mass of loose waves. She carried a massive, slouchy black bag over one shoulder. Not the usual clientele Helen saw in the shop.

A cough brought Helen back to herself and she realised she had been staring impolitely, the bookmarks still clutched in her hands. The old woman was waiting patiently to be served, holding a copy of one of Helen's books, a Rick Stein recipe book and Richard Osman's debut novel.

"So sorry, away with the fairies there," Helen said to hide her embarrassment. She stacked the bookmarks hurriedly and none too tidily, and returned to stand behind the desk.

The old woman looked from the girl back to Helen curiously.

Helen rang up the sale and packed the books into a canvas tote bag emblazoned with the name of the shop, The Owl and The Pussycat. Holding up her own book, Helen said, "Do let me know what you think of this one. The writer is a friend of mine, so I can pass on your feedback."

"I will, thank you. Particularly looking forward to this one though. Heard lots of good things about it," she said, pointing to the Osman book.

"Ah, yes, another celebrity author, probably has a ghost writer," Helen replied. She was about to say more but swallowed down the words at seeing the now disapproving look on the woman's face.

"I think he is just lovely. I'm a big *Pointless* fan," the woman said and tucked the tote bag into her pull-along grocery carrier. She headed out of the shop, leaving Helen alone with the young girl, who was also now looking at Helen's books.

"Did I hear you say you know the author?" she said suddenly in a deep, throaty voice.

"Er, yes, I know her quite well actually."

"What is she like?"

"Very nice, friendly. Um…"

The girl nodded, picked up another book, set it down

again. "I picture her as quite an eccentric woman, a martini drinker who wears big hats and has large breasts. Am I right?"

Helen laughed. "Not in the slightest."

She nodded again. "Do you have any history of art books?"

"Um, the shelves towards the back are our reference section. There may be some there."

Helen could feel the girl's eyes on her as she walked past, but Helen kept her head down, looking at but not seeing the computer screen in front of her.

Helen wiped a hand across the back of her neck, which was damp with sweat.

Minutes later, the girl appeared from behind the shelves again and said, "You don't have what I'm looking for," before walking towards the door.

"I can order titles in if you—"

"That's ok, I'll be back. I like it here." She paused with her hand on the door, smiled angelically, then floated out, leaving just the smell of cherries in the air.

She watched Helen move about in the shop. She seemed stiff and tense today though, her movements jerked and forced as she rearranged shelves, unpacked new orders, served customers.

Occasionally, she'd sit and drink a cup of tea, her fingers aimlessly scratching at her arms or her hands rummaging in packets of biscuits.

Those habits lingered, the only real signs that she was affected by it all.

Helen couldn't see her from where she was sitting. She liked to do this most days, just watch her moving around, waiting for the weight of it all to come crashing down on her. The guilt, the sense of wrongdoing, the retribution.

But it never did.

Helen went about her business, then returned home to her big family and their comfortable life. She would watch the family sometimes too, from the garden late at night when the sea was at its loudest, shouting in her ears. She would look up at them moving between the windows of the house. She had to stop herself from screaming at them all.

It wasn't fair.

None of this was fair.

10

THEN

I'm still annoyed when we finish school. I saw Tracey come into my English class after lunch, her shirt smeared red like she'd been stabbed, despite her obvious attempts to wash it off. She avoided all of us and sat at the back. The school photos were a nightmare, with Eloise, Steph and Emily insisting that the photographer take extra shots so that they were in the best light, while Tracey had to cover up with a borrowed jumper from lost property that smelled strongly of sweat.

I should've known better than to invite her to sit with us. Not without checking with Eloise first. What she says, goes. It's always been that way and I've never questioned it, but now I'm starting to think there should be more to our friendship than endless conversations about boys and fashion trends after all these years. I feel like I have been hurtled onto a completely different path to them.

Thank god we are nearly done with all of this and I can get out of here, far away from their small-mindedness.

As I walk towards the bus queue, my feet trailing behind the other three, I notice Tracey head out of the main entrance and turn towards the gates.

"Shit, I've forgotten my history book. I have to go back inside," I say.

"Well, hurry up. I'll keep you your usual seat."

The bus is pulling up in front of us, people piling in. I can see Brian in the back row. He is looking out of the back window and waving at us.

"No, you go on – Brian clearly wants you to sit next to him. I think I'll walk today anyway. I could do with it after eating that toasted cheese at lunch." Except I didn't eat it, but they wouldn't have noticed that. They were too busy fluttering their eyelashes at Brian and his mates or laughing at Tracey.

"Actually, yes, you probably should. All that grease will go straight on your hips," Eloise says and pushes past the younger kids as usual. Steph and Em follow suit. The younger kids just make room, none of them brave enough to take her on.

I wait for the bus to pull away, then follow the route Tracey took. I walk fast, trying to catch up to her. I can smell the sea salt in the air, tangy, fresh. Soon enough, I see her ahead of me and the bus well ahead in the distance.

"Tracey!" I call out. Maybe she didn't hear me because she keeps walking. In fact, I think she has sped up, because I have to accelerate to get closer. "Tracey!" I call again.

This time her feet hesitate and I see her shoulders droop, which makes me feel even more wretched.

I run the last few yards and I'm a little out of breath when I do catch up to her.

"Hey, Tracey, I thought it was you," I say, attempting nonchalance.

She turns weary eyes on me and I can see she has pulled her coat tight across the stain on her shirt.

"Listen, sorry about lunchtime. El can be..."

"A bitch?" she says with ferocity.

I nod in agreement. "Yeah, a bitch." I smile sympathetically. She looks at me for a moment, probably trying to work out whether I am being genuine or if there is something else coming her way. She even looks over my shoulder, checking to see if the others are going to appear out of nowhere, perhaps jump her or something.

Then her shoulders relax and she says, "It's ok, I'm used to people like her," and we carry on walking.

"No, it's not ok. Don't you want to catch the bus?" I ask.

"I prefer walking. It gives me headspace. I usually listen to music and I like being on my own." She pats her coat pocket and I see a Walkman sticking out. "It's usually a madhouse at mine because I have a younger brother and he's... not well."

"Right." I'm not sure what to say next. Should I ask about him? Leave well alone? It's different to my house. All I get is my own space.

"So what are you listening to?" I ask instead.

We start chatting about music as we walk. She is a Depeche Mode fan too – and The Cure. Then we get onto books and I find out she hasn't read any Stephen King yet, so I offer to lend her *It* while she tells me to read Mary Shelley's *Frankenstein*. All too quickly, we are near to the coastal path and I take her the long way around, past our house. I point out the house and she tells me it looks weird, spooky. From her lips it sounds like a compliment.

I don't want to go in just yet, so we keep walking. At the far end of the coastal path, the little chip van is parked up in its usual spot and I realise I'm starving after my lack of lunch. I buy us chips and we smother them in salt and vinegar – no ketchup this time – and sit on a bench overlooking the sea, the rocks below us, laughing and chatting.

I realise as we talk that her eyes are different colours. One brown; one green. They're beautiful. She's beautiful. In an understated way, unlike Eloise's artificial beauty that is painted on every morning and removed every night. Her deep caramel skin is clean and smooth, and I find myself wondering what it would feel like under my fingertips. I'm immediately shocked at myself.

When she says she has to get home for dinner, I feel inexplicably sad. I've had fun today. More fun than I've had in a long time.

We part ways and walk in opposite directions. I stop and turn to watch her go.

I let myself into the house and throw my schoolbag at the foot of the stairs. Martha appears almost immediately and greets me warmly.

In contrast, my mother is thumping around in her bedroom, oblivious that I am there, flinging outfits from her wardrobe and moaning about not having anything to wear for the trip to America. This has become a daily event – either over-the-top excited or stressing about things like how many clutch bags to pack. Her moods lurch and dip, at once delirious and then anguished. Father has been even scarcer than usual, as though the promise of a holiday has given him the permission he needs to spend even less time at home.

She says nothing to me when I step into her bedroom.

I stub out the cigarette left dangling precariously over the edge of the ashtray that is tossed onto her bed. She screams at me, "Can't you see I'm busy here? Get out! Get out!" Her face is pulled into an ugly snarl. I leave quickly and she kicks the door shut behind me.

I can't wait to see the back of them.

I push the Rice Krispies around the bowl. The snap, crackle and pop has long since stopped. They are mushy and sodden now, unappetising. Still my father drones on. He's not normally here on a Friday morning. In fact, it's been ages since we actually shared the same air. He usually breezes past me without so much as a glance on his way back to London or in a rush to close himself in his office across the hall.

Today he is on an epic rant. My grades aren't good enough. I'll never make something of myself. The good universities will be closed to me if I don't start taking school more seriously.

Yawn.

He is such a hypocrite, sitting there, spooning scrambled eggs into his tight mouth. His lips are so used to being pursed, I'm surprised he can get the fork in.

I know what this is really about. Pamela Stewart's father managed to secure her an early interview at Oxford. And if his business rival has a successful daughter, then so must my father. It wouldn't do to fail on that score. So the pressure on me has ramped up, but I'm sure he'll lose interest again soon enough when he realises I am a lost cause.

Martha is in a bit of a flurry around us. There must be an important dinner at the house tonight. I'll be told to make myself scarce, of course. I'll just sneak a bottle of something up to the attic and read in peace. Actually, maybe I should invite Tracey over. They won't notice she is here.

Father pats the side of his mouth with a napkin and I think he is done. I'm about to push back my chair, but he was only taking a breath. I wait patiently.

The truth is I would love to go to Oxford, maybe study English literature or consider a career in journalism, something like that. But I would never tell him that. He wants another lawyer in the family or, failing that, a stockbroker or investment banker, someone with a high-paying city job like his. But his job doesn't seem much fun to me.

Finally, he stops talking. I look up and I'm about to say that I'd happily work harder if it means I can go to Oxford to study English when he picks up his newspaper and obscures his disapproval with the headlines. He hasn't asked me about school per se or how things are going.

I pick up my bowl and rise from the table, leaving without a word. I haven't said anything to him apart from, "Morning, Father." He hasn't noticed my silence.

Martha is at the kitchen sink, washing a large vase.

I set the bowl down on the counter next to her. "Thanks, Martha, I'm heading out to school."

"But you've hardly eaten anything! Can I make you something else?"

"No, thank you, I'm not hungry. See you later though."

I turn to go, then ask over my shoulder, "I guess there's something on tonight?"

"Yes, a dinner, your father's partners and their wives." She looks at me with such pity that I feel like bursting into tears on the spot, but instead I swallow and nod, before heading out through the back door and down the garden.

I open the gate past the pool house and step out onto the path. The sky is a menacing grey today, the clouds rolling as much as the waves below, matching my mood like a co-ordinated outfit. I walk along, my hands shoved deep into my pockets, my head bowed. I have loads of time before school starts, but I just needed to be out of there.

At the end of the wall, the path curves away towards the farm and on a whim I decide to walk in that direction. Maybe I can catch Tracey before she has left for school. I had a really nice afternoon yesterday and right now I just want to see a friendly face.

After about ten minutes of walking, I can see the farm in the distance. It is quite isolated here – just fields, hedgerows and the grey sky. I approach the gate to the farm and contemplate the incredibly muddy path that stretches up to the farmhouse. My school shoes will not come out of that mud unscathed. I step back and look up at the house again, then see the front door open and a number of bodies emerge. They are being bundled into an old Land Rover and I realise with embarrassment that Tracey is getting a lift to school and I am stood at the bottom of her driveway like a loser. I turn and hurry away before anyone notices me, but the ground is soggy and I slip, landing painfully on my hip. One of my hands has landed in a splat of what I hope is mud but on closer inspection is cow shit.

"Shit," I mutter, then start to giggle.

I hear the Land Rover approach the gate and stop.

"Helen?"

I look up and see Tracey peering down at me, her forehead knotted in confusion.

"Hey, Tracey, I was... just wondering if you wanted to walk to school together, but then I slipped and..."

And then she is laughing. Really hard. So hard she is snorting. More people emerge from the Land Rover and peer down at me, but I can't make out their faces as I am now laughing hysterically too. Tears are starting to rush down my cheeks and every time I move to get up, I keel over again.

Eventually, a man with a kind face and a bald head reaches under my armpits and hauls me to my feet.

I manage to mumble my thanks as the laughter subsides.

"You must be Helen," he says. "I'm Terry, Tracey's dad. Let's get you inside and cleaned up, then I'll give you all a lift to school. Did you hurt yourself when you fell?"

"No, I just got a bit filthy."

"I'll walk back to the house with her, Dad. Helen, you can borrow one of my school skirts for today if you want?"

Her little brother is still sitting in the back of the car, giggling, his shoulders shaking as her dad reaches in and lifts him out. I can see from looking at him that what Tracey said about him not being well isn't strictly true. He has Down's Syndrome and is disabled. I look away as her dad helps him out of the car.

The kitchen of their house couldn't be more different to

ours. It is warm, the heat from the Aga radiating cosiness, and the counters are strewn with all sorts of random objects – books, unopened post, sunglasses, a baseball cap, batteries, bowls of fruit, lengths of cable. There is a long table down the middle of the room that also seems to be covered in various household objects, including the end of a vacuum cleaner, as well as breakfast cereal boxes, empty bowls and splatters of milk.

Tracey's mum, who introduces herself as Gloria, is simultaneously fussing around me, clearing the breakfast bowls, wiping the table and running a sink of hot water for me to wash my hands. Doing a million little things at once, all with a warm smile on her face, which is free of any discernible make-up. Her afro is held back from her coffee-coloured face with a brightly coloured scarf knotted at the nape of her neck and she is wearing baggy jeans and a sweatshirt. I have never seen my mother in denim. A radio is playing and she is humming along to the song – 'Wake Me Up Before You Go Go' by Wham – her ample hips shimmying to the beat.

Tracey is rummaging through a basket of clean clothes stashed in the corner. She pulls out a skirt and hands it to me.

"I hope it fits ok – you're much smaller than me."

I don't think I am. I think I have quite sizeable hips, especially compared to Eloise, and I start to worry that the skirt won't fit and then I'll be mortified all over again.

"The downstairs loo is just through there if you want to change," Tracey says and points down a narrow corridor off the kitchen.

The loo is a tiny room, painted in a bright sunshine yellow

with small, framed pictures of Tracey and her brother that hang haphazardly on the walls. Photos of sunshine, holidays and stolen family moments. There is a basket on the floor full of comic books and the smell of vanilla wafts from an air freshener on the windowsill.

I wiggle out of my dirty skirt and into Tracey's clean one, then hold in my stomach as much as I can while I pull up the zip at the back. It just fits, but it is a bit tight and I will have to be careful not to breathe out too much when I'm at school.

When I emerge from the loo, I stand in the doorway for a moment and watch them. Her mother is telling her father something, her hands animated and her smile wide. He is listening to her with intensity, then he reaches out a hand, pale against her dark skin, and touches her face with affection. Tracey's little brother says something then and they all look at him and laugh. He has a yellow ribbon in his hand and points to Tracey's hair, which is pulled into a low ponytail again. She leans over and he ties the yellow ribbon around her hair in a big bow.

Tracey beams at him and he claps his hands in delight.

As she straightens up, she notices me standing in the doorway and says, "Great! The skirt fits!"

"Yes, thanks. Nice ribbon."

"Yellow is his favourite colour and he wants me to wear it in my hair today." She is unapologetic about it, about him.

"Excellent," her father says. "It looks amazing, Alistair. Right, let's get going then as I have to get back for a delivery."

"Helen, you are welcome any time to come and visit," her mother says as we file out of the house. "Come for tea one day after school – I'm sure Tracey would love it if you could. I make a mean chicken curry." I smile politely back at her.

I pile into the back seat of the Land Rover. Tracey sits in between me and Alistair, who is watching me with curiosity. I don't want to stare at him, with his open face and big brown eyes, so I look out of the window instead and see her mother waving us off enthusiastically. My dirty school skirt is tucked into my school bag at my feet and suddenly I'm really pleased I ended up in the mud.

The engine starts up simultaneously with the radio, and Tracey and her dad start singing along to the song playing. By the time we pull up to school, we are all singing and laughing, my earlier dark mood and argument with my own father a distant memory.

11

NOW

"I'm just not feeling it yet, Hels," Sharon said.

Helen rubbed at her forehead. The headache that she thought had dispersed this morning was back with an insistent vengeance. She had headed home from the bookshop soon after her assistant, Jenni, had arrived for her afternoon shift. Jenni covered the shop for Helen a few afternoons a week and on Saturdays so that Helen could write. The village was still small enough that during the winter it was closed on Sundays.

A sweet girl, only eighteen, Jenni was eager to please and pleasant with the customers. She had a quirky dress sense, favouring obscure hats, mismatched prints and layers of bracelets on her tiny wrists that clattered as she moved. She had big, red-framed glasses that magnified her brown eyes and made her look not unlike the owl on the shop signage, and she always had her nose in a book. It was like she had walked out of a Beatrix Potter story, but she was unapologetic about her chosen style and Helen envied her for that. Today Jenni had been dressed in double animal print, but with a cheetah print on the top and zebra print on the bottom, it went against the laws of nature. When she walked, it looked like her jacket was trying to eat her skirt.

Helen sat at her desk in her attic. Sharon was still talking down the phone. "It's just too similar to the last plot. There's no... surprises."

Helen leaned back in her chair, which groaned in response. Secretly Helen agreed with Sharon. She'd known when she was writing it how flat it was. But it annoyed her to hear Sharon say it out loud. It made the clawing panic that sometimes inched its long, bony fingers around her throat tighten its grip just a little bit more.

Is this it? Have I finally run out of ideas? Will they all see I am a fake after all?

Imposter syndrome at its best.

Helen wrote romance novels. Bodice rippers. Hence Hugh's relief that she wrote under a pseudonym. He would hate it if the school committee knew his wife was behind such steamy titles. Nothing too risqué – they weren't on the Fifty Shades level of smut – but there were plenty of heaving chests and quivering limbs, mixed with a good dollop of innuendo. There was nothing literary about the books, but she found it liberating to write the kind of things that would never happen to her, to create characters with life and vigour, all under a cloak of secrecy. And if readers kept buying them, she would keep writing them. Villains and heroes, brooding, misunderstood men and empowered, feisty women, taking what they want from whomever they choose.

Her real life may be tedious domestic humdrum at best, but her alter ego got to have a lot of fun.

"Should I just go back to the drawing board?" she said to Sharon.

Sharon sighed down the phone. "Maybe. Have you had any other ideas?"

Helen thought about the photograph, thought about how long that story had been hidden – and how freeing it would be to finally let it out, tell it her way. "What if I said I did? But it would be completely different to what I've written before?"

"Oh? What is it about?" Helen could picture Sharon sitting higher in her seat.

"A house – and a secret. A teenage girl and a murder." Helen hesitated. "I don't know. It's still vague at this stage."

"Sounds intriguing. We can push the deadline out. I'll talk to the publisher, get you some more time. I think it might be worth it." Sharon paused again. "Look, truth time. Sales are down; reviews haven't been great. It's like…"

"Say it, Sharon."

"The publisher thinks you need to change things up a bit. The formula is getting a bit… stale. So if this new idea has legs, then run with it. Get some new chapters over to me and we can take it from there."

She'd said it. Stale. That summed everything up. The shop was stale. The books were stale. Helen was stale.

"I'm not trying to hurt your feelings here, Helen. I'm on your side. I still think you are great at what you do. We just need to change it up a bit, that's all. Have a think, do some planning and call me later, ok?"

Helen sighed and shifted her weight. The chair groaned again, as if in agreement with Sharon. "Ok, I will."

Helen ended the call and sat in the silence. Her writing room was at the very top of the house in the attic. It was a turret-shaped room tucked into the eaves, only accessible by a rickety staircase attached to a trapdoor in the furthest corner of the house, which had to be pulled down from the ceiling by a long pole. It was dark and musty, with a steeply pointed roof and very little natural light coming in from one small window set high into the turret. Helen could just make out the sea in the distance if she stretched up onto her toes and strained her neck. Today it was a swirling, endless greyness, choppy and angry.

Boxes were piled precariously along one curved wall, creating deep shadows, and the wall lights were a hazy yellow under old, fringed lampshades that offered no useful illumination. This wasn't a glamourous writing space, but it was all hers. She had commandeered the attic as a child when she had needed a place to hide. She didn't think her parents ever knew she had taken over this space. They never came up here looking for her.

In those days it was bean bags and blankets on the floor, posters on the walls and books everywhere. Their housekeeper at the time, Martha, had helped her to find various bits and pieces to make the space more comfortable, most of it from things her parents had discarded in the basement. Now though, there was a vivid pink velvet couch in front of the desk, usually adorned with a sleeping bulldog lying with his head propped up on the multitude of bright cushions. Clive had to be helped up and down, which was no easy feat, but he insisted on being by her side. This couch was where she sat to think about plot holes and character traits, her fingers lightly stroking his ears. The covers of all nine of her books hung in small frames on the walls. There were two low side tables at either end of the couch with old-fashioned, Tiffany-style lamps that helped to bring some light into the gloom.

Dominating the room and facing the fuchsia pink couch was her father's old desk. A solid, heavy mahogany behemoth of a desk, with drawers down both sides, ostentatious gold handles and clawed feet. Hugh originally had his eye on it for his study, but Helen had insisted on moving it up here, which was an accomplishment in itself. It had to be dismantled and brought up in sections, but what made all the effort of rebuilding it in this small room worth it was knowing that she was writing her trashy novels on the desk that had brought her father such notable success in business. He would be spinning in his grave.

He certainly wouldn't think writing was a suitable career for her. Helen would like to think she was shoving it in his face, accompanied by her middle finger.

She rocked gently in the chair, listening to it creak while she tapped her fingernails against the dark wood. Why had she told Sharon that?

That story wasn't for telling. Not yet anyway.

But it also might be nice to get it out of her head, finally expose the nasty ugliness of it.

Her eyes scanned the boxes piled against the far wall. Most were full of her parents' paperwork and bits from her childhood that had been relocated to the attic at her parents' request when they cleared out her old bedroom in a rush to rid the house of her presence after she left hastily under a cloud of disgrace.

The shoebox wasn't in there though. It contained the diaries, disguised beneath fake book covers. She scratched absent-mindedly at the old scar on her wrist, faint now when once it was an angry red.

No, Helen needed to come up with a new idea instead. That story was best left buried in the past where it belonged.

With the kids due home at any moment, Helen emerged from the attic with Clive at her feet, creeping his way slowly down the stairs with bulldog grace. As she passed Hugh's closed office door on the ground floor, she hesitated a moment, then pushed open the door and stepped into the room.

This room was originally the old library and her father's office, with bookshelves lining the walls and a large picture window looking out over the garden to the side of the house. There was an air of severity in the room and it still felt like the headmaster's office now that Hugh had taken residence, like the bookshelves were looking down on you in disappointment.

Must do better, Helen.

You would think it would've been her favourite room of all when she was younger and that she would've claimed it as her own when Hugh and the kids moved in, but this had always been her father's domain. It reminded her of tense negotiations and shouted exchanges filtering through a door that was always firmly closed to her unless she was in trouble.

Hugh loved it. The door was still always firmly closed.

The air smelled faintly of Imperial Leather soap and old paper. There was a mug on the desk, a mouthful of coffee left in the bottom, ringing the white porcelain with a dark stain. Helen stepped around the desk and picked up the mug, but her fingers were moving slower than her brain and the mug slipped from her grip. The cold dregs of coffee splashed onto Hugh's keyboard.

"Shit," she muttered and grabbed a handful of tissues from a box on the desk. As she dabbed at the keyboard, the screen came to life and Hugh's private Gmail inbox popped up.

Helen didn't even know he had a Gmail account. He still walked around with an old Nokia phone into which he would shout as though he was on the moon.

Inexplicably, Helen looked over towards the open office door, even though she knew she was alone in the house. She glanced at the emails. One address seemed to have sent him a few emails in the last day or two, but Helen didn't recognise it – *dsto4@gmail.com*. None of the emails had a subject line, but they did have attachments. Helen reached for the mouse to open one of the messages just as the front door slammed.

Hastily she snatched her hand back, finished wiping down the keyboard and emerged from the office, dirty mug in hand and a flush in her cheeks.

Mills was in the hallway. She dumped her school bag under the console table before shrugging out of her coat. She looked over as Helen closed the office door behind her, excuses ready on the tip of her tongue.

"Hey, Mum," Mills said.

"Hi, how was your day?" Helen felt like she had been caught doing something she shouldn't, even though all she did was nudge a mouse and spill some coffee.

Clive was shuffling around Mills' feet, his substantial bum wiggling in greeting. Mills fawned over him, stroking his ears and crooning at him, before replying, "Fine. I'm starving. Is there anything to eat?"

She kicked off her shoes, left them in the middle of the floor and glided to the kitchen on stockinged feet. Clive grabbed a shoe in his mouth and followed her, but Helen snatched it from him as he lumbered past.

She put the shoes neatly under the console table and followed Mills.

The kitchen was immaculate and smelled of bleach and lemon. Every surface sparkled after Pauline's hard work, but before long it would all be undone.

Mills had her face in the fridge, muttering about there never being anything to eat, and Helen had an overwhelming urge to hug her. She wrapped her arms around her from behind and squeezed, love for her daughter making her feel dizzy.

In return Mills tapped at Helen's cold hands on her chest like she was petting Clive. Helen pulled away and went to fill the kettle.

"Cup of tea?"

"Yeah, thanks. Rubbish day. Had a physics test."

"Did you revise for it?"

Mills looked at Helen with narrowed eyes, before saying, "Yeah, course I did," which made Helen think she hadn't.

She was a smart kid, quick to pick things up, but prone to only doing enough to get by. Helen had been the same at school, only really putting any effort into English, and it had done Helen no favours. She had found school as tedious as Mills did, just something to be humoured until she could get out into the wide world and find her place in it. Helen had many regrets about that time in her life, but she had clawed her way back from rock bottom and was now living a contented life, albeit dull, uninteresting and predominantly funded by her dead parents who had never had any faith in her.

That was not what she wanted for Mills, whose whole future was stretching out ahead of her. Helen wanted that life to be everything hers had not been.

"Lydia didn't walk home with you?" Helen said as she poured boiling water into a mug.

"No, she has hockey practice today."

Helen wanted Mills and Lydia to be friends, sisters even, but there was a distance, a reluctance to get close.

"I think—" The front door slammed again, followed by uncharacteristic giggling.

Helen frowned, her hands pausing in the process of wringing the life out of a teabag. Clive lurched away again, ready to greet whoever was next. Feet thudded across the parquet floor in the hallway, heavy and rushed, and a husky feminine voice exclaimed, "Oh wow, who's this?"

Matt's deep voice replied, "This is the legend that is Clive. Come on boy, let's go. Leave her alone."

Helen turned with a smile on her face as Matt walked into the kitchen, followed by an extremely pretty girl.

The girl from the shop.

They screeched to a halt and just stood, looking at Helen, whose face had frozen in surprise.

"Hi," Helen said cheerfully.

Matt looked at his feet, coughed a little, but said nothing.

Helen stepped towards them. "I'm Helen, Matt's stepmum. We—"

"I'm Diana," the girl interrupted.

"Beautiful name," Helen said.

Beautiful face, she thought.

Diana shrugged. "My mother had a thing for the royal family. If I had a brother, he'd be called Charles. Hey, Mills."

Mills raised a hand in reply. Helen was surprised that they knew each other. Matt's art college was a half-hour inland while Mills was doing her A-levels at the private school where Hugh taught just outside the village. The same school Helen had attended back in the day.

Mills had finished making the tea. She took one of the mugs in her hand and left the kitchen without another word.

"I've just boiled the kettle if you would like some tea?" Helen said to cover Mills' rudeness.

"We're going to my room," Matt said instead. He sloped over to the pantry, grabbed a large bag of crisps and returned to stand next to Diana, who was still staring at Helen, a strange half-smile on her lips. Matt took her hand and they left the room. Helen could hear giggling again and snatches of whispered words, Matt saying something about Helen being "lame" and "awkward".

Helen's heart was hammering in her chest and her cheeks burned. She took the remaining mug of tea with a trembling hand.

Something about that girl. Not just the coincidence of seeing her twice in one day. Helen had felt it earlier too. The glossy hair, full rose lips, swaying hips demanding that all eyes were on her.

She reminded Helen of someone she knew a long time ago.

She felt like she was suffocating, the air in the kitchen closing in on her like a poisonous gas. She had to get out. She didn't notice the tea spilling over the rim of the cup as she burst through the glass doors into the garden, filling her lungs with fresh air as soon as she stepped outside.

The air was chilly, a salty breeze carrying in from the sea. She could see the water, a navy blue stripe against the grey sky. There was one faint shape far out on the ocean and she imagined a small ship, bobbing in the waves, alone, isolated, just the boat and the expanse of water around it. Thinking about all that space and solitude made her feel calmer and her breathing slowed a little. She walked over to a bench, pulling her cardigan tight around her for warmth and the feeling of security, of being held, contained. The wood of the bench was cold and damp beneath her legs after a rain shower earlier. A shadow stepped into the light of the kitchen doorway and her heart sank at the thought that someone wanted something from her, a need that required satiating on demand, but it was just Clive, watching from the back door, reluctant to come outside into the frigid garden but desperate to make sure she was safe.

Helen smiled and sipped at her cooling tea. She looked up at the windows above her. Bedroom windows on either side of the huge stained glass masterpiece running down the centre of the back wall like a painted mouth. She could see Mills walking past her window, swigging from the neck of a bottle. Helen knew she kept vodka in her room, could often smell the cigarette smoke in her hair too, thinly disguised by a spritz of body spray. Helen should probably add it to the list of things to talk to her about, but the idea left her feeling enervated. Hugh wouldn't get involved – they had an unspoken rule that he disciplined his kids and she did hers – but after a childhood like Helen's had been, she knew all of the best hiding places for contraband and didn't think it was a big enough problem to address just yet. Some clandestine booze and cigarettes were the least of her sins back then.

Helen's eyes moved over to Matt's window. Just shapes and shadows moving beyond curtains that had been closed again.

She checked her watch, drained her mug and got to her feet with a sigh. It was 4:30 p.m. She needed to get some writing time in before making a start on dinner. Hugh liked his dinner on time at 7:30 p.m. every evening and she had been on the receiving end of his terse looks before, the way the sides of his face pinched in when he was made to wait. He was a stickler for good manners and punctuality.

But happy life, happy husband.

Her limbs felt heavy and lethargic as she headed back indoors, past Clive who had positioned himself right in the doorway. She had to climb over him to get inside, but he remained where he was, fast asleep, oblivious. She had a thought then, fleeting and thin, of Clive and her a few years from now, just the two of them in their little house by the sea, everyone else gone, and it made her feel wistful.

Mills could see her mother in the garden, the way she sat

heavily on the bench, clutching at her cardigan like it was a straitjacket. The way her eyes flitted around anxiously as she checked her watch, always conscious that there was something she should be doing rather than just sitting in the garden enjoying a cup of tea.

Sometimes Mills wanted to tell her to chill, take a moment for herself. The only time she did indulge herself was when she was swimming. Even the writing seemed to be a chore these days, something to distract her and agonise over rather than enjoy like in the early days when she would call Mills over and excitedly open the box of freshly published paperbacks, take one out, proud and thrilled, showing it to Mills with a big smile on her face.

These days she just seemed sad.

Mills knew there were things going on she didn't understand. Like her mother's relationship with Hugh. She did not get what her mother saw in him. He was everything she was not and she waited on him hand and foot. He was stuffy, dull, old-fashioned and set in his ways. He liked to speak in clichés and she imagined that was what her grandfather must've been like. Not that her mother ever said much about him.

Mills often did stuff just to get a rise out of Hugh, but all he would do was tut and hand it over to her mother to deal with – and then Mills felt bad because her mother and her were a team, a unit.

Well, they used to be.

A thump through the bedroom wall and loud music started up. Matt had brought Diana home for the first time and Mills didn't like it one bit.

Mills knew her from school last year. She was weird – too

inquisitive, like she wanted to know everything about you. She had a way of staring at you when she talked, like she was evaluating your response or judging you, staring into your very soul to establish if you were telling the truth. Considering that Mills was a school year below her, it had seemed unnatural for her to take so much interest in Mills' life.

And yet here she was in her house, having apparently moved on to Matt as her point of interest.

Mills necked more of the vodka, her brain in overdrive. It tasted funny, thin, but she drank deeply again anyway.

She knew the booze was probably a bad idea. She had homework and revision to do, but some days she just felt lost, adrift, unsure of everything.

And now she had her mother to worry about too.

12

THEN

Eloise is waiting for me by my locker and scowls as she sees me walk in with Tracey.

"You weren't on the bus," she says, completely ignoring Tracey's presence.

"No, Tracey's dad gave us a lift this morning."

She glares at Tracey, looks her up and down as though she is a science experiment, then says, "You hair looks cute, Tracey. That ribbon is very... fetching. It really stands out, what with your colouring and everything."

"Thanks," Tracey says with a big smile, but I know from El's tone that she isn't being kind.

Right now, I hate Eloise. This girl who has been my friend for as long as I can remember, with her perfectly peachy skin and luscious hair, her privileges and prejudices. She would never understand the simple pleasure of wearing a ribbon in your hair because your little brother gave it to you.

I want to say something to her, tell her to leave Tracey alone, but the bell is ringing and the corridor is filling up rapidly, bodies rushing to class, shoving and bumping. One of them is Brian, who links arms with El and leads her away. He looks over his shoulder and sneers, "Ridiculous ribbon, Tracey, what are you? Like, three?"

Their laughter bounces off the walls as they walk away.

Tracey looks bereft and reaches up to pull the ribbon from her hair, but I say, "Ignore them, I think it's lovely and so does your brother. Who cares what they think?"

She smiles weakly at me, but leaves the ribbon in place as we head into class.

At lunchtime I have a dilemma. I know Tracey will be on her own, but if I choose not to sit with El, it will make things harder for Tracey in the long run. When El gets someone in her sights, she can be unrelenting. Just before the lunchtime bell, I write Tracey a hasty note and pass it to her as she walks past my desk when I am packing up. The note explains that I can't sit with her at lunch, but asking if she wants to stay at my house tonight.

She reads it quickly, then smiles and nods, before whispering, "I'll talk to you later. Walk home from school together?"

I nod, just as El sticks her head over my shoulder and says, "Are you coming or what? Tracey, I'm sure you have somewhere else to be, don't you?"

In the canteen, I poke at my yoghurt and try to see where Tracey has ended up sitting. Then I see her across the room with a very quiet girl who is in my English class. They are laughing at something in a book. I wonder what is so funny as I watch them. She looks happy, her hair bouncing with her shoulders, the yellow ribbon still in place. Who is that girl she's with though? I can't even remember her name. Tina, maybe? Yes, that's it.

El is rambling on about something and nothing, but I'm not listening. Tracey and her new friend are now sharing the girl's chips, dipping them in ketchup and chatting between mouthfuls. I push my yoghurt away, untouched. Then I hear El say, "I know! We should have a party. Invite some of the boys! It'll be fun and we only have a little bit of time left together before we break for study leave. What do you think?"

"Yes, yes!" Steph and Emily squeal in excitement.

I merely shrug. None of the boys at this school hold any interest for me.

"Aren't your parents going on their trip to America soon, Hels?"

Tracey and her friend are packing up their trays. They are still chatting and laughing. They seem to have a lot to say to each other.

"Yeah, they leave next week," I say absent-mindedly.

"Great! We'll have the party in your pool house!"

"Wait, what?"

"It's perfect – there will be no adults around and the pool house is so ideal. I have a lovely new bikini that I bought in Santorini that I need to wear at least once this year."

"That is a brilliant idea, El!" Steph says, her face so lit up with excitement that the spot on her chin glows even redder. El could suggest planting a bomb under the school and Steph would clap her hands and say it's a good idea though.

"I don't know, my folks would be fuming if they found out," I say.

"How would they know? You could tell the staff that they have agreed to it. There's no way they will check and I promise we will leave the pool house the way we find it."

I look over at Tracey again, but she is walking out of the canteen. My eyes follow the yellow ribbon. El narrows her eyes.

"I'll even let you invite *her* if you want? You're paying her more attention than us anyway."

Not that it's up to Eloise who I invite to a party that I am hosting, but the idea of being able to invite Tracey without any aggro from El means I might actually have fun after all.

"No, I'm not. I just… have some stuff to ask her for French homework, that's all. Ok, you're on for the party, but any damage or mess and you have to help me tidy it up. I cannot have my father on my case for anything else."

My parents will be away for about six weeks, so plenty of time to get the party organised and spread the word. Of course, El will take over all of the arrangements. She already has plenty of ideas.

I'll need to get a new bikini – and maybe not eat anything between now and then. El is drinking this detox green tea at the moment and only eating celery from what I can see. Negative calories in celery apparently. Maybe I should try that. I wish I had her willpower. She can be really single-minded when it comes to food. If she says she is not going to eat for a day, she will clamp her lips shut and they will stay that way. I make these declarations, then end up thinking so much about food that I end up eating anything I can get my hands on. I start each day thinking I will be good and only eat fruit and vegetables, and then by the time I get home from school, Martha is there with a plate of freshly baked cookies or a Victoria sponge and it all goes out the window, not to mention her lovely dinners. By bedtime, I lie there with my hands on my rounded belly, berating my weak willpower and promising myself I will do better tomorrow.

But I never learn.

Of course, if El doesn't see me eating, the calories don't count, right?

I could tell Martha that I only want salads, but she gives me these pinched lip looks and tells me there is nothing wrong with the way I look and then I feel awful that she has spent time cooking for me when I am the only one eating. My mother hasn't eaten a proper meal since 1972.

Tracey walks past us as we head into class after lunch. El is still talking about the party before loudly shushing us all when she sees Tracey, which is incredibly awkward. I'll tell Tracey about the party after school anyway. I hope she comes.

I really don't know what El's problem with Tracey is, unless it's just petty jealousy. El has always been a bit possessive of me. Frankly, Tracey is far nicer than her – and pretty too. Obviously El is beautiful, which is annoying in itself, with her auburn hair and big blue eyes, but Tracey is pretty *and* nice. That's the difference. El is just a bitch. But we've known each other for so long that I've never thought about not being friends with El. Steph and Emily are just background noise, but El and I have been friends since we were little.

And yet I don't actually know if I even like her anymore.

She is so obsessed with how she looks and boys, whereas I'm not that interested, but I have to pretend to be. I can't remember the last time El and I had a conversation that wasn't about boys and clothes.

Spending time with Tracey is easy. It feels *normal*. I can enjoy myself without having to put other people down, laugh at jokes that aren't at someone else's expense, eat chips out of the wrapper with salt and vinegar rather than worry about how many calories there are in a banana.

Being friends with El is hard work. You are constantly on your guard in case she has changed her mind about what is the latest thing to wear or you speak to the wrong person, someone she has decided she will pick on this week. She can cut you down with one sharp comment and leave you withering on the floor. I've seen her do it so often to Steph and Emily, but they keep coming back for more as they hang their self-worth on El's approval. She does it less to me, but there is always that element of danger, knowing she could turn on me at any moment. It's like hanging out with a hand grenade with a loose pin.

Let's not forget what she did to that girl Mandy for doing nothing more than smile at a boy El liked at the time. El spent the next few weeks slipping notes into everyone's lockers saying awful things about Mandy, so that every time she showed her face in the corridors, people would laugh at her and point. In the canteen, she would slip her foot out as Mandy walked past, so that she fell or tripped and spilled her drink, or she would hide her underwear while she was in the shower after PE, then tease her and try to lift her skirt in class, knowing she had nothing on underneath. Eventually El got bored of toying with her, but the change in Mandy over those two weeks was obvious. She went from being bubbly and chatty to walking everywhere with her head down, her hair covering her face, and jumping any time anyone spoke to her.

And I admit, I was a part of it – me, Steph and Emily. It had started out as a laugh. We would help El come up with the nasty rumours to write on the notes. It was my bag that El hid her underwear in. I might have even pushed my bag out in front of her once and laughed as she tripped over it and dropped her tray.

But El has a way of pulling you in and making you complicit. And anyway, Mandy was nothing to me. Just a girl I had seen around.

But I actually *like* Tracey. I like her family and the things we talk about, the way I can relax around her. And I've only known her for one day.

I'm going to invite Tracey to the party. I'll tell her to stay over that night too, so that she doesn't have to worry about getting home. Because she has the kind of parents that would worry about parties at rich kids' houses. And who knows? Maybe El will like her too and she can join our group.

El has a long list of boys she wants to invite, including Jason who she thinks I should get together with, but his nose is too big for his face, almost as big as the inflated opinion he has of himself. He's all big talk about his skiing holidays and how much his new trainers cost. I couldn't care less. I hate skiing. My parents go every year and, although I am fairly competent at it, I spend most of the holiday in ski school hanging out with the same kind of kids I hang out with at home, but with helmet hair for a week. I'd rather be at home with a good book.

At least with Tracey at the party, I might actually have a laugh while El is busy cosying up to Brian and his mates. She will try and match me up with Jason though, so I need to have a strategy for that.

13

NOW

Helen had one foot on the stairs when Lydia arrived home, covered in dirt, hockey stick under one arm and with very little to say. She fussed over Clive, but hardly spared Helen a look, just cut in front of her and went to head straight upstairs. Then she paused, her head cocked like a puppy, her ears pricked. "Who's here?"

"Matt has a friend over. Diana," Helen replied.

Lydia looked taken aback for a second, then it passed. She ran up the stairs and Helen heard her bedroom door slam seconds later.

Helen followed up the stairs and paused outside Mills' room, thought about knocking and maybe taking a moment to talk to her about the drinking. Her hand hovered over the wood, then dropped to her side. Instead, she headed up another floor to the main bedroom.

This was once her parents' room, her parents' bed. Helen still thought of it as her mother's domain, no matter how many times she decorated, painted, stripped away the pomp and frills. More of a suite than a room, complete with a separate dressing room, en suite bathroom, a large stone fireplace that dominated one wall and a huge four-poster bed that held court over the rest of the space. It was all a bit ostentatious and heavy, like something out of a television period drama. The bed itself was a bit of a relic. It creaked loudly when you moved, like it was objecting to your presence, and was claustrophobically sombre. Helen had strung fairy lights around the frame before Hugh moved in, in a bid to lighten it and differentiate it from the bed in which her mother would spend days on end curled up, crying into the pillows or flinging herself around in a fit of rage at her father's latest indiscretion. Hugh hated the fairy lights, said he couldn't sleep with them twinkling above him, so they were on a strict timer switch. It wasn't like Blackpool illuminations or anything, but Hugh liked simple, plain, unadorned.

Helen lay back on the bed and stared up into the darkness above her, the lights twinkling gaily. She knew her head was not in the right place for writing or planning. Another thing Hugh didn't understand. He thought it was simply a case of sitting down and starting to write, but there was a specific mental space Helen had to occupy first. In her imagination it looked a little bit like the land where the Teletubbies lived, probably because a lot of Helen's early writing was done to a Laa-Laa and Po backdrop when Mills was young. Right now though, Helen's head was full of images of The Time Before, bashing together like bumper cars, leaving dents and purple bruises. That was happening a lot lately.

Maybe she should ask Mills for some of her vodka. The idea made her smile. The truth was Helen was proud of who Mills was turning into. She wasn't perfect, but she was a part of Helen. The better part.

She could hear music thumping up through the floorboards, the occasional laugh and rumble of conversation from Matt's room directly beneath her. It was soporific and Helen could feel herself dozing off. But if she did that, there would certainly be no dinner ready for Hugh – and he considered ordering a takeaway to be an admission of failure.

Helen heaved to her feet with a sigh.

She turned on the radio in the kitchen and listened to random chat while she began prepping dinner. As she lifted a casserole dish into the oven and started wiping down the surfaces, she heard the front door again. Clive let out a small, gruff bark from where he had positioned himself at her feet, perfectly placed to catch any falling scraps. He heaved to his feet and waddled from the room.

"Hi, Clive, old boy. How's things? No, leave it. Leave it! Helen!"

Helen walked into the hallway, wiping her hands on her apron. Hugh was wrestling with Clive, who had his shoe firmly clamped between his teeth.

"Clive, behave," she said and Clive glanced at her witheringly before dropping the shoe and lying flat on the floor, his legs stretched out behind him and his soulful eyes searching hers. "Good boy."

She gave Hugh a small kiss on his cold cheek. "How was your day, darling?"

"Fine, fine, lots of marking to do though and a governors' meeting to prep for tonight."

"At least sit for a minute and relax. You work too hard,"

she said, taking his coat from him and hanging it in the cupboard under the stairs.

"Dinner nearly ready? Something smells good."

"Yes, not long to go."

"Great, I'll catch up on the news then."

He disappeared into the family room. "My day was good too, thank you for asking," Helen muttered to herself.

She followed him. He had collapsed onto the couch and was loosening his tie at the neck.

"Matt has a friend over. A girl," she said casually.

"Oh?"

"Yes, do you know her? Diana somebody or other. I think she went to Seahaven."

His eyes darted towards her. "Diana? I… er… maybe, er, yes, she was in one of my classes a couple of years back."

"Oh, right. Is she nice?"

"Um, I guess." He was fussing with the cushions on the couch, pulling tiny white Clive hairs from the fabric. He reached up to pull at the collar of his shirt.

"Are you ok?" Helen asked.

"Yes, yes, just tired and need to get out of this tie. Um, is she staying for dinner?"

Helen hesitated. "I don't know actually. I'll ask her."

"No, no, no need. I'm sure she has plans to eat at home."

"No, it would be polite to ask."

"True, true, the more the merrier and all that." He coughed. "I'll, er, freshen up."

He disappeared upstairs.

The thud of overlapping music was coming from the bedrooms on the second floor. Each one of them was playing a different soundtrack through closed doors. Helen approached Matt's door, feeling weirdly uncomfortable. She could hear very little through the wood other than the bass beat of a song she wasn't expecting to know. She raised her hand, ready to knock, then wondered if she should just burst in.

What were they doing in there? Did she really want to see? Oh god, what if they were having sex?

She reached for the handle just as Lydia emerged from her own bedroom down the hall, wrapped in a bathrobe, puffs of steam wafting through the open doorway from her bathroom. Her hair was wrapped in a towel. She stopped in her tracks when she saw Helen.

"What are you doing?"

"I... er... was going to ask Diana if she wants to stay for dinner."

"Oh, right," she said, then disappeared back into her room.

Helen frowned, then knocked loudly on Matt's door and turned the handle simultaneously.

Matt and Diana were sitting on his double bed, the bag of crisps spilling onto the duvet and a magazine open in front of them. They were the picture of innocence and Helen felt strangely disappointed. Diana looked at her with big eyes, a small smile on her lips.

"Sorry to interrupt, but I was wondering if Diana will be staying for dinner?"

"Yes, thank you, I'd like that," Diana said without hesitation or even looking at Matt to see if he agreed.

The look on his face was one of surprise, followed quickly by delight, before settling back into his usual expressionless mask.

"Great, I'll set an extra place at the table. It'll be ready in about fifteen minutes."

Back in the kitchen she found herself prepping a salad with extra care, ridiculously pulling out all the stops for the surprise guest with the addition of feta cheese, croutons and crispy fried onions. On a normal evening, it would be iceberg lettuce, cucumber and tomatoes, maybe red pepper if she could be bothered. By the time the timer buzzed on the oven, the dining room table was set, with the salad taking pride of place in the middle alongside a bowl of warmed slices of baguette.

Helen called "Dinner!" up the stairs, then took her place at the head of the dining room table, Clive tucked neatly under her chair at her feet. She sat patiently, her hands clasped in front of her, itching to shovel down a slice of bread while she waited.

She was just brushing away the crumbs of evidence from her plate and swallowing the last hastily chewed mouthful when Hugh walked in, straight-backed and looking like he might have brushed his hair. He had removed his tie and loosened a button, even uncharacteristically rolled up the sleeves of his shirt. He sat in his usual place at the other end of the table.

There was a sudden waft of lavender and Lydia floated in, her hair no longer wet from the bath. In fact, it was neatly blow-dried in loose curls around her face. It seemed Hugh wasn't the only one who had made an effort for their guest. "Hey, Dad," she said and went to give him a hug before taking her seat to his right.

"Hi there, good day?" he said.

She shrugged.

"Your hair looks lovely, Lydia," Helen said and Lydia blushed, but gave her a small smile. Helen noticed she had also put on some mascara and pink lip gloss. Helen had never seen her in make-up before. It brought out her blue eyes.

Mills was next to the table, now dressed in loose jogging bottoms and a tight cropped t-shirt. She smelled vaguely minty, like she had just brushed her teeth. Her hair was piled on top of her head in a messy bun and her eyes were glued to the phone in her hand. "Hey, Hugh, how was your shift down the pit?" she said.

"Another tough day at the coal face, Millie, I'm not going to lie," he replied. Her jaw clenched when he called her Millie, but other than that, her attention was entirely on the phone. Helen could hear the tinny sounds of TikTok and realised she had her earphones in. She propped one foot up on her chair and leaned on her knee, an Instagram picture of posed chill. She reached for a slice of baguette, nibbled on the corner, then discarded it on her plate, still staring at the screen.

More giggling filtered in from the hallway and Matt appeared with Diana behind him, the two of them clearly sharing a private joke.

Hugh sat up a little higher in his chair, if that was even possible given his ramrod-straight back. "Diana, how lovely to see you again."

"Hey, Mr Whitmore. Thanks for inviting me to stay for dinner."

"Not at all, any time. A friend of Matt's is a friend of ours."

Helen wanted to cringe at his formalities – and even more childishly point out it was her idea to invite Diana to stay.

Instead, Helen said, "Please help yourself, Diana. Cottage pie, salad, French bread. Mills, the earphones out please." Mills sighed, but put the phone face down on the table and removed the earphones, tossing them casually next to the phone.

Diana sat in the chair next to Helen and facing Mills, then looked scathingly at the food on the table. "Just salad for me, thank you. I'm vegetarian."

"Oh, I'm sorry, I had no idea," Helen said awkwardly.

"Why would you? It's not like we've met before." Diana's eyes glinted at Helen, unblinking, and she held her stare for a moment longer than was comfortable before turning away and reaching for the salad bowl.

Helen inspected her hands, feeling foolish and chastised in equal measure.

Mills watched Diana, her eyes narrowed, then reached for the cottage pie and dished up a large helping, more than she would normally eat, before smothering it with HP Sauce. Helen's heart swelled. Diana took no notice of Mills.

Lydia was taking notice though and dished up only salad for herself too.

"Lydia, would you like some cottage pie? It's usually one of your favourites. The brown sauce is there too," Helen said.

Lydia flushed a deep red and said, "No thanks, I'm trying to eat healthily, less red meat. Just salad tonight, I think."

Helen frowned, but said nothing more. She tried to catch Hugh's eye, but he was busying himself with putting a napkin in his lap. Lydia was watching Diana like a hawk, her eyes wide.

Cutlery clattered against china as everyone dished up in silence. It was stilted, certainly not companionable. The extra person in the room had tilted the dynamic. Helen looked up from dishing up salad for herself and saw Diana watching her, her head tilted slightly to the side, as though studying her curiously. Helen smiled back thinly, but Diana didn't seem at all embarrassed at being caught in the act of staring. She didn't immediately look away. Instead, Helen broke eye contact first.

Hugh coughed and said, "So, Diana, I'm guessing you are at college with Matt now? How are you enjoying it? Miles better than those dreadfully dull school days when I was teaching you history, I imagine?"

Diana giggled coyly. "Oh, you were never boring, Mr Whitmore. You were very charismatic."

Hugh smiled delightedly and puffed out his chest. He had no idea that he was being mocked, but Matt and Diana were clearly on the same wavelength. Matt had to shove a large forkful of cottage pie into his mouth to stop himself from smirking.

"What are you studying, Diana?" Helen asked, hoping to take control.

"Fine art."

"She draws the most amazing pencil sketches and portraits," Matt said with pride.

"You're not a stranger to the creative process yourself, I believe, Mrs Whitmore," Diana said to Helen. "Matt tells me you are behind the Portia Deane novels."

Helen was taken aback that Matt had told her anything

about her at all. She wouldn't have thought his stepmother was one of his chosen topics of conversation. "Yes, well, they are not literary in any way, but I love writing them – and call me Helen," she replied, awkwardly remembering their conversation in the bookshop.

"Is that why you write under a pseudonym? Because they are so... erotic?" As Diana said the word, she bit her bottom lip. Hugh coughed uncomfortably and Helen shuffled in her chair and swallowed the cottage pie, which felt like mud in her mouth, cloying and stodgy.

"I don't know if I would call them *erotic*. Scandalous maybe. No, I... er... I value my privacy, that's all. I didn't expect the books to be as successful as they have been over the years and I don't like attracting undue attention to myself."

"Why's that then? Too many secrets in your closet that you don't want exposed?" Was she mocking Helen now? If so, no one else seemed to have noticed. Hugh was pointedly focusing on his plate. Lydia was talking quietly to him, something about a test she had had at school today, but his eyes kept flicking over to Diana while Lydia talked. Mills was ploughing through her dinner, her leg still up on her chair.

Helen ignored Diana's question and said, just to hear her own voice more than anything else, "Mills, can you sit properly please?"

Mills glared at her in return and dropped her leg dramatically.

Helen hardly touched her dinner. Her appetite had fled for the hills, along with any sense of humour she may have had when they all sat down. She felt uncomfortable, annoyed at this brazen girl sitting next to her, who was now speaking in quiet tones to Matt, touching his hand intermittently as they chatted.

Hugh began to tell whoever would listen what he deemed to be a humorous anecdote from school, but there was an edge to his voice, slightly elevating it as though he was desperate for everyone to listen. Perhaps he had had a stressful day. Helen was finding it difficult to focus on what he was saying, something about "batting with a straight bat" and "calling a spade a spade". Hugh tended to talk in clichés at the best of times, letting the old favourites roll off his tongue, to the point where Helen switched off. She couldn't peel her eyes away from Diana's fingers, now resting millimetres away from hers on the white tablecloth, the index finger stroking the cotton almost intimately.

When she did drag her eyes away, she noticed Hugh had gone quiet and was watching Diana too.

The evenings were getting darker earlier and what Helen wanted to do was get out onto the beach with Clive for a walk to flush out her head, but the idea of the darkness closing in on her as she walked along the coastal path put her off. Instead, she headed into the garden again once she had cleared away the dinner dishes and shovelled another four slices of baguette into her mouth without tasting them. She needed to breathe in fresh, clear air. The automatic lighting system meant the garden was mostly illuminated in what should seem a romantic and ethereal glow, but tonight it felt oppressive and secretive, the shadows taking over and joining together.

There was a stone bench towards the end of the garden by the pool house, a lovely place to sit in summer when it was framed by climbing rosebushes and scented jasmine. Helen clutched a cup of jasmine tea in her hand, at least trying to recreate the fragrance, but it was overwhelmed by the headiness of salty sea spray. Helen sat on the numbing stone bench, facing towards the house, and wrapped her thick cardigan around herself, making herself small against the cold.

She looked up at the house. It was an imposing building, always had been. One of grandeur but eccentricity, with its strange additions and pointy edges. You couldn't see the eye-shaped windows from this side, but you still got the impression from this angle that the house was looking over its shoulder at you. A house used to keeping secrets. Or maybe that was just the way it made Helen feel, a ghost of a memory of when she had lived here as a child, constantly being evaluated and proving herself below par, then later hiding the truth from everyone, the house the only witness to events that played out in the year before she left.

She had always said she would never be the kind of parent whose child would not feel comfortable talking to them. She hoped her child would always feel like she was good enough, worthy, no matter what she did, and could feel safe enough to talk, like she was seen and heard, not shooed away like a mouse.

Helen liked to think that she had succeeded in that, but the older Mills got, the less they shared.

The house was laughing at her.

Look at you, turning into your mother.

Those childhood feelings lingered, even at the age of forty-seven. The feeling that no matter how hard she tried, she just didn't measure up, couldn't get things right. The house was looking at her disapprovingly now, out here in the dark on her own, juxtaposing a jasmine tea with a few puffs on an illicit cigarette she had smuggled out in her cardigan pocket. The orange end glowed fierce and angry as she pulled on the filter, breathing in the nicotine and relishing the dizziness that followed. She rarely smoked these days. Hugh hated it. Helen hated it. The smell, the taste. But sometimes she needed to feel the childish rebellion that the cigarette represented, taking her back to the days when she would hang out of that top right-hand window, breathing the smoke into the night air and wafting it away with one hand while gripping onto the edge of the window ledge with the other, hoping her disinterested mother wouldn't smell it through the floorboards and get angry, which would end in a slap or a kick, while hoping that her increasingly distant father might. Maybe then he would come up to her room, look her in the eye for once and shout at her rather than dismissing her or looking straight through her.

The irony was that Helen now recognised that vacant disregard on Hugh's face sometimes. Maybe it's true that you end up marrying your father.

She took one last puff on the cigarette, then ground it against the underside of the bench. Her thighs had numbed to the cold, but she didn't want to go in just yet. She put her empty mug down and looked up at the house again, now almost completely dark apart from the lights blazing on the second floor. The stained glass window was a dark yawn and Lydia's room had the curtains drawn, the light behind it rose-tinted from her fairy lights, but next to it was Matt's room, the light piercing against inky black edges.

While Lydia may be a quiet, introverted, solitary soul, Matt was all sharp edges, confrontational one moment and surly the next. Helen couldn't remember a moment in the last seven years in which she had felt any sort of affection or fondness from him. His loyalty had always been to his mother, despite Hugh being the injured party when his first marriage dissolved. Matt had always viewed Helen as an imposter in his family.

Ironic considering he was living in her family's house. Perhaps that was part of it. If they lived in his father's house, he may find her easier to stomach.

Helen watched the window without really seeing it, her mind churning over the characters behind those walls, the ones physically present and living out their lives, encased in the same brick and cement exterior that she found herself stifled by, and those that were merely ghosts imprinting on the rooms, like the faded shape left behind by an old picture frame when a family leaves.

She jolted unexpectedly when she realised someone was watching her from Matt's window. Merely a shape against the light, but she knew instinctively it was Diana.

It felt like she was staring right at her, naked and exposed, even though there was no way she could see her all the way down this end of the garden and sitting in shadow as Helen was.

She didn't move for some time. Her skin felt prickly, like she'd been caught snooping, but Helen stared straight back, wanting to look away but finding she couldn't.

She thought she could hear the ring of a bell, carrying on the breeze from the house.

The ring of a bicycle bell.

She pulled her eyes away from the window and stared towards the kitchen door. Was someone in there? The person who had left the bell for her to find. Had they come into her house? Where they there now, taunting her with the tinny sound? She froze, her heart thumping in her throat.

There it was again, barely audible but definitely there. But if there was someone in the house, Clive would've barked, alerted her.

Unless it was someone he knew. Someone inside the family.

She strained to listen again, but she heard nothing more other than the sounds of the sea in the distance, the waves calling and answering.

She looked back at Matt's window, but the blind had been pulled again, blocking out the light and cutting her out.

Matt stood in the kitchen and stared at the bicycle bell on the table. He picked it up, turned it over in his hands, felt the weight of it. He pressed the lever, heard the metallic rasp of the ring and smiled. He could see his reflection in it, a distorted image of his face, gurning into the silver, making him look misshapen, deformed.

The smile froze.

He rang it one more time, then gripped it tightly in his fist, the metal cold against his warm palm, before dropping it back on the table and heading upstairs.

14

THEN

I take my time packing up after the last bell, but Eloise is hovering, wanting to talk about plans for the party on the bus home.

"Hurry up, Hels, or we'll miss the bus!"

"Oh, I'm walking again today." I don't meet her eyes.

"What? Why? It's raining."

"I know, but if I want to get into a new bikini, I need to start doing a bit more exercise, so I think I should walk every day for a bit."

El is watching me closely and I'm sure she is about to say that I'm lying, but she says instead, "Yeah, you're right. You could do with losing a few pounds. Especially here." She reaches out and prods my waist. "Fine, I'll call you later to talk through some more party ideas, like where we are going to get the booze from."

"You can't!" I practically shout after her.

"What has got into you? Why not?"

"Erm, because my dad has called an emergency meeting

tonight to discuss my grades and stuff. He's really on my case about it and he'll be really mad if I'm on the phone to you tonight instead of pretending to study." I roll my eyes, but it doesn't feel convincing. "Besides, we don't want him to get even more mad with me in case they decide not to go on their trip." I hold my breath, hoping she'll take the bait.

"They wouldn't do that though, would they?"

"He has been pretty mad with me."

She thinks about it for a moment, her mouth gurning as she chews on her lip.

"Yeah, you're right. You need to keep your nose clean until they leave. Ok, I'll see you tomorrow. I'll make notes and we can talk then." She sweeps from the classroom and I exhale.

I wait a little longer until I am sure the bus will have left before emerging into the rain. Tracey is sitting on the wall by the school gate under the shelter of a tree, but she is still quite wet by the time I join her.

"Sorry, Tracey, I got held up."

She looks annoyed at me, but says, "That's fine. I wasn't going to wait much longer though."

El would've had a right go at me for making her wait.

She slides off the wall. I pull my hood up. The rain pelts my face.

"Um, so you know Eloise?" I say.

"Yeah, she hates me, doesn't she?"

I shrug. "I think she just doesn't know you."

"She hasn't tried to get to know me."

"She can be... prickly I guess, especially with new people."

"Especially new people like me."

"What do you mean?"

She looks at me like she thinks I'm being sarcastic. "You must've noticed that there are very few people that look like me at this school."

I hadn't noticed until she started. I don't know what to say.

"How long have you known her?" she says.

"Since the first day of school. We've always been best friends."

"But you're nothing alike from what I can see. What about the other two?"

"Steph and Emily? They joined our group last year. They're ok – a bit vacant sometimes, but alright, I guess."

"I don't get you and Eloise."

"I suppose it's just that we've been friends for so long that I can't imagine not hanging out with her, you know?"

"It doesn't seem a good reason for a friendship to me."

"She's harmless," I say, knowing that's not true.

"It isn't harmless when you're on the end of the comments, stares, jibes. You know, someone deliberately left a banana skin in my bag the other day. Luckily I found it, but it was tucked right to the bottom."

We walk along in silence for a bit, with Tracey walking straight through the puddles in her worn trainers and me dancing about, avoiding splashing my new white ones.

"She's asked me to invite you to a party we're having in a few weeks," I say.

"Oh, really? *She* asked you to?"

"Yeah, she told me earlier. It'll be at my house – my parents are going to America, so while they're away, we thought we'd have a party before we go off on study leave."

She hesitates, then smiles. "Cool."

My stomach flips in panic. I really hope Eloise doesn't cause trouble.

"You could ask your parents if you could stay over afterwards if you want? There won't be any adults at the party, if that's a problem? I mean, my housekeeper lives at the house, but the party will be in the pool house."

"Sure, that's a good idea. Um, does that mean I need a swimming costume? I don't have one. The last time I swam was when my brother was a toddler and we went to local pool – I think it was in Retford. Like a verruca fest."

"I have a few swimming costumes. I could lend you one. We can try some on this afternoon if you want – and go swimming!"

"Isn't it too cold?"

"The pool is heated." I hear myself saying the words and I realise how flippant I am about a heated swimming pool. The sense of shame I feel is new. She's made me aware of that, of how extravagant my life sounds compared to hers. But I didn't ask to be born into privilege, so is it my fault? Looking from the outside into Tracey's family home, I would rather have parents who actually took notice of me than all the money in the world, but that's the hand I've been dealt. So I'll carry on swimming in the heated pool, but I'll include her too, so she can enjoy some of it.

It's raining hard by the time we reach the house and we are soaked through. Martha greets us at the door with her usual warm smile.

"Hello, who's this then? Welcome!" she says.

"Hi, Mrs Tillsbury," Tracey says before I can introduce them.

"Oh, no, Tracey, she's not my mother. This is Martha,

our housekeeper. Martha, this is Tracey. She's new to the school."

Tracey flushes in embarrassment. I fling my bag down and kick off my wet shoes, leaving them lying on the floor where they land. Tracey is looking around, her body rigid as her eyes roam over the expansive front hall, the antique sideboard with its elaborate flower arrangement and gleaming parquet floor that reflects our faces back at us. The light is creating rainbows down the staircase from the towering stained glass window.

Her feet remain glued to the doormat.

Martha sweeps her in with an arm around her shoulder and is rewarded with a nervous smile from Tracey.

"Make yourself at home and let me know if you need anything. Here, give me those wet coats and throw your shoes down there where Madame has left hers. You should take those wet things off and I'll get them dried for you."

"Thank you, but I have to head home to get some stuff as I'm staying over tonight," Tracey says as she pulls off her soaked trainers. She has a hole in her sock and one toe is sticking out, its nail painted a vivid red.

"I can lend you anything you need?" I say. "Maybe just phone your parents and ask them now instead of having to go out in the rain again?"

"Um, yeah, ok, thanks." She's still uncomfortable, her words stilted, like she's wary of me now.

Wary of this house.

"There's carrot cake in the kitchen," Martha says.

"Oh, that sounds yum, thank you," Tracey says just as I'm about to turn it down.

"Shall I make some hot chocolate to go with it? Yes, I think so – with cream and marshmallows. It's very wet out there." Martha heads into the kitchen.

Tracey watches her go and says to me without making eye contact, "She's really nice."

I can't read her expression, whether she's judging me for even having a housekeeper or just envious. "She's been with us since I was born, so she's like a mum to me." More so than my real one, but I don't say it. "There's a phone in the kitchen you can use."

I sit at the kitchen table as she makes her call. I catch snippets of it. "Hi, Mum… yeah, good thanks. How was your day? Uh huh… yeah… I'm at Helen's house. It's the big one on the coastal path… Yeah… You should see it on the inside. Listen, can I sleep over here tonight? Helen's… um… mum said it was ok. She says she can lend me some clothes and things… No, don't worry, you don't have to. It's fine, I can borrow stuff… Yeah… yeah, I will. Thanks Mum. Love you."

I look away. I can't remember the last time I said that many words to my mother.

"Is Mother home?" I ask Martha.

"Yes, she's upstairs, I believe, getting ready for this evening."

The dinner party. I'd forgotten.

Martha places tiny china plates in front of us with miniature silver cake forks, at odds with the huge slabs of cake she has cut.

Tracey tucks straight into hers. I play around the edges, my mouth watering and my brain fighting with itself. "Tracey, I forgot to say, my parents are having a dinner party tonight.

I hope that's ok? We're not invited or anything, but there'll be old folk here."

"Oh, are you sure they're fine with me staying over then? Your parents?"

"They won't care. I usually stay well out of the way when they have people over. That's how they like it. I just thought it would be nice to have someone to hang with for a change."

"Ok, I'm cool with that."

"I have pizza for you girls for later, before the guests arrive – I'll bring it up for you. And I'll see what snacks I can rustle up, make it a real slumber party," Martha says as she puts a pan of milk on to warm up for the hot chocolate and I love her for it.

"Thanks, Martha." I jump up and give her a hug.

"Oh, you silly thing," she says, but her cheeks are glowing.

The smell of hairspray and menthol cigarettes enters the room before my mother does. Her eyes narrow as she sees me with my arms still around Martha. "Martha, talk me through tonight's menu," she says, her voice tight. Her eyes fall on Tracey, but her face is expressionless under the mask of make-up.

"Hi, Mother. This is my friend, Tracey," I say.

Tracey gets to her feet and the look on her face makes me think she is about to curtsey. "Hi, Mrs Tillsbury, nice to meet you."

Mother dismisses her outright, turns to me and says, "Helen, darling, you do know we have guests this evening."

"Yes, I know and we will be up in my room all evening."

"Fine, make sure you are." She turns back to Martha. "The menu, Martha."

"Let's go up to my room," I say and I take my plate, even though I don't want the cake.

My mother's ice blue eyes look at the cake, then at me as we walk past.

"Thank you for having me, Mrs Tillsbury," Tracey says as she passes.

Mother responds with a thin smile.

I can hear her saying to Martha as we leave, "You spoil her too much, Martha. She certainly doesn't need that cake and is that hot chocolate you are making? I don't think so."

I push open my bedroom door, then stand back, wrapping my arms around myself. At first she just wanders around, her eyes sweeping over it all. Floor to ceiling wardrobes on one wall; fairy-tale four-poster bed against the other. The floor is covered in discarded clothes, like it has been ransacked. The desk is covered in open books and novels are thrown on every surface. I ditch my plate of cake on top of a poetry anthology as she picks up a battered copy of *Wuthering Heights*.

"I love this book," she says, then puts it down again reverently.

I scramble around, picking up clothes and underwear to expose the fluffy pink rug underneath.

"Excuse the mess," I mumble.

"It's fine, mine is much worse."

I don't believe her.

"You have a really lovely bedroom. It's huge." She goes over to the window and looks out at the sea in the distance. The glass roof of the pool house is reflecting the sun as it breaks through the rain clouds finally. Shards of white cutting through the grey. "Is that the pool house?"

"Yeah." I walk over and open the window, letting in a sharp, salty tang of sea that flushes out the stale air in my room. "We can go down there in a bit if you want?"

She nods, turns away from the window and continues her survey of the room.

I chew on my lip, my arms automatically clasping to my waist again. She is peering at photos pinned to the board above my desk now. I can't tell what she is thinking about all that pouting, all those pretty ponytails and pink lips.

I busy myself with opening the wardrobe and chucking the pile of clothes in quickly. I slam the doors shut on the carnage inside.

It's getting awkward. There's an elephant in this pretty pink room.

I go to say, "Don't mind my—" as she says, "Are you sure—".

I go first. "I'm sorry about my mother. She's… well, she's like that with everyone."

"Is she though?"

"What do you mean?"

"Nothing. Are you sure she's ok with me staying?"

"Trust me, she cares more about impressing her rich friends than anything I do."

Tracey sits on the edge of the bed. Her knee is grazed, the redness vivid against her dark skin. "It must be hard – with your mother, I mean."

I shrug. "It's never been any different, so you don't miss what you don't have, I guess."

"What about your dad?"

"He's hardly ever here. If you're lucky, you won't meet him."

I turn on the radio in an attempt to dispel the clumsy atmosphere. Disappointingly, there are only adverts playing, the jingles harsh in our ears as we eat cake without speaking. I'm wondering if maybe this was a bad idea.

"So where are these swimming costumes then?" she says as she pushes her plate away. I still have most of my cake left, but I'm pleased for the excuse to put it aside.

I jump up, rummage in one of my drawers and pull out four or five options.

"I don't know what size. You're much smaller than me, so these will probably be massive on you," I say.

"Seriously? What do you actually see when you look in the mirror? You're tiny!"

I keep my eyes on the drawer so she can't see the heat in my cheeks. "I'm not at all. El is tiny."

"Eloise probably doesn't eat."

"Yeah, I wish I had her willpower."

I turn to see Tracey shaking her head. "Nah, I like food too much. And frankly, if someone doesn't love me for being myself, then they aren't worth my attention. We are what we are. If they don't like it, that's their problem, not mine."

I hold out several swimming costumes and she reaches for a bright red one piece with a halter neck. "I'll try this one, I think."

"There's a bathroom there." I point at the wardrobe doors.

"What? In the wardrobe?"

I laugh and pull open the middle two doors to reveal

a hidden en suite. "This is a weird house. Lots of hidden rooms."

She steps into my bathroom. White marble, gold fittings, plush but damp towels left on the floor. "Impressive."

I suppose it is. I've never thought about it.

"I share a bathroom with my brother. It's gross," she says. "He pees on the seat, but it's not his fault. He can't help it."

She closes the door behind her and I look around me, starting to see what she sees. A spoilt brat? Someone to envy? Or someone to pity?

I quickly change into a swimming costume and throw on my dressing gown over the top.

When she comes out of the bathroom, the red material striking against her dark skin, I try not to stare at her long legs and flat stomach. I try not to make comparisons with my wide hips and big, flabby tits, but it is obvious that my swimming costume looks much better on her than it ever did on me.

"You look great in that. You should keep it."

She looks down at herself. "Thanks, but I don't have any reason to need a swimming costume unless I'm here."

"Then keep it here. Wear it whenever you want."

She smiles, happy.

"Come on then, let's go."

"Don't we need towels?"

"There's towels in the pool house."

We run out into the cold garden in bare feet, feel the wet grass squelch under our toes, ignoring the numbing chill of it. She doesn't seem to mind being in just a costume. She gallops across the grass in front of me, while I follow along clutching the dressing gown to me.

The humidity of the pool house smothers us as I throw open the doors. The glass roof is blinding with the sun bouncing off it and throwing shapes onto the water. I drop my gown onto one of the loungers lined up facing the water. Tracey hurls herself into the water, squealing. I laugh and follow her, flinging my body into the deep end, feeling it engulf me, pull me down momentarily before I bob back up. She splashes me as I break the surface and I cough, the chlorine coating my lips, then splash her back before kicking with my feet and propelling forward.

She swims with long strokes next to me, her arms like pistons. "Race you to the end." She is off and I hesitate before swimming after her. I can't catch her, her long legs and muscular arms giving her an advantage.

I am panting when we reach the end, but she seems unaffected. I pull myself onto one of the wide steps in the shallow end. "God, I am so unfit. How are you not out of breath?"

"I work on a dairy farm when I'm not at school. It keeps me fit." She flexes her arm and I can see the toned bicep.

"You have amazing arms."

"Lifting bales will do that. My parents need all the help they can get with the farm and looking after my brother. They can't afford to hire someone else to help right now, so we make do with the few workers we have and do the rest ourselves."

I run my fingers through the water.

"But if I had this at the bottom of my garden, I'd be swimming every day!"

I shrug. "I guess I don't because it's not much fun on your own."

She throws a wet arm around my shoulders, "Well, you've got a swimming buddy now," and smiles widely before pushing back into the water and kicking hard with her feet. A torrent of water hits me, leaving me coughing.

I laugh and launch under water, grabbing at her ankles and pulling her down.

15

This morning's sky was cornflower blue, exacerbating the lingering feeling of wanting to be free of the oppressive walls of the house and out in the wide open. After Helen had returned indoors last night, she had gone straight up to her room, ran a hot bath and soaked for a long time, trying to rinse the awkwardness from her skin and put Diana from her mind. She had only half succeeded. Images of her plagued her dreams through the night and she had woken feeling clammy, groggy and with the girl still imprinted on her eyelids.

There was something about Diana that unsettled her. Her brazenness maybe, or the openly challenging way she looked at Helen. It was like Diana was daring her to find a connection, a reason why she should feel like she knew Diana. Was it that she reminded her of someone? That frustratingly unsettling feeling of a thought being just out of reach. The best Helen could hope for was that this was just a fleeting flirtation for Matt and nothing more serious.

Perhaps he would tire of her soon enough. Teenage boys could be fickle.

Then Diana would become insignificant, a name not to be mentioned again when he moved on.

Helen decided to walk to work rather than cycle, her feet itching to move. There was a wooden gate at the far end of the garden behind the pool house that would take her straight onto the coastal path, shaving a good ten minutes off her journey, but she never went that way these days. The gate was padlocked, had been for years, the lock rusted from disuse. Hidden as it was from the house and overgrown with ivy, she didn't think anyone else even knew the gate was there, which suited her just fine.

After leaving Clive safely tucked up in his bed with a treat, she locked the front door behind her and headed down the driveway. Even though it was almost 9 a.m., Matt's car was still parked in its usual spot. Helen hadn't seen Matt at breakfast though. She assumed Diana had left last night when Helen was in the bath, but perhaps his absence at breakfast meant that Diana had stayed over. She wasn't sure what to do with that. Matt was technically an adult, as was Diana, but it was her house. And the more she stayed over, the less likely Matt would grow tired of her.

Not that Helen would dare to check up on Matt and whether he had girls sleeping over. That was Hugh's job, but Hugh liked to stick his head under the covers and hide from any truly hard-hitting conversations with his children. He preferred the "*if I don't mention it, then it hasn't happened*" approach to parenting.

At the end of the long driveway, Helen paused at the letterbox, her breath hitching, but it was empty. She turned right and walked along the narrow road. There was no pavement for much of the way along this stretch. In summer, the road tended to be backed up with cars trying to wind down the narrow lanes to the beaches further along the coast, packed to the hilt with surfboards and bicycles, but this late into autumn it was quiet, with only the occasional supermarket delivery van or local's Range Rover rumbling past.

Helen inhaled deeply, letting the crisp air fill her lungs and breathing out the strangeness that had cloaked her for the last few days. She walked blindly past houses that had been there since she was a kid, mostly modernised now for the holiday rental market, her mind empty, taking her time to let her eyes rest on the sea to her left as she tried to shake off the poor night's rest. This was the kind of long and winding lane that tourists were nervous to drive along as you couldn't see around the corners until you were right on top of them, but Helen knew the road from muscle memory after all these years. Further along the road, tall hedgerows and trees lined the lane like sentinels, separating the traffic from endless fields on one side and the sea on the other.

Today everything seemed muffled, the subtle rumble of the sea, the gentle moaning voices of the livestock in the fields, with only the seagulls jarring in their vocal discontent. The sea was an ever constant of this landscape. The tangy smell of it in her nostrils; the salty taste of it on her lips; the coarseness of it permanently coating her skin. Helen hadn't realised she would miss it as much as she had when she had finally got away from this place. And much like the tide, it had pulled her back again.

She strolled along, feeling lighter than she had done in a

while, letting her mind mull over her manuscript and where she should take it, loosely fleshing out a new plot, licking the salt from her lips as her hair tickled her face in the chilly breeze.

Maybe because she was distracted, deep in thought, but she didn't hear the car until she was almost at a sharp bend in the road. She stopped abruptly at the revving of an engine, realising that the car was coming fast. The road ahead of her was completely obscured from view and any vehicle coming towards her at speed would not see her until the last minute, so she pushed herself back against the hedge, feeling the branches catch in her hair.

She edged along, letting the branches scrape the back of her coat, trying to get around the corner to where she knew the road widened a little to allow cars to pass each other. She could still hear the engine, louder now.

Then she realised her mistake. The car wasn't in front of her. It was coming from behind her. She turned, startled, and saw the car approaching, for some reason with its headlights on full beam, even though the morning was bright with sunshine. She had a moment to think it would be fine because from this direction the car would have seen her. It would slow at any moment to enter the corner and pass her safely. Then panic set in as she realised the car was accelerating.

She gasped and threw herself backwards. The hedge gave way and she tumbled into it, branches scratching at her face and poking into her eyes. The car shot past so close that the side mirror clipped her hand as she fell backwards, the speed of the car propelling her further into the bushes.

There were no sounds of braking and no tail lights flashing. All she could see was the car speeding away.

She remained spreadeagled in the hedge for a minute, trying to catch her breath, then pulled herself upright, aware that she was shaking and gulping air. Not just because of the close call with the car, but also with the unsettling realisation that the car had looked familiar as it had sped away.

It had looked like the one parked in her driveway this morning.

His hands were shaking as he gripped the steering wheel. He knew he should stop, turn around, make sure she was ok, but another part of him told him to just keep driving.

It was too late. The damage had been done.

He felt like he was going to throw up. He wound down the window, gulped in air.

He hadn't seen her. He had been going too fast. He could admit that, at least. But he knew these roads well now and he had overslept this morning. He was late, annoyed that he had had to phone Diana and tell her he couldn't pick her up after all because he'd slept through his alarm. That's the kind of thing a schoolkid would do.

He'd reached down on to the passenger seat for a bottle of water, opened it and dropped it in his lap as he approached the corner. Water went everywhere, spilling into the footwell where his sketch book was with the drawings he'd done of Diana.

Beautiful images of her face, her hands, her hair, all

from memory, her features imprinted on his brain like photographs.

He'd leaned down to grab the bottle, trying to save the drawings, not realising his foot was pressing harder on the accelerator as he did. His arm had snagged on the headlights lever, flicking them on in the process. When he sat back up after finally grasping the bottle, he saw the hedges and the bend in the road, figured it would be better to take it at speed than risk skidding if he braked too hard.

Then he saw her.

And he had kept going.

He thought he had heard a dull thud, like he might have hit something, but he pushed the thought away. Because he couldn't go back now.

Oh god, what had he done?

Just for a moment, a fleeting second of time, he had seen her and not reacted. He didn't brake, didn't swerve. Just kept going.

He knew it was her and had kept going.

Who did that? To their stepmother? Their family?

She'll be fine. He didn't hit her.

It wasn't her. Just someone who looked like her.

That thud? It was nothing.

It'll be fine.

16

THEN

We sit on the pool steps, dripping, laughing. The sky is darkening outside, the shadows lengthening across the tiled floor. She has her legs out in front of her, aimlessly kicking in the water. Droplets of water slide off the smooth skin of her legs.

I sit with my arms crossed over my belly, conscious of the roll that forms if I sit forward. "What was your other school like?" I ask her.

"It was just a regular state school. There were some nice kids, some not so nice. Not so different to where I am now, except that most of the kids didn't have mansions and swimming pools. A bit more diverse too."

"What do you mean by diverse?"

She shakes her head at me, like I'm a child asking a silly question.

"What about your friends?"

"Nice. I had a couple of close girlfriends – we stay in

touch on the phone and write letters. My parents have said I can go and visit when my exams are over."

"It must be hard coming into a new school this late in the year."

"I guess, but we had no choice. My grandad died unexpectedly. The choice was all move here or my dad trying to run the farm on his own. It was never really discussed. Besides, all the actual schoolwork is done now, isn't it? It's just revision and exam practice. They are using the money from selling our old house to pay for my school fees at Seahaven. It's also a great move for my brother. He was in a mainstream school back home, but the place he's at now has much better provision for his special needs and he's happy there. It was the right thing to do."

Her life is so different to mine. Is it weird that I wish I had hers? Parents who think about what might be best for their children. Framed happy memories on the walls and yellow ribbon.

"Is it hard – with your brother, I mean?"

"It can be, but that doesn't matter. I mean, he has good and bad days, but then we all do. His bad day is just as much a part of him as mine would be. I don't see him as any different. I mean, if you think about it, most days it's easier to get on with him than it is to get on with someone like Eloise."

"You have a good point there," I say.

"You probably don't get it though."

"What do you mean?"

"Well, look at your life. You have everything you could want – money, luxury, private school, a housekeeper to cook and clean for you – a fucking pool, for god's sake!

Wall-to-wall privilege. You don't have to worry about anything."

"Money doesn't make you happy though."

"No, but it's a good place to start. I see how much my parents struggle sometimes. Not just financially, but with my brother, his mood swings as he gets older, that kind of thing."

"From where I'm sitting, you are still much better off than me."

It's getting dark outside now, the air cooling rapidly as the sun disappears, and I realise that if we don't go in soon, we will be getting dangerously close to bumping into the guests for my parents' dinner party in our wet swimming costumes.

"We should go in."

"Yeah, sure."

We walk back to the house against a soundtrack of rumbling waves in the distance, ominous in the darkness and in stark contrast to the silence between us.

We let ourselves into the kitchen, which is a flurry of activity, with Martha making sauces, dressing salads and buzzing around.

"There you are!" she says. "Your pizza is ready – take it up with you, but best you make yourself scarce. Everyone will be here soon."

She points at two trays, one laden with pizza and the other with sweets, crisps, chocolate and drinks. We take a tray each and Tracey follows me as I creep out into the hallway.

It is empty, but I can see the dining room through the open door, set with limitless cutlery, beautiful white flowers down the middle of the table and crystal glasses sparkling in the light of the fire. Martha always outdoes herself on these occasions.

Halfway up the stairs, we hear an aggressive voice from the floor above, shouting, "Not now!" and a door slamming.

"Come on," I say to Tracey quickly.

I close my bedroom door firmly behind us and put the tray down on the bed.

"Was that your dad?" Tracey asks.

"Yeah."

"He didn't come to find you when he got home? To say hello?"

"He never does. Sometimes it's like he forgets I'm here at all. I can go days without seeing or speaking to him. Once I counted and it was thirteen days before he saw me at dinner one Sunday and asked me to pass the salt."

"Seriously?"

I shrug.

"It must get lonely."

"I guess that's why I rely on people like Eloise, Emily and Steph. I know they can be... you know... but they understand. El in particular. Her father isn't that much better than mine, so she knows where I'm coming from and what it can be like sometimes. Her mother is nice enough, but she hardly sees her dad too. And Eloise is honest – you always know where you stand with her. She tells you what you need to hear. Steph and Emily are ok – both airheads, really dumb and will say what they think you want them to say – but El is smart. I know she doesn't seem like it, but she is."

Why am I telling her all of this? Trying to justify my friendship?

"I'm sure she is. I just don't think she's the kind of person I could be friends with – and she certainly doesn't want to be friends with me."

"She just a bit protective of me, I think."

"What does she think I'm going to do to you?"

"I don't know."

She looks like she wants to say more, but instead reaches over and grabs some pizza. "Can I?"

"Yeah, of course."

She takes an enthusiastic bite. "God, this is amazing."

My mouth is watering as I watch her. I can smell the cheese, can taste the pepperoni in my mouth already. I reach out, then pull my hand back.

"You not having any?"

"I shouldn't."

"Who says?"

"No one – it's just that I have to wear a bikini for the pool party…"

"So?"

"So look at me!" Colour rises in my cheeks. I stand up and throw off the robe. I feel naked despite the still damp swimsuit. "Look at these huge hips, these ridiculous boobs that you can see more of from the back than the front, these chubby arms!"

"What are you talking about?" Tracey puts the pizza slice down and comes to stand in front of me.

"Here, look." She turns me towards the full-length

mirror by the window. "Let me tell you what I see." Her face is framed over my shoulder and I search it for clues as to whether she is going to tell me the truth or spin me some barely disguised lie. *Be nice to the rich girl.* Her hands are on the tops of my arms, her palms warm, her fingers long. "I see curves to die for, boobs that make a statement, sure, but skin that is clear, like milk, and thick wavy hair. I see beautiful eyes and a lovely, open, heart-shaped face." Her hand reaches up and brushes my hair from my face. "I think you're lovely."

I feel awkward, uncomfortable. But I'm also tingling, the skin beneath her fingers alive, the nerve ends firing.

"So if you want to eat pizza, then eat the fucking pizza," she says, then grabs her slice and shoves it into her grinning mouth.

I laugh, more to break the awkwardness I'm feeling. "Fine, I'll eat the pizza."

We change into pyjamas and I turn on the small television on my desk, flicking through the channels as we finish off the pizza. There isn't much to watch. Tracey goes through my music collection and chooses something to listen to, but I stop her from putting it on, saying, "They'll hear it downstairs. But we can go up to the attic. They won't hear us up there. Wait here."

I creep out of my room. At the top of the stairs, I can hear the steady thrum of polite conversation and the chink of crystal, smell the nicotine in the air and feel the warmth from a fire that has been lit in the stone fireplace in the dining room, despite it not really being cold enough. There is a door under the stairs that leads to the basement where all sorts of things are stored, including my parents' alcohol collection. I reach the bottom of the stairs without seeing anyone. The dining room door is open, but I can only see the backs of heads, shoulder pads and straight backs. A loud guffaw cuts through the room – my dad laughing at his own joke, no doubt. I quietly open the basement door and let the darkness swallow me as I close it behind me. Only then do I flick on the light switch. The stairs are steep, leading down into a room that is full of random objects, unused furniture and rails of my mother's clothes that she no longer wears. The smell of gas is strong from the huge, cranky boiler that squats like an angry fat man in the far corner of the room. Boxes of champagne and racks of red wine line another wall, along with bottles of the vodka my mother prefers served ice-cold in her afternoon martinis.

I grab a bottle of red wine and a bottle of vodka, then tuck an extra bottle of vodka under my arm.

I turn off the light before I open the door again and emerge back into the hallway. Halfway back up the stairs I freeze at the sound of footsteps. I turn slowly to see a man I don't know heading towards the downstairs toilet. His hair is combed back from a large forehead and his mouth is wide, like a letterbox. He looks up at me over his shoulder and winks, the letterbox opening wide, then disappears into the cloakroom. I run the rest of the way back to my bedroom.

"Ok, grab the food and let's go," I say, out of breath. Tracey looks at the alcohol and I think she's going to tell me she's not interested, but instead she smiles conspiratorially and loads up her arms with Martha's snacks.

She follows close on my heels as we head upstairs, past the door to my parents' bedroom. It is the only room on this floor and incorporates a bathroom and a large dressing room, as well as the expansive bedroom and a wide window that draws your eyes out towards the sea. As we go past, Tracey says, "Can I peek?" and I nod.

She sticks her head around the door and gasps.

"Come on." I'm impatient – I want to open the wine and take myself away from here.

The door to the attic is tucked into the corner, the room accessible by a staircase that you pull down from above. The air is already colder in the stairwell. I reach the top and turn on the lamp closest to the door, then step aside for Tracey.

There is only a tiny porthole window letting light into the room. I have covered the walls in posters of my favourite bands and there are bean bags to sit on. The Persian rug on the floor is an old one that my mother grew bored with and it is anchored down by an old coffee table I found in the basement. On it is a record player, album sleeves tossed about, lying where they fall when I rifle through them.

The far wall is lined with shelves and I have slowly pilfered books from my father's study, the local library, school and second-hand shops to fill them. I have read and loved every single book in this room.

This is my space, all my taste, every inch of it reflecting my personality. I have never brought Eloise up here. I don't think she would understand this side of me. She would prefer the fairy-lit brightness of my bedroom to this cold, dark space.

Tracey is walking around, taking in the bookshelves and the record sleeves.

"What do you think?"

"I love it! Did you do all of this yourself?"

"Yeah, this is like my private space. I don't even think my parents have been up here in years. It wasn't used for anything except storage, so I started out in one corner and slowly took over the rest of the space. The furniture is all old stuff that my parents don't use anymore that I found in the basement. I like that it is at the top of the house, private, you know? A bit like a treehouse, but with electricity."

I put the bottles on the table and drag the bean bags together, grab two blankets from the corner.

"Wow, this house is something else."

"I guess. It has a weird vibe though. Sometimes it feels like…" I stop, knowing it sounds daft. I feel it the most up here in this space. The sense that the walls are inhaling and exhaling, expanding and contracting with every breath, and using me for oxygen.

"Feels like what?"

"Don't laugh, but sometimes it feels like the house is *alive*, watching, listening, taking it all in." My voice is low. "Stupid, I know, but it doesn't feel like a happy house. It feels like a house plotting something."

"They say houses can absorb the energy of those who live in them, so maybe there has been a tragedy here or something."

"You know this will all be mine one day."

"Sure, because you're an only child."

"Not just that, but when my mother dies, the house passes straight to me, bypasses my father. It's something that was written into one of my great-great-grandmothers' wills – that the house can only be passed down the female side of the family and to the oldest surviving woman. She had some beef with her husband and swore that the women that came after her would never be without a home."

"That's cool! All this is yours and you will never have to pay rent or save for a deposit like the rest of us? You are so lucky," she says.

I reach for the wine, rummage in a drawer under the coffee table for the bottle opener. "But it means I'm tied here. I can't go anywhere else."

"You could sell it."

"It can only be sold if there is no one to pass it on to."

"So it's like you're handcuffed to the place?"

"Yes, that's exactly what it feels like. I want to go places, see the world, and I can't."

"Well, just because it's yours doesn't mean you have to live here. You could rent it out or something."

I put the bottle to my mouth and drink long and deep. The wine is warm, thick and fruity yet bitter. I hand it to Tracey, who takes it gingerly. I can tell she hasn't had a drink before.

"What do you want to do, after school I mean?" she says before drinking from the bottle. She coughs a little, then drinks some more, wincing.

"I want to write. Whether it's books or journalism, I don't know, but I want to write things that people will want to read. My father wants me to go to university and get some sort of business or financial degree and I can think of nothing worse."

"Will they let you do what you want?"

"They will probably have something to say if they are paying the fees."

Tracey hands me the bottle and I drink more, feeling warmth spreading through me from my toes.

"What about you? What do you want to do?"

"I think I want to do something with animals, not a vet but maybe an agricultural degree of sorts. I've really enjoyed the last few weeks working with my dad, but I'm sure there are ways of running the farm that would be more efficient, would make it more profitable. That side of it interests me, you know? The business side of it. I'd study locally though, to help with the farm and my brother and stuff."

I guess that's one of the big differences between us. I'm trying to get away from my home and she's desperate to stay at hers.

17

NOW

By the time she reached the village, Helen's breathing had slowed a little, but she still felt shaky and on edge. She had spent the rest of the walk checking over her shoulder and peeking around hedges, her skin tight around her throat, her mind scrambling for an explanation.

Helen knew she and Matt weren't exactly close, but surely he didn't dislike her that much? But then, how well did she really know him? He was very much a closed book and it wasn't like she had tried that hard to bond with him. He had made it clear very early into her relationship with Hugh that he would always be on his mother's side and she hadn't pushed it further. So she didn't really know him or understand his feelings towards her.

But he surely couldn't hate her enough to want to hurt her? She must've been mistaken. There were plenty of silver Renault-style cars around. She hadn't seen the licence plate because the headlights were blindingly bright, so she couldn't be sure of anything.

The skin under her eye was stinging. It felt like there was a scratch where the hedge branches had raked across her face and it was tacky to the touch. Definitely bleeding. She could feel the back of her hand throbbing too, the skin already looking discoloured and purpling. Instead of going straight to the shop to open up, she headed over to the small tea shop on the square and ordered a latte and a big slice of carrot cake. The woman serving her winced when she looked up, said, "Are you ok, Helen? That's a nasty scratch."

Helen couldn't remember her name, had bought coffee and cakes from her for years but had never bothered to ask her name. "I'm fine, just stupidly didn't see a low hanging branch."

"You should get that cleaned. You don't want it getting infected. Something like that happened to my cousin Gina and she got lockjaw."

Helen smiled thinly and fumbled her change into her pocket. Her hand shook as she carried the plate and mug back outside.

She sat at a table in a patch of weak sunshine. She exhaled as she cradled the cup. Her eyes flitted around her. For a small town, there was plenty of activity. The laughter of children playing in the nursery playground to her left and the clatter of a van roller door as the driver unloaded kegs of beer for the pub across the square. An old man on a bench, staring ahead of him, shopping bags at his feet. A mother chasing a small girl on a scooter, her hair in high pigtails flying out behind her as she bumped and raced down the cobbled street. Helen focused on the details around her in the hope that her mind would still, along with her trembling hands. She scoffed down the carrot cake without tasting it. It was meant to make her feel better, but lodged in her throat like cotton wool.

She became aware of ice cold pin pricks on the back of her neck. She spun around in her chair, the metal legs scraping. There was no one behind her, but the feeling persisted. Then she noticed the eyes watching her from inside the post office over the road. She squinted to see if she could make out who it was, but their face was obscured by an advert in the window for salsa classes.

Helen knew who it was though. She got to her feet, considered waving, then changed her mind. For a second she wondered if they were behind the Polaroid, then she dismissed the idea.

She drained the mug of tea and balled up her napkin, discarding it on the plate. She took one last, long stare at the eyes in the window, then went to open the shop.

Helen kept a small first aid box stashed under the sink in the tiny kitchen at the back of the shop in case of serious paper cuts. She used it to clean the graze on her cheek, which stung as she swiped at it with a disinfectant wipe, her eyes watering. Something was caught in her hair and she pulled loose a twig from the hedge. She sighed, packed away the first aid box and put the kettle on. There was a packet of fancy chocolate biscuits in the cupboard and she opened the box, even though she wasn't hungry after the cake.

She sat at the shop counter with a cup of tea she didn't want, eating biscuits she had no appetite for, staring out at the people walking past the window. For the first time she could remember, she wanted to close up the shop and head back home, shut the door on the world and hide in her bed, the covers over her throbbing head.

Who would notice if she did?

The bell jangled and she walked in. Helen was not surprised. She had grown used to her appearing over the years, saying very little, then disappearing again. Like she was reminding Helen she was there. As if Helen could forget.

After flicking her eyes at Helen, she said, "You look like you've been in a fight."

"You should see the other person," Helen replied without humour.

She walked further into the shop, paused by the table of Helen's books, took another step forward. "Written anything good lately?" Her voice was little over a whisper.

"Was it you?" Helen asked.

"Was what?"

"The photo."

She frowned, looked directly at Helen fleetingly with those strange eyes of hers, then looked away just as quickly. "I don't know what you're talking about."

"Someone sent me a photo – of her."

She paled, stepped back, edging towards the door. "Well, it wasn't me. Why would I?"

"Yeah, you're right. Why would you?" Helen's voice was calm, steady, but her heart was not. It was jumping and thudding with anger, fear, anxiety. She wanted to scream at her, shout, tell her to do something, say something, after all this time. Swear at her and see her flinch. Hit her.

Push her.

"That means someone else knows. The photos." Her body stiffened in realisation.

Helen sighed. It wasn't worth it. "It doesn't mean anything. It could be just a coincidence or something."

Her hair was a mess as usual, unruly, sticking out in places, flattened or thinning in others. More grey strands ran through it these days and over the years she had lost much of the youthful beauty Helen had envied when they were younger. Now she looked folded in on herself.

She backed away and left the shop without another word.

Helen watched her walk away with narrowed eyes.

Helen managed to make it through to the afternoon on autopilot, stuck to her chair, her hands slotting biscuit after biscuit between her lips like letters in a postbox. She was not even tasting them. They were just filling the void in her gut.

Someone knew something. What did they want? Just to torment her? Play with her?

Or some sort of revenge? Drive her crazy with paranoia before throwing her to the wolves? And did Matt have something to do with it?

She looked down and the biscuit packet was empty. She pushed it to the bottom of the wastepaper bin in disgust.

She heard the bell jangle again. It was Jenni, bundled up in a thick fur coat and hat, as though it was the middle of winter instead of early October.

"Hi, Helen," she said, unwrapping her layers as she walked through to the back room.

Helen immediately started to pack up her things, shrugging into her own coat, but not relishing the walk home. She could hear Jenni babbling from through the doorway. "You know, I was thinking about the new book coming in next week. You know, the one about the two women. What if we recreate the front cover as a display? Knock over a glass of red wine on the wooden table over there, like on the book cover?" She emerged from the back room, her eyes fizzing. "Tie it in with Halloween?" She tilted her head. Helen could see her brain working. "Hmmm, no, could get messy though, couldn't it? And someone might slip, hurt themselves, sue us. Yeah, probably not."

Jenni could sometimes get carried away with her ideas for displays. Helen usually let her rattle through them before reining her in. Today Helen cut off her ramblings.

"I'm not feeling great today, Jenni, so I'm going to go straight off home, if that's ok."

"Oh." Jenni's forehead creased with concern. "Are you ok?"

"Yes, just maybe coming down with something."

"Ouch, how did you scratch yourself?"

Helen lifted a gentle finger to her face. "Er, gardening."

Her eye was caught by an email notification that popped up on the shop computer. Helen opened the email, meaning to ask Jenni to respond if it was a customer enquiry. The subject line was blank, but the body of the email was typed in capitals:

HOW DOES IT FEEL TO KNOW YOUR SECRET IS OUT? I KNOW WHAT YOU DID.

She didn't hear Jenni come up behind her. "Ooooh, what's this?" Jenni said, reading over Helen's shoulder.

"I don't know," Helen said, her voice tiny.

"Must be marketing for a new thriller. Who sent it?"

Helen looked at the details: *schoolisoutforsummer@ gmail.com*.

"That's good marketing, isn't it? Even the email address is creepy. A bit like those horror movies – *I Know What You Did Last Summer*, wasn't it? Sounds great – have to keep our eyes open for this one. God, these publishers can be so clever."

Helen grabbed her bag, said a hurried goodbye and rushed out of the shop, sucking air into her lungs. She paused, then set off across the square, ignoring Harry from the florist when he waved at her.

She took the shorter route home with its wider pavements, even though it would take her along the coastal path. She rushed along, not looking to the left or right, until she reached the bottom of her garden. She turned and followed the wall around to the driveway leading up to the front of the house.

Once inside the house, she leaned her back against the front door, shutting the world out.

Maybe it was a coincidence. As Jenni said, a marketing ploy for a new book.

No, Helen knew better.

Regardless, she muttered the word *coincidence* to herself over and over, like a mantra, hoping to calm her flailing insides. She caught sight of herself in the large mirror over the hallway console table. Hair ruffled, skin deathly pale except for the red gash on her cheek, muttering to herself like a mad woman.

She looked away again quickly.

How many coincidences could there possibly be before she had to realise that someone was trying to tell her something? The coincidences were stacking up, one on top of the other, teetering, and at some point they would topple down on top of her, drown her, cut off her breath and suffocate her. No less than she deserved.

Helen lit the wood burner in the family room, even though it wasn't cold enough for it, and curled up in the armchair with a book, hugging her knees to her chest, hoping someone else's story would distract her churning mind. Instead, she found herself cradling her throbbing hand to her chest and staring into space, her eyes full of unshed tears and her mind hurtling from one thing to the next.

She heard a dull thud from somewhere in the house. It sounded like it was coming from upstairs.

No one should be home yet.

She crept out of the family room and into the hallway, listening intently. Clive was at her feet, had been since she had barrelled into the house. He didn't seem to share her concern at the idea of a possible intruder. Helen climbed the stairs slowly, her eyes scanning for weapons within grabbing distance. She saw a moving shadow in the hallway, felt her breath stop altogether. She debated going back downstairs, maybe locking herself in the cloakroom or running out to the pool house before calling the police. It was only Clive's chilled demeanour that made her continue up the stairs and around the corner.

She gasped at the sight of a woman standing with her back to Helen. Then Clive lumbered over to her and Helen realised it was Lydia standing outside her bedroom door. Helen exhaled and felt inexplicable anger directed at Clive. He could've told her that Lydia was home.

"Lydia! What are you doing home?"

Lydia jumped and paled as she saw her. She was clearly expecting to be alone too. "I'm not feeling well and I have a project to hand in tomorrow, so I came home. I'm... er, just going to go to my room to lie down for a bit."

"Can I get you anything? Cup of tea?"

"No, thanks." Lydia's phone buzzed in her hand. She jumped again, alarmed eyes flicking to the screen and back at Helen.

"Ok, well, I might go for a swim, but come and find me if you need anything."

"Yeah," Lydia said and hurried into her room, Clive tripping along after her.

Helen paused, then followed her. She stopped outside Lydia's bedroom door. She could hear more notifications on her phone, buzzing in one after another.

Unusual. Lydia was hardly ever on her phone and never seemed to get texts or messages, but she was especially popular today. Perhaps it was because of her new look. Helen couldn't help but notice that she had attempted to copy Mills' flicked eyeliner this morning. However, rather than having the desired effect of maturity, it had made her look strangely young, like a girl playing dress up.

Helen continued up to her bedroom and sat on the bed, thinking about the swim she had voiced a commitment to, still trying to wrap her head around the fact that someone had tried to run her over this morning.

She had no doubt it was intentional now.

Someone wanted her to remember, but Helen wanted to forget.

And the more she thought about it, the more she realised that everything had begun to spiral out of control when Diana walked into their lives.

The air in the pool house was thick, condensed, the smell of chlorine comforting. She glided up and down the pool, pulling herself through the water as though she was swimming away from her demons as fast as she could. She could feel them tugging at her heels as she kicked out, pushing them away just enough but knowing they were still behind her, even if she was putting a little distance between them. Her happy place. After half an hour she felt better, more grounded.

She let herself back into the kitchen, a towel wrapped around her hair and her feet in her outdoor slip-ons. She ditched the shoes at the kitchen door and padded quietly across the stone floor and into the hallway. The house was quiet, no sound coming from upstairs.

She went to stand outside Lydia's closed bedroom door for a moment, listening. She could hear Clive snoring loudly, imagined him stretched out on the bed, his legs twitching as he dreamed about chasing squirrels and pilfering sausages. Helen gently turned the handle and peeked into the room. Lydia was curled up next to Clive, her arm draped over his rotund belly. He opened one eye and looked at Helen before dropping straight back to sleep. Lydia was also asleep and at first Helen thought she looked peaceful, calm. But then she noticed her forehead wrinkled in a tight frown and there were tear tracks drying on her cheeks, smudging the black eyeliner, with a small wet patch of black sadness soiling the purple pillowcase.

Helen tilted her head to the side, wondered what had upset her. Lydia was a very quiet, unassuming girl, so unlike her stepsister Mills in every way. There was nothing showy or loud about Lydia. She was perpetually calm, understated. The hand not wrapped around Clive was holding her phone. Helen wanted to reach out and take it from her, see what the messages had been about. But was this really her place? The evil stepmother checking up on her. Maybe she should just mention it to Hugh, let him sort it out. It was probably nothing anyway.

Helen looked around the room, taking in the fairy lights draped across the headboard of the bed, the neat desk in the corner, the pinboard covered with photos of her and her best friend, Lucy, pulling childish faces and grinning beneath cat ear filters. No pouting, posing or duck lips yet. Everything was neat and tidy, no clothes strewn on the floor or books out of place. Her school bag was at the foot of her bed and Helen reached out to open it, then changed her mind.

She retreated, closing the door gently behind her.

Later Helen took up a tray with a bowl of tomato soup, some buttered toast and a glass of chocolate milk. She knocked hesitantly this time, but didn't wait for Lydia to answer before she walked in. Lydia was still on the bed, but now sitting up, surrounded by books. She shoved something aside as Helen walked in, then shuffled higher up against the pillows. Clive was still snoring, lying stretched across the bed at her feet.

"I brought you some soup and toast if you're hungry?"

"Thanks." Lydia looked miserable.

"Do you want to talk about it?"

"No, I told you. I just don't feel well. Bad cramps."

She didn't meet Helen's eyes.

"Ok, but if you want to talk, I'm here."

Helen left the tray on the bed and turned to go, then said over her shoulder, "What's the project about?"

"What?" Lydia's head jerked up.

"The project? You said you have a big project to hand in. What's it about?"

"Oh, er, it's about families and stuff. Genealogy."

"Well, your dad would be able to help with that."

"Yeah, I know."

Helen stood a little longer, hoping for something more but getting nothing. She stepped towards the door, but Lydia's voice stopped her. "You know, I know nothing about you."

"What do you mean?"

"You – where you're from, who you are – or were. You just…" Curious eyes stared at Helen, trying to figure her out. "You're just some woman who my dad met and then we all had to uproot and move in here." Her arm swept across the extravagant bedroom with its large picture window and stone fireplace.

Yeah, it's a hardship for you alright. So much worse

than the bungalow you were living in when your dad was married to Francesca.

Helen took a moment to find the words she should say rather than what she wanted to say. "I didn't realise you felt that way." She sat on the edge of the bed. Lydia scuttled further away. "Let's be honest, Lydia, it's not that much of a change. You are still in the same village you grew up in and going to the same school. You just happen to have moved into a bigger house with a few extra family members, that's all. I thought you liked it here – with Mills especially? You two get along, don't you?"

She shrugged, her face a picture of sadness.

"What is this really about?"

Lydia didn't answer, just picked at a thread on her duvet cover.

Helen sighed. "Ok, I'll tell you a bit about myself – but there's not much to tell other than what you see. I grew up in this village, went to the same school as you, then moved away for a bit after school, had Mills, moved back and opened my shop where I met your dad. Nothing else to tell."

"So how come when I have to do a project on family, I can't add any details about your side because you haven't shared any of them?"

"I wasn't exactly close to my parents – and they've been dead for some time now. I have no siblings, it's just me and Mills. There's nothing else to tell. No secret past or anything like that."

"Do you have any photos? Of what you looked like at school?"

Helen could feel her teeth pulling at the skin on the inside of her cheek, gnawing away.

"Um, I think I might somewhere. I could have a look."

She nodded. "Thanks."

"What else is going on, Lydia?"

She looked like she was going to say something else, the moment hanging in the air like a comma, but then mumbled, "Nothing, I just feel like I should know more about you, that's all."

"Ok." Helen stood up, hesitated, then said, "You know, you can talk to me about anything. I am here for you."

Lydia ignored her.

Helen headed up to the attic room. The wooden stairs creaked and groaned as she dragged them down into place, the familiar smells of paper, stuffy air and dust welcoming her as she ascended into the darkness at the top of the house.

She paced across the old carpeted floor, the floorboards creaking in familiar places. She felt restless again, unable to settle. She looked over at the far end of the room where the boxes were stacked and stopped in her tracks. Had the boxes moved? Did they look straighter, neater, less haphazard than before, less like they would topple over at any moment? Pauline never came up here to clean. Helen didn't even think she knew this room existed.

Had Lydia come looking for information? She wouldn't find much in the boxes though. It was the loose panel behind that hid the real secrets. Her childhood hiding place. Helen hadn't looked in there since she had closed the panel all those years ago.

She sat at the desk, leaned back in the chair and closed her eyes. Taking a deep breath, she opened her laptop and tried to write, to still her brain and get herself into a better mindset. She managed to get some words down, but she knew they were rubbish, thin, two dimensional. She had very little to say.

She headed back downstairs in frustration and went straight to the kitchen cupboard, pulled out a large bag of crisps and made short work of them before shoving the empty bag to the bottom of the bin. The tang of artificial cheese and onion was sharp on her tongue and made her feel a little more fulfilled, but that quickly morphed into nausea and disgust, and she immediately regretted eating them. Before long, everyone else would be home, the house full of voices and energy, all demanding something from her and most of the time she would fail in the delivery. She would have to pretend to be their version of her for the rest of the evening and the thought made her want to reach for more food. Then she heard the front door opening and voices. It sounded like Matt and Diana.

Helen's heart sank into her stomach.

She exhaled, then walked purposefully into the hallway to greet them, a largely fake smile on her face.

Diana was shrugging out of her pink fluffy coat, her legs stick-thin in the same tight jeans and Doc Martin boots as the other day. Matt looked pale as he saw her approach.

"Hi, how was your day?" Helen tried to keep her tone even, but instead it came out high-pitched. "Everything ok?"

"Fine." Matt avoided her eyes, but that wasn't unusual.

"Um, did you go in your car this morning, Matt?"

"I do every day, why?" He crouched down and fussed with his shoes, seemingly struggling with unknotting the laces when normally he would kick them off still tied.

Helen shrugged, aiming for nonchalance but looking

more like she had a twitch. "No reason, just thought I saw you this morning a bit later than normal."

"I doubt it. I left really early. Had to hand something in."

Diana was looking at him weirdly, like she wanted to say something but was holding herself back.

The awkward silence sat heavy on them.

"How did you hurt yourself?" Diana said to Helen eventually.

"What do you mean?"

"Your cheek."

Helen reached up to her eye and said, "Oh nothing, just a bit of gardening. The roses, you know…"

Matt stood and shuffled from foot to foot.

"Matt said you have a gardener."

"That doesn't mean I can't prune the roses if I feel like it," Helen snipped back. She stared at Matt, willing him to look at her so that she could see if there was guilt in his eyes, but his face was blank, difficult to read as always. Surely if he had driven into her, he would be acting more amused than he was, or – she hoped – relieved that she was ok, but she saw neither emotion.

"It must be nice to be able to afford to pay someone to do all the jobs you can't be bothered to do," Diana said.

"I guess it is," Helen replied. "Arthur has worked here since I was a child though. He's part of the furniture now. More a family member than an employee."

"So you can afford a cleaner, a gardener and a pool guy?"

How did she know that? What had Matt been saying?

"Yes, well, the house is too big for us to manage it all ourselves."

Diana was making her feel uncomfortable. "Your family has owned this house for generations, haven't they? You obviously come from a very wealthy background."

"Well, it's nice to not have to worry about money, I guess, but there are more important things in life."

"Only a rich person would say that," she said.

"It's really none of your business."

Diana smiled icily and walked away. Matt followed her, leaving Helen standing in the hallway.

She thought she heard Diana whisper something about lying as they headed up the stairs.

She waited for a moment, then followed and stood outside Matt's closed bedroom door. She pressed her ear to the wood, trying to hear what was being said, but the voices were muffled, any words unclear. As she stepped back, Lydia's door opened and Helen jumped back. Clive shuffled out, stopped and looked up at her, as if asking her what she was doing.

"You're right, Clive. I know, I need to leave it," she said quietly, as though he had indeed spoken. Some of Helen's best conversations were with Clive.

She returned to Lydia's bedroom and retrieved the tray from her bed. Lydia was now sitting at her desk, her back to Helen, and said nothing as she picked up the tray and left. Her phone was tossed on the bed, face down. Lydia had eaten at least and Helen took that as a small victory. She paused outside Matt's door again on the way past. She leaned towards it just as the door flew open and she almost toppled into the room. The bowl slid dangerously towards the edge of the tray.

"Are you listening in on us?" Matt said in anger.

"No! I... er... came to collect the tray from Lydia's room. She wasn't well earlier and I made her some soup." She was rambling at him in embarrassment.

"You were! You were listening in!" Now he sounded amused. "Hey, Diana, maybe we should give my delightful stepmother a bit of a show, what do you say? She's so sad that she has to listen in on us to get her thrills."

"Wow, that is sad," Diana said, a sickening grin on her face.

"No, that's not what—"

"That is exactly what it looks like."

"Matt, this is my house and I think you should show some more respect, don't you?" Helen said, but her voice lacked conviction.

He smirked and said, "Come on, Diana, let's give the landlord what she wants."

He leaned into Diana, but Diana stopped him with a firm hand on his chest and said, "Don't be childish, Matt. I am not a toy."

Diana flopped back onto the bed and flicked casually through a magazine, but Matt remained rooted to the spot, hurt paling his cheeks, mortified at being called out in front of Helen of all people.

Helen wanted to smile, but instead she turned her back on him and walked with a calm she didn't feel back down the corridor.

She fled downstairs and slammed the tray on the kitchen table. She reached into the cupboard for another bag of crisps, her chest heaving as she stuffed handful after handful into her mouth, not tasting the salty vinegar, only swallowing in order to make room for more while feeling the acidic sting of tears on her cheeks. When the bag was empty, she thrust it into the bottom of the bin and opened the cupboard again, but heard the front door slam before she could pull anything else out. She paused, her hand still in the cupboard, and took a breath, trying to slow the pulse in her throat and settle her heaving chest.

Mills can't see me like this.

She rushed over to the sink, splashed water on her face hurriedly and dried her hands just as Mills came in.

"Hey, Mum," Mills said behind Helen.

Helen spun around, feigning cheerfulness. "Hi, how was your day?"

Mills was looking down at her phone anyway. "Fine, I guess. Although Olivia was being a right bitch all day. Then she blew me off after school to go and hang out with some guy she's just met."

"Oh, that's not good. Cup of tea?" Helen filled the kettle, fussed about wiping down the already clean countertop, trying to stop the ridiculous tears she could feel hovering on her eyelashes.

"Yeah, thanks. I've got loads of work to do, a test tomorrow."

"Ok, well, best you get to it then."

Would Matt tell Mills he had found her snooping? Probably. He liked to get a rise out of Mills as much as Helen.

Will it ever stop feeling like it's them against us?

"Matt is upstairs with Diana and he's in one of his moods," Helen said.

Mills rolled her eyes. "I'll stay out of his way. And she's a right cow. What does he see in her?"

"Is she?" Helen asked innocently. "Why do you say that?"

"I dunno, she's just…" She shrugged. "Weird, I guess. She tried to be friends with me last year, but she's the year ahead of me and I just thought it was a bit creepy, you know? She was asking questions all the time, like I was being interviewed, but she never wanted to tell me anything about herself." She shrugged again and then looked up from her phone. She tilted her head. "Are you ok, Mum?"

Helen smoothed out the frown lines on her face and smiled at her, "Yes, fine, all good. Just trying to stay out of their way too."

Her eyes were boring into her. "You're scratching at your arm."

Helen looked down and saw that she was, her nails scraping across her forearm, leaving angry red lines. "Oh, I—" The kettle clicked off loudly and Helen busied herself with the tea, but her brain was swirling in ever tightening circles.

Mills disappeared upstairs with her bag over one shoulder and her mug of tea in her hand. Helen watched her go, then locked herself in the downstairs cloakroom, knelt in front of the toilet and made herself sick, her fingers probing, tickling the back of her throat, punishing herself for her overindulgence, then relishing in the calming relief when her stomach was empty again.

She took a minute to steady herself, breathing deeply, wiping her eyes, splashing more water on her flaming cheeks. She was still not sure what to make of what Mills had said about Diana, but purging herself had given her a moment of clarity.

A few more deep breaths and she felt almost normal

again. She unlocked the cloakroom door quietly and stepped back into the hallway. She noticed Hugh's study door was partially ajar, where she was sure it had been closed a moment ago. A shadow was moving around, barely visible inside, but Hugh wasn't home yet, wouldn't be for some time.

Helen stepped back into the gloom of the cloakroom and pulled the door almost completely closed. She had a sinking feeling, as though she knew she didn't want to see who was in the study, couldn't bear being humiliated again, accompanied by the certainty that after this, nothing would be the same again. Before she could change her mind and flee upstairs in blissful ignorance, the study door opened. Helen panicked and stepped backwards out of sight in reflex. She heard the door click shut and soft, padded footsteps move away. By the time she edged open the cloakroom door again, whoever had been in there was out of sight.

Helen waited for a moment, then crept over to the study, her heart pounding. She reminded herself, as she often had to do, that this was her house. She could go into any room she liked. But she still felt like a criminal as she pushed open the door. Everything looked as it should on the surface. Nothing out of place. Hugh's desk was tidy, with paperwork stacked neatly and his favourite brand of pens lined up like soldiers. Helen closed the door behind her and moved over to the desk.

She opened the desk drawers one by one, all except the bottom one, which was locked. That wasn't unusual though. He always kept it locked because he said his confidential school paperwork was in there, student records and the like.

She shook her head and turned to go. She was letting her

paranoia get the better of her. Maybe whoever it was had actually been looking for a book from the tightly packed shelves or a spare pen. Something inane and ordinary. This was just a boring, book-lined history teacher's study after all. Nothing controversial in here apart from Hugh's taste in short-sleeved shirts.

Helen's hip caught the edge of the desk as she turned to go. She hissed and rubbed the spot where the corner had poked into her skin, knowing it would leave yet another bruise. Her hand caught the pile of papers on the desk and they cascaded to the floor like confetti.

"Shit!" she muttered and crouched down to gather them back up.

Then she noticed the Polaroid that had fallen from the pile.

A Polaroid of a girl.

A girl with a cloud of hair around her face as she lay back, her face turned away from the camera, her legs splayed.

Mills watched her mother from the shadows at the top of the stairs. She had heard her in the toilet, the sounds of muffled retching, the water running, the toilet flushing. She knew what she had been doing.

Mills had known about Helen's eating disorder for some time, but she had never spoken to her about it. It was one of a list of unspoken vices between them – Mills' smoking and drinking, which she figured her mother knew about, and Helen's tendency to binge and purge when something was bothering her. She had thought things had settled, but when she saw the crumbs on her mother's shirt earlier, then heard her vanish into the toilet as soon as Mills turned her back, she knew.

She hovered on the stairs, debating whether to talk to her, to check in. The two of them came as a pair after all. She started down the stairs, then heard a noise behind her, a door opening, and changed her mind, darting back into her own room.

She could talk to her another time, when they had the house to themselves.

18

Crisp crumbs stick to the blanket as we huddle together and listen to music. The wine bottle is empty, the vodka bottle open. Tracey is drunk. I can tell from her slurring words and giggling laugh. I think I am too. I feel almost out of my body, like the air around me is buzzing and rotating of its own accord. I don't know what time it is.

"I need to pee," Tracey says.

"We should probably go downstairs, back to my room anyway. I'm cold."

Tracey heaves to her feet, stumbles, falls back into the bean bag and snorts. I pull her to her feet again and she puts her hands on my waist as we leave the attic in a conga line, Tracey giggling in my ear and weaving, making me stagger and lurch as I try to keep us from pitching forward down the steep stairs. Outside my parents' room I put a finger to my lips to silence her. The door to their room is closed, so I don't know if they are in there, but I suspect the dinner party is still going on downstairs, brandy and cigars in my father's study for the men, a Baileys or Amaretto in the lounge for the wives, bowls of salted peanuts and rum truffles being passed around and politely declined.

Tracey is still sniggering into my shoulder. "I really need to pee," she whispers.

We run the rest of the way and as I shut my bedroom door behind me, she lurches into the bathroom, pauses, then throws up on the white marble floor. Bright red splashes like an abstract painting.

"Oh god," she says, "I am so sorry," then throws up into the bath. The puke is rancid in my nostrils and I swallow hard so that I don't follow suit. I grab a towel from the laundry basket and throw it over the sick on the floor and manoeuvre her to the toilet before she wets herself too. She pulls down her pyjama bottoms and slumps heavily on the toilet. I look anywhere else.

"Oh god, do you hate me?" she says.

"Of course not, you silly cow. It's fine." I wipe up the sick as best I can, but my own head is spinning and my stomach lurches with every inhale.

I throw the towel in the bath and run the taps as Tracey hauls herself from the toilet. Pouring a glass of water at the sink, I hand it to her. "Here, drink this, then rinse your mouth out with the mouthwash over there."

I close the curtains in the bedroom and pull back the covers on the queen-size bed. She staggers from the bathroom, swiping at her mouth, and collapses into the bed. I crawl beneath the covers with her, leaving a space between us, but she pulls me towards her, throws an arm over me, her feet intertwining with mine.

"I'm really glad I met you, Helen. I love you. I think we are going to be lifelong friends."

"I'm really pleased I met you too." I smile into the darkness.

Then her breathing slows, her body deflates and I know she has passed out.

I lie for a while, my head spinning from both the wine and the feeling of her lying so close. When Eloise sleeps over, we top and tail, so that we never actually touch at any point. She would snigger and call me gay if my foot even brushed hers.

But lying here with Tracey, it feels warm, comforting. I reach out and gently brush a curl from her face. A strand is caught in the corner of her mouth and I release it, smooth the skin on her cheek. She sighs in her sleep.

19

NOW

Helen had wandered through the last few days like a ghost, lacking substance and purpose. All she could think about was the photo, but she was struggling to process what it might mean. She hadn't looked too closely at it, but it was still burned into her eyelids. She had stared at it like it was tainted, poisonous, then picked it up again with her fingertips and shoved it back where she assumed it had fallen from, appalled, disgusted, her mind swirling as she fled the room. Now she wished she had looked closer.

She had never seen the photo before, she was sure of it, but she knew who the girl was. The question was, why did Hugh have it?

The faces around the dining room table tonight were smiling and engaging for a change. No teenage angst or sullenness. No barbed comments or loaded questions. Lydia seemed more cheerful than she had been in a while, chatting happily to Diana, her voice giddy and babbling. She had upped her make-up game again and was sporting a full face of colour. She looked like she had borrowed one of Mills' cropped t-shirts too and was baring a lily white, concave stomach above the waistband of skinny jeans. Her phone was next to her on the table and her eyes kept straying over to it like a nervous tic.

Diana and Lydia were laughing, talking about things they had seen on TikTok. Matt was desperately trying to join in the conversation, laughing and adding little quips, but his voice was more forced, like he was trying to muscle his way in. Diana had eaten with them every night for a week now, but Helen seemed to be the only one irked by this. And maybe Mills, who rarely said two words to Diana. Meanwhile, Hugh looked delighted every time he saw her, his face flushing, his sweaty palms patting down his wayward hair.

She had figured it was a harmless middle age crush until she had seen the photo in his office. She found herself watching Hugh closely as he removed his glasses and wiped them vigorously on the handkerchief he kept in his pocket. He was certainly acting as pompous as usual, if not even more so, in a pathetic bid to impress their guest. Maybe someone had left the photo for him. Maybe he hadn't seen it yet, tucked as it was between the papers on his desk. Either way, none of it made sense. Why involve Hugh unless it was meant to harm her by dragging him into what happened all those years ago?

She could feel Mills watching her as she chewed on the skin around her fingers instead of her dinner, so she forced herself to stop. She had waded through a pile of food earlier when she was alone at the bookshop – crisps, biscuits, a dozen doughnuts – all of it in a bid to stop her mind from lurching from one ridiculous theory to the next. Now her stomach felt stretched and bloated, her throat scratched and raw from the aftermath. Her binges and purges were escalating again and she could feel herself teetering on the edge of what was controllable. She had been here before.

Mills' hand reached out and touched Helen's arm. Mills nodded at Helen's hand and Helen noticed the red pinpricks of blood on her forearm where she had begun scratching absent-mindedly. The scratch marks on her right wrist had only just scabbed over. Older scars on her arms were pale, ghostly memories of a past imprinted on her skin. Her fingertips still strayed towards those scars now and then, a braille history to remind her of those years after she left home, of the punishment she had inflicted on herself.

Helen willed herself to stop scratching, chewing, pulling at herself, but her fingers twitched in frustration. They wanted to scratch away the skin, down to the bones, to feel the snap and sear of pain, to punish herself over and over.

She sighed and smiled absently at Mills, put her hands in her lap under the table and forced herself to focus on the conversation in the air, but she felt like she was smiling maniacally while shit rained down around her and she wanted to run screaming from the room.

Diana was sitting at the other end of the table to Hugh's left. Helen watched her, her full lips smiling at Lydia, her long fingers gripping her knife, the deep red nails perfectly manicured to sharp points. Helen watched as she raised her fork to her mouth, parted her lips and bit a small piece of potato from the prongs. Helen's eyes tracked up her face and she realised with a jolt that Diana was now looking directly at her.

Diana chewed calmly, a slight smile on her lips, then put down her fork and said, without taking her eyes off Helen, "Tell me about how you and Helen met, Hugh."

When did she start calling him Hugh?

"I walked into the bookshop in the village one day, looking for a book on Lee Harvey Oswald for a class I was teaching on 1960s American history. Behind the counter was an extremely pretty woman who had her nose buried deep in *Wuthering Heights*. So taken by the book was she that she didn't even look up and I felt awful interrupting her to enquire about the book I was looking for. But needs must and I grabbed the bull by the horns, as it were, and ploughed straight ahead with my query. She didn't have the book, but ordered it in and I made an excuse to go back to the shop every day for a week under the pretence of seeing if the book had arrived, but actually just to see her. I was like a dog with a bone, I tell you." He chuckled, proud of himself.

He had certainly been persistent, Helen would give him that. Their courtship, as it were, was more a case of him wearing her down rather than sweeping her off her feet. There was nothing chest-heaving about their relationship, even back then in the early days.

Helen kept her eyes on the peas and chicken pie in front of her. She would be damned if she was going to make vegetarian food every time Diana was here.

"I think that's very romantic," Diana said. "I've seen your shop, Helen. It's very... quaint."

"It doesn't need to be big and fancy for our village. There is a Waterstones in Padstow if people want a wider choice and, as Hugh says, I can order in any title someone

is looking for. I prefer the cosy, intimate feel of my shop."
Helen tried to keep her voice light, but her teeth were biting
off the ends of her words. Why had Diana not admitted to
everyone that they had met in the shop? It would be very
awkward for Helen to admit it now of course, so she would
keep up the pretence for as long as Diana did, but it was
certainly odd.

Helen changed the subject. "Mills, have you sorted out
that nonsense with Olivia yet?"

"Nah, she's still acting weird, but won't tell me why. I've
obviously done or said something, but if she doesn't want to
tell me, then there's nothing I can do to fix it. I'm not losing
sleep over it though. She gets like this sometimes. It'll blow
over. It's probably got something to do with this new guy. It
usually does." Mills' best friend, Olivia, had always been as
changeable as the wind for as long as they had been friends,
all the way back to when they were in nursery together.
They reminded Helen of her friendships from school, all
artifice and passive aggression, borne out of circumstance.
Helen had tried to foster a friendship with Olivia's mother
when the girls were in nursery, but her heart hadn't been in
it and after a while she had let it fizzle out. Helen preferred
her own company to that of others who would only want to
get to know her – and there was a lot Helen didn't want
people to know. So she stuck to casual acquaintances rather
than deep friendships, always keeping a safe distance.

"Teenage friendships can be so toxic sometimes, can't
they?" Diana said.

Helen was still looking at Mills and she raised her
eyebrows, to which Mills giggled around her fork.

"You should let her know how you feel, Mills. Sometimes

people just don't realise when they are hurting you. It's often based on a misunderstanding or something else going on, maybe an assumption she has made about you, and all it takes is a simple conversation to clear it all up. You don't want to end up in a situation where you aren't speaking at all or, even worse, end up hurting each other." As she said this, Helen could feel Diana staring at her, but when Helen met her gaze, her eyes were wide and innocent.

"That is very true, Diana. Talking is important," Hugh added, nodding sagely. "A problem shared is a problem halved. One should always bat with a straight bat, let people know where they stand." Hugh and his clichés.

"Right, thanks for that cricketing analogy," Mills said, barely disguising her sarcasm.

Diana's words were clanging in Helen's ears, images of the photo dancing to the beat, making her question every word Diana was saying, why she was here in her house, what motive she had for getting close to her stepson, her husband, her family.

'If you were a bloke, you could just punch her and get it all sorted," Matt said unhelpfully. "It worked for me and Tommy Green in primary school."

"Violence is never the answer, Matt," Hugh said predictably. "The pen is mightier than the sword."

"I don't think a strongly worded letter will do the trick, Hugh," Helen said. "I think you're right, Matt. The only way to stop a bully is to stand up to them, show them strength. Maybe she does just need a hard slap."

Silence fell over the table as all eyes swivelled towards Helen. They were trying to work out if she was being serious.

Then Mills started to laugh. "Imagine her face if I did!" She laughed harder and Lydia joined in nervously.

Hugh sighed deeply at the other end of the table and shook his head. "Not the right message to be sending to our impressionable young family, darling," he said, exasperated. "Let's talk about something else."

Helen looked over at Diana and smiled sardonically. For the first time, it was Diana who looked away first.

Screw her. Time for Helen Whitmore to step back into the shadows where she belonged and for Helen Tillsbury to reappear. If Diana wanted to fuck with Helen, then bring it on.

Later that evening, Helen overheard Matt saying goodbye to Diana.

"Do you have to go? You can stay over if you like," he said, his voice surprisingly needling and pathetic. He was normally so determinedly in control of himself, rarely showing any emotion at all.

"I have loads to do on my portfolio for next week. Besides, we've spent every day together for the last week." Her voice sounded impatient.

He was standing over her, almost leaning into her so that she was pushed up against the front door. "But you've been hanging out in Lydia's room all night. I haven't seen you."

"She wanted me to do makeovers and stuff – and she's a sweet kid. You should spend more time with her yourself. I think she's lonely."

Helen was thrilled at the thought that perhaps their little love affair was losing its sparkle and shine already.

"Seriously, Matt, it's like you want to monopolise my time. I need space to breathe." She put a hand on his chest and pushed him away from her, but he closed the small gap again, towering over her.

"Right, space. You need space," he said, his voice rising. "Fine, have all the fucking space you want."

"Don't be like that, Matt. You're a good friend and I enjoy hanging out with you."

Ouch.

Helen felt uncomfortable listening in, so she stepped towards the kitchen doors, stared out into the night instead, at the rain racing down the glass.

The garden was dark, with only muted lighting here and there to cast circles of illumination into the night. Movement caught her eye and she stood up a little straighter. Down towards the far end, an adjustment of the light against the dark, a shape sticking to the shadows. She reached for the handle, just as she heard the front door open, feet walking quickly across the gravel and then the door slam shut.

She hesitated, torn between seeing if anyone was outside and checking in on Matt. She turned away from the garden. It was probably nothing anyway.

She grabbed a tea towel on her way out of the kitchen and pretended to wipe her hands unnecessarily. Matt was standing with his hands splayed on the heavy wooden front door, his head bowed.

"Has Diana gone? Does she need a lift somewhere?"

"She's fine," he said without lifting his head.

"But it's dark and wet out there. You normally take her home, don't you." She knew she was pushing.

He shoved away from the door, pulled himself up to his full height. "She's a big girl, she'll be fine," he growled.

Helen lifted her hands in surrender. He stalked off into the family room. The television blared into life.

Against her better judgement, she followed him. He was stretched out on the largest of the two couches, an arm flung over his forehead, the remote control pointed at the television as channel after channel flicked past.

"Are you ok, Matt? Did you have an argument?"

"No."

"It sounded to me like you did."

"Then you shouldn't have been listening. Again. You're making a nasty habit of that."

"Look, Matt, maybe it's for the best. She seems... I don't know..."

He sat up suddenly, anger flaring his cheeks red. "She seems what?"

Damaged.

Helen sighed. "It's just... how well do you know her? She seems to have come from nowhere."

"I know her, alright? She was at my school. Dad taught her. Mills knows her." His voiced dropped. "And it was brilliant when she finally paid me some attention."

Bingo. He had finally revealed something. "You mean you haven't actually known her for long?"

He flopped back down onto the couch and sighed. "No. She was just someone I had seen around, you know? She was in my art class last year, but we didn't really talk. Then I saw her at college and she just starts talking to me and..." He shrugged nonchalantly, but his forehead was furrowed and his mouth pinched.

"So what's the problem?"

"I guess I pushed her too hard."

She thought about him leaning over her at the front door, his height and weight so much more than she could fight back against, his sheer physicality that could be threatening in certain circumstances.

No, he wouldn't.

Would he?

Silver cars and blind corners.

"Matt, did you try to force her into—"

"Bloody hell, what do you think of me?" Spittle flew from his lips as he snarled at her.

"Sorry, I just… I misunderstood what you were saying."

"That's just it though. I haven't tried anything until now." His voice dropped low again and he looked down at his hands. "I haven't pushed it. We've just been chatting, hanging out, talking about music and books and stuff. So tonight, I tried…" His voice was now barely above a whisper.

"You tried what? To kiss her? More than that?"

"To kiss her," he mumbled. "But she knocked me back, said she's just interested in being friends, nothing else."

"Friend zone, huh?"

"Yup."

"Well, that's better than nothing, isn't it? And maybe she'll come around to your… charm." She paused. "Where does she live?"

He looked up. "Why? What does that have to do with anything?"

"I just worry about her walking home, that's all."

"I don't know where she lives," he admitted.

"But…?"

"I usually drop her in the village and she catches the bus from there. I haven't been to her house yet."

"So you don't really know her at all?"

"What are you getting at?"

"Well, you don't know where she lives, who her parents are or anything. She seems quite keen to keep you at arm's length from where I'm standing. Maybe there's a reason for that. Maybe she isn't the kind of girl you want to know after all. Maybe you're better off without her. Mills doesn't seem to like her very much."

He lurched to his feet.

"I know her, ok? I know how funny and smart and insightful she is. That's enough for me. And she's great with Lydia, not that you would notice that. Fuck what Mills thinks! That's probably because of you anyway. You just don't like her and I don't know why, but I wish you'd leave her the fuck alone. She probably doesn't want to take it any further with me because you've made her feel unwelcome. You had a scabby face on you all through dinner and every time she said something, you scowled at her."

"No, I didn't!"

"Actually, I do know why you don't like her. It's because of the way she looks, isn't it? It's because she is hot and young and fit, and look at you!" He sneered at her. "You're old, a has-been with no talent, a failing career and a fat arse. Do people even read your pathetic books anymore? If it wasn't for your parents' money and Dad funding you, you'd be nothing. No wonder you were so happy to marry Dad, the poor, sad fuck. He was so much better off with Mum."

"Matthew!" Helen reeled at the hatred in his words.

Before she could say anything else, he stormed out of the room, leaving her with burning cheeks and reproach hanging heavy in the air.

Hugh leaned over Helen as she sat at her dressing table, brushing her hair and smearing night cream into her rapidly ageing face. He smiled and kissed the top of her head, then disappeared into the bathroom. She could hear the water running as he brushed his teeth and she wanted to scream at him to stop wasting water, turn the bloody tap off while he was brushing, but she clamped down on the rant so hard that her jaw ached.

The gargling noise now coming through the door made her stomach heave.

He emerged, wiping his mouth with a towel that he then tossed aside, and went into the adjoining dressing room to set out his clothes for the next day. This from a man who owned three pairs of the same corduroy trousers for work, the same style of white shirt in duplicate, with a short sleeve version for the warmer summer months, and one suit for funerals. He reappeared in his sensible, button-down pyjamas and threw the cushions onto the floor from the bed. They scattered across the carpet until the room resembled a kid's soft play area. Helen had to pick her way between them to reach the bed.

When she climbed into bed next to him, he had already turned on his side, his back to her. She reached for her book and started to read, then reread the sentences again.

She gave up, put the book down and said, "Darling, what do you make of Diana?"

Did she hear his breathing pause or was she imagining it? "What do you mean?" he said eventually, still with his back to her.

"I just thought, since you taught her, that you would have an opinion. I overheard her and Matt arguing after dinner."

"She is an intelligent girl from what I remember, but I don't know too much. Doesn't come from much, but is doing her best. Scholarship, if I remember correctly."

"She was in your class though?"

"For one year, yes, but how much do teachers really get to know their students? You see one side of them, that's all. Now, darling, if you don't mind…" He exaggerated a yawn that made his shoulders heave.

"Um, one more thing, have you noticed anything different about Lydia? You know, the make-up and clothes?"

"She's just experimenting, trying new things. Millie has probably been encouraging her. It's harmless. As long as Millie doesn't introduce her to any of her other bad habits."

Helen sat up straighter. "What do you mean?"

"Well, Millie can be rather rebellious and I don't want her rubbing off on lovely, sweet Lydia. Now really, darling, I am exhausted, so can we talk about this another time?"

Helen's jaw ached from being clenched so tightly. She turned off her lamp and shuffled down onto her pillow, but stared straight ahead into the darkness, all tiredness forgotten.

She expected to hear Hugh's snores begin as usual. He had a knack for falling asleep as soon as his head hit a pillow or his arse a chair.

But tonight his breathing didn't change; the snores didn't begin.

She suspected he was staring into the dark too.

Hugh lay like cement, his back to Helen, listening intently for her breathing to slow and her body to do that jerky thing it always did when she dropped into sleep. It was taking longer than usual and he suspected she was doing the same, the two of them caught in a passive-aggressive battle for sleepless supremacy.

His nose began to itch, a sneeze coming, and he clenched his teeth and wriggled his nose, hoping it would go away. A sneeze now could pull her back from the brink of dropping off.

Eventually he felt her body jerk as she fell off the edge into sleep and he gave it a few more minutes before sliding gently out of bed. He slipped his feet into his still-warm slippers and rather gracefully slinked to the door. His efforts were nearly undone when his slipper caught on a scatter cushion and he stumbled, bumping against Helen's dressing table, but he held his nerve and emerged into the hallway triumphant before exhaling audibly.

He avoided all the creaky spots as he descended the stairs. He paused on the landing outside the teenagers' rooms, but everything seemed quiet, no blue light flickering under closed doors. He crept on, reached the stained glass window and paused again. The house was awake. It was always awake, creaking, groaning, clanking away, and tonight was no different. The boiler in the basement hissed into action;

the pipes clanked as the heating came on; wind rattled the glass. Just letting him know it was watching, listening.

He hated this house. But he wasn't one to look a gift horse in the mouth and moving in here when he married Helen meant he could sell the bungalow and save on the mortgage repayments.

He carried on past the judging gaze of the window to the ground floor. He could hear Clive snoring in his bed in the kitchen, the noise loud enough to wake the dead.

He closed the study door soundlessly behind him and lowered himself into his chair. Only then did he start to breathe normally, allowing the oxygen to settle the drumming in his ears. He sat for a moment, his hands flat on the desk in front of him, his eyes closed. Then he reached under the lip of the desk to where a small key balanced in the groove. The key opened the bottom drawer of his desk. Sitting on top of the papers and folders was the photograph that had tumbled out of his pile of marking. He looked at the girl in the photo, his hands shaking. He couldn't see her face, but her long legs were positioned in such a way that left very little to the imagination. One breast had crudely escaped from the fabric of her costume. He turned the photo over and read the words written on the back again:

YOU HAVE A SECRET.

He tossed it back in the drawer and rubbed at his eyes, as if to dispel the image. He was confused. This, on top of the emails he'd received recently, could ruin him. One sniff of impropriety and his career would be over.

He slammed the drawer shut and stood on unsteady legs. Reaching into the bookcase, he pulled out a weighty hardback copy of *War and Peace* and grabbed the bottle of whiskey hidden behind it.

20

THEN

The next morning when I open my eyes, she is not in bed next to me. She has left an imprint on the pillow though, so I know it hadn't been a dream.

I sit up and regret the sudden movement. My head is thumping, my mouth dry, my tongue swollen. I sit for a moment, waiting for a dizzy spell to pass, then swing my legs from the bed. As I take a few tentative steps towards the bathroom, the door opens and Tracey is standing in front of me.

"Hey, how are you feeling? God, my head hurts," she says. "I am so sorry about last night. I'm mortified."

"Don't be – we drank a lot. I need to pee though," I say, more because I can feel my cheeks flushing than anything else.

She climbs back into bed and I disappear into the bathroom. She has cleaned up all the vomit, washed out the bath and rinsed the towel, which is hanging over the shower door to dry. I take a minute, stare at myself in the mirror, tell myself to be cool.

I climb back into bed. "You didn't need to clean all that up. Martha would've sorted it."

"No, that's not fair on her. It was my mess to clean." She snuggles down under the duvet. "I hope I didn't say anything embarrassing. I was really drunk." I thought back to her telling me she loved me and how warmed I had felt, how something in my stomach had shifted and rolled over.

"No, no, you just went straight to sleep."

"Ok, good, because I really like hanging out with you. I'd hate it if you didn't want to be friends after this."

"I do. It's all good. I gave you the booze anyway, so it's my fault."

"You didn't force me to neck it though." She closes her eyes, her hair fanning around her on the pillow.

"We just need to build up your resistance a bit, that's all."

"No, I'm never drinking again!"

"We'll see... Come on, a bacon sandwich and a cup of tea from Martha will sort you out."

"Does Martha ever get a day off?"

"Not many."

Martha has her back to us, washing pans, but she turns when she hears us, smiling around a yawn.

"Hi, girls, did you have fun?"

"Yes, thanks, but we would kill for a bacon sandwich and a cup of tea," I reply.

"Um, would that have anything to do with the bottles I saw someone sneaking upstairs last night?"

"You saw me?"

"Eyes in the back of my head, Helen. Just be careful. Your father will be fuming if he finds out."

"He won't care."

"Well, I care – and you should take better care of your lovely young bodies. Now then, bacon sandwiches coming right up."

Tracey leaves soon after, the house immediately quiet and sombre without her in it. I go up to my attic and sit, listening to music, thinking about her, us. I have revision to do, but I can't concentrate on anything concrete, so I let my mind wander.

I imagine us at the party, the centre of attention, her in the bright red swimming costume, her dark legs long and lean, everyone laughing at her jokes and wanting to be near her, then I find myself getting annoyed at the idea, not wanting to share her with people who would not appreciate her – people like Steph, Emily and Eloise.

As if reading my mind, Martha calls up to me that there is a phone call for me. I trudge back to my bedroom and pick up the phone extension on my bedside table, hear the click as Martha puts down the receiver in the kitchen.

"Hello?"

"Hels, it's me. I'm sooooo bored! What are you doing? Let's make some plans for the party. You have no idea how excited I am. I'm thinking it should have a theme, like Club Tropicana or something. Of course, we could go with the haunted house theme since we're having it at your house. Ha!" El has never liked my house, is convinced it's haunted. That suits me fine as it means she rarely wants to sleep over. We usually go to her house, which is clean, modern and predominantly painted magnolia. I don't like having people over in general. I can never tell what kind of mood my mother will be in, if she will be sweetness and light or scathing and scratching at me like a feral cat. Eloise doesn't know the full extent of what my mother is capable of. No one does.

Last night was safe because my mother was in entertaining mode.

"Hey, El, um, maybe we should just let people come as they are instead of a theme?"

"Where's the fun in that?" She pauses. "You do want this party, don't you? You don't sound very excited." I can hear her pout down the phone line.

"Yes, I do. Sorry, I'm just in the middle of revision and it's doing my head in a bit."

"Which is exactly why we need this to distract us! Now, let's talk booze…"

We talk for over an hour – or rather, El talks at me and I nod, grunt, mumble in agreement, but I stop concentrating when she suggests that the four of us wear co-ordinated bikinis.

The silences start to stretch between her monologues and my replies, so I tell her Martha is calling me for lunch and end the call.

I feel weary. Not just from the hangover, but with the whole process of being me, of juggling the different sides of myself, without fully understanding which one should take top billing, which face will be liked the most, which face *I* would like the most.

Am I the version of myself that I am with Eloise? I used

to think that was ok, but I'm starting to prefer the version that hangs out with Tracey. She is more open, engaging and actually has opinions of her own. She doesn't have to dumb herself down. What I'm worried about is that the Eloise version is slowly morphing into my mother.

But how do I amalgamate the two?

And which of my friends will still want to know me if I do?

21

NOW

It felt like the pool house was her only sanctuary. The thick, heady air; the oppressive quiet; the darkened glass windows despite the bright daylight outside. She lay on her back in the warm water, floating with her eyes closed, supported, safe despite the visions of photographs dancing behind her tightly squeezed lids.

The more she thought about it, the more she thought the photo was put there for Hugh's enjoyment. Maybe that was why Diana didn't want to take things further with Matt. So Hugh had his secrets like the rest of them. Why was she so surprised? We never really get to know other people fully, do we? Most of us don't even know ourselves, let alone anyone else. We only learn what they want us to see.

Helen was surprised at how upset she felt about it all. She and Hugh hadn't been close for a while. He lived his life and she lived hers, albeit in the same house, and as long as there was no scandal or gossip and a quick fumble on a Friday evening, he was content to pretend they were a happily married couple.

So why did she marry him?

At the time, she had needed stability. She was a single mum with a young child. She had moved back to her hometown shortly after her parents' death after years of what could only be described as rebellious debauchery in self-exile. Men, alcohol, short-lived jobs and even shorter-lived relationships. Periods when she had lived in her car, hopped from one couch to another, ate out of polystyrene containers and showered in community centre bathrooms.

Then, after a night where she actually couldn't remember very much of anything at all, along came Mills, with her head of dark hair, green eyes and angry screams, and Helen knew she had to make some changes. Her second chance. Her parents were dead – her dad from a heart attack and her mother shortly after following a short illness, probably exacerbated by using alcohol and pills as her only nourishment for years – and Helen had inherited a home she hated, with all its trauma and secrets. But she needed a stable home for Mills, so she had returned.

The childish gossip that had swirled around her when she had left fizzled out over the years once the village grapevine had grown bored, so she kept her head down and focused on her baby girl, in the process setting up a respectable bookshop, complete with children's story time every afternoon at 3 p.m. and a sensible monthly book club pick.

Hugh was the icing on her respectable cake. If anything could well and truly bury her past for good, it was quietly marrying an unassuming, well-respected history teacher at the registry office.

If he could love her, then she must be ok.

And it had been quiet ever since. Settled. Safe. The community had accepted her; she was a familiar face in the square; her shop was well loved by the locals; and no one was any the wiser about what had gone on before.

Until now.

But now even Hugh wasn't what he seemed, apparently.

She flipped onto her front and swam back to the side. Her towel was draped across a lounger and she wrapped herself in it like a cocoon, breathing in the scent of the fabric softener. She dried quickly before reaching for her bathrobe.

But before she could, her arms were pinned to her sides as someone grabbed her roughly from behind, forcing the air from her lungs.

Matt lay in bed, his face turned to the wall. Diana was airing him, leaving his messages unread, even though her Stories said she was on her way to college already. She'd posted herself saying hello to a Shetland pony in a field before she headed into the village. He knew the pony. Lydia had ridden him when she was younger and fancied having a pony. Helen had encouraged his dad to let her have riding lessons and look after the ponies before investing in one for herself. She had lasted a few weeks until they realised that even just the smell of horses and hay on her clothes had made his dad sneeze and his eyes stream with allergies.

Lydia had been devastated, but had kept it to herself as always. He had heard her crying through the bedroom walls though, could see how the light had dimmed behind her eyes just a little bit.

He hadn't said anything. He struggled to relate her, to relate to anyone since his mother had left. She was the only one that really got him.

He rolled over and was blinded by a beam of sunlight shining through a gap in his curtains. The dust danced in the glare, tiny little pieces of dead skin flinging themselves around in a last-ditch attempt to find where they belonged.

He dragged himself to sitting, looked at the clock and thought about lying down again. He had missed his early class, so there was no point in going in at all today. But his full bladder forced him into the bathroom.

He emerged from the bathroom and pulled open the curtains. The weight of his argument with Diana was sitting on his chest like an anvil. Maybe he needed a session with his weights to flush it out of him. Or maybe a day in bed with Netflix was what he needed. As he stretched and yawned, he thought he saw movement towards the bottom end of the garden. He leaned towards the glass. Probably Helen coming out of the pool house or Clive snuffling in the grass.

There it was again. Definitely someone at the pool house, but it wasn't Helen.

He smiled when he realised who it was.

Interesting.

Sometimes you really didn't know the people you lived with as well as you thought.

22

THEN

I had actually forgotten about their trip, what with Tracey staying over and everything, but Sunday brings with it the joyous news that my parents are leaving today. There is an unusual amount of activity. Suitcases being carried down, rushing around, instructions bellowed out.

I sit in the kitchen, listening to it all unfold around me. Wondering if they'll remember to say goodbye. I don't actually know how I feel about it. I will enjoy not having to tiptoe around, worried about whether my mother has had enough coffee today, or not enough; whether her bath was too hot and made her cranky; or if my dad's tone on the telephone was dismissive; whether I can jump away quick enough before her rings catch my face or the back of my legs.

Martha bustles in and out, fetching this, carrying that, her cheeks ruddied, her hair ruffled. Eventually, there are shouts of, "The driver is here!" I stand in the kitchen doorway, willing them to see me, but also hoping they forget. Just one more thing to add to the list I can discuss with my therapist in future years. One more transgression to hold up and say, "See? This is why I am the way I am."

But my mother is coming towards me, her arms outstretched. She is animated, excitement at the decadence of her trip putting colour in her cheeks and a sparkle in her eye. Unless she's taken something to help her cope.

"Darling, do be good for Martha. I know you will. You always are." There's an air kiss on each cheek, a brief hug. Not too close; not too long. "We'll be in touch."

"Have fun, Mother. Say hi to New York for me. Bring me back a t-shirt."

"Make sure you study when we are away. Martha will be keeping us informed of your progress," Father says, but doesn't come closer than the doorway.

"Straight A's all the way, Father," I say. Then I rush at him, throw my arms around him. "I'll miss you, Daddy."

I feel him stiffen in my arms and lean away from me in horror, so I squeeze tighter, smirking into his shoulder. I let go and smile angelically. He looks mortified. He coughs, puts his hand out as though he is going to pat me on the head like a dog, thinks better of it and rushes to the car.

Then the car is pulling away. I stand in the driveway, waving enthusiastically as it disappears out of the gate, no one looking back. I have the urge to laugh loudly.

Martha is watching me from the door, concern wrinkling her brow.

"I'm fine, Martha," I say as I walk past her. "We'll have fun without them. And I hope they are paying you enough for this! I'll put in a good word." I wink as I go inside.

23

Helen struggled against the strong arms, twisting and turning to free herself, but the grip tightened as her wet swimsuit bunched and gaped, cutting into her. She could feel someone's breath on her neck as she was dragged back towards the edge of the pool, her feet slipping in the puddles of water on the tiles.

She screamed in frustration and fear, pushed herself hard backwards. The crown of her head connected with something with a thump and the arms loosened enough for her to spin around and strike out again. Her hand made contact this time and she heard a squeal of pain.

"What did you do that for?"

"What the hell, Peter?"

Her chest was heaving, her breath coming in pants and gasps, the chlorine in the air and shock making her dizzy. Peter, the man who maintained the pool house, was crouched down on the tiles, holding his hands over his nose as blood dripped between his fingers. He had a red mark on his forehead from where she had headbutted him. "I was just messing about," he said, his words muffled.

She sighed. "Come here, sit down," she said and led him to a lounger. He sat obediently on the end as she straightened her swimming costume and threw on her robe. She used the end of her towel to wipe his nose, swallowing down a flare of annoyance at soiling a clean towel, then tilted his head back to try and stop the bleeding.

"You frightened the hell out of me," she said, her voice steadier.

"Sorry, I just saw you in here and thought I'd surprise you. I haven't seen you for a while."

She was standing between his legs, still wiping at the blood while holding his head back. His hands moved up the back of her bare legs.

"You've been away," she said. "How was your family holiday?"

"I missed you." His hands moved higher, his fingers feather-light.

"Peter…"

"Ah, come on, it's been ages. You haven't called since I got back."

"I've been busy."

He looked at her, his eyes big, aiming for puppy dog but coming across as pleading. "So why does it feel like you're avoiding me? Don't you like me anymore?"

His fingers were working their way under the fabric of her swimsuit.

"You've just been on holiday with your wife and child." She squirmed away, but he pulled her back hard.

"Oh, playing hard to get today, are we? You're usually

gagging for it." His voice was low and throaty and, instead of making her feel desirable, she felt nauseous.

She pushed his hands away again and stepped back decisively.

"No, Peter, not today. I have a lot going on." She turned away and faffed with folding the soiled towel.

"Right." His voice had chilled now. She could feel his eyes boring into her, as though her intentions were written as clear as day on the back of her swimming costume.

"Peter, we should probably not do this anymore…" She used to be so much better at breaking hearts, but this felt cumbersome.

"Oh, I get it. You've had your fun and now you're bored." He was sulking like a school boy. The sulk quickly turned into a scowl. "You rich bitches are all the same."

"Don't let your wife hear you say that. We pay her mortgage." Helen couldn't keep the chill from her voice. She was starting to wonder what she had ever seen in him, if anything. He'd scratched an itch. Now the itch had turned septic.

Peter launched off the lounger towards her and she stepped backwards, feeling the edge of the pool beneath her heels. "Don't you dare mention my wife. You have a helluva lot more to lose than me. That teacher husband of yours – I wonder what he would think if this little *arrangement* was made public. No doubt that fancy school wouldn't be too pleased if you were the talk of the village. *Again*. And you could probably kiss this lovely big manor house goodbye."

That was where he was wrong. This lovely big manor house belonged to Helen. It had nothing to do with Hugh, but men always liked to assume it was the woman that was financially dependent.

"What do you mean by *again*?"

"Oh, come on, we all remember the stories about you. Part of me was curious more than anything else. You know, whether you're still as much of a goer as you used to be. I guess once a slut, always a slut."

He was right up in her face, to the point that she was arching her back to put space between them, but not so far that she fell backwards into the pool again.

"Peter, you're fired. You need to leave."

He stared at her, loathing her. A complete contrast to the way he had looked at her before. All those times here, in this pool house, on these loungers, with the ivy providing camouflage. Now he was all spite and bruised ego.

"Oh, I'll go," he growled, "but I'll be back. You owe me. Not just my wages, but compensation for all those times you used me like a piece of meat. Some would call it sexual harassment, abuse of power. Watch your back, *Mrs Whitmore*," he sneered. "I'll be back to collect."

And then he was gone, the ivy shimmering in discontent as he slammed the glass door.

She sank to her knees on the tiles, her body shaking in disbelief.

How did she get herself into these situations?

The affair had started purely out of loneliness. She had needed someone to help Arthur with the grounds, since he was slowing down in his old age, and Peter seemed perfect for the job. But it wasn't the stereotypical *rich older lady flirts with young, handsome pool boy in bid to alleviate boredom* kind of thing. Peter was Helen's age, had gone to the local comp when they were kids, and now had a young wife who worked in the local supermarket and a little girl at the village nursery school. He had his own business doing gardening, pool maintenance and general DIY in the village. He was well known and well liked. God knows why. Clearly there was a side to him that he kept hidden too.

Helen had employed him to maintain the pool and found herself chatting to him when she brought him cups of tea while he was working. They would laugh over things they had seen on television and stories of other people in the village, things she wished she could laugh and chat about with Hugh, but he was always so preoccupied with his students and hobbies, closed away in his study most nights or sleeping in front of the news, or just not interested in gossip.

Peter was charming and funny, so when he made the first move one day, his fingers lingering on hers over a steaming brew, she thought, *Why not?* It's not like things were hot and heavy with Hugh. The best he could manage was an occasional Friday night fumble every couple of weeks with the lights off and his socks still on.

Then things started growing more intense. Peter would turn up on days when he wasn't working, knocking on the kitchen door to be let into the house, calling into the shop and lingering while she served customers. She started to avoid him. If she saw him coming along the street, she would ask Jenni to cover the shop and would sneak out the back until he had left or she would keep the kitchen curtains closed so that he couldn't see if she was at home. One day when he knocked, she actually hid in the kitchen cupboard among the brooms and mops. She started to feel stalked, like prey.

Then he let into conversation one day that he thought they had a mutual friend from all those years ago, someone in common, and Helen knew she had to end it. Preferably without a scene. She naively thought a few weeks apart would do it – out of sight, out of mind. So when his wife conveniently won first prize in a competition that the bookshop ran to celebrate the launch of the new Portia Deane novel, Helen was delighted. The prize was a two-week holiday in the Lake District, where the book was set.

Jenni was annoyed that Helen drew the winning name without her because she loved to make an occasion of everything. She wanted fanfare and an Instagram story to announce the winner; Helen needed to get Peter as far away from her as she could, at least for a little while, and as quickly as possible, so she fixed the draw. For two weeks she could breathe freely again, the suffocation of his advances alleviated, the worry about what he did or did not know dissolving away for a while. In fact, she had almost forgotten about him completely, what with everything else going on.

But it would seem out of sight was not out of mind after all and some men didn't like to be told no. They didn't like to have their cake taken away from them when they were still hungry. They were like toddlers in that respect.

Now she had something else to worry about – and how would she explain to Hugh why she had fired him?

She let herself into the house and got dressed for work, her mood low. She had been late into the pool this morning and regretted not going earlier as she would've avoided the run-in with Peter if she had. Having said that, he was not normally here so early. He must've been waiting for her.

Still, it was over now. She just needed to manage the situation. And if he confronted Hugh and laid bare their affair, Helen guessed Hugh had a few secrets of his own that she could bring up to even the score. That photograph of a semi-naked woman in his possession, for instance.

The idea of a confrontation did not fill her with joy though. Her life had been quiet and settled for some time now and she generally liked it that way. Yes, she could feel lonely, but that was only because Mills was older now and living a more independent life, leaving Helen behind. She didn't need Helen as much. But that was what you were supposed to want for your children, wasn't it? Independence, a free spirit, to make their own way in the world? For so long, it had been just Helen and Mills against the world. Even when Helen married Hugh and they found themselves catapulted into a ready-made family, it felt like the others circled them warily, freaks in a cage, never quite getting close. Now it felt like Mills was pulling away from Helen too, leaving her behind.

Helen remembered when she had lost Mills for all of ten minutes once. That desperate feeling of not knowing where she was, if she was safe, if she was hurt, had haunted her ever since. Mills had been three years old and had wandered out of the bookshop door one sunny summer afternoon when Helen had nipped for a wee in the toilet at the back of the shop. When she had looked around for Mills, she had found the shop door open and had rushed outside. The cobbled street was busy as it was peak tourist season. All she could see were men in shorts and socks, pale legs on show, and women with straining t-shirts and wedge-heeled sandals teetering across the cobbles. Helen had the horrible decision of going left or right. She left the shop door wide open and ran down the road to the right, hoping she had chosen wisely. The panic had made breathing impossible, fear gripping at her diaphragm and making her lightheaded. She couldn't get her eyes to focus. Then, at the bottom of the street, she saw a woman walking up the hill, holding Mills by the hand. Helen had raced towards her, grabbed Mills and crushed her in a vice-like hug, while repeating, *Thank you, thank you*, over and over to the startled woman.

Thank you for not being a paedophile. Thank you for not running off with her. Thank you for seeing her and bringing her back.

That feeling, that sense of utter, gaping, unfillable loss – she never wanted to feel that ever again.

But before she knew it, it would be just her and Hugh in this house, rattling around and avoiding each other. Mills would be off living her own life.

Helen had watched her that morning, sitting at the table, a plate of toast in front of her. Two slices of wholemeal, one with cream cheese, one with marmalade, cut down the middle into triangles, like she had had it since she was little. Helen watched her eat one half with cream cheese before eating one half with marmalade, savoury then sweet, followed by the savoury again. Still her little girl, with her familiar habits and eccentricities, yet now unapologetically wearing the body of a woman. In that moment, Helen had had an overwhelming urge to cry – with pride, fear, yearning, love – and had had to get up and fuss over the dishwasher in order to compose herself.

Helen let herself into the shop through the back door and immediately set about making a strong cup of tea to try and warm the chill that had settled in her stomach after the confrontation with Peter. Tonight was Helen's regular Friday date night with Hugh. She would have to tell him that she had fired Peter. Maybe then he would confess himself.

As she carried the tea out to the front, ready to open up, she noticed a package on the mat inside the front door, which was still locked, the sign reading "Closed".

Helen picked up the package, feeling the weight of it in her hands. It was wrapped in brown paper and A4 in size, most likely a book. Curiously, it was far too big to have come through the letterbox. Her name was handwritten in capital letters on the brown paper in black Sharpie, the handwriting vaguely familiar, but there was no postmark or courier label. She was used to locals dropping off copies of their self-penned manuscripts in the hope that she might have a contact in the publishing world to get it into print, but this didn't feel like a manuscript.

She sipped at the tea, sat down at the desk and tore open the paper. It was a book, not too thick, but heavy and encased in a leathery cover.

She turned it over so that it was face up – and stopped breathing.

It was the yearbook from her last year at school. The Seahaven crest and motto were etched into the burgundy leather in pretentious gold foil. She dropped the book onto the desk with a thud. A jaunty pink tag was sticking out from between the pages and she couldn't stop herself from reaching out with a tentative hand and turning to the marked page, even though instinctively she knew she should just put the book aside, throw it into the recycling bin, set fire to it, anything but open it.

A large red circle was drawn around a photograph halfway down the page. Helen knew that photo well. It was *her*. The girl with her hair in a high ponytail that hung long over one shoulder. The girl with the black and red tie knotted perfectly at her throat. The girl with the crisp white school shirt, clean for school photos day, but soon would have specks of blood staining it.

Helen's own photo was just below it. Her face was missing. Someone had scratched at the photograph with something sharp, leaving a scarred, torn mess in its place.

Underneath, written in red, was the word MURDERER.

She pushed the book away. It slid to the floor with a sound like a judge's gavel.

Her ears whistled and her chest tightened, like a strap was being pulled taut, to the point where she could feel her ribs and lungs constricting. She rushed into the back room and retched over the sink, nothing coming up but bile and regret.

She remembered that day so well. The day the school photos were taken. Stains on the white shirt almost as damning as the stains left on their souls when it was all over.

Helen remained leaning over the sink, breathing in the smell of bleach that barely covered the sour stench of the blocked drain beneath it. She ran some cold water and splashed her face, but her cheeks continued to burn.

She approached the desk again like she was expecting a landmine. She could see the book lying spreadeagled on the floor, open, exposed. She bent to pick it up, ready to toss it into the bin where it belonged when she noticed that other pages had been vandalised too.

She sat on the floor beneath the desk and flicked through the rest of it.

Every group photo that Helen featured in had been scratched, her face obliterated.

Every photo of *her* was circled with a red ink heart.

24

THEN

It is decided that we will have the party next weekend. Well, Eloise has decided. That gives me next to no time to lose more weight before I have to parade around in a bikini. I'll have to mention the party to Martha. She will certainly notice if a crowd of teenagers turns up. It's too late for her to object though.

"Martha, I'm having a party next weekend. Nothing big – just a few friends around to hang out at the pool house. A belated birthday party since I didn't do anything for it in June. My parents know about it. I told them before they left and they were fine with it." I look at my fingers, suddenly interested in a speck of dirt under my nail.

"Oh, ok, that sounds fine. As long as there aren't too many people. Can I prepare some food for it? Would you like a cake?"

"No, no cake, thanks, but some food would be great – we could order in a pile of pizzas so that you don't have to go to any trouble though?"

"We'll see, shall we? I think it will do you good to let your hair down and have some fun. You haven't been yourself lately." She runs her hand affectionately over my hair and I feel guilt rumble into my stomach, knowing I am lying to her.

I close myself in my bedroom and call El, tell her Martha is on board. "But seriously, El, we can't have too many people over, ok?"

"We won't! It will just be Brian and a few of his mates. Have you invited Tracey?"

"Yes, she said she's coming too."

"Oh, fun!"

I wonder if there's a reason she's asking.

When I hang up, I call Tracey and the conversation couldn't be more different. We talk about my parents leaving, how different the house feels, lighter, less like it's slowly suffocating me.

"Why did they even have kids then?" she asks honestly.

It's a question I've often asked myself. "I don't think I was planned. They are older, much older than most of my friends' parents, and I was an unfortunate development when they were more interested in socialising, I guess." I should ask them one day, find out whether I was planned or not.

"Anyway, the party is next weekend. You are still coming, aren't you?"

"Um, about that, I don't know if I should."

"Why? I really want you to."

"I don't know. I don't want to cause trouble with Eloise."

"She knows you're coming and she will be too busy with Brian to be bothered with you, trust me. Please come."

There is silence, only her breath faintly audible along the line.

"Ok."

"Great! Now I just need to lose a few pounds before then."

"No, you don't. You need to be at that party the way you are, as yourself and no one else."

She doesn't know what she's talking about. I don't have her confidence. I've had nothing to eat all day and I am now ravenous and doing everything I can to distract myself from heading down to the kitchen to see what Martha has cooked up.

We start talking about books, movies that are on that we want to see. We tentatively arrange to go to the cinema in town later in the week. She says her dad is happy to give us a lift and I'm envious that her dad will do anything for her, whereas mine would arrange for Arthur to take me where I need to be, would just throw some cash at me without a glance or a thought.

When we've finished talking and hang up, I stand in front of the mirror and try to see what she sees. I'm not sure if I've ever properly looked before. At parts of me, yes. Twisting and turning as I try on new jeans maybe. But not a head-to-toe analysis.

I'm wearing loose jeans that sit high above my waist and a baggy t-shirt, the words "Choose Life" shouting from it. All of it hides my shape well. I pull the t-shirt tight across my chest, trying to understand how I feel about the shapes and undulations that are exposed. I see medium-sized boobs that splurge at the sides like fleshy doughnuts, nothing like Eloise's pert, tiny bee stings. I see a curved belly beneath the waistband, like a mound. Nothing like El's concave stomach and exposed ribs above a waist you could wrap both hands around and still have your fingers overlap. I pull the legs of the jeans tight and see substantial thighs, built more for lifting heavy things than modelling swimwear. Nothing like Eloise with her thigh gap so wide you could drive a small vehicle through it.

And yet Tracey says she sees something different.

I wish I could see it too.

Maybe my mother has a pool cover-all that I can wear next week. Something sheer that shows a suggestion of what's underneath without giving it all away.

I creep into the main bedroom, feeling like an intruder in my parents' private space. I rarely come up here and if I do, I'm focused on Mother's amateur dramatics rather than what is around me. It feels strange being in their space without them. I can still smell her perfume in the air, like she was there seconds ago. The room is in disarray – shoes abandoned on the thick blue carpet; handbags discarded on the bed; make-up and jewellery scattered across my mother's dressing table in the window. I sit at the dressing table now, looking at the diamond earrings and cheap necklaces jumbled together, marvelling at my mother's lack of concern at the sheer materiality of what she owns. Much of the expensive stuff has been gifted to her by my father over the years. I assume the idea is that if he buys her sparkly things, she will stay happy and will keep her eyes closed to his transgressions. And I have no doubt there are some.

I open the dressing table drawers to rows and rows of intimate lingerie, things I can't imagine my mother wearing, lace, silk, colour. I push the drawer closed again.

The bedside tables are vastly different from each other. My father's side bare except for a small alarm clock and a paperback of *A Brief History of Time*. My mother's side is a jumble of things – fashion magazines, an old paperback of a Mills and Boon novel, tissues, more earrings, a hairbrush. I open the bedside drawer and marvel at the tiny pill boxes inside. There is a pill for everything – happiness, sadness, insomnia, exhaustion. It is an apothecary's chest of drugs and I wonder how she manages to get her hands on them all. Most of them look to be prescription drugs. I pull out one plastic bottle, this one for extreme fatigue according to the label, consider the tiny white pills inside and slip the bottle into my pocket. I also pocket the sleeping pills and anti-depressants. Sometimes I feel sad. These may take the edge off. If they are good enough for my mother, then they should work for me. If they were important, she would've taken them with her.

Off the main bedroom with its vast bed is her dressing room and it is a similar picture. One of extravagant chaos as she rifled and discarded items not worthy of ending up in her suitcases. There is something about the decadence of all this that is sitting uneasily with me today. Perhaps because it comes on the back of talking to Tracey with her humble outlook and modest family, but this show of wealth is making me queasy.

Is this what Tracey sees when she looks at me? Is she lying about my worth when she actually sees a spoilt little rich girl in front of her? Is she friends with me only because I am rich?

I open the wardrobes, marvel at the rows of coloured material, hearing the clatter and chink of the empty hangers, naked, their outfits now packed into the underbelly of an aeroplane. One wardrobe is entirely dedicated to my mother's shoe obsession. On good days, I have seen her teetering about the house in thin heels, leaving little circles of damage on the parquet floor like a breadcrumb trail of her aimless wanderings.

At the top of the wardrobe are even more shoeboxes. I tug on one I can reach on my tiptoes and it is released in a rush, the boxes above it thudding and settling once more. Something shifts around inside the box and I realise it doesn't have shoes in it. Inside are two bundles, wrapped in silver paper and tied with different coloured ribbon. I untie a pink ribbon and lift a corner of the paper to reveal a bundle of letters. I take the box and throw myself onto the huge bed, shoving aside the bags, scarves and shoes, hearing them clatter to the floor. Someone will sweep through this room in the next few days and it will be straightened and tidied, dusted and cleaned, as though my parents had never made a mess. As though they were never here in the first place.

I pause, wondering if I should really be reading these letters, then shrug and open the first envelope.

25

NOW

Helen wanted to lock up the shop and rush home, but the bell above the door jangled. She closed the yearbook and slipped it under the desk. A man walked in with purpose in sensible shoes, his heavy coat rustling as he headed over to the latest releases. He took his time reading the backs of a number of books, paging through others, even reading chunks from some, and Helen wanted to shout at him to hurry up, to just pick something and get out, that this wasn't a library. In the end, he bought five books, four of them hardbacks, which was a good haul, and he left satisfied with his tote bag of literature swinging from his shoulder, only for a woman to come in straight after him.

And so it was for the next few hours, uncharacteristically busy and no chance for Helen to close up. All she could do was sit at her desk, chewing on her pen, her brain swooping from one theory to the next as it tried to fathom where the yearbook had come from, who had sent it and what they wanted from her. Helen had a copy of the yearbook herself – everyone was given one just before they went on study leave for their exams. Of course, there was a whole memorial page near the front dedicated to *her* after what happened, all angelic smiles and *Rest in Peace* missives. Everyone saccharine sweet in their comments. That probably wasn't what they were saying in private. Helen assumed her own copy was in the same place it had always been, hidden with the shoebox, in which case this was someone else's yearbook.

Someone who knew what happened.

Or thought they did.

Helen left as soon as Jenni arrived for her shift, once more not hanging around to chat. If Jenni thought anything of it, she didn't let on, but her face was tight with concern. Helen walked home quickly. There were people around for most of the walk, thanks to the unusually warm sunshine, but Helen felt exposed, like there were eyes on her, tracking every step she took. She spun around every now and then like a madwoman, but couldn't see anyone following her, watching her. She felt singled out, yet alone, like there was a solitary spotlight shining on her, blinding her to what was going on.

She walked with her keys in one hand and her mobile in the other, her eyes alert, her head swivelling from side to side.

On a whim, she continued past the bottom of the garden and along the coastal path behind the house. Once, years ago, she had found herself here almost by accident. Mills was a toddler and they had been out walking with Clive. Mills had run off along the path and Helen had chased her, only realising where they were when she caught up with

Mills. That was the first time Helen noticed the memorial plaque. Simple, plain. Just a name and dates on black slate. It was almost completely obscured by sand and grass, set into cement on the edge of the worn footpath, teetering on the edge of the sheer drop into the ocean below and the angry, jagged rocks.

Today, as Helen drew closer, she noticed the differences time had brought with it. The path itself was narrower than ever, now more a worn track than a path. A sign attached to a wooden post told walkers to be careful of the drop, to stay away from the edge. The plaque was still there; the grass around it had been cleared, but now there was an additional flash of colour.

Someone had laid a bunch of lurid red roses on the plaque.

As Helen stood and looked at the words carved into the slate, the waves below shouted and snarled at her, as furious as they had always been as they flung themselves in anger at the landscape.

She suddenly felt vulnerable, standing so close to the edge. She spun around, expecting to see someone right behind her, their hands outstretched, but there was no one there. Just the flowers lying in cellophane that moved in the breeze, the petals fresh, vibrant, the colour of blood. As she stared down at them, it started to rain big, fat drops that fell on the petals. She felt like she was intruding on someone's moment, someone's grief.

Of course, the flowers could be for anyone. Surely others who had walked along this path over the years had slipped in the wet sand, perhaps tripped over an exposed root, felt themselves plummeting down, unable to stop, hands reaching up, reaching out, trying to grab onto something, anything...

Helen stepped back from the edge, stinging bile rising in her throat. She turned to go and noticed a figure in the distance, standing, watching. Helen couldn't make out who it was. They were wearing a heavy padded coat over a dark sweatshirt with the hood pulled up, their face in shadow. She couldn't even make out if they were male or female as they were standing too far away. Helen assumed female from their height. She stepped towards them, held out her hand, but they turned and walked away.

It may have been yet another coincidence, perhaps just a walker looking for solitude, who saw a crazy woman with wild eyes gesturing to them and decided to go a different way, or changed their minds about using the coastal path after seeing how close to the edge it was. How sheer the drop was.

A certain plummet to your death.

But Helen also couldn't deny that there were too many things happening to her now to be coincidental any longer.

She headed back to the house. Over the wall, she could see the shape of the pool house, lurking in the ivy, obscured from view. The ivy engulfed all of it like a living, breathing blanket, claiming more for itself with every passing year. Helen almost didn't register the gap in the ivy draping over the back wall until she had walked past. She stopped short and retraced her steps. The ivy that had grown over the gate had been pulled back.

The gate was open. Just enough for someone to squeeze into the garden.

That gate hadn't been open in years. As Helen stepped towards it, her shoe kicked at something hard lying in the dead leaves. She reached down and pull out the padlock that had kept it locked on the inside. It was broken.

She edged through the gate and past the pool house, her brain whirling. It must've been Peter. That was how he had got to the pool house so early. He must've noticed the gate when he was tidying the bushes along the back wall. Was that who was watching her on the coastal path? Was he trying to freak her out? Or was it her again?

Peter would make himself known. He wanted her to know he was threatening her.

Even so, she was annoyed. What did she say to Mills? That bullies only understood strength? Then she would have to show him strength.

Without a key for the kitchen doors, she had to walk around and let herself into the house through the front door. By the time she reached it, her hands were tight fists at her sides. She had decided it was perhaps time to visit Peter's wife, let him know she could be threatening too. As she opened the front door, she could hear voices coming from somewhere in the house. Helen pushed the door closed very quietly, stopped at the bottom of the staircase and strained to hear.

One of the voices was Lydia's, high and distressed.

"I have to tell her."

"No, you don't. You can use this to your advantage. She deserves everything she gets."

"But Dad…"

"Oh come on, do you really think it would upset him that much? He probably knows already anyway. I thought you wanted her gone? This is how you do it."

The other voice sounded like Diana – but it couldn't be, surely.

Helen stepped closer to the door. The floorboard under her foot creaked loudly.

"Is someone here?" Diana asked.

"No, I don't think so. It must be Clive."

"I'm going to check."

Helen rushed into the kitchen and looked around frantically for somewhere to hide. The cupboard she had hidden in from Peter was in the far corner. She pushed herself inside and pulled the door almost closed behind her before rearranging some of the hanging aprons over herself. Through the crack in the door she could see most of the kitchen. The pungent smell of spices was heady and overpowering in the small space. She could feel them tickling her nose, threatening to make her sneeze. She screwed her eyes up tight to stave off the sneeze. Her heart hammered loudly in her throat.

Just when she thought she had gotten away with it, that no one would come looking, she heard footsteps and saw Diana step into the kitchen and look around. She nipped her itchy nose and held her breath, praying Diana wouldn't think to look in the pantry. What would Helen say if she did though? No lie could explain why she was crouched in a cupboard, holding her nose against the spices and hiding behind some dirty aprons with a mop handle poking in her back.

But Diana didn't come any closer. Instead, Lydia came

up behind her and Helen saw Diana turn and reach out to touch Lydia's face. Lydia smiled beautifully and they kissed – long, deep, passionately – before leaving again.

Helen held her breath as long as she could, then crept out of the pantry, headed straight over to the French doors and quietly let herself into the garden. She breathed in deeply, shock making her pulse race. As she stepped outside, she heard footsteps behind her and spun around ready to defend herself, but it was Clive sloping towards her, his bum wiggling in excitement.

He followed her into the garden and they walked quickly towards the pool house. Helen needed space and quiet to think about what the hell was going on.

Why was Diana with Lydia? Where was Matt? Did he know about their relationship? The way she stroked Lydia's face, the passion in the kiss... Lydia was only a baby, too young to understand such a relationship, surely.

It felt like there was a meteor hurtling towards her and every way she turned, she found herself still in the strike zone.

Peter. Lydia and Diana. The yearbook. It couldn't all be connected, but somehow she thought it was. They say, *The truth will out.* Helen had the overwhelming feeling that her time was up.

The pool house was in darkness. Helen opened the door and immediately felt calmer as the hot air hit her. She reached around to turn on the lights. The sudden illumination blinded her. She blinked, thinking it was just her unfocused eyes, but it wasn't.

Someone had painted the word WHORE in bright red paint across the tiles.

The paint was still wet, drips running down the white tiles like blood, the word screaming at her.

There was something stuck to the wall. Another photograph. Not a Polaroid this time, but a poorly focused photo, grainy and of poor quality. It was of Helen and Peter on the loungers. They were certainly not practising their swimming strokes.

How had he taken the photo? Did he have a camera or phone rigged up somewhere? Were there more?

Helen sat heavily on the lounger closest to her, feeling it shift along the tiles as she fell onto it. Her eyes remained glued to the wall.

This was turning out to be one hell of a day. A helluva few weeks. Not too long ago, she had been content living her less than extraordinary life with her dull husband and disconnected family. Now it felt like she had been shoved off course. Everything was tilting and she couldn't make sense of anything anymore. She couldn't work out who was a hero and who was a villain.

And what was she?

She felt like she was slowly going mad. Polaroid photos, yearbooks, Hugh, Diana, Lydia. It was all too much. Her throat was closing in panic and she gasped in air. Clive was oblivious to her distress as he snuffled at her feet, licking at the tiles and drinking from the small puddles along the edge of the pool. She reached up to claw at the collar of her shirt, desperate to get more air, but her phone was still in her hand, as were her front door keys. She still had her bag over her shoulder too. Poking out of it was the yearbook.

The phone started to vibrate, the ringtone stabbing at the silence. She dropped the keys in fright, almost dropped the phone too. She looked at the screen and jabbed at it, suddenly furious.

"You got my message then?" Peter said, his voice low and threatening.

"Very subtle, Peter." Was he watching her now? She walked over to the door, peered out, but the garden was empty, the gate to the path closed again.

"I thought so too. Did you like the photograph? I don't think it quite captures your best side though, do you? I prefer you from behind."

"How did you take that photo?"

"Ah, Helen, I needed some security, that's all. I had a feeling things might pan out the way they did, so I made a few... let's say, *home videos* for my own enjoyment."

"You filmed us?" She felt sick.

"Among other things. They're quite good actually. Lots of action. The dialogue is a bit flimsy though." He chuckled, clearly enjoying tormenting her.

"What do you want, Peter?"

"I told you. I want compensation for lost earnings."

"Money? This is all about money? How grubby of you."

"I'm not the grubby one, Helen."

"And if I don't pay up?"

"I'll leak these videos on social media. I'm sure your customers will be delighted to see what you've been up to, not to mention your lovely husband, your children. I bet they will be thrilled."

"How much?"

"Patience, my darling. All in good time. I'll be in touch."

★

Lydia sat on her bed, hugging her unicorn pillow and thinking about the afternoon with Diana. If her dad or Helen found out she had cut school to spend time with her, they'd be furious, but she couldn't say no. She didn't want Diana to think she was childish, scared to break a rule or two. She wanted Diana to think she was cool, edgy.

And for the most part, the afternoon had been fun. When her dad had dropped her off at school, she had feigned a migraine and walked straight home again, then called Diana once she was sure Helen had left for work. They had drunk herbal tea, eaten the oat biscuits Diana had brought – they tasted like cardboard, but she ate them anyway – and they talked for ages about everything and nothing.

Diana was mesmerising, from her long hair and full, pink lips to her ideas on the world, her love of expressionism, her sense of injustice at the world in which they lived – social inequality, gender inequality, racial inequality. She made Lydia feel ashamed that she hadn't been taking enough notice of what was going on in the world around her and Lydia wanted to do better, to understand it all more and try to make sense of it. Despite Lydia's naivety, Diana wanted to hear her opinions and she finally felt like someone saw her, cared what she thought, listened to her when she spoke.

The first time they met was just before Diana came for dinner. Lydia had been in the square. She needed to pop into Helen's shop for a spare key because she'd left hers at home. She had been looking down at her phone, more messages from those bitches at school blowing up her Snapchat, and she had walked straight into Diana.

When she looked up, her stomach flipped like she was in an elevator. Diana had been annoyed at first, then pretty cool about it. She said she recognised Lydia, that she was a friend of Mills and they had made small talk before Diana had sauntered away. Lydia had watched her go, feeling like she had been sprinkled with fairy dust.

Then Diana turned up at the house with Matt. They had chatted a little at the table, literally bumped into each other again later in the corridor outside Matt's room. Diana had quipped that they had to stop running into each other and Lydia had heard herself laugh like it was the funniest joke in the world and wanted to die of embarrassment at how lame she sounded.

Lydia had been carrying a copy of *Lord of the Flies* that she had to read for school and they got talking about it, right there in the hallway. Eventually Matt had got annoyed and stole Diana away again, but after that Lydia couldn't stop thinking about her, started casually being around whenever Diana came over, until eventually Diana was coming over to spend time with Lydia and not Matt.

She wasn't sure what was going on between Matt and Diana now, but she knew they didn't talk much. Matt was still obsessed with her by the sounds of it, constantly phoning, messaging and pestering Diana at college. Diana had explained to Lydia that she was bi and Lydia thought it must be so nice to be that secure in yourself, able to be confidently fluid, letting yourself feel what you wanted to feel without adhering to societal constructs and stereotypes. Even so, she had asked Lydia to keep their relationship a secret as Matt wouldn't understand and Lydia was fine with that. She wanted this all to herself anyway.

She smiled into the pillow, had to fight the urge to laugh

out loud in delight. She thought she could smell Diana's perfume in the fabric of it.

She grabbed her phone and scrolled through to the selfie they had taken, lying back against the pillow, hugging, Diana looking straight at the camera but Lydia unable to peel her eyes away from Diana's face.

Then she frowned and her stomach bubbled with anxiety as she remembered what they had talked about just before Diana left.

What Diana had asked Lydia to do.

26

THEN

I sit on the bed and carefully unwrap the paper around each bundle. The letters tied with a pink ribbon are in my father's handwriting and addressed to my mother; those tied with a blue ribbon written by my mother to my father. I sort them into date order, curiosity overcoming any feelings I may have of guilt at intruding into their private correspondence.

The letters all date from the months leading up to when my mother was pregnant with me. I remember hearing that my father had been sent to work in the Netherlands for some time. He had stayed for six months, travelling backwards and forwards when he could, my mother waiting patiently at home. She was doing what many privileged, bored women did then, hosting society events in the name of fundraising for charities, but if I know my mother, it was the excuse to host an event and show off that appealed more than the causes she was supposedly championing. I have never known her to be selfless.

I page through the letters, feeling a sense of disbelief and curiosity at the voice narrating the words – my mother's proclamations of affection that border on obsession, asking endless questions about who he is spending his days and nights with, proclaiming that she can't live without him, begging him to reconsider the job, yearning for him, her loneliness seeping into the page in blue ink.

In contrast, the letters bound by the pink ribbon begin with the heady, raw passion of a man in love, his words declaring the physical void where his adored wife should be, then tapering into impatience and annoyance at having to explain his movements, addressing her declarations with claims of hard work, endless evenings in monotonous business meetings, living out of a suitcase and the joyless existence of hotel life, before morphing into the passive aggression of someone who has tired of providing a constant alibi. The final letters become companionable, as though he is penning a postcard to a favourite aunt, and I almost feel pity for the woman my mother was. I can see ripples of that woman now, when she is sprawled on her bed, wailing at the injustice of her lonely life, swearing to anyone that will listen that he is having an affair, won't take her anywhere, doesn't love her anymore. When she is snarling at me because I am there and he isn't, lashing out in anger and leaving bruises that she will forget about pretty quickly, but I will feel for days. Until he sends her a sparkly gift and he is her husband again, the man she adores, the one she cannot be without, and I get a temporary reprieve from being her scratching post.

The last two letters to him share the news that she is pregnant. It would seem a brief sojourn back to England one weekend and a bottle of expensive champagne resulted in me being brought into existence. My mother is overjoyed, her words rushing over themselves, talk of bringing them closer to each other, demands that he has to return home now, that she cannot do this alone. The second letter was sent soon after, before he had even had time to respond to the previous one. In it, she accuses him of ignoring her previous letter, her anguish at knowing he didn't want children, swearing that she hadn't planned the pregnancy, that it is a happy miracle. She promises the child won't get in his way, won't stifle him at all.

The words, "It will very likely not be a girl, so we can still sell the house and return to London as you want," blur in front of my eyes.

I open the last few letters in a hurry, the pages catching on the envelope as I tug them free. He addresses the news of her pregnancy, saying his silence was because he needed time to get his head around the news, that she knew of his decision to not have children, that he wanted a long and successful career, one where he could travel, they could see the world together without the burden of having a child in tow. He ended it by saying he would be home soon and they could discuss the options available to them.

Her last letter to him is brief, the ink smudged in places, and I imagine her tears falling melodramatically onto the thin paper, evidence of her anguish. She tells him she has not gone through with "it", but doesn't say what "it" is. I have a fair idea though. She goes to some lengths to say that a child won't change anything. If anything, it will bring them closer together, that a son will bring him joy. I wonder if she is trying to convince him or herself.

His final letter is even shorter, the words punched onto the page, the pen leaving small tears in places, his hand heavy as he expresses his disappointment that she went against his wishes. He tells her his placement will be over in another two months and that they will address it when he returns to England. His final words are the hope that she is carrying a son.

27

NOW

Helen sat at her dressing table under a cloud of Chanel. It reminded her of her mother, this perfume, and she hated it, but Hugh was a creature of habit. He had presented her with a small bottle for their first Valentine's Day together and she had politely said it was one of her favourites. Since then he had bought it for her every year. She'd tried wearing a different fragrance for their date nights, just to spice things up, but he'd noticed every time and let her know in his characteristic passive-aggressive way that he was disappointed by sneezing repeatedly and commenting on how her alternative perfume was affecting his sinuses.

So now she tolerated the headache-inducing smell, just so that she didn't have to endure his sullen expression over the dinner table. Tonight the perfume was masking the smell of bleach after she had removed all traces of the red paint from the pool house, scrubbing until her arms ached and then scrubbing some more, long after the paint had gone.

She checked her make-up, making sure it was sufficiently understated because he hated to see her "painted like a doll", as he described it. Not too much, but enough to disguise the tiredness and worry lines. Her hair was loose and blow-dried around her shoulders, just how he liked it. He liked to sit and stroke it sometimes and in those moments she felt like Clive, fussed over, petted. She had finally chosen an outfit of muted colours, nothing too bright to offend his sensitivities, after discarding a rainbow-coloured skirt that she had struggled to zip up, the waistband constricting her, payback from her binges. She wasn't sure why she went to such lengths to fit in with all his little preferences, considering that he would likely turn up in the same pair of trousers and shirt he had worn to school, would maybe have run his hands through his hair if she was lucky.

She pushed away from the dressing table and made her way downstairs in leopard print, kitten-heeled shoes, a tiny cry of rebellion that she couldn't quell. She expected him to be in the lounge, sipping on a whiskey from a crystal glass and looking more like her father every day, but the lounge was empty.

She approached the closed study door and knocked before opening it. His chair was turned away and he swung around at the sound of the door opening.

He was sweaty and pale, his eyes wide like he was staring down an oncoming train.

"Darling, are you nearly ready?" Helen asked.

"Oh, um, is it that time already?" His hands were grappling with something under the desk. "Give me a few minutes to get ready."

She narrowed her eyes, but closed the door behind her and stood in the hallway, unsure what to do with herself.

All dressed up and nowhere to go, as her mother would say.

She shrugged into her jacket. "Mills?" she called up the stairs. She heard her footfall almost immediately. Mills appeared on the landing, dressed in a leopard print onesie, her hair pulled into a messy bun perched on the top of her head.

"We're going," Helen said. "There's leftovers in the fridge. Can you make sure Lydia gets something too?"

Mills pulled a face. "Can we order a takeaway?"

The study door opened and Hugh emerged, looking a little less sweaty but still pale and distracted, his hair Boris Johnson-esque in its unruliness.

"Right, right," he blustered. "Ready, darling?"

"You might want to..." Helen said, then decided against it. She turned back to Mills. "Yes, you can order in a takeaway. There's money in the jar in the kitchen."

She ignored Hugh's tight lips.

"Thanks, Mum." Mills came all the way down and gave her a hug. "Have fun, Hugh. Don't do anything I wouldn't do. Oh, and you might want to do something about your hair." She disappeared into the kitchen, already on the hunt for takeout menus.

Hugh was frantically patting down his wayward hair.

"Matt, Lydia!" Helen called. Their response was slower. Matt sloped down, barefoot and wearing only baggy tracksuit bottoms, his chest bare and his face sullen. He had been like this since his argument with Diana. Barely saying a word to anyone, closing himself away in his room.

Helen assumed he didn't know Diana had been at the house earlier with Lydia.

Lydia appeared over his shoulder. In contrast, she was looking almost buoyant. She was wearing childish pyjamas, SpongeBob SquarePants frolicking across her legs, her face scrubbed clean of the make-up she had been layering on with a trowel lately.

"We're off to dinner. Mills is ordering in takeaway if you can all agree on something."

Matt pushed past them without a word. Lydia gave Hugh a kiss on the cheek, but ignored Helen. Her eyes were glued to her phone as she walked past, then she stopped in front of the long mirror on the wall, pulled the pyjama top tight against her midriff and took a photo of her reflection, lips pouting like a fish. Hugh didn't notice. He was too busy checking his pockets for his wallet, keys, handkerchief.

The car journey was short but quiet. Neither of them had much to say. Helen made small talk about the weather, how the nights were getting shorter and the wind over the cliffs colder. He nodded in agreement, his hands gripping the wheel as they drove the dark and twisty roads into the village. They could've called a taxi, but Hugh preferred to drive himself, which meant he only ever had one drink with dinner. Helen couldn't remember ever seeing Hugh drunk. He had managed to get a bit tipsy on champagne at their wedding, but the idea of him ever being inebriated was laughable.

She, on the other hand, often had an overwhelming urge to fall into a large bottle and tread water in it. She didn't, but the urge was there all the same.

"Darling, are you ok?" she said to him as he stared ahead.

"Yes, yes, fine," he said.

He parked on the village square. Helen could see her shop across the way, in darkness apart from the light above the sign. She had named the shop "The Owl and The Pussycat" after Mills' favourite poem when she was younger and the shop's location close to the sea. The sign was hand-painted by a local artist and illustrated an owl and a pussycat in a pea green boat sailing atop bobbing waves. Tonight it was swaying in the stiff wind, making it look like the boat really was sailing of its own accord.

As Helen looked away, movement inside the shop caught her eye. She stared hard at the window, but could only make out darkness behind. A trick of the light perhaps. Probably a shadow from the trees in the square. She kept her eyes fixed on the window for a little longer, just to be sure, until she heard a subtle cough and turned to see Hugh standing with his hand out impatiently, waiting for her to join him.

The aroma of garlic, basil and sweet tomatoes overwhelmed them as they opened the restaurant door to deep conversations and companionable warmth. Benito, the owner, looked up and smiled in delight under his statement moustache. "Ah, you're here! Wonderful to see you again." He always greeted them in the same way, as though he hadn't seen them in weeks rather than days. He was a regular in Helen's shop too, often poring over cookery books or asking her to order in books on his other passion, gardening. He lived on a small holding just outside of the village and grew a lot of the produce used in the restaurant.

He directed them to their usual table in the corner by the window and Hugh held out the chair for Helen. The restaurant was full, every table taken, the air buzzing. Helen didn't look around, but Hugh made a show of smiling at some of the faces he recognised, looking more like himself now that they were inside.

Benito rattled through the specials unnecessarily, since they always ordered the same thing: bruschetta, followed by spaghetti carbonara for Hugh; garlic prawns followed by spinach and ricotta cannelloni for Helen. Then Benito subtly disappeared, leaving the menus on the table.

Hugh immediately picked his up and pored over it, despite knowing it backwards. His face was a studious mix of concentration and indecision. Helen looked over the wine list, decided on the usual house white, of which she would limit herself to two glasses, then cast her eye over the dessert menu first before pulling her eyes to the mains.

Benito was back, pad and pencil in hand. "So, my lovely friends, the usual? Or something different tonight?"

Hugh made a show of turning the menu over, considering the options, before handing it to Benito and saying, "Two glasses of your house white please, and then bruschetta for me, followed by the carbonara, I think."

"A man who knows what he likes," Benito said, although Helen was sure he was sighing in frustration on the inside.

Helen was.

Then Hugh said, "And my lovely wife will have—"

"You know, Benito, I think I will have something different tonight," Helen interrupted.

They both looked at her like she had uttered a stream of profanities.

"I think I will start with the arancini, followed by linguine amatriciana."

Hugh was frowning at her, but Benito looked delighted. "Excellent choice, my friend, excellent!"

He gathered the menus and weaved through the tables with a smile.

Helen kept her eyes on the window, staring out into the night, trying to see over to the shop, but she couldn't see it from this angle.

Benito returned with the wine and they clinked their glasses together before Helen took a long drink. She bit down on an audible sigh of satisfaction.

Hugh reached over and took hold of her hand. His was clammy and warm. They sat in silence. He released her hand when a parent of one of his students wandered over and said hello, smiling politely as they made small talk. She returned to her table and Hugh asked Helen how the shop was doing. She returned the favour by asking how school was going.

The same conversations every Friday evening; the same answers provided. Nothing new or interesting or exciting. And she wondered why she had been tempted into an affair. Was it the same for him? He was certainly distracted tonight, not his usual self. His eyes were pinched at the edges, little lines that weren't there before, his hands fidgeting, fussing with the napkin, brushing non-existent crumbs from the tablecloth.

She knew what she was marrying when she had accepted Hugh's proposal. A quiet life of domesticity, nights in front of the television and buttoned-up pyjamas in bed. At the time, she thought it was what she wanted. To have someone to take care of her for a change. She had never had that before. Growing up, the closest person she had had to a parent was Martha, the housekeeper. So the idea of a man who wanted to take care of her, who offered her stability, security, safety – that idea had been appealing. And not just for her. For Mills too. A stable family life, with siblings and a father figure, routine and structure.

Now that Helen's life was spiralling again, she should be finding these moments of mundanity nice, but she didn't. There was a feeling building inside her, like she wanted to fight her way out of the mess she was in, instead of lying down quietly and letting it happen.

Hugh hadn't asked too many questions about her past before. He didn't like sordidness, so she hadn't volunteered anything. He knew the bare minimum about Mills' dad, but then Helen knew very little herself. He was a man, a bunk-up in a car park, never to be seen again. Mills knew that – Helen had been honest with her at least. She'd told her as a cautionary tale, considering that Helen couldn't actually remember many details about the night. One day Mills might want to know more, but for now she seemed content with knowing that her mother had made mistakes, but had done her best.

Now the fear was that Hugh – everyone – was about to find out a whole lot more about Helen. That getting pregnant after a tacky one night stand while drunk on tequila was not the worst she had done.

The silence between them was squashing her into her cushioned seat. She sipped at the wine, tried to talk about Lydia again, but Hugh cut her off and changed the subject, letting her know in unspoken terms that Lydia was not Helen's concern.

Their food arrived and they ate predominantly without words. Helen ordered another glass of wine after the first disappeared rather quickly. Hugh ordered a jug of tap water. It arrived with slices of lemon and lime bobbing between the ice cubes that clattered into the glass as he poured for both of them. He pushed her glass towards her and nodded at it around a mouthful of bruschetta.

By the time they had finished their main meal, Helen had been on the receiving end of a disapproving glare from him when she called Benito over to order a third glass of wine. She was now feeling rebellious, mostly because she was annoyed that the linguine was not as good as her usual choice of cannelloni and it irked her to think she should've stuck with what she knew after all. She then ordered tiramisu on a whim instead of a cup of peppermint tea. Benito raised a bushy eyebrow and smiled.

The tiramisu arrived with two shots of limoncello on the side.

"She didn't order that," Hugh said, but Benito merely winked at Helen and said, "On the house."

"I can't, I'm driving," he insisted, pushing it away.

Helen knocked back her limoncello before Hugh could send it back, then downed his as well.

She was now feeling quite tipsy and the conversation she knew they had to have was perched on the end of her tongue, ready to dive off. Probably not the best time to bring up Peter, Lydia, Diana, but she was going to anyway.

"By the way, I had to let Peter go," she said as Hugh sipped on his filter coffee.

"Oh? Why?"

"I just don't think he was doing a good enough job."

"Well, you should've discussed it with me first." He was in a disagreeable mood now.

Helen could count on one hand how many times Hugh had ventured into the pool house. He hated the smell of chlorine and humidity brought him out in a rash. The maintenance of the house and the staff had always been her concern, as though he was embarrassed to live in a house that came with staff, but quite happy to let them pick up after him.

Helen was annoyed at his reaction. "Well, no, not really. I use the pool every day, so I expect it to be maintained properly and I think standards were slipping."

She could feel his eyes on her. She spooned pudding into her mouth and steadily met his gaze.

"Do you though?"

The spoon paused in front of her mouth. "What do you mean?"

"Do you use it every day? I mean, you say you do and I see you head down there often enough, but..."

She waited for him to continue. "But what?"

"Well, let's be honest, darling, you don't look like Rebecca Adlington, do you? So what are you actually doing in the pool house if you're not swimming?"

"I am swimming. Every day."

He nodded, sipped at his coffee. Helen put down her spoon.

"So how did he take it?"

"Who?"

"Peter. How did he take being fired? By you?"

It seemed a strange question. "Why do you ask that?"

"Just because he is well known in the village and has worked with us for quite some time. We don't want to be the subject of *rumours* or *gossip*, do we?"

"He was fine... disappointed, I suppose, but my decision is final."

"Right." He sipped on his coffee again, but his eyes didn't leave her face. She could feel them on her skin like laser pointers. "It just seems a rather sudden decision to have made."

She sighed. He wasn't letting this go. "Not really. I've been thinking about it for a while. Arthur says he is fine to carry on with maintaining the pool and I was thinking that maybe we should consider a gardening company to come in and maintain the grounds instead, lighten Arthur's workload that way."

"Well, well, speak of the devil," Hugh said and got to his feet. Helen looked up to see Peter helping his wife into her jacket as they emerged from the back end of the restaurant. Hugh called out, "Peter!"

"What are you doing?" Helen hissed.

"You said he was fine with it. I just want to make sure. Knock any bad feeling on the head." Hugh had an odd look on his face.

Helen could feel her skin burning through her clothes. She drained most of the wine left in the glass as Peter walked over.

"Hugh, long time, no see. Helen, not so much. You remember my wife, Sally?"

"I do, yes, how are you both?" Hugh replied.

Sally smiled politely at Hugh, but glared icily at Helen.

"Listen, I just wanted to say no hard feelings about the… you know… *dismissal*." Hugh said it like a dirty word, shameful. "Helen has explained and I'm sorry, but I have to bow to her wishes on this." Hugh was looking theatrically sheepish, as though he was mortified at the situation, but helpless to change it.

"Yes, well, these things happen," Peter said with a knowing glance at Helen.

"I'm pleased you understand," Hugh said with a surprisingly smug smile.

"Of course, Helen and I understand each other perfectly well," Peter said, equally smug. Helen scowled at him and drained the rest of her wine. This was the most polite male pissing contest she had ever witnessed.

"Well, I don't understand," Sally said then, ice coating her words. She plonked her hands on her hips and puffed out her non-existent chest. She was a tiny slip of a thing, all bones and no substance. Helen could take her in a second, but she admired her bravado. The dress she was wearing had an awful purple and yellow print repeating on it, which was making Helen's eyes want to bleed. It looked like a television test pattern.

Hugh smiled politely at Sally. "I'm sorry?"

"She can't just fire him like that. It's not acceptable," Sally said, adding an extra centimetre to her height. "I won't have it."

Peter put a hand on her arm. "Sally."

Helen wanted to laugh. "You might want to rein in your guard dog, Peter," she muttered with a quiet snort.

"No, Pete, I'm not having it. He should know what you told me, about what she—"

"Sally!" Peter raised his voice. The couple at the next table turned to stare.

"To what are you referring, Sally? As far as I understand it, Peter was unfortunately not doing a good enough job, so it was an inevitable course of action for Helen," Hugh said calmly, bringing out his teacher's voice to illustrate the severity of the situation.

"Oh, is that what she told you?" Sally's voice was rising. Small dogs around the village could probably hear it at the pitch it had now reached. Other faces turned towards them, eyes glowing with undisguised curiosity. Helen felt sweat run down her back. Sally flicked her short bob away from her wide eyes. "I call it sexual harassment!"

"Sally, you've said enough. Come on, let's go," Peter said, trying to pull her away.

"No, Pete, that rich bitch can't get away with it, using you like that, forcing you to... you know... and then tossing you aside, just because they can afford to. We need that job." She was on the verge of crying now, her face crumpling into ugliness.

"I'm sorry, Sally," Helen said quietly, "but I haven't done anything wrong."

Sally clamped her with one more glare and for a second Helen thought she was going to grab the jug of water and fling it in her face. Instead, Sally reached out, grabbed the back of Helen's head by the hair and thrust her face into the plate of tiramisu. Helen gasped and shot to her feet, alcohol-tinged cream stinging her eyes and coffee pushing up her nostrils. There was a collective held breath in the restaurant.

"Sally!" Peter shouted, then dragged his wife by the arm out into the street. Helen could hear her arguing with him all the way out of the door.

Benito rushed over with some napkins as Helen swiped at her face. Hugh asked Benito for the bill and she slumped in her chair, avoided looking around.

Well, that had escalated quickly. Helen didn't know Sally had it in her.

At least the cream was hiding the redness in Helen's cheeks. Another waiter rushed over and attempted to wipe her nose, but she waved him away. Hugh was flapping around, unsure what to do. He followed Benito to the bar area to settle the bill, his embarrassment apparent in his stiff back and reddened neck.

Helen wanted to laugh out loud again, was about to do just that when she noticed someone standing outside the restaurant window. Thinking it was Sally again, Helen turned to the window, licking cream from her fingers, this time more prepared for round two.

But it was her. She was standing metres away on the other side of the thin glass, smiling in amusement.

Helen stared in disbelief.

Then she turned and walked away slowly, her hands tucked into her sleeves, her head bowed.

They sat in the car in silence. Helen's hair was cloying and sticky, her cheeks still enflamed. Hugh started the car, his eyes determinedly focused straight ahead.

"Why did she say that? Why did she do that?" he asked then.

"I don't know," Helen replied, knowing it sounded thin. Her fighting spirit was rapidly deflating, like a collapsing pool inflatable at the end of the summer holiday. The excitement over; reality kicking in; excuses to be made. "I guess he must've told her a story about why he was fired. Maybe he was embarrassed – you know, male pride. He didn't want to admit he had failed, so he told her something else, spun her a lie about why I fired him. Who knows."

"Maybe," he said, lacking conviction.

They drove the rest of the way in silence.

Helen let herself out of the car rather than waiting for him to open her door for her. They needed to talk, but Hugh was stoically non-confrontational at the best of times and it was annoying her tonight. She would've preferred shouting, accusations, anything but his polite dismissal. Everything indicated that he knew about her and Peter – or suspected – so why not challenge her on it?

But then, she knew there was something going on between him and Diana, and yet she had said nothing. She was as bad as he was. Best to just keep calm and carry on as though everything was fine.

She was disappointed in herself.

He was still sitting in the car, his hands clutching the steering wheel even though the engine was off, when she rooted in her small handbag for her front door keys. She pushed open the door onto chaos.

Matt and Lydia stood in the hallway, screaming at each other, mouths spitting, hands waving, him towering over her but her not backing down. Mills sat on the stairs, watching it play out in front of her as though she was at

Wimbledon, ridiculously with her hand tucked into a large bag of popcorn.

"What on earth is going on?" Helen shouted as she waded between them.

Matt and Lydia fell silent.

Helen noticed Clive peep his head out from the kitchen doorway where he was hiding in his bed. He woofed once and returned to his safe haven.

"Matt? Lydia?"

They both started shouting at each other again, Helen not able to make sense of the words, but the name Diana came up.

Lydia managed to get the last word in by saying, "He's a filthy fucking liar," just as Hugh stepped into the house.

He roared, "Enough! Everyone, to your rooms!" in an unusual display of authority.

Matt and Lydia glared at each other once more before Lydia stomped past Mills and up the stairs. Matt sloped off after her.

Mills remained on the stairs, shovelling in popcorn, her face a mask of amusement.

"Mills, what was that about?" Helen asked, shocked at the sudden display of ferocity she had seen in Lydia.

Mills shrugged. "Dunno, but it kept me entertained." She sniggered.

"Amelia, go!" Hugh said.

She rolled her eyes and disappeared upstairs.

Helen ran a hand through her hair. "Wow. I don't—"

But Hugh just pushed past her into his study and closed the door.

She stood in the hallway, alone, anger on a simmer.

Hands clenched, she exhaled and followed, not waiting to knock as she stormed into the study. "Are we going to talk about this?"

"Talk about what?" He was staring at his computer screen, his mouth tight.

"What's going on! The kids, Lydia, us."

"Teenage hormones, that's all."

"And us?"

He looked up then. "Helen, I have more important things to worry about than whether you have fired one of your staff and what goes on in the grounds of *your* house. Now, if you'll excuse me, I have work to do."

"On a Friday evening?"

"Yes." He looked back at his computer, the conversation clearly over.

She glowered at the top of his head. He ignored her presence.

She left, slamming the door behind her.

Helen slept restlessly, images of Sally and Peter doing a dance in her head. Hugh didn't come to bed. She woke too early the next morning with gritty eyes, a dull head and the smell of sour cream on her pillow. She stood under a hot shower for longer than necessary, just letting the hot water pour over her.

She knew she had to do something about Peter. If he was spreading rumours about her, it would harm her business, her family life, everything. What she couldn't work out was how he connected to Diana, if they were in on it together. Was this really all about money? It just seemed so tacky.

She sat on the side of the bed, towel drying her hair. Her phone buzzed on her bedside table and she turned it over to see an email notification for the shop's email account.

Another email from the same sender, this time saying:

THE TIME HAS COME. TRUTH. SOON.

Dramatic, certainly.

She remembered the figure she thought she had seen at the shop last night. It was Saturday and Jenni was due to work today, but something told Helen she needed to get there first. It was still early, only just gone 7 a.m. She could get to the shop before Jenni arrived to open up at 9 a.m.

It was quiet downstairs. She expected to see Hugh lying on the couch, his shoes kicked off and his face slack in sleep. But he wasn't. There was a light on under the study door – he must still be there, either asleep in the armchair or up early like her. She couldn't possibly see what was keeping him so busy though.

She had thrown on some jeans and a jumper already. Shoving her feet into trainers, she grabbed Clive's lead and knocked on the study door. She poked her head into the room, not waiting for an answer. Hugh was at his desk. He looked dreadful. His hair was dishevelled and he was wearing last night's clothes, now creased and crumpled. He jumped and flinched as the door creaked and she saw him quickly click the mouse in front of him.

"Morning," she said. "Um, you didn't come to bed."

"Er, yes, paperwork to catch up on."

He looked sweaty, almost feverish, despite a chill in the room. "Are you ok? You look pale."

"Tired, that's all. I'll finish this, then lie down for a bit." He ran a hand through his hair, making it stand up even more.

"Ok, well, I'm taking Clive out for an early walk. See you in a bit."

He said nothing further, so she closed the door again. She zipped herself into a raincoat as Clive wiggled at her feet, excited at the sight of the lead in her hand and the prospect of some morning air. "Come on, boy," she said, clipping it onto his collar. "Let's go."

It was crisp outside, the breeze off the sea growing ever more wintry with the passing days. Helen and Clive walked past the pool house, with Helen resisting the urge to check inside for any new graffiti. The gate was still unlocked and Helen pulled it towards her, feeling the wood catch on the grass and soil. There were fresh gouges in the earth where it had been opened recently. Helen made a mental note to speak to Arthur about making it more secure again. Anyone could find their way into the garden and on into the house.

They emerged onto the coastal path, the wind catching their breath. Instead of heading towards the beach, Helen led Clive along the path and into the village. It was quiet, the village empty apart from the newsagents putting out the morning papers. The bookshop was dark and from the front everything looked as it should.

Clive sat at her feet as she unlocked the front door. The bell jangled as always and she was hit with the familiar smell of paper and leather. She loved that smell. It was comforting, like a hug.

There was nothing on the welcome mat. No envelopes

containing yearbooks or photos. But something had changed in the room. She could feel it.

Then she saw it.

Taped in a haphazard pattern across the top of the serving desk were Polaroid photos. About twenty in total. She may not have seen these photos before, but she knew when they were taken. She had been there that night.

She did not know how they had got here.

The person who took them had been dead for thirty years.

Helen started ripping the photos from the desk, her mind whirling, her breath coming in gasps as she fought off dizziness. She spun between various scenarios of how this could've happened. But she kept coming back to the same answer.

Maybe she wasn't dead after all.

Hugh had been up all night, thinking things over, trying to find a solution, but the more he sat, the worse it looked. Whiskey coated his tongue and his eyes were husks.

When Helen had knocked and walked in, he had already put his only plan into action, but he didn't feel any better.

He knew it was risky. He had history with this. It had been the catalyst in the breakdown of his marriage to Francesca, had pretty much pushed her into the arms of tantric Todd.

He reached out and touched the photo frame next to him, drank in the smiling faces of his children, his ex-wife. Ice cream dripping, sunburnt noses, freckles on shoulders.

Yes, the game he was playing was dangerous, but he had no other choice.

As long as Helen didn't find out, he'd be ok.

It was just for a little while.

He could stop whenever he wanted to.

28

I toss the last letter aside, my cheeks burning and acid in my throat. I look for later letters, but there aren't any. I wonder what their discussions were when he returned home to a woman who was in her second trimester of a pregnancy he wanted no involvement in.

The realisation that sweeps over me is one of relief. I always suspected there was more to his distance and disinterest than just not liking me. The fact is he never actually wanted me in the first place. Part of me takes the relief and holds onto it, taking comfort in the knowledge that he wouldn't have liked any child and that it has not been personal after all. But another part of me latches onto the idea that this is not actually true. A son may have been different. Archaic as the idea seems, a son may not have been such a disappointment.

I almost want to laugh at how ridiculously Henry VIII it all is. I mechanically pack the letters away into their silver paper and retie the ribbons. I go to put the box back in the wardrobe where I found it, but change my mind and take it up to the attic. I feel strangely calm as I pull back the loose wooden panel in the far corner of the room and put the box in the space behind it. I pull out my diary and begin to process my new knowledge in the only way I know how, by letting words fall onto a page and form a discernible pattern of comprehension. As I write, I realise that my mother has been trying to make it up to him for seventeen years, but he has never forgiven her. He has kept her at arm's length, treating her like a needy pet, appeasing her with sparkly toys when all she really wanted was his forgiveness and the adoration they shared when their story began.

The truth of it is he has never bothered to get to know me, to see if he could love me. He dismisses me outright, like an object he never asked for, never wanted. And she has come to see me as the personification of her biggest mistake. No wonder she rarely looks at me. Regret and resentment are the threads that tie me to her rather than any bonds of affection or love.

This house. I once looked at it with quirky affection, enjoying its twisted rooms and eccentric silhouette. I was secretly proud of living in a house that others feared, gawped at, whispered about. I liked the idea of not conforming without having to change myself in any way. It was as though the house awarded me enough peculiarity that meant I could conform with the likes of Eloise, Steph and Emily, safe in the knowledge that part of me was different after all.

Now I look around me and feel anger at this building, these walls, for taking away from me the family I could've had. The idea that one piece of paper can have such a long reach and influence the lives of people for so many generations is astounding.

Hell hath no fury like a woman scorned. Well, that one disgruntled woman all those decades ago, who decided that no man would ever control the women in her family, didn't realise that there are more ways to ruin a life than just money.

A son would've been tolerable, but a daughter was inconceivable. My father didn't want a daughter because he wanted to sell the house. The house can only be sold if there are no female heirs to pass it down to. I ruined his future, so he has disregarded mine.

I realise I am crying only when the tears fall onto the ink and make puddles similar to those left in the ink in my mother's letters.

I swipe at my eyes angrily.

Why can't I have a family like Tracey's? With kind, loving parents who may not have financial security but know how to love their kids, regardless of their strengths and weaknesses. I think of Tracey's brother Alistair, with his gentle, confused eyes and the way his mother looks at him with bottomless, unconditional love. I think of her mother dancing in the kitchen, her face alight with happiness as her hips sway.

Then I think of the way my father looks through me, his eyes always fixed just over my shoulder, never actually on my face. And my mother's gaze, always blank, glassed over, her mouth pulling down at the corners like a painted mannequin.

I am intelligent, articulate, witty and perceptive, and yet they don't see any of it, don't recognise any value in me.

Perhaps this is what Tracey has been saying all along. It is hard for me to see myself if those who are supposed to love me the most don't see me either. But now it is time I do start acknowledging my strengths and recognising my weaknesses not as failure, but as potential. It is time to stop doing everything I can to get *them* to notice me and start doing everything I can to notice myself.

This is what I write down anyway, but believing it is harder.

The tears are running freely now and I can't seem to stop them, even when I hear Martha calling me for dinner. I climb down from the attic and shout that I am running a bath and that I will eat later, ask her to put it on a tray for me as I might get an early night. She replies that she will bring it straight up and that I should leave the tray outside my room as an early night is a good idea for both of us. She says she will see me in the morning, but to knock if I need anything in the night, and I have to clamp my hand over my mouth to stop from sobbing out loud. Someone does care after all. But she is paid to.

A muffled, dense fog has filled my head. The walls of my bedroom feel like they are closing in, the house trying to suffocate me now that I know the truth. I go into the bathroom and push the plug into the bath, turn on the hot tap as far as it will go and pour deeply purple foam bath into the torrent of scalding water. I stare as the water runs so darkly purple, it is almost black. It is as though I am looking through a window on a rainy evening, everything blurred and distorted.

Steam builds, fogging up the mirror as I begin to undress. My hands fall on the pill bottles in my pockets, forgotten amid a bigger discovery. I consider each one, then line them up on the side of the bath.

I throw on my robe and, closing the bathroom door behind me, I leave my room, climb back up the stairs to the attic and dig behind the loose panel again, pulling out the bottle of vodka I opened with Tracey, most of the liquid still there, only a few mouthfuls missing.

I return to my bedroom. The tray of food is already on my desk, Martha filling a plate with lasagne and salad, a bowl of strawberries swimming in cream on the side. All things I love, but have no taste for tonight.

I close my bedroom door, then close the bathroom door firmly before dropping the robe and slipping into the water, the vodka bottle clutched in my hand. The water is scalding. I inhale sharply, feel my skin tingle and sting as I sink into it. It is almost unbearable until I turn on the cold tap and feel it splash and pour over me, taking the searing edge off. My skin is bright red below the water, peach white above. I think of Tracey's dark skin, such a contrast to mine, and the way the water clung to her in droplets. I turn off the water and line the vodka bottle up next to the pills.

I lie back, my long hair fanning out around me, the bubbles clinging desperately to my scorched skin. The smell of lavender is inebriating, overpowering me into not thinking.

But not for long. My mind returns to the letters, to my father's face when I hugged him as he left. Sure, I was trying to evoke a reaction from him, but I also recognise the tiny part of me that really wanted him to actually hug me back, properly, intentionally, with feeling. Instead, I can see the alarm, dread and revulsion that flickered across his usually blank face in a matter of seconds, like a ripple in a puddle.

Now I understand.

I reach out and grab the bottle of vodka, my hand gripping the cap so tightly, the metal teeth cut into my skin, leaving little speckles of blood. I drink long and deep, the burn in my throat matching the burn of my skin in the water.

I lie in the water for what feels like a lifetime, my mind moving between thoughts, revelations and accusations, the vodka slipping further down the bottle. When the water has cooled to the point where I feel shivery, I sit up. It is too much, too quick and I fall back into the water as dizziness unsettles me. The purple water splashes over the edge of the bath onto the tiles. I lean over the side and see myself reflected back in the puddle, my face a moving, blurring, distorted mask that I find hideous. I pull myself onto my knees, screw the lid back on the vodka and slowly get to my feet. Taking deep breaths, I step onto the mat, but my foot catches one of the pill bottles and it clatters to the floor. I grab at it as it rolls away.

Without thinking, I fumble with the child-safe lid until it finally loosens. I shake some pills into my hand and swallow them quickly, chasing them with a slug of the vodka.

I am naked, water still streaming from my limbs, soaking the floor. I wrap myself in a warmed towel and weave to my bed.

29

NOW

The walk back with Clive was brisk, his little legs pummelling along to keep pace with her, and they were both panting when she let them back into the house. Helen felt like she was coming unravelled at the seams. Nothing made sense.

It was like her life had morphed into the bundle of Christmas lights you pull from the loft every year, never sure whether you can untangle the knot and find the end, giving yourself one more go to undo the mess before you give up, only to plug them in and find that most of the bulbs are broken or missing.

She kicked off her trainers as Mills tore down the stairs, fully dressed and looking like she was going out. That in itself was weird. She was never up and dressed before noon on a weekend. She slammed to a stop when she saw Helen.

"Where are you going?" Helen said.

"Where have you been?"

"I took Clive out."

Mills hadn't returned the favour by answering Helen's question.

"So where are you going?" she repeated.

Mills sighed and came up close to Helen, saying in a stage whisper, "I'm worried about Lydia."

"Ok?" Helen's heart was beating a little faster now, and not just from the walk.

"She's just gone out. On her own."

Lydia never went out on her own.

"I thought I would follow her," Mills said. "See what she's up to. She's been acting weird – and after last night... the argument..."

"What are you not telling me? If she's in trouble, I should know about it."

"I can't, not yet, because I don't really know. But that's why I want to follow her." She looked earnest, genuinely concerned.

"Fine, go, but let me know what's going on."

Mills kissed Helen on the cheek and left in a flash of padded coat and Impulse body spray.

"Where's she going?" Matt was standing on the stairs, looking half asleep.

"I don't know," Helen half-lied. "You're up early." Had she wandered into the Twilight Zone? A parallel universe where all the teenagers actually got up and did something constructive on the weekend?

"There was a lot of thumping going on. It woke me up. Where's Dad?"

"In his study, I think."

Matt pushed past her into the kitchen and started to make himself some coffee. He didn't offer Helen one.

"I'll have one of those if you're making?" she said, sitting at the table.

He grabbed another mug and slammed it onto the countertop.

"So how are things with Diana?" Helen said carefully.

"They aren't," he replied, his voice a low rumble.

"Oh, I'm sorry. I just... thought I saw her last night, that's all." Helen thought back to the shape moving in the shadows of the shop.

"You couldn't have. She was here."

"At the house?"

"She's been hanging out with Lydia a lot."

"Oh? That would explain the dramatic makeover."

"Yeah."

"So what's that about then?" Helen pushed.

He kept his back to her, but his shoulders were stiff, drawn up to his shoulders.

"Matt, I'm worried about her. Your dad says to leave it, but I don't know. Something doesn't feel right. If you know something..."

"She's being bullied. Online stuff mostly. Diana saw her phone, saw some of the stuff she was getting, has been *supporting* her, I guess."

"Is that all she's doing?"

"What do you mean?" He spun around, his eyes dangerous.

"I saw them, the other day. They didn't know I was here and... they were kissing." Helen's voice was as quiet and gentle as she could make it.

"No. You're lying. Lydia said she's a friend, that's all."

Helen paused, not wanting to push it further, but needing to let him know.

"Why didn't you tell me about the bullying then? I could've helped, talked to your dad."

"Because she doesn't want you to know. You don't even see her most days. You look straight through her. Why would she confide in you?"

He was right, of course.

"And Dad would say, *Turn the other cheek*. What fucking good is that? Anyway, you two have enough going on."

"What do you mean?"

He paused, went to say more. Instead, said, "Nothing," his eyes sparking.

Helen stood up, took a step towards him. "Look, Matt, I'm not lying. There's something going on here and it... it must be Diana. I did see them kissing and I'm worried about Lydia. She's young and playing a dangerous game that she doesn't understand."

"No, you're lying! Diana would never – not with Lydia!" Before Helen could say anything else, he stalked from the room, leaving the coffee unmade on the counter.

Helen leaned against the table, hanging her head. Hugh needed to know what was going on. He couldn't hide from this.

She knocked on the study door, but there was no answer. She pushed open the door. The room was empty. Perhaps he had gone upstairs to bed after all. She closed the door gently and approached his desk. What was he looking at this morning that had made him look so ill, so stressed? Had he finally found the photo? Something else?

She pushed the mouse and the computer screen jumped to life. There was now a password on it when there wasn't one the other day.

What would Hugh use? He lacked imagination in most things. She tried their anniversary year. Nothing.

Then she tried the kids' birthdays. Still nothing.

She was about to give up when her eye fell on an old photo frame perched on the end of his desk. It was askew, not in line with the edge of the desk as he would normally have it. The photo had been taken years ago when Lydia was a toddler. She was sitting on Hugh's lap on a sunshine-happy day in Spain, wearing a swimming costume covered with watermelons and holding a dripping ice cream. Sitting next to him was Francesca, with a very young Matt in her lap, his face covered in ice cream and everyone laughing at the camera. Francesca was wearing a huge sun hat that covered her thick dark hair and big sunglasses obscuring her eyes. She looked like a voluptuous Audrey Hepburn, full of smiles. From what she remembered, Hugh had said that that had been their one and only holiday abroad and shortly after the photo was taken by a fellow holidaymaker, Hugh had developed severe sunstroke and had stayed indoors for the remainder of the holiday.

Helen had never questioned the photo's existence, on show as it always had been on his desk. She assumed it was because of his children, carefree and happy on the beach, their cute faces bright with smiles.

Helen typed in the date of Hugh's anniversary to Francesca. Valentine's Day in 1998. He used to tell the kids that story so often – how his romantic proposal went so wrong with a power cut, food poisoning from their takeaway and her tripping over in shock at his grand gesture and fracturing her wrist. He said he should've known their marriage was doomed, but there was always a wistfulness to his voice when he recounted it.

The screen came to life. It would seem Matt was perhaps not the only man in this house pining for someone he couldn't have.

The first page was Hugh's Gmail. There were two email addresses sending him repeated messages. She opened the top email, received yesterday morning, and found a video attachment. She watched the first few seconds and had to turn it off. Peter had made good on his threat to tell Hugh about them, had even sent video evidence. He wanted money, was threatening to drop the video onto the internet. But why hadn't Hugh said anything last night?

Helen felt sick to her stomach. That explained his pallor when she interrupted him before they left for the restaurant.

And why had Peter changed his mind to go straight to Hugh with his threats instead of her? He probably thought Hugh was the one with the money and the big house. Fool.

She opened another email, this one from a different sender. It was another demand for money. An even larger sum. The request was backed by a threat to disclose what they knew, to spread malicious gossip through the school about photographs found in the history teacher's home.

Attached to the email was one of the photographs. Different to the one that fell out onto the carpet the other day, but the same girl in her swimsuit, her legs spread, a thin strip of material protecting her modesty and leaving very little to the imagination.

Helen looked closer this time. The girl's eyes were closed, but there was no denying who it was.

She opened some more emails. More requests for money

in return for silence – and from the replies, it looked like Hugh had been paying up.

Helen then clicked on Hugh's search history. It was full of online gambling sites from last night. So that was what Hugh was doing instead of sleeping.

On a whim, she opened his desk drawers and started rummaging through the papers. Eventually she found what she was looking for, shoved to the back of the drawer. His bank statement.

The bank account was in overdraft. Helen had never known him to go into overdraft. He was the kind of person that paid off his credit card completely every month, never overstretching himself, never living above his means.

They shared a joint bank account too, into which Helen paid money each month out of whatever profits there were from the bookshop. It was used for groceries and paying for the household bills. She pulled her mobile phone from her pocket and signed into her banking app..

The joint account was empty too.

Hugh had transferred the last few hundred pounds from it as recently as last night.

Helen sat heavily in the desk chair. Her foot kicked out, catching the handle of the bottom drawer of his desk, the one that was usually locked. It flew open. Inside the drawer were more photos underneath an almost empty bottle of whiskey.

She picked up the top photo. There were other faces in this one – wide smiles, posing for the camera, innocent until you looked closely at what they were doing.

A night that was forever imprinted on her brain, no matter how hard she had tried to forget.

★

Lydia was out of breath. Halfway into the village where she had arranged to meet Diana, she had the feeling that she was being followed. A creeping sensation on her skin, like tiny ants crawling over the back of her neck.

Diana had asked to meet her outside the bookshop. Lydia was carrying the bag with everything Diana had asked for, the weight of it swinging against her hip as she walked quickly. The air was crisp, the smell of the sea very strong. Seagulls swooped and cried out, like they were telling her to turn back, warning her that this couldn't end well.

She saw movement behind her reflected in the window as she passed the post office. She recognised that coat, that hair. Mills was following her. She took out her mobile, messaged Diana that there was a change of plan and told her to meet her on the coastal path by the gate instead.

Then she ran, looped in and out of the side streets, criss-crossed and danced between buildings, her feet slapping the cobblestones until she was sure she had lost Mills.

Her heart racing, she looped back around to the coastal path and made her way carefully along the sandy track to the bench overlooking the cliff. She dropped the bag on the seat next to her and smoothed her hair, tightened her ponytail and took a moment to catch her breath, her hungry eyes watching out for Diana.

And there she was. Her beautiful auburn hair flowing out behind her in the wind, her eyes smoky and dark with eyeliner, thin legs that stretched on forever. A broad smile cut Lydia's face in two and she jumped up and ran over to Diana, threw her arms around her.

"Woah! Not here. Anyone can see us," Diana said and pushed her away. Lydia felt a stab of hurt, cutting deep, but swallowed it down.

"Sorry, I had to change the meeting place. Mills followed me and I know you said not to tell anyone where I was going."

"That's fine, you did well, but we are very exposed here. Anyone could come along. Mills could still be watching."

"No, I lost her, I made sure of it." Lydia said quickly.

"Did you though, Lydia?"

Lydia started to doubt herself. She strained to look over Diana's shoulder, panic gripping her. She didn't want to disappoint Diana. She thought quickly. "Ok, come on, the pool house is open."

She pulled on Diana's hand. They pushed and ducked through the ivy-covered gate.

"We should just tell people," Lydia said, breathless. "About us, I mean. Fuck everyone if they don't like it. Fuck those little bitches at school – they can spread as many rumours as they want, call me whatever. I don't care. I've accepted who I am and I'm ready to own it. Isn't that what you've been telling me I should do? To own my own truth?"

She felt alive, empowered, stronger than she thought she could be, and it was all because of Diana.

Diana stopped just outside the pool house door. "I've explained this to you, Lydia. We can't go public, not yet. It wouldn't go down well with anyone. I don't want things to get hard for us when it is going so well. There is a difference between being empowered and being impatient. You have to choose your moment to shine. We still have so much to accomplish. You're too young to understand yet."

Lydia felt her heart plummet to the floor of her stomach. They stepped inside. Condensation clouded the glass.

"Did you bring it?" Diana asked.

Lydia stepped back, saw the hungry look on Diana's face. "That's all you care about."

Diana sighed. "What are you talking about?"

"This!" She brandished the tote bag. "It's all you talk about now. These stupid diaries!" Ironically, the bag was from The Owl and The Pussycat bookshop. "Why are you so obsessed with her? It's like you're in love with her or something."

"Lydia, now you're being childish."

"I could just tell them anyway, you know. I don't care what they say." She reached out with trembling hands. "I love you."

The words hovered in the air, suspended, like a held breath. She waited for Diana to say the words back to her, but instead they fell onto the tiles and shattered into a million tiny pieces.

"Lydia, give me the bag. We can talk about the rest of it when you are less emotional."

Diana snatched at it and the strap broke, spilling the contents onto the lounger between them like a loaded bomb, its timer ticking loudly.

30

THEN

Iwake in the early hours of the morning to the feeling that someone has a hold on my throat, slowly tightening their grip, the air wheezing from me in a thin stream that will be cut off at any second. The face looking down at me is that of my father. My heart is racing in panic and I claw at his hands, but there is nothing there.

I lurch upright, gasping, and turn on the lamp next to my bed. The room is empty. I am alone, still wrapped in my towel, lying on top of the bed. My skin is prickled with goosebumps of cold, but I am bathed in sweaty fear. Images of my father leaning over me dance behind my eyes and I can hear his voice telling my mother that she should kill me, get rid of me, that I am not wanted. The voice grows fainter as my heart rate slows and the sweat cools on my skin, but the fear roots itself in my stomach.

I climb under the duvet and turn to face the closed bedroom door. I lie that way, my eyes on the door, knowing it won't open but still not believing it. I fall asleep again with my eyes trained on the door.

Then it is daylight. My alarm is blaring. 7 a.m. My curtains are open and a weak sun is illuminating the dust dancing in the air. I sit up and feel my brain clash against my skull, leaving behind a dull and persistent throb. My eyes are itchy, my mouth dry, my tongue clinging to my lips. I feel exposed and vulnerable in my nudity under the duvet. I stagger to the bathroom and wrap my mouth around the basin tap, sucking down long gulps of water. I shrug into my thick dressing gown before returning to bed.

I'm hungry, my stomach gurgling now that the water has woken it up. The tray of last night's dinner is still sitting on my desk. The lasagne is cold, the oil congealed onto the plate, but I grab the tray, prop myself up on my pillows and eat it without tasting it. I finish with the strawberries, ignoring how soft they are, how the juice has bled into the cream.

I push the tray aside and check the time. I need to get ready for school. I think about Tracey, finding her by her locker, telling her everything I found out last night. She'll hug me, wrap her arms around me as she asks how I'm feeling, her breath in my hair as I cry into her shoulder, oblivious to the people around us.

I'll hug her back, can already feel her curls tickling my face.

I can already see her pity when she looks at me.

No, I don't want to talk about it with her. She won't understand. I think I know what her opinion will be: that I should analyse my feelings, discuss how I can process it. She'll probably suggest that I talk to my parents, discuss the implications, the rumbling after-shocks. But I don't want to. I want her to hug me, hold me, not try and bolster me, safe as she is in the knowledge that she is loved.

I don't want this to define me. I want to forget about it, at least while my parents are on the other side of the world and I don't have to face up to it yet. I want to pretend I don't know about the letters, maybe even pretend that my parents actually love me, are missing me. I want to think about something trivial and petty. I would rather call Eloise and talk about inanities, like the party, what she is wearing, what I should wear, whether Brian will make his move on her.

That calms me and my hand is steady as I grab the phone and dial Eloise's number.

Her housekeeper answers and it takes a moment before the extension is picked up and I hear her honeyed voice, "Hey, Hels. I'm still in bed, it's a bit early, isn't it?"

"Sorry El, my parents have just been on the phone and woke me up – they've just arrived at their hotel and didn't realise the time difference, I guess. They were missing me already, so called to check in, make sure everything is ok." The words are rattling out of me.

El yawns down the phone in response, so I gabble on some more.

"So yeah, I guess they're worrying about me since they've never left me on my own before. Ha, it's been one night and they're already on the phone. Can you believe it? Well, Martha is here, of course, to look after me, but still, they worry."

"God, I wish my parents would bugger off and leave me here alone."

"Anyway, I told them I was fine and they said they would probably call me every day to check in. So you know those pills you've been taking to lose weight? Have they worked?"

"Yeah, I've lost two pounds this week, but they're laxatives, so you end up in the toilet quite a lot. A few cramps, but I think it's worth it as it means you can eat and still lose weight. Why? You decided you still need to lose a few pounds before Saturday? It can't hurt, can it? You can never be too rich or too thin, as they say. And you do have that round stomach of yours, like you've swallowed a beach ball some days. Just telling it like it is, babes, because you're my best friend."

I reach down and put my hand on my stomach, now full of cold lasagne. "You're right, I need to try and lose it before Saturday if I can."

"I can get you some – they're my mother's, but she doesn't notice if I take them. She has loads of them, is always popping them back, especially before one of her dinner parties so that she can eat in front of people, but not show it the next day on the scales. It's ingenious really. I'll bring them to school today."

"Great, thanks. I'll see you in a bit then."

I run into the bathroom and stick cold, accusatory fingers down my throat. Nothing happens at first, my body refusing to give up what I've invested in it, but then the lasagne, strawberries and cream surge from me, leaving me breathless and coughing. I wash my face, get dressed quickly and plait my hair to hide the mess it dried into after last night's bath. While I'm in the bathroom, I see the pill bottles and scoop them into my school bag before hiding the vodka bottle in my bedside table in case Martha comes in.

She has tea and toast waiting for me, with a couple of digestive biscuits on the side of the plate. The pit of my stomach is gloriously empty, like there is a gaping chasm that wasn't there yesterday morning. I take a few bites of the toast without tasting it, nibble on one of the biscuits, then rush out of the house down to the meet point for the school bus.

The school corridors are a cacophony of shouting, laughter, whistling, thumping feet, slapping hands. I stride straight over to my locker, not looking around me, shoving past the bodies in my way. I grab some of the books I'll need and turn to go, bashing into the person behind me.

"Fuck, careful, Hels!" Eloise is rubbing her arm where I collided with her.

"Sorry, didn't see you."

"Whatever," she sighs. "Look," she looks around surreptitiously, "here's those pills." She hands me a white box.

"Great, thanks." I open the packet, push out two small white tablets and put them straight into my mouth. "Got any water?"

"Sure." She hands me her bottle and I swig at it, feel the pills slip down. "I meant to say, you're only supposed to take one at a time after meals."

I shrug.

Brian and some of his mates are striding along the corridor. Bodies part for them, like they are gods. They stop at a bank of lockers, shoving and grabbing at each other, head-locks and dead arm punches. Then Brian nods with his head and starts making low monkey noises. The others join in, the noises growing in volume, and I see Tracey walking along the corridor towards them, her cheeks flaming.

Eloise is watching too, a smirk on her lips. "Come on, let's go," she says and steers me away.

Half an hour later and I am in a world of pain. I have to run from my maths class, claiming that I'm feeling sick. My stomach is in cramped knots, like an iron fist has hold of my intestine and is making a balloon animal out of it. I see the look of concern on Tracey's face as I rush past her desk. I have avoided her all morning and hope she doesn't follow me to the bathroom to check up on me.

I make it to the toilet in time and thankfully it is empty because what comes out of me is frightening in its intensity. The cramps slowly subside and by the time I stagger from the cubicle, I feel purged but weak. My stomach is already flatter though, even if my heart is hammering like I'm having a heart attack.

I leave the bathroom on shaky legs, but feeling in control for the first time since finding those letters. It is a powerful feeling.

The lesson is almost over when I return to the classroom. I ignore Tracey's curious glance, but smile knowingly at Eloise, who winks back.

Tracey sits with her other friends at lunch, but I can feel her eyes on me across the canteen. I don't look over. Brian and his friends come to sit at our table and I chat to Jason, the boy Eloise is trying to hook me up with, while ignoring the salad on my tray. He tries to make me laugh, but his jokes are lame, pathetic. I laugh anyway and notice how his smile widens when I do. I am making him happy just by pretending to like him.

That feeling of control grows. I assess the satisfying weight of it in my hands. Something I've not considered before. I move ever so slightly closer to him, let my knee rest against his and his cheeks flush. I smile to myself.

The bell rings and we file out. He is pressed up against my back in the queue out of the hall and I can feel his hand on my waist, light, tentative. It's pathetic really. How easy it is to manipulate him. No wonder Eloise enjoys it so much. Pretending to be what they want you to be, the play-acting in return for adoration. It's strangely compelling.

Tracey is waiting by my locker.

"Hey, you ok? How are you feeling?" She has concern all over her face. It wrinkles her brow and sits heavy in her eyes.

I shrug, avoid it. "Fine, just tired."

"Just when I saw you rush out like that—"

"It was nothing, just felt a bit weird, that's all." My voice is sharper than I intended.

"Oh, ok." She looks down at her feet, shuffles a bit. "You want to hang out later?"

Eloise comes up behind her. "I think she has party plans to be finalising, don't you, Hels?" She looks at me pointedly, makes a face behind Tracey's back.

Tracey flushes at the sound of El's voice. "Yes, of course." She walks away, her head down.

"God, she's a bit desperate for friends, isn't she? She's so weird. Come on, Hels." El loops her arm through mine and marches me down the corridor, directly past Tracey's locker. She looks up as we walk past and I see the hurt on her face. I feel wretched, remembering how much fun we had the other night, how free I felt with her. She looks away before I can mouth an apology.

I pull out of Eloise's grip and tell her I need to go to the bathroom again before class starts.

I close myself into a stall, drop the lid of the toilet seat and sit on it, my head in my hands. What is the matter with me today? I feel like I am stumbling around, not quite there, not really focusing on anything, at once on high alert and then in a dense fog, voices muffled, movements blurred.

I scrabble around in my bag and find my mother's anti-depressants, shake three into my hand and knock them back with a swig of water.

I emerge from the toilet stall and stand in front of the row of basins, looking at the reflection I see in the mirror. I look like myself, but not a version I recognise. It is unsettling to think I am changing so quickly, time passing and leaving its mark, my face changing with every second that passes. Tomorrow I will be ever so slightly altered from what I see today and that disturbs me. I lean forward and stare so hard that my eyes glass over and the details smudge together, like I have swiped my finger through a pencil drawing of my face.

Someone charges into the bathroom, laughing. A Year 7, giggling with her friend. They stop when they see me, look at each other, look back at me.

I push away from the mirror, scowl at them and leave with a deep breath fuelling my feet.

I settle into the science lab, everyone around me unpacking books and donning the unflattering lab coat made to fit giants, not skinny teenage girls. Tracey is picking at the skin on her finger, the movements sharp and destructive. Her hair is loose today, like a cloud of tight curls around her face. I like it like that.

I hastily scribble a note on a piece of paper torn out of the back of my lab book, telling Tracey to meet me on the bench on the coastal path after school. I wait, on edge, for a suitable moment to pass it to her. The moment comes when she has to walk past my desk to collect her protective glasses from the front of the room. When she does, I slip it into her hand. She stumbles, frowns at me and I shake my head ever so slightly. She crumples the note into her fist and continues past.

The teacher's voice is soporific, interminably dull, and I close my eyes. I can feel the drugs dispersing through my bloodstream, imagine them like a vapour, curling tendrils teasing and tickling. I lay my head on my arms and listen to my breath.

"Don't let me keep you from your nap, Miss Tillsbury."

My eyes snap open and I see that everyone is staring at me, laughing, the teacher standing with his arms crossed, glaring.

"Sorry, sir," I mumble, flushing.

"Maybe an experiment will wake you up. On your feet, everyone. Pair up, please."

Eloise is straight at my side. "What's going on with you?"

"Nothing. I'm just tired. I drank a bit last night while I was watching TV – you know, since my parents are away and I can do what I like – so I'm a bit hungover today. And he is so boring, his voice is killing me."

"God, I know! You are so lucky! I wish I was staying on my own."

She has no idea. I wish I had parents who worried, who didn't want to leave me, wanted to spend their evenings in my company, discussing our day and playing board games, lamely arguing over what television programme to watch as a family.

But I've never had that. And I now know I never will.

In fact, I wish my parents were dead.

31

NOW

Mills arrived back just as Helen emerged from the study.

"Did you find her?"

"She was in the village, but then I think she saw me because she took off and I lost her. Mum, what's going on?" Her voice was diminished with worry.

"I don't know," Helen replied truthfully. "But the one person who does is Diana." Helen thought for a moment, then said, "Do you still have her phone number?"

"I have her on Snapchat. Why?"

"I think it's time I met up with Diana, had a conversation with her, find out what her intentions are with Lydia. I saw them the other day, Mills. It's weird. It's not right."

"You really think they are together?" It was Matt, standing on the stairs, the stained glass window casting sharp shards of garish colour across his anguished face.

Helen looked up at him. "I know what I saw. But I don't fully understand it."

His hands were clenched in fists by his sides and his body was rigid. He stormed down the stairs and on towards the kitchen.

"Matt!" Helen called after him.

"I need some air," he shouted back and she heard the kitchen door slam.

Helen thought for a moment, then said to Mills, "Send Diana a message. Tell her to meet you in an hour at the pool house. But instead of you it will be me."

Mills' fingers flew over the screen on her phone. "Done." She looked at Helen closely. "What are you going to do now?"

"I need to talk to Hugh."

Mills nodded. "I'm going to see if Matt is ok."

Helen paused on the stairs and pulled her phone from her back pocket. Why hadn't she thought about it sooner? Everyone had social media these days. Surely Diana had a profile on Facebook or Instagram. Perhaps Helen could work out what the connection was. It felt like the walls of the house were leaning in, watching over her shoulder as she opened her Facebook app and typed in the name Diana before realising she didn't know Diana's surname. Frustrated, she shoved the phone back in her pocket.

She sighed and trudged up the stairs on heavy legs, like she was walking to the gallows.

Hugh was lying on their bed, still fully clothed, his eyes closed and an arm slung over his face. The air was stuffy and pungent with sweat.

"Hugh?"

He opened one eye.

"Can we talk?" she said.

He sighed melodramatically.

"You know, don't you?" Helen said.

He pulled himself up to sitting, the pillows pressed into his back, and shrugged, his mouth pulled down in a sulk. "How long?" was all he said, his voice low.

"Not long, a couple of months."

"It's Francesca all over again."

"No, no, it's nothing like that." She sat on the bed next to him, reached out her hand, but he pulled out of her reach. "I feel nothing for Peter," she continued. It wasn't a lie. "It was just... I don't know, a mid-life crisis? Stupid and stereotypical, but it was just to alleviate the boredom."

She sounded awful in her own ears.

"Anyway, it's done now. We need to call the police, tell them about him blackmailing you."

Hugh's head shot up. "You know about that?"

She nodded. "I know about the photos too."

He surprised her by starting to cry. Big heaving gulps and gasps. Helen recoiled.

"I've lost it all, Helen. All our savings, everything. All we've got is this house, which isn't even mine! And I haven't done anything wrong. It's all lies. Someone is setting me up." His voice was wretched.

"But then why did you pay up?"

"Because it doesn't take much to ruin a man's reputation. Not these days. I'm a teacher, a male teacher. Just a hint of anything inappropriate and I would be finished. Where there's smoke, there's fire, they'll say. Diana said she had loads of evidence against me. I don't even know who the girl in the photo is, but that won't matter."

"Diana? She's the one leaving the photographs everywhere?" Helen had hoped for clarity but instead was more confused than ever. How had Diana got hold of the photographs? How much did she know? And why go after Hugh? It had nothing to do with him.

He was still crying, big, ugly sobs that made his body shudder and his nose stream. Helen reached out and wrapped her arms around his heaving shoulders awkwardly. "This is all my fault. I'll sort it out, I promise."

The pool house was quiet, but the lights were on, fluorescent white. Mills thought Matt had headed in this direction, but now she wasn't so sure. The glass door was standing open, the humidity escaping like a fog. Oily fingerprints smudged the glass.

Diana might already be inside, waiting for Helen, ready with her excuses and explanations. Mills hesitated. Maybe she should talk to Diana first, let her know she couldn't mess around with her family like this. What had Mum said? Show a bully strength and they will run a mile? Maybe Diana just needed to be taught a lesson.

She took a deep breath and stepped through the glass door.

It took a moment for her eyes to adjust to the piercing light.

And that's when she saw her.

Diana was floating face down in the pool.

32

THEN

The rest of the afternoon passes without memory of it. I can hear myself laughing riotously at times, tickled by obscurity, then feeling serene and calm, silently enjoying the sensation of a blade of grass running between my fingers at break time or the fresh, alive, tingling taste of minty chewing gum in my mouth. Then a surge of energy so that I have to tap my foot and click my pen, anything to release it. I think a teacher tells me off for fidgeting, but I grin back and carry on regardless. I catch Steph and Emily elbowing each other and nodding at me, but I don't care.

I don't care about anything at all. I feel like I am floating through the rest of the school day, at once enjoying the weightlessness while desperate for it to end so that I can go home. To nothing. To no one.

Then I swing to desperately wanting to go swimming, to feel the warm water against my skin and the pull of the resistance as I glide over the surface. I know it is the pills dulling the edges of my reality, but I like it this way. No wonder my mother sometimes looks so relaxed she could be vertical, sliding through the house as if on an invisible cloud. That's what it feels like. But I also know what it's like when she would come back down to earth, usually with a melodramatic wail or thundering crash, her mood heavy, the cloud underneath her turning to a thunderstorm. That's when she rants at nothing, closes herself in her room, cries into the pillow. That's when I have learned to give her space or I'll feel the sting of her palm against my skin. That's when Martha leaves a tray of food outside her door, which is still there the next morning.

That isn't me though. I am in control.

I forget about meeting Tracey and it is only when I get off the bus and come over the rise in the path that I see her sitting on the bench in the distance. Part of me wants to duck into the gate and pretend I didn't see her. I hesitate. She looks over and sees me, waves. She is huddled into her coat, the wind blasting from across the sea and blowing her hair wildly around her face.

I walk over and sit next to her. We stare out at the sea, which is exceptionally unsettled and angry today. I can sympathise.

"I'm sorry about earlier," I say, the wind taking the words and twisting them inside out. "I've been in a bit of a strange mood since my parents left."

"Oh, shit, yeah, well, that's understandable, isn't it? You're probably missing them like mad."

I swallow, trying to dislodge the pebble that has settled in my throat. "Yeah, sure." The wind is making my eyes water. That's what I tell myself anyway. I swipe at them.

"You know, you can come and stay with us any time

while they're away. My mum would be totally fine with it. I don't have a huge bedroom or anything, but at least you won't be on your own."

"Thanks, I'm fine, really. I'm kind of enjoying having my own space."

I can feel the wetness on my cheeks and tell myself it's the sea spray.

I want to tell her the truth – about the letters, my sense of abandonment, the thoughts constantly in the back of my mind about my father's intentions all those years ago, what he could've done to get rid of me, my brain making each of the scenarios bigger and scarier every time I think about it.

And now I am crying. She puts her arms around me and holds me like I knew she would, but also like I don't think anyone ever has before. Her hair is tickling my face. I can smell the apple scent of it. I can't stop the tears, so I burrow into her even more.

I don't know how long we sit there, but eventually my tears slow and I feel my shoulders sag in exhaustion. My breath is still hitching, but I feel composure is within reach. She releases me and I feel the space between us, gaping and open, letting the wind through. I want to close the gap again.

"There, you ok?" she says.

I nod, unsure if I can speak yet. Her arm is around my neck, light, comforting. She reaches out with her other hand and takes hold of mine. I look down, light against dark.

"Want to tell me what's going on?"

"You wouldn't understand. Your family is so lovely and mine is just toxic."

"My grandfather didn't speak to my father for years

because he married a black woman, so I know a little bit about toxic. Try me."

And I do, every messy little detail of it, how angry and hurt I feel, how I now hate that house and everything it represents. The house that is rearing up behind me as we talk.

She sits and listens. No one has ever listened to me like that before. No one has given me the time to just talk. When I'm finished, every last word wrung out of me, I wait for the criticism, the judgements, for her to tell me I'm being melodramatic or that other people have a much harder life than me, that I need to put on my big girl pants and get on with my privileged life without complaining.

But she doesn't. She looks aghast, outraged at what she has heard.

"Wow, I can't imagine what that must feel like. How betrayed you must feel." She sits back against the bench, stares out at the snarling sea. "Have you told anyone else about what's going on?"

"Eloise, you mean? Or Steph and Emily? No, they wouldn't understand. And we don't really have that kind of friendship."

I'm beginning to realise that the friendship I share with them is all falsehoods and pretence, of saying what I'm expected to and creating a carbon copy of each other, not veering off the path of popular conformity, that different is bad.

"I think you should talk to someone."

"I'm talking to you."

"I know. It's just... What about your mother?"

"No, absolutely not." I can feel anger building again.

I knew she would do this. Tell me that talking is best, honesty will help. That's fine for her. She has a family that does talk to each other, that discusses their feelings and comforts each other when they've a bad day, supports each other when her brother is struggling or the load is tilted too far in one direction.

It's only good to talk if they are willing to listen though.

"No, it'll be fine. I'll be fine. It's just the shock, you know? Of finding the letters. Actually, I'm relieved. Now I know what they think and feel. No more wondering if I've done something or said something. Now I know it is my sheer existence that is to blame. It's not personal. And I can live with that."

"I don't know…"

"I don't want to talk about it anymore."

"You can't just forget it happened, bottle it up. I know when I'm feeling angry or conflicted about my brother and what he needs, how sometimes everything in our house revolves around him, I talk about it – to my parents mostly – and it lightens the load. I'm always here to listen, but perhaps your parents should hear some of it too."

I launch to my feet, my voice strained. "I don't want to talk about this anymore."

"Ok, ok, I'm sorry."

I sit down again. There is just the wind, the sea, the awkwardness.

"Oh, I finished the book you suggested," she says in a quiet voice, so quiet that even the wind can't steal it away.

"What did you think?"

"I loved it, thought it was dramatic, tragic, very atmospheric."

And just like that we are talking about fictional problems in fictional worlds, where there is usually a happy ending and narrative growth for the protagonist; not sadness, solitude and more of the same as far as the eye can see.

We go our separate ways when the sky is starting to turn a darker shade of grey and the wind is too cold to bear the sting on our cheeks. I let myself into the bottom gate, my legs heavy. The pool house is in darkness, but I can feel the warmth leaking from the glass as I walk past, smell the tang of chlorine in the air. I remember my earlier urge to swim and I open the door, feel the heat wash over me like a blanket. I close the door to the cold and leave the lights off, throw my stuff on a lounger and remove all of my clothes, the gloom making me feel safe, unseen.

I slip naked into the water and just stand for a moment, breathing in. Then I plunge under the water, feel it close over my head as I sink to the bottom. I weigh myself down, try to remain on the bottom for as long as I can. My eyes are open, my hands opaque in front of me as I tread water. Only when my lungs start to burn do I allow myself to bob to the surface again, annoyed that I couldn't stay down there longer. I swim backwards and forwards, diving beneath the surface, seeing how far I can go in one breath, relishing that feeling of panic when my lungs run out of air.

When I let myself into the kitchen door, Martha is waiting, a tea towel wringing in her hands and a troubled look on her face.

"Oh, there you are! I was worried as it's getting so late!"

I smile despite my sombre mood. "I'm fine, I just met

Tracey after school, then went for a swim before coming in." My hair is dripping down my back and I am cold from the walk back to the house.

She exhales with relief. "Let me make you a nice cup of tea. Pork chops for your tea tonight."

"Thanks, Martha, but I have loads of revision to do and I'm not really hungry."

She looks disappointed. "You might be later though. I'll keep it under foil. You have to eat."

"Thanks. Um, did anyone phone today? My parents maybe?"

"Sorry, love, not today, but with the time difference and everything, I guess it's hard to find the right time."

"Yeah, of course. No problem." I'm annoyed at myself for asking the question and expecting a different answer.

That night I take a couple of my mother's sleeping pills, just in case I have more dreams about my father's cold hands around my neck, squeezing the air out of me.

33

NOW

Helen pulled the boxes away from the wall, but didn't open them. They contained mostly paperwork relating to the house, her parents' deaths, the subsequent inheritance and legal papers. None of that mattered right now.

There had been nothing unusual or strange about her parents' deaths. One day Helen had received a call from a solicitor telling her that her mother had died from a relatively short illness and that she had inherited the family estate. Her mother had been in hospital with pneumonia before she died. Helen had had no idea she was ill. They hadn't spoken in years. Helen was not surprised her mother had died so soon after her father. She had needed his very existence to get out of bed every day and once he was gone, her lungs couldn't breathe on their own.

Helen had been sleeping on a friend's couch at the time, working as a waitress with a pay-as-you-go phone that was hardly ever in credit. She had asked about her father and been coldly informed that he had passed away a few months earlier from a heart attack.

There were no tears or dramatic displays of affection. No big funerals with men in sombre suits eating vol-au-vents and women in hats weeping into handkerchiefs.

Nothing like that funeral thirty years ago.

She'll never forget that.

Helen left all the details to her mother's legal team and stayed away. She felt no remorse at that. They hadn't had that kind of relationship – or any relationship at all by then. Her mother couldn't even bring herself to get in touch with Helen to tell her that her father had died. That was how little she was considered.

Out of sight, out of mind. How they had always liked it.

They had never met Mills, despite the letter Helen sent when she was born. And the telephone calls afterwards, none of which were taken or returned. Their only grandchild. A girl, in keeping with tradition.

When Helen thought about her childhood and those years after she left – and she tried not to as much as possible – she felt utter sadness at what she didn't have more than regret at what she did. She would've liked the opportunity to introduce them to Mills, to show them what they were missing out on. A vibrant, colourful force of nature; the one success of Helen's life. But there was no point in wasting energy on what could've been. She needed to focus on what was happening right now.

As she moved the boxes around, she noticed fingerprints in the thick dust coating them. The dust on the labels had been swiped away too.

Someone had been inside these boxes, had rifled through them.

Unease rippled through her, then she steadied herself. These boxes held nothing incriminating. If someone wanted to spend their time reading up on the ins and outs of Helen's weird inheritance and who would get the house when she was gone, then they were welcome to do so.

It was the stuff stashed in the wall behind the loose panel that she didn't want seeing the light of day. Everything dating back to a period of time she would do anything to forget, had done everything to forget since it happened. The diaries, school yearbooks, photos of memories shared – all of it hidden away.

She should've burnt it all back when it had happened. She didn't honestly know why she had kept all of it. It would have done no one any good if the truth had come out.

Murder.

Plain and simple.

Once the boxes had been dragged aside, she pushed on the bottom corner of the wooden panel so that the top corner popped out. She wormed her fingertips into the gap and pulled the panel away.

She felt the familiar puff of cold air on her face from the gap in the roof tiles beyond the panel, carrying with it the smell of mouse droppings and age-old dirt. She reached in. There was space, cool air, darkness... but nothing else. Helen turned on her phone flashlight, but it only confirmed her suspicions.

It was all gone.

★

The body floated gently in the otherwise still water. She was face down, like she was bobbing for apples, her hair fanning out around her, her legs splayed. Puddles of water had collected on the tiles, lightly marbled with blood.

Seagulls shrieked outside, shocking Mills into action. She rushed over to the side of the pool, reached in and grabbed a leg, pulling it towards her.

The body was surprisingly heavy as Mills flipped it over and tried to get her arms underneath to pull her from the water.

Mills fell backwards as she heaved Diana from the pool, wet jeans and Doc Martins weighing her down. Diana was left slumped on her side. Helen could see a gash on her head where blood had seeped into her wet hair. She reached out and touched it gingerly. Her fingers came away red and slick. Mills fought the urge to heave.

"Oh god, oh god, oh god," she moaned.

She looked around, her head spinning, trying to make sense of what had happened. Who had been in here? Who had met Diana? Lydia had probably been with her earlier and Matt had also headed in this direction. They could've fought. He could've lost his cool. She had seen him punch doors before. He was furious when he found out about Lydia and Diana.

Furious enough to kill her?

And what about her mother? Had she already been here to confront Diana? Was she just covering her tracks by asking Mills to message Diana?

She staggered to her feet, a thousand questions running through her brain. Should she leave her here? Call someone? The police? Run?

There was a bag lying on the floor. It looked like one of the bookshop tote bags. A pile of notebooks lay on a lounger. And lying in a pool of water on the tiles was one solitary Polaroid photo.

Mills reached out and picked it up.

34

THEN

The rest of the week is a jumble of sights and sounds, nothing distinct and yet interspersed with moments of absolute clarity. Martha has taken to shaking me awake every morning because the sleeping pills are making me sleep through my alarm. But I am enjoying the dreamless sleep of the intoxicated dead, for which I am grateful.

Jason is still keen, keeping himself physically close whenever he can, moving his chair next to mine in the canteen, resting his knee at an angle that brushes my thigh, letting his hand touch mine when I walk past his desk. I don't mind. At least he's paying me some attention.

I've taken to eating everything Martha puts out for me so that she isn't disappointed, then swallowing El's pills afterwards or throwing up until it is purged from my body before any of it can lay down a base. My fingers tickling the back of my throat has become a familiar feeling and the emptiness afterwards worth the constant raw sting in my throat. I think it is working because I'm sure my jeans are feeling looser in the waistband, my stomach flatter. Not quite concave yet, but I can feel a difference. I'm sure of it. And that makes the discomfort and awful cramps easier to bear.

I forgot that we had a maths test yesterday, could feel panic inching up my spine, but a couple of little white pills swallowed hastily before the lesson and I was back in control, the test paper swimming in front of me as I tried to write something legible. I have vague recollections of writing smiley faces instead of numbers for some answers and making a pattern with the multiple choice answers – I'm sure the teacher will smile at that.

Or not. I don't care.

Tracey has met me a couple of times, but her concern is now bordering on irritating. She asks me constantly if I'm ok, how I'm feeling, if I want to talk. I don't. I wish I hadn't told her any of it – and that I hadn't invited her to the party. She phoned me last night, upset because her brother had had a tantrum and smashed some of her favourite records. She was saying that she shouldn't be angry with him, but couldn't help herself, that his tantrums have been worse lately and it is exhausting trying to pre-empt what is going to set him off. He is physically growing in strength too, which makes it harder to control him. He hit her mum when he was flailing his arms around. It left a bruise on her cheek.

I laughed. Probably shouldn't have. I've had a few of those bruises. I told her I could give her mother some tips on covering it up with make-up.

I wanted to be supportive, to listen to Tracey like she listened to me, but I struggled to focus on her voice because I'd just taken a pill and my brain was fogging up. I told her that the party would make her feel better, that some time away, dancing, drinking, would help, but she seemed annoyed and said that it would all still be there when she got home. The bruise will still be there when she takes the make-up off. I know that.

I hung up soon after, telling her that Martha was calling me, but in fact Martha had already turned in for the night and I was on my own in bed with a bottle of vodka and trash on TV.

I'm now really looking forward to the party. I have raided my parents' alcohol stash in the cellar and already put boxes of vodka and wine, and some random bottles of Kahlua and Baileys, in the storeroom at the back of the pool house. I don't think Arthur, the caretaker, will be going in there any time soon as it is just full of lounger cushions and towels. Martha has planned the food and I have asked her to find some tropical decorations in the village. Club Tropicana it is, just like El wants.

I'll ask Arthur to set up the music system on Friday and make sure the pool is ready. Then all I have to do is decorate and get myself ready on Saturday. Tracey has said she will come early to help set up and that's fine because when I asked El, Steph and Emily to come and help, they moaned about needing time to get themselves ready. Selfish cows.

Since Tracey is staying over, it makes sense that she comes earlier anyway. I just hope she isn't too much of a prude about the booze and boys, but I think she'll be ok after the other night when she threw up everywhere. She is still claiming she won't drink after that, but we'll see.

I've also made sure I have plenty of film for my Polaroid camera so that I can take photos of the night. This could be the last party we have before things change forever, before my parents return and exams take over.

I intend to do it right.

35

NOW

The house was quiet. Helen stood at the top of the stairs, looking down, listening. Hugh was still in the bedroom. She had no idea where the kids were. She needed to search their rooms and would rather not have to come up with a plausible excuse if she was caught, but there was nothing to hear except the inhales and exhales of the house, the walls and floors creaking, the pipes stretching and settling.

She peered through the stained glass window towards the pool house, could see light shining from between the ivy leaves. They must be in there with Diana. She didn't have long.

The first room she went into was Lydia's. This was where she expected to find the answers to her questions. She was the one who had changed the most and there had to be a reason behind the transformation. A reason why Diana was pursuing her. Helen rummaged under the bed and through her dressing table, but there was nothing. No incriminating evidence. No contraband. Just a regular fourteen-year-old's bedroom. She found some leaflets in her bedside table offering advice on how to discuss homosexuality openly as a family and she felt a twinge of guilt. Regret. She knew Lydia would not choose to discuss such a thing with her. But then she wasn't her mother.

She moved on to Matt's room. Marginally tidier than the last time she was in there. The first thing she looked for was his laptop. Password protected of course. She thought about what mattered to him, how creative he was and typed in the year he was born.

Apparently not that creative after all. The laptop sprung into life, his emails open on the screen. A lot of college-related content. Emails backwards and forwards with Francesca. Except that Francesca hadn't replied to the last few he had sent. His tone was pleading, almost begging her to let him come and live with her. Helen hadn't realised he was so unhappy. She doubted Hugh had noticed either. It made her sad to think he didn't want to be here – and even sadder that Francesca hadn't answered him. Earlier responses she gave said to stick it out, that the café demanded a lot of her time and her new home with Todd wasn't big enough for him too. Empty excuses.

If Helen thought Mills was unhappy and reaching out to her, she would grip on and pull her in, arms open wide.

She recognised the same email address she had seen on Hugh's email. She opened a message dated this morning to see an email from Diana with an attachment.

More photos.

Of Diana and Lydia, giggling, taking selfies. She had been taunting him with her relationship, putting it front and centre. But why? It didn't make sense. Why did she want to hurt him like that? What had he done to her to deserve that?

She called up his internet history, maybe hoping to answer the question of what he did late into the evening. It was not porn as she had suspected, but a chat room about Fortnite and gaming.

And another offering support for mental health issues. Helen slammed the laptop shut, now feeling like an intruder, the knowledge that he had reached out to strangers for help leaving her feeling filthy with shame.

She was about to head into Mills' room when she heard a noise downstairs.

She turned and rushed out of the room, hoping it was Clive coming to find her.

Someone was in the kitchen.

She peered around the door. Mills was leaning on the kitchen table, her hands splayed, a tote bag in front of her. Clive was at her feet, peering up at her in adoration. She turned when she heard Helen behind her.

Mills pulled a shoebox from the bag, shoved it towards Helen.

Helen said nothing, just reached out with a trembling hand.

"But before we talk about that, there's something you need to see. In the pool house."

"I'm going there anyway – to meet Diana like we planned," Helen said, confused.

"Someone else got there first."

36

THEN

Friday is a fizz of excitement. We sit in the canteen, the air around us humming as we talk plans, details, what each of us will wear. The boys saunter over and join in, talking about bringing beer and beach balls, discussing the possibility of a girls vs boys volleyball tournament. Eloise looks like she'd rather pull out her own fingernails than splash around with a volleyball in the pool, but she smiles half-heartedly at Brian anyway.

I look over as Tracey walks into the canteen with Tina. She has been spending more and more time with her this week since I've been so distant and monopolised by Eloise. I can hear her laugh at something Tina has said and I want to know what it is. My ears are buzzing, like there is a bee stuck deep down that is wrestling to get free.

I should maybe lay off my mother's pills for a bit as I'm struggling to concentrate on any one thing. My mind jumps around, jittery, easily spooked, and I find myself twitching and looking over my shoulder, expecting someone to be right behind me when they aren't or staring at a shape in the corner of the room, knowing it is someone watching me, only to realise it is a coat or a shadow, but not before my hands are visibly shaking and my breath is coming in short, sharp gasps.

I've kept some distance from Tracey because I think she will notice and probably disapprove. Eloise, Emily and Steph haven't noticed anything other than that I am looking thinner. El actually told me I looked great yesterday and that filled me with warmth that spread from my toes and stayed with me for the rest of the day. Sad.

When I did bump into Tracey, she told me I looked tired.

"Oh god, Tracey is coming over with that weirdo, Tina. You know, from English. She's like a mouse. I could squash her," Eloise says and scowls into her green salad.

I look up and see that Tracey and Tina are weaving between the tables towards us.

"Hi, Helen, really looking forward to the party tomorrow," Tracey says.

"Wait, you're coming?" Brian says, then snorts derisively. "Bloody hell, Helen, did you invite every loser in the jungle?"

Tracey throws him a withering look and says, "She must have if she's invited you."

Brian flushes and I look away with a smirk.

"Anyway," she continues, talking only to me, "I was wondering if Tina can come too? It's only one more."

The silence is deafening as they all turn to look at me. I don't need to look at Eloise to know she is throwing me a warning glare.

"Um, well, we've already planned the food and everything

and I think we're pretty much maxed out, so um... maybe next time?"

Tina looks deflated, as does Tracey, who replies sharply, "Oh, ok, well, thanks anyway."

"Unless you want to come and serve the drinks for us, Tina?" El says snidely.

Em and Steph giggle.

"Fuck off, Eloise," Tracey replies with venom.

They turn to go and I can hear Tina say in a whisper that's loud enough for us all to hear, "See, I told you she would say no. I don't get what you like about Helen – or any of them. They're such stuck-up sluts, all plastic and no brains."

Brian says, "You're not going to let her get away with talking about you like that, are you, El?"

Eloise gets to her feet in anger, but I put a hand on her arm. "Leave it, El, she's just mouthing off because she can't come to the party of the decade."

"She needs to be taken down. They both do. Especially that Tracey! How dare she swear at me!"

"Look, she's had a rough week, ok?" The words are out of my mouth before I even know I am going to verbalise them.

"Why? What's happened?" El's face lights up at the thought of finding out some gossip. She sits back down hungrily.

"It's nothing. She probably wouldn't want me to tell you."

El sits forwards, puts her hands on my knees, her long nails digging into my skin. "Then it is your very duty as my best friend to tell me."

"I thought I was your best friend, El," Emily says, trying to crack an ill-timed joke.

"No, Em, you are like a mosquito buzzing around my head."

Emily gapes while the rest of us laugh. I laugh the loudest, hoping the conversation can steer away from Tracey. "I don't know why you're laughing, Steph. You're like shit on the bottom of her shoe that she can't scrape off," I say and laugh some more.

Some of the boys laugh and say, "Oooh, harsh."

Steph looks like she is going to cry.

"Oh, come on, Steph, I'm joking. You big baby, you're going to cry!"

"I'm not," she says, looking at her feet. "I know you're joking."

"You're so sensitive, bloody hell! Can't take a joke anymore." I tighten my ponytail, feeling awful in my stomach at insulting Steph, but pleased to have successfully steered us away from Tracey.

"So you were saying?" El says pointedly to me and my heart sinks.

Maybe El will be kind if she hears about Tracey's brother.

"Her brother has... special needs, ok? He's got Down's Syndrome and she looks after him a lot. It's been a difficult week. He's been lashing out and stuff."

The bell rings then and we all get to our feet. "Please don't tell her I told you though," I say to all of them.

"Why would we?" El replies, but there is a glint in her eye and I know she has filed the information, ready to be tossed like a grenade when necessary.

After school, we pile out of the doors into the throng of

kids milling around, waiting. El grabs me and says, "Look, over there."

Tracey and Tina are hugging and smiling.

"Right little lesbians, aren't they?"

I frown. "They're just hugging."

"Oh, come on, I think there's more to it than that. Look at them. I think they're into each other."

Brian and Jason come up behind us. "Who is?"

Eloise nods at them. "I think they're lezzas," she says in her *I'm talking to boys*, high-pitched voice.

"No, they're not, El. Leave them alone."

"Seriously, Helen? After what they said earlier? No, I'm not leaving it alone."

She stalks off, making a beeline straight for them, with the rest of the group following, mob mentality kicking in at the thought of a bit of drama.

"Hey, you two. Are you lesbians?" Eloise shouts loudly as she gets closer to them.

Tracey and Tina spin around and I see Tina pale as the mob moves in. I stay at the back, keeping a distance, torn between stepping in between them and not wanting to stand out, draw attention to myself.

"What are you on about, Eloise?" Tracey says, but her voice is uncertain. The mob creates a semi-circle around them.

"Well, that was quite a hug there. I don't know if we should be condoning that kind of thing here at Seahaven. What do you think, guys?"

There are rumbles of laughter and agreement. I say nothing.

"This is quite tiresome, Eloise. Go home." Tracey says and turns her back on them. She starts to walk away, just as Tina says, "Yes, you brainless slag. Go home."

Eloise flushes a shade of red that I don't think I've ever seen on her pale skin, but Tina doesn't see it as she has turned her back on El too. She is looking down the driveway at the car that has stopped next to her. A Year 8 is climbing into the back seat.

The woman driving it is looking into her rear-view mirror, smiling, and I can hear her in my head, asking her son if he has had a good day.

Eloise is watching too and takes a step closer to Tina.

The woman pulls away, her eyes still on her mirror, chatting to her son.

As the car accelerates forward, I see El reach out and grab Tina, then go to shove her in front of the quickening car. It is all happening in slow motion. I can see my hand reach up to pull at Eloise's coat at the same time that I hear Tracey shout out.

Eloise's hands push Tina towards the car and immediately pull her back in. The car screeches to a halt, the woman's face a mask of fear and shock. There is silence around us until El says, "Tell your mother I saved your life, Tina," and she lets her go.

Tina crumples into a heap on the ground and Tracey stoops to help her up. The mother scrambles from the car, her apologies running over each other. Students stand and gape, talking behind their hands and watching as the mother helps Tina up, asking her again and again if she's ok.

Tracey launches at Eloise and slaps her hard, catching

her nose, which spurts blood onto her shirt. Eloise gasps, but then recovers, smiles sweetly and walks away casually, turning back only to say, "Watch your back, Tracey."

37

NOW

The garden was cold, the grass wet, but that wasn't why Helen was shivering. There was something about Mills' face, like she was barely holding herself together, pulling in the threads of her sanity before it unravelled completely. Helen had never seen her look this way before. She trailed behind Helen, as though her legs really did not want to take her where they were going. Helen had a sudden expectation that she would walk into the pool house and see *her* sitting on a lounger, still in the bikini she wore that night, her hair pulled into an impossibly high ponytail and her lips shimmering in pink gloss, then a Polaroid flash as she documented the shock on Helen's face and that laugh, loud, cackling.

They were halfway down the garden when she heard Clive barking aggressively back at the house.

Helen stopped and turned back. He hardly ever barked.

Someone was in the house. Someone who shouldn't be there.

"Leave it, Mum. This is important," Mills said.

Clive's barking grew more animated.

"Something is wrong. He never barks like that."

"Hugh is there, isn't he? He can check – he's probably just been spooked by Arthur or Matt or something."

Then Clive yelped in pain.

Helen tore back to the house and burst into the kitchen.

Clive was cowering in the corner, with Peter standing over him.

"Peter! Don't you dare touch him!"

Peter swung around to face them, his eyes blazing.

"Here she is!" He was smiling, but it was the smile of a lunatic. He stepped closer towards them. "The woman who ruined my life."

"Peter, go home. Now is not a good time."

"Home! Ha! I don't have a home, thanks to you!" He stepped closer again, close enough that Helen could smell the alcohol coming off him in toxic clouds.

"Mum?" Mills said behind her.

"Go and find Matt, Mills," she said, but Peter rushed past them and slammed the kitchen door, blocking her exit.

"No one is going anywhere."

"Peter, this is ridiculous. Hugh has paid you, I know he has, so let's leave it at that, ok?"

"She's left me! Because of you – took my little girl and went to live with her mother. She wants a divorce."

"And that's my fault? You started this – the blackmail, everything. You could've just walked away. This is on you."

She was surprised to find that she wasn't frightened of Peter at all, with his masculine bravado and pathetic attempts to manhandle them into submission. She'd dealt with men like this before, when she left here and survived on her own. She'd had men trying to intimidate her, hurt her, but they were just small-minded bullies. You had to show them strength because they were cowards on the inside.

Helen stepped towards him. He was much taller than her, but she looked straight up at him, her shoulders squared.

"Mum..." Mills said warily.

"It's ok, Mills, he's just a coward, like all bullies are. He's frightened because he's on his own and he's looking to blame someone. Aren't you, Peter? But you know deep down that this is your fault. You made a choice to sleep with me and now that your wife knows, you can't look at yourself in the mirror, so it's easier to blame me."

He was glaring down at her, the alcohol rancid on his breath.

He lashed out, struck her with the flat of his hand. Her head rocketed to the side, the pain pleasurable in its intensity.

Her mother's slap had hurt more.

Mills shouted out, Clive launched from his bed and darted behind Helen's legs, but Helen stood her ground, challenging Peter to do it again. She could take it.

Then his face crumbled. He launched at her and for a split second she thought he was going to strangle her.

He wrapped his arms around her and started crying into her shoulders, big gulping sobs. She staggered under the weight of him. Even Clive sat with his head on the side, wondering how they had gone from violence to emotional breakdown in ten seconds flat.

"Mills, let's get him into a chair."

Mills jumped forward to pull out the chair and Helen pushed him into it.

"She found the videos. On my phone – she said she was looking for a phone number, but I know she was checking up on me. I'd told her you had used me, told me I would be fired if I didn't sleep with you."

Helen rolled her eyes.

"Then she saw the videos and said it didn't look like I needed much persuasion." His shoulders shuddered. "And now she's taken my little girl, says I can't see her."

"You slept with *him*?" Mills asked. "Really?"

Helen looked at him now, his head bowed so that you could see the start of a bald patch in his thinning dark hair, snot dripping from his nose and sweat stains on his dirty t-shirt, and she couldn't understand why either.

She sighed and patted him on the shoulder awkwardly. Even Clive took a few tentative steps forward to sniff at him, then left to find a quiet corner somewhere else where there was less drama.

"Mum," Mills insisted impatiently. "We need to go. This is more important than your boyfriend's breakdown." Helen heard the disappointment in Mills' voice.

"Peter, I have to sort something out, but sit here, get yourself together, then go. You can't be here. Give Sally some time, she might come around." She patted him one more time for emphasis and he nodded around a sob. "Oh, and don't ever come back – because if you do, I'll hurt you."

Helen walked away.

Once outside, she exhaled heavily and looked at Mills. "Don't say a word, ok? We all make mistakes."

38

THEN

I feel awful. I must have overdone the laxatives yesterday because my stomach is hard and sore. I'm light-headed, but also very headachey, a dull, constant thump behind my eyes. The morning light is glaring, not helping at all.

Typical. Today of all days. It's the party tonight and I want to be at my best.

I crawl from bed and run a hot bath, hoping it will alleviate the cramps. I get on the scale and I'm pleased to see I have lost four pounds this week. So I was right in thinking my stomach was flatter. I twist and turn in front of the mirror while the water runs and steam fills the air, liking some of what I see and hoping I can disguise the bits I don't.

Maybe I shouldn't eat anything today. Lay off the laxatives, but keep away from food so that my stomach is as flat as possible. I should probably not take any pills today either. I took some when I got home yesterday, still shaking a little at the stunt Eloise pulled on Tina. But that's Eloise all over. She has had plenty of moments like those over the years, taking things too far when exacting revenge on someone she thinks – rightly or wrongly – has offended her.

Yesterday was an overreaction and I probably should've stepped in and done something, said something, but I didn't. Maybe my reactions were slow. Maybe I didn't want trouble before tonight. Either way, deep down I know it was cowardly of me.

When everyone had dispersed yesterday, I went to check that Tina was ok. She was furious, wiping the dust from her knees with still trembling hands.

"Tina, are you ok?"

"I'm fine, no thanks to your friend." Her hands swiped furiously at her legs. "She's fucking dangerous," she seethed.

"I'm sorry, I don't know what came over her."

Tracey looked at me with such disappointment that I wanted to wither away. "I'm sorry, really. I have to go." I left, not looking back.

I have no idea if Tracey is still going to come to the party. I hope she does. I want to explain that I had nothing to do with what Eloise did.

I slip into the bath and think about the other day, talking to Tracey on the bench, the relief at letting out all that hurt, letting the words tumble into her lap while she let me cry. How nice it felt to have someone hold me, comfort me, listen to me. How strange and unfamiliar it was. I'm only just realising how much I crave that physical and emotional connection. You would think you wouldn't miss what you've never had, but apparently you do.

*

Hours later, I stand in front of the mirror in my bikini. I am feeling empty. Hungry, certainly, and on edge. My stomach feels cavernous after very little food all day and my head is still full of cotton wool, but the dull ache has retreated a bit.

People will start arriving soon. I need to open the bottom gate. Everyone has strict instructions to come straight into the pool house and not bother Martha up at the house – mostly so that she doesn't see how many people turn up. I hope it's not a lot, but I can't trust Eloise. She will have been burning up the phone lines with invitations all week.

I grab the flimsy lilac throw I found in my mother's wardrobe and put it over my orange bikini. My hair is tied in a high ponytail with ringlets around my face and I have very little make-up on. If I do go in the pool, I don't want to come out with panda eyes.

I hear Martha calling me from downstairs.

I shout from my bedroom door. "Yes? What is it? I'm getting ready."

"Tracey is here!" she calls back.

My stomach flips over. She came after all. I pause, feeling my pulse jump erratically in my wrist, then reach into my bedside table and pull out the bottle of vodka stashed in there. It's nearly empty. A bottle of pills falls out onto the carpet and I pick them up, take a second to see they are the happy pills, the ones that make me feel light and floaty, and quickly neck a couple with a big swig of vodka.

I stash everything back where it was just as I hear her feet on the stairs.

Then she is standing in the door, looking as awkward and uncomfortable as I feel.

I don't know what to say. "Hey."

"Hey," she replies.

"You came."

"I said I would."

I nod, look away.

She says, "I really like you, Helen. And I know you're good friends with Eloise, which makes it difficult, but I would like to be friends."

Warmth spreads through me. "I'd like that too! I know she's a bitch and a bully. To be honest, we aren't as close as we used to be. Yesterday was just... mad, really. So I can put some distance between me and her if that's what you want. Anyway, in a few months we'll all be off to uni and going our separate ways."

"Tina is going to report Eloise at school."

"Oh, right, yeah."

She has an overnight bag over her shoulder and is still standing in the doorway. "So do you want to...?" I nod at the bedroom.

She smiles and comes towards me, gives me a fierce hug. "Let's get this party started," she whispers in my ear.

When she has changed into the red swimming costume and a peacock blue throw I put aside for her from my mother's endless wardrobe, we wave to Martha and run down to the pool house. I have already stashed booze in the storeroom, which I drag out now by the box full.

"Wow! Do you think we'll need this much?"

"Probably not, but better too much than too little, as my mother would say." I don't mention the bottle of pills I've stashed there too, along with some make-up for touch-ups later. All the essentials covered.

I think about my mother, wonder what she's doing now.

Is she in Central Park, walking in the sunshine, enjoying the sights and smells of the Big Apple? Or sitting in her hotel room while my father works, drinking endless martinis and eating pills like sweets as she waits for him to return, sleepy, her head drooping over her untouched prawn cocktail?

I don't know and I want to kid myself that I don't care.

I care even less about what my father is doing.

I hope he's having a shit time.

They haven't called once.

I can feel my mood souring, so I pull out the first bottle I put my hand on. It is champagne, richly yellow with its elaborate gold foil cap and tiny bubbles.

"Champagne?" I say.

Tracey laughs. "Sure, why not? You know, I've never had it before."

"Well, today is your lucky day."

The cork is stiff in the neck of the bottle, not yielding at all. I give it a twist and a hard pull, and it shoots out, the champagne frothing and spurting from the neck.

Tracey giggles and claps her hands.

Martha has been busy. There is a table set up in the corner and she has laid out plastic cups, brightly coloured paper plates and bowls, with trays of food. Bless her, there's even a happy birthday banner strung across the front of the table, just like a real birthday party but for a ten-year-old.

"It's not actually your birthday, is it?" Tracey asks.

"No, but I had to tell Martha something so that I could have the party." I pour some champagne into two cups and hand one to Tracey before pulling down the banner and tossing it aside.

"Cheers! Let's have some fun!"

"Cheers," she says and sips at the cup, wrinkling her nose as the bubbles pop in her face.

I gulp at mine, not tasting it, just wanting to get it into me, feel it take over my body. When I've finished it, I pour some more and say, "Right, you put some music on and I'll go and open the gate."

I can feel the champagne mixing with the pills already, my heart rate tripping up as I walk out of the oppressive humidity of the pool house and into the cooling night air. Goosebumps spring up on my skin and I traipse across the grass quickly. There are balloons tied to the gate so that everyone will know where to come to. I open the gate and run back to the pool house. Tracey is sitting on the edge of the pool, her feet dangling in the water as she munches on crisps.

"Sorry, I'm really hungry. I didn't have dinner before I left," she says.

I forget myself for a second, grab a handful too and sit next to her. The water surrounds my feet. I shovel the crisps into my mouth. "Me neither. I'm starving."

Her toenails are painted postbox red to match her swimsuit and I am mesmerised as I watch them peep through the surface of the water, then disappear again. She is wearing a delicate ankle chain with tiny beads and a silver conch shell dangling just above her heel. It glints in the fluorescent lighting bouncing off the water. Her hand is resting on the tiles, her fingers millimetres from mine, and I suddenly want to close that distance, touch her fingertips.

Instead, I take another big drink of champagne. "I really hope tonight is fun," I say. "And if El or anyone gives you a hard time, let me know."

She smiles sweetly. "Don't worry, I can look after myself."

39

NOW

This time it was Mills leading the way down the garden. She pushed through the pool house door, but then ground to halt, staring around her in confusion.

Matt and Lydia were sitting on the loungers. Matt had his arms around Lydia, who was sobbing uncontrollably.

"Where is she?" Mills said. "Where's the body?"

Helen spun to face her. "The *body*?"

Her eyes frantically searched the room. "She was here. Floating. I pulled her from the pool. There was blood." Mills took a tentative step forwards, then pointed at a faint red swirl in a puddle of water on the tiles.

Lydia started to wail.

Matt was on his feet. "What the fuck is going on?"

"I came in here earlier and Diana – she was floating face down in the pool. She had blood on her head and..."

"What? You didn't say that!"

"Well, I would've shown you if your boyfriend hadn't turned up!"

Helen turned on Matt. "What did you do?"

"Me? I didn't do anything!"

"You were furious. You came marching down here – what did you do?" she shouted.

Lydia cried even harder.

"You were angry, you left because you had found out about Lydia and Diana. Did you attack her, hit her?"

"No, I—"

"And where is she now? What did you do with the body?" Mills asked again.

"Nothing! It wasn't me!" Matt shrieked.

"It was me."

Lydia had stopped crying, but her breath was still hitching and gulping. She looked at them with eyes wide open, black mascara rimming them like face paint. "I killed her."

Standing in front of Diana in the pool house, the contents of the bag spilling out in front of them, Lydia heard the silence, felt her heart crashing from her body as Diana dismissed her. She had been so wrong about everything.

Everything Diana has asked of her, she had done. She'd stolen, she'd lied – all of it because she thought Diana loved her.

When Diana had said she needed a quiet place to work because her parents were constantly arguing and it was affecting her creativity, Lydia had said how nice the bookshop was for quiet moments, how Helen had created a reading space in the far corner full of armchairs and bean bags where customers could sit and take a moment.

Diana had asked if Helen would let her use it after hours,

but Lydia knew that was out of the question. She'd seen how Helen bristled when Diana was in the room, could feel the snapping tension between them. Instead, she had stolen the spare keys to the shop from the kitchen drawer. Helen had waved the keys at her once when she had brought up the idea of Lydia helping her out in the shop after school. All Helen wanted was cheap labour, someone to do the lifting and carrying for her, someone she could pay next to nothing and chalk it up to "work experience". Lydia hadn't fallen for it. She was not going to let her stepmother use her like that. Diana was all about taking control, standing up for yourself, not letting yourself be used by those in positions of power. Lydia needed to be more like Diana.

So she'd swiped the keys and given them to Diana.

She warned her that there was someone living in the flat upstairs, but if she kept quiet and out of sight, she could use it whenever she wanted.

Diana had given her so much advice and help that she just wanted to do something worthwhile back.

You be you, Diana would say to Lydia. *Don't waste energy on other people's feelings. That's their problem, not yours. Your happiness is the only thing that matters.*

And she was right. For too long, Lydia had let people walk all over her, had remained silent so as to spare other people's feelings, had swallowed down what she really wanted to say.

Now it was time to be heard, to act, to take control.

There was a captivating light about Diana when she smiled in pleasure, like the day Lydia gave her the keys. The whole room was illuminated by her smile. However, she'd also seen that light fade rapidly when Diana didn't get what she wanted. There was a darkness to her too, like a light switch flicking on and off. She could be morose and melodramatic, wallowing in deep emotional outbursts when she declared the world was against her, that Lydia was drifting away from her, that she wasn't worthy of the pureness that was in Lydia. And Lydia would do anything to lift the black cloud. There was a lot that Diana didn't talk about or explain when the curtain fell. Lydia suspected there was more going on at home than Diana would admit and Lydia wanted to be her person, the one who made her feel better, the one she couldn't live without.

Then Diana had told her that she had found something disturbing when she had been looking for a pen in the shop one evening. Something that would expose the real Helen, she had said, pull back Helen's mask to reveal the side that no one else knew about. She had said that their family was in real danger.

Lydia felt alive. Not scared or worried, but like every nerve was tingling inside of her, firing her up. Someone needed her. Someone had asked for her help. Someone had confided in her. Diana had chosen her out of everyone else – not Matt, her dad or even Mills.

Those bitches at school were wrong. She wasn't weak and pathetic after all. When they had started teasing her because she didn't want to go out and drink vodka straight from the bottle on the beach with random boys every night, she had shrugged it off. Then they stopped inviting her, which was actually a relief. But it soon escalated into more than just teasing. It became a consistent, stinging attack for her lack of interest in the make-up they wanted to wear, the short skirts and tight clothes, the need to prove they were cool by vaping and lacing their Lucozade with enough alcohol to make them pass out. She had stood her ground, put some distance between herself and them, tried to drown it all out, but when they noticed her lack of interest in boys altogether, the attack became all-out warfare, a bombardment of abuse across messaging groups and Snapchat private stories, notes in her locker and sniggered comments in the corridors as she walked past. She could've probably ignored all of that too, except that she was uncomfortable in the knowledge that they were poking at a newly discovered and exposed nerve.

Yes, she was different to them, but she didn't know how to deal with it yet. She hadn't got her own head around who she was, so that made isolating herself and retreating her only option. The more she retreated, the quicker the bullying had picked up speed. They began hurtling insults at her like grenades, spreading rumours, hitting out at her with their hockey sticks when the coach's back was turned and pinching her skin until it bruised as they ganged up and surrounded her in the toilet block.

But then she had met Diana and suddenly she didn't care about the bruises. This beautiful, smart, confident woman was actually interested in talking to *her*! Wanted to spend time with *her*! It gave her the power and confidence to stand up to her tormentors. When they texted abuse and insults, she replied with selfies of her with Diana or a selfie of her staring straight into the screen, flipping her middle finger at them.

If they prodded, she poked back, started kicking out her feet and laughing as they pinched. And it felt good. Their power diminished while hers grew.

Diana was not pleased when she found out that Lydia

had texted out the selfie of them together. She wanted their relationship to be kept a secret, saying that Matt wouldn't understand. He would be heartbroken, considering how much he liked Diana himself. Lydia knew she was right. Matt had a weirdly unhealthy obsession with Diana, stalked her socials, constantly texted her, apparently wouldn't leave her alone at college.

And then she told Diana she loved her – and Diana had stood silent for a moment.

Then Diana laughed, a cruel, patronising laugh.

One moment. One bad decision that sets off a domino reaction.

And before you know it, you have blood on your hands.

40

THEN

"Hey, losers!" A voice rips through the moment, just as I am about to reach out and take Tracey's hand. I jump. Brian and his three mates tumble through the door, pushing and shoving at each other, already drinking from cans of beer. I get to my feet, but Tracey stays where she is.

"Hey, guys," I say brightly.

"Is this it?" he says, looking around. "Cool pool, but where is everyone?"

"You're the first here."

I can see Jason over his shoulder. He smiles when he sees me.

"Lads, pool time!" Brian starts taking his clothes off, dropping them at his feet, until he is wearing only a pair of brightly coloured surf shorts, his skinny torso transparently white against the neon fabric. He runs and launches himself into the pool, splashing Tracey in the process.

"Guys! Chill, would you?" I say.

"This is a party, isn't it?" he replies.

The rest of them follow Brian, shedding clothes everywhere. I notice Jason as he takes his shirt off. In contrast to Brian, his chest is more defined, less boyish. Still pasty white, but he has the beginnings of stomach muscles, faint lines rippling under his skin. He's also being more reserved, not rushing into the water like a toddler.

I drink some more champagne and sit back down next to Tracey. She rolls her eyes at me, but then I notice her watching Jason too as he bobs in the water. One of them has produced a beach ball from somewhere and an impromptu game of volleyball breaks out.

"Who knew he had that hidden under his school shirt?" Tracey says to me quietly and we giggle.

"Ladies!" Eloise, Steph and Emily walk through the door, looking like they're attending the Oscars. El is wearing bizarre, massive sunglasses that cover most of her face, despite it being dark outside. Steph and Emily are like identical twins in matching purple bikinis beneath denim jackets. It is my turn to roll my eyes.

I get up again, pour some more champagne into cups and hand it around. I think El was expecting more fanfare when she arrived, but the boys are too engrossed in dunking each other and pelting the beach ball around to notice her, so she is scowling already.

She puts her huge beach bag on a lounger and flings off her long coat to reveal a very skimpy yellow bikini underneath. "Hi, Brian," she says, waving her fingers at him. He looks over, momentarily stunned. The beach ball smacks him on the side of the face. The rest of the boys start laughing and, embarrassed, he turns his attention back to his friends.

El rips off the sunglasses in annoyance and drains her

cup before indicating I should refill it. I drain my cup too. She sees my Polaroid camera on the table.

"Emily, take a photo," she commands.

"Cool, of all of us?"

"No, just me and Hels."

"Oh," Emily says, her face falling.

Eloise puts her arm around me and poses, her other hand on her jutting hip, her eyes wide, her boobs pushed forward. The flash blinds us as we smile. I see Brian watching us and El gives me a knowing smirk as she takes the photo from Emily. She wafts it dramatically, like she is wielding a fan, looks at it and shakes her head.

"For god's sake, Emily. Not just our faces. You never get anything right." She tosses the photo aside and snatches the camera from Emily before she can take another photo and stalks off. Steph and Em follow her like sheep as she sets herself up on the loungers, right next to where the boys are throwing themselves around.

I look at the photo and it's a nice one. We are both smiling and look pretty, happy.

I slip the photo into the waistband of my wraparound as more people arrive. Some I know; others I don't. Small groups of girls from school, mostly the popular ones, those on the sports teams and in drama club with Eloise, alongside groups of boys from Seahaven and the local comp in the next village over, friends of Brian's, the news of the party having apparently reached them too. Before long, the pool house is busy with bodies, noise and music. The boys have momentarily halted the volleyball and got out of the pool. They are throwing crisps at each other, seeing who can catch the most in their open mouths. I lose sight of Tracey while I say hello to the various faces I recognise, but then I see her on a lounger on the other side of the pool, talking to a girl with French plaits in her hair and ridiculously large hoop earrings.

I go into the storeroom for another bottle of champagne and shove the photo in my bag. I open the bottle and wander around with it in my hand, having ditched the cup in favour of swigging straight from the neck of the bottle. Eloise's camp now includes three loungers pulled together, on which Steph and Emily are reclining like they are in the south of France, while Eloise is making out with Brian. She breaks for air and smiles at me, thrilled that she has finally got her claws into him. I'm torn between wanting to find out what Tracey is talking about and knowing I should be paying El the appropriate amount of attention. If I talk to her now, maybe she'll leave me alone later so that I can hang out with Tracey.

I sit down, perched on the end of El's lounger, as though I'm worshipping at her perfectly pedicured feet. Steph and Emily are gabbling and giggling, swatting the air lamely as the boys splash them, twirling their hair between their fingers and fawning over everything Eloise says.

"You're soooo funny, El."

"Oh, I wish I had your beautiful skin, El. You are soooo radiant."

How have I not noticed before now how insubstantial they are? How lacking in opinion or purpose? I turn away from them, survey the room, the people milling about, jumping in the pool, splashing water, necking booze and gobbling handfuls of Monster Munch. How many of these people do I actually know? And how many actually know me? A lot of them have been school friends for years, but when I think about it, they aren't my friends. They don't know me anymore. I feel like I've quietly been changing, evolving, morphing into a completely different person in the last few weeks, the final ingredient in my transformation being the knowledge that my parents never wanted me, that my father actively investigated getting rid of me.

My father wanted me dead.

None of these people, these *kids*, would understand it, with their privileged lives and happy families. Eloise, Emily, Steph – could I tell any of them what has been going on? Would they even try to understand or care?

Tracey understands. She knows me – and yet she has been my friend for the least amount of time.

Jason sidles up to me while I'm watching Tracey from the other side of the pool.

"Hey, Helen. You look nice."

"Thanks," I say, although I don't want to talk to him right now. Tracey is laughing at something the girl has said. I strain to hear too, but can't make it out over the music.

"So do you want a drink?" Jason says. He blushes, looks at his feet, then back at me. I can smell his aftershave, heady and strong in my nose, like he's bathed in it.

I hold up the bottle. "I've got one," I say and walk away from him, over to where Tracey is.

"Hey, how's it going?" I say.

"Good thanks. Do you know Julie? She's in the netball team with me."

I didn't know Tracey played netball.

"Er, no, I don't. Hi." I give her a steely look, hoping she'll get up and move, but she is oblivious, her eyes now on a boy in the pool with big blue eyes and spots on his chin.

"What to do you think about Thomas, Tracey?" she says and they resume their conversation. I feel dismissed, like I'm surplus to requirements.

I'm about to speak again, maybe try and manoeuvre myself into sitting with them, when I hear Eloise calling me. She is standing with her hands on her tiny hips, pushing her boobs out as much as possible. "Can we change this music please? It's so lame. And is there more champagne?"

"Sure." I walk away. Tracey and Julie continue their conversation. I see the boy with the Bambi eyes swim over to them. He leans onto the edge of the pool, his muscles flexed, starts chatting to them. I stop, watch them, annoyance rumbling in my throat, then walk away.

Jason tries to intercept me as I weave through bodies, but I ignore him again.

I go into the storeroom and lean against the wall, closing my eyes for a minute. I can hear Steph and Emily, their laughter like nails on a chalkboard, screeching through the thin walls. My head is spinning and I feel sick. There is a small changing room with a toilet at the other end of the pool house, but I can't bring myself to walk that far, past everyone. But my stomach is lurching like the sea outside and I know I'm going to throw up soon. I grab a bottle of champagne, shove past the people standing just outside the storeroom and practically throw the bottle at El before charging for the changing room.

I notice Tracey look up as I rush past. I'm pleased she is concerned at least. I lock myself into the small toilet and collapse to the floor, breathing deeply.

I hear someone on the other side of the door. "Are you ok?" It's Tracey.

"Yeah, thanks, just too much champagne and not enough food."

"I'll get you something to eat."

There is silence again. The spinning in my head slows down and I get to my feet slowly. The changing room is wood-panelled with bench-style seats built into the walls and a small shower in the corner. I sit on one of the benches and lean my head back. Closing my eyes, I listen to the sounds of the party. The laughter, shouting, splashing water, champagne corks popping. Everyone sounds like they are having fun. Then I hear glass breaking. I should be worried about that, glass getting into the pool or on the tiles, no one cleaning it up. But I don't have the energy. I can hear someone apologising loudly, voices raised, someone saying, "It was an accident!" It sounds like Tracey.

I open my eyes and think about going to see what's going on, but then Tracey is back with a plate of food and a cup of water.

"What's going on out there?"

"Nothing," she says. "I just knocked over a bottle when I walked past. It's fine, I'll clean it up in a minute. Eat this first."

I bite into a small sandwich triangle, ham and cheese wilted and warm from the humidity. There are cheese squares and tiny pickled onions on sticks, Monster Munch and little sausages on the plate, and suddenly I am ravenous. Tracey sits and watches me as I eat, her hand on my hair, stroking it like I'm a child. It is comforting. When I'm finished, I lean my head on her shoulder and we sit like that for a moment as I sip at the water. I don't notice my hand coming to rest on her bare thigh, the skin soft and warm beneath my palm.

The door bursts open and Eloise storms in, then comes to a sudden stop.

"What the fuck is this?" she says. Her voice is sharp with icicles.

I lift my head. "What do you mean?"

"Why are you sitting there cuddling her like that?"

I sigh. "We're not cuddling," I say. "I wasn't feeling well. Tracey is looking after me."

"Oh, is she now? Looks like more than that to me. You've practically got your hand up her fanny." I snatch my hand away as she turns and says with a sneer over her shoulder, "Looks like we've got a lesbian show going on in here."

Faces appear around the door. I can hear someone wolf-whistling and a boy's voice say, "Go on, give her a kiss."

I push away from Tracey. "Don't be so childish."

"Oh, please," El continues, her voice dangerously pitched, "I've seen how you can't take your eyes off her at school, following her around like a puppy dog, practically panting after her. I can't believe I didn't notice sooner. You are, aren't you? You're a lesbian!"

I lurch to my feet. "I'm not! You're being ridiculous. We're just friends."

"Yeah, friends with benefits."

The crowd behind her is whispering and giggling, excited by the drunken drama on show.

Then I notice blood on El's foot.

"Eloise, you're bleeding."

Eloise looks down, then suddenly remembers why she was here in the first place. She points a wavering finger at

Tracey. "She broke a bottle and now I've cut myself. You would think she of all people would know how to clean up."

"What's that supposed to mean?" Tracey growls.

"Eloise, stop it. I'm sure it was an accident. She was just about to come back and sort it."

"But you lost track of time, is that it? Gazing into each other's eyes? And now I'm bleeding all over the place."

"It's not that bad. There's a first aid kit over there in the cupboard. Put a plaster on and it'll be fine." I'm worn out by the confrontation already.

The faces start to disperse now that some of the excitement has dissipated. I push past Eloise and head back towards the pool, grabbing a half-empty bottle of champagne from a small table as I pass. Tracey follows me and goes to clean up the glass, but it looks like the girl with the hoop earrings has done it already.

The music is loud now, the glass walls throbbing to the beat. As I walk, it feels like everyone is looking, whispering, gossiping. I can feel them judging me. I start to realise how this could get out of hand, how they'll whisper and talk. My paranoia kicks up a gear at the thought of the rumours that will circulate, at first a low rumble, then a deafening roar as they strengthen and mutate. I have never been the subject of unkind rumours before. I've started them, but never had to endure it. My pulse begins to gallop. I find my bag, take two more pills and a deep breath. I look at my watch. It is only 9:30 p.m. It feels like it should be much later. I turn to find Eloise standing right behind me.

"What are those?"

I look down at the pill bottle still in my hand. "Just some of my mother's happy pills."

"And why haven't you shared them?"

I think about telling her they could be dangerous, that she shouldn't take them, that they are making me crazy, but I don't really care anymore.

I shrug and hand over the pills, then take a swig from the champagne and leave her to it.

Jason is sitting on the pool steps, drinking from a bottle of beer and chatting to a girl I recognise from my maths class.

I slide onto the step, dangerously close to him. "Hi," I say.

He looks a little taken aback. "Um, hi."

"Having fun?"

"Yeah."

The girl on the other side of him – I think her name is Cheryl – glares at me, then pushes off the step and into the water to join the volleyball game.

"So, you and Tracey, huh?"

"No, we're just friends."

"Really? That's not what Eloise says."

"Oh yeah?"

"She says you've been together for a while in secret. That you've tried it on with her too."

"Right." Why am I surprised? I think about Mandy, the girls we broke with our careless gossiping and childish taunts. "You shouldn't believe everything you hear. I can prove it to you if you like." I'm not sure why I do it, but I lean forward and start to kiss him, throwing everything I've got at him, pressing my body against his. I can feel him recoil at first, then respond, and soon he is pushing back, his hands on my back and his leg pushing between mine. I clamp down the thought that it doesn't feel as nice as I thought it would.

We break apart and he looks like all of his Christmases have come at once. "So you're not a lesbian then. Are you bi? I don't mind or anything." He looks excited by the idea.

I hit him playfully on the arm, then lean in to kiss him again. I open my eyes and see Tracey watching us. She walks away, back to where she was sitting before, but the girl with the hoop earrings gets up and moves away as Tracey approaches.

Guilt turns my stomach, but I pull out of the kiss and make a play of cuddling into Jason's shoulder instead. I am acutely aware of his hand high on my waist, his fingers very close to the underside of my bikini top, and I want to push him away, but Eloise is watching me closely. Brian goes up to her and she says something to him I can't hear. She looks over at Tracey, her face a mask of hatred.

Then Jason is leaning in again, blocking my view. When I pull back again, Eloise has disappeared.

She reappears a few minutes later and walks over to Tracey, a cup in her hand. Cold washes over me as I think she is going to throw the drink at Tracey, but instead she hands her the cup with a smile. I can't hear what they are saying, but Tracey looks nervous, then visibly relaxes and accepts the drink. El holds her cup up and they toast each other.

Jason's hands are starting to wander, but I'm more interested in what is going on at the other side of the pool. I push him away, ignoring the look on his face. He is persistent, comes straight back.

"Jason, can you get me a drink please?" I say to distract him. He adjusts his baggy shorts and leaps out of the pool, happy to play the role of gallant gentleman if it means he might get lucky. I keep my eyes on Tracey and Eloise. They are chatting and look almost friendly. Tracey is a little stiff, probably keeping her guard up, but Eloise appears to be all charm.

Jason is back with a cup of neat vodka and I knock it back with a grimace. I know El is up to something, but I don't know what. She chats to Tracey for a little while longer, then walks away. I don't like the look on her face or the knowing smirk she gives me as she comes over to us. Brian pads over behind her and they climb into the water next to Jason and me.

"Decided to swing back to boys then, Hels?"

"Oh, grow up, Brian."

Eloise sniggers.

"Why would I be interested in someone like Tracey anyway?" I hear myself say.

I look over at Tracey with her long hair and legs that go on for miles. She is leaning back on the lounger, her feet dancing to the music, her eyes closed.

"Yeah, you're right. You'd at least choose someone more like us. So are you two an item now then?" Eloise indicates Jason, who has his hand on my waist again, his thumb rubbing at the bottom of my bikini top. I am trying to ignore him, but I'm getting irritated by his roaming hands.

I shrug in reply.

"Why are you still staring at her?" Tracey has slumped further down the lounger. She looks like she might be drunk, her face softened, as though it is melting, and she is grinning goofily at no one as she stares vacantly around her.

"Give it a rest, El. I'm not gay, ok? You know that. I'm

just worried. She looks like she's had a lot to drink. She's not used to it."

"Hasn't everyone? Isn't that the point of this party? I don't see you worrying about how much I've had – or Steph or Em."

I look over at them now and they are definitely drunk, swaying in a gormless way. But El is right. I don't really care about them like I do Tracey.

Eloise is annoyed again. "Do I really know you, Helen? Do I know anything about you anymore? Apparently you and her have been spending loads of time together. Sleepovers and everything, she says. Tell me, do you share the same bed when you're together? That's sounds... cosy. Frankly, I worry about what you've been thinking about me all this time, if you've been watching me change at school, staring at me naked. If word got around school about this, you'd be finished."

El is now making me sound like a pervert. Her eyes are blazing with fury and in that moment I know that our long friendship would not stop her ruining me in a second. Her need to be top dog, to be right, means she would spread it around the school before I could blink. I can already imagine her telling everyone she caught me spying on her in the showers, that I tried something on with her, even assaulted her. I've known her for long enough to know she would happily lie if it served her cause. I can picture it now. The whispering, the endless comments, notes through my locker and snide remarks as I walk past, sitting alone at lunchtime as everyone laughs and jeers.

"Come on, Jason. I think you and I need some time alone, don't you?" I say suddenly with a pointed look at Eloise.

I don't know what I'm doing, but my head is telling me to show her, show them all. I grab his hand and pull him from the pool. Eloise watches me, smiling knowingly, challenging me, as though she thinks I won't go through with it.

I lead him like a puppy from the pool house into the cold air outside. It slaps into me, my body responding with aching goosebumps. I guide him over to the bench in the garden. He is practically panting. I push him onto the bench and straddle his lap, letting him touch me, kiss me. His hands grapple at my bikini straps, pull at my bikini bottoms, his surprise and delight making him clumsy and rough.

I'm glad of the darkness. I don't want to think he can see me. I don't want to think anyone can see me. But I have a feeling we are being watched.

The house is glaring at me over my shoulder, the windows wide and unblinking.

I keep my eyes closed. I want the black night to swallow me whole.

I empty my mind, try to take myself away from this place, this moment. I can feel his insistent hands on me, smell the stale beer on his breath. I shudder at the feel of him on my skin. He mistakes it as a sign to carry on.

He pushes me onto my back on the bench. The wood is spiky and rough. He presses his cheek to mine and I can see a lump of wax in his ear, making me want to gag. I close my eyes. I let it happen. I focus on the ringing in my head and the sounds of the party, even though every part of me wants to scream, "STOP!". The song playing is Madonna, 'Like a Virgin'. The irony is not lost on me. I know that I will never be able to listen to this song again.

But I don't say a word. I don't say yes. I don't say no. I let him carry on. He doesn't hesitate. He rushes on as though he's worried I'll stop him at any second.

At one point I see a flash of light behind my eyelids, but I ignore it because I know that if I open my eyes, I will panic and it's too late now. It's happening.

It will be over soon. I sob, but it comes out like a moan. He says, "Yeah baby."

Then it is over. Those few minutes felt like hours. He is slumped on top of me, heavy, sweaty despite the cold, his skin sticking to mine. I can't breathe beneath him. I push him away, fix my bikini top, which is garrotting me, straighten my bikini bottom from where it has been pushed aside, cutting into my skin. My hands are shaking.

I get to my feet, don't look back as I walk straight back into the pool house, my head held high. Knowing eyes turn to me, the word travelling fast on loose tongues. The sounds of the party seem to hush momentarily, but I ignore them all. I climb into the pool and dive underwater, swim as far as I can before my lungs start to burn. I come up for air, turn around and do the same again in the other direction. Then I climb from the water, dripping wet, my hair now plastered to my head and mascara probably running down my cheeks. I find the nearest cup of alcohol and neck it, then go in search of more.

I pass El, who is smirking. "I can't believe you just did that," she says.

"Fuck off, Eloise."

When I come back out of the storeroom with a full cup of vodka, I look over to where Tracey is still sitting on the lounger, her body at a strange angle that does not look comfortable. She tries to get to her feet, but the lounger tips up and she seems to collapse in on herself. She slides into the deep end of the pool, as if in slow motion. People around her start snorting with laughter and pointing.

For a moment I watch, waiting for her to come back up to the surface, hoping to see her laughing at her clumsiness. But she doesn't.

Jason comes up behind me, slides an arm around my waist, his cheeks flushed, his smile wide.

I push him away and take a step forward, peering into the water. I can see Tracey on the bottom of the pool, but she doesn't seem to be moving. A ghastly feeling of dread crawls over my tainted skin as I realise she is not coming back up. I drop the cup, feel the vodka splash across my toes. I dive under the water and swim as hard as I can to where she is floating, her eyes closed. I loop my arms under her armpits and pull her to the surface.

"Help!" I cry out to someone, anyone. Heads turn, disinterested. Someone actually turns the music up.

"Help!" I shout again. "Jason! Jason!" He looks at me vacantly. "Help me get her out!" I am kicking as hard as I can to stay afloat, to keep her head above the water, but I can't keep it up for long. Jason walks around the edge of the pool and leans down to pull her from my arms onto the wet tiles. I pull myself out of the water and check to see if she is breathing. I can feel the panic in my throat.

El's voice carries over to me as she says, "Looks like someone can't handle their drink."

"Jason, can you carry her into the changing room? Please?"

He nods and scoops her up into his arms like a doll. I follow him and lay a towel down on the bench before he lays her on top of it. "Turn her on her side," I say. Her chest is rising and falling, so I know she is breathing, but she is out cold.

"Tracey! Tracey! Can you hear me?"

There is no response. I try slapping her cheek. Nothing. I grab an empty cup discarded on the floor and go into the toilet to fill it with cold water from the basin. I let the water run for a bit to get it as cold as possible.

Then I feel like I'm going to pass out myself. I crouch down, put my head between my legs and breathe deeply for a moment, willing the spinning to stop. It takes a few moments though. The world is on a fast rotation.

By the time I return to Tracey, a little group has gathered around her. El is standing over her with my Polaroid camera, taking photos. It looks like someone has posed her, manipulating her limbs so that she is exposed. She is on her back, her legs splayed, pubic hair sticking out from the bottom of her swimsuit obscenely and one breast falling out of the halter neck top.

Steph and Em are laughing and making faces of disgust.

"El! What the fuck are you doing?" Jason, Brian and the boy Emily has been stuck to all night are standing around, laughing and pointing, posing with their hands on her boob, gyrating obscenely against her and sticking their tongues out as El snaps away like she's the paparazzi.

"Stop it! All of you!" I screech. I rush over to intervene, maybe cover her up, but Steph grabs me and spins me away. I slip on the wet floor and land painfully on all fours.

"Come on Hels, she deserves it! People like her deserve it," El says. Her face is contorted into a mask of frenzied depravity.

Then something clicks into place. The little chat on the lounger. The cup she passed to Tracey. The maniacal grin afterwards. I scramble to my feet.

"Wait, Eloise, what have you done? Did you give her something? Earlier when you were talking? What did you give her?" El doesn't deny it. Just smiles that knowing smile. I want to scratch it from her lips, tear it from her face.

I grab a towel from the side and push past Steph to stand right in front of Eloise, hating her with every fibre of my being. I throw the towel over Tracey. My voice is a low rumble, deep in my throat. "What did you give her?"

"Just some of your mother's happy pills. I guess they didn't make her very happy though."

Eloise steps back and cackles like a witch. Jason is now on the outskirts of the group, looking unsure. He is still smiling, but hesitantly, his eyes flicking from me to Eloise and back to me. Brian is laughing riotously as he looks through the photos El has handed him.

"Oh my god, these ones on the lounger are hilarious. She looks like she's dead!" he says. "I can actually see everything in this one!" He grabs all of the photos and rushes out, Eloise at his heels, saying loudly as a group forms around him, "Come and see these! Oh my god, the fucking state of her!"

I glare at Jason, who has said nothing to his friends while they openly assaulted an unconscious girl. I can't believe I let him touch me. I feel sick to my stomach, dirty. I want to plunge into a bath of bleach and scrub every part of me, rinse the scent of him from my nostrils and the taste of him from my tongue.

Instead, I turn my attention back to Tracey. I'm still

holding the cup of water. Tracey's eyes are flickering behind her eyelids. I splash the cold water on her face and she gurgles in response, then leans over and throws up onto the floor. The smell is acrid and bitter in the air.

Jason dry heaves and leaves in disgust.

He is pathetic.

I am relieved.

I cradle her head as she throws up some more, until she is just retching, dry heaving gulps of air.

It is my turn to stroke her hair this time.

We sit for what feels like hours but is probably only ten minutes or so. The songs change, the noise peaks and rolls, the shouts and laughter grow in volume as the booze takes its toll. No one else comes in.

Eventually I sit her up, hand her some more water and tell her to drink.

"What happened?" she asks, her words slurred and strung together.

"You were sick." The smell of vomit is coating our skin and clinging to our hair. I ask her if she can walk, if she can make it outside.

She leans on me and I help her to her feet, where she sways, as though she is dancing with me to the Wham song that's now playing. I half drag her out of the changing room, ignoring the pointing and sniggering as we make our way to the door of the pool house.

The air outside clouts us. I can see awareness begin to creep back into her eyes as I tell her to breathe deeply. We stand, our arms around each other, swaying in the night air, the sound of the sea barely audible above the thud of the music.

"I'm ok," Tracey says after a moment. "I can't believe I threw up again. You must think I'm such a loser." She bows her head, starts to cry quietly. Her words are still slurred, running into each other, indistinct.

"No, I'm the loser. I didn't look after you."

My skin is alive with goosebumps once more, but now it is sobering.

I'm angry.

Beyond angry.

I don't want to tell Tracey about what El was saying, about Jason, my stupidity with the pills or that El slipped those same pills into Tracey's drink. The photos, taken with my camera. The boys' hands on her body.

She will hate me. She has every right to.

I'm suddenly exhausted. I want everyone to leave. I want to get Tracey up to the house where it is safe, let her sleep it off.

I can see the lights on in the kitchen. Martha is still up, pottering around. She will know what to do.

I walk Tracey over to the garden bench, where only minutes before I was stupendously falling from grace. "Stay here," I say. I run up to the house, feeling naked and sullied in the tiny bikini, the edges of which are stretched from Jason's heavy hands.

I burst into the kitchen, surprising Martha as she sits at the table with a cup of tea and a biscuit, listening to the radio.

"Oh! Helen! You frightened me!" She pauses, then says, "Are you ok?"

"Sorry, Martha, but I need your help. Do you think you could come down to the pool house and tell everyone to leave? It's getting a bit out of hand and I'm scared."

"What do you mean, out of hand? Of course!" She draws herself up to her full five-foot height and storms out of the kitchen in her slippers, her back straight and her shoulders squared.

I remain in the doorway, cowardly, holding my breath and listening intently. The music cuts out abruptly and soon I see bodies scurrying from the pool house like little ants. When the last little ant has fled, I see Martha helping Tracey up the garden.

"Oh dear, oh dear! You didn't tell me there would be alcohol, Helen!" She shakes her head and tuts under her breath. "Let's get both of you up to bed and we'll talk about this tomorrow."

We help her up to my bedroom and I run a hot shower. Tracey is shivering and deathly pale.

"I'll go and lock everything up," Martha says.

"Thanks Martha – and… please don't tell my parents about this."

She looks at me for a moment and I try to read her expression – disappointment maybe, or sympathy? Then she smiles and pats me on the arm before heading back downstairs.

I help Tracey to the shower. "Can you get in yourself? Do you need me to help you?"

"I'm ok, I think. Just feel very sleepy."

"Ok, get in the shower. It'll help."

I leave her for a moment and go into the bedroom to take my bikini off. I bundle it into a ball and throw it in the bin.

I'll never wear it again. I throw on my dressing gown and go back to her when I hear her thin voice call out.

She is wrapped in a towel and sitting on the toilet seat. I perch on the edge of the bath and we sit in silence. I can see she is struggling to stay awake, her eyelids heavy and drooping.

"Come on, let's get you into bed. I can sleep in another room if you want?"

"No, please, stay with me."

She gets up to her feet and the towel gapes open. I look away, Eloise's voice loud in my head.

Once she is in her pyjamas and tucked into bed, I tell her that I think she may have got some sick on me so I'm going to climb into the shower too. She nods, but is already closing her eyes. I close the bathroom door, shed the gown and turn on the taps.

The water is immediately hot and I turn my face to the spray. Then I start to cry, big gulps of air that I swallow down with the water so that she can't hear me. I feel like someone has ripped my insides out, hollow, bruised, thumped.

I sit on the floor of the shower, hunched over, until the water runs cold and I start to shiver.

41

NOW

Helen wanted to laugh. "Don't be ridiculous, Lydia. Now is not the time."

"I'm telling the truth. We argued and I pushed her. She slipped on the tiles, banged her head on the edge of the pool and lay really still. I panicked, didn't know what to do, so I pushed her into the water. I thought someone would think she had had an accident."

Silence fell over the group.

Then Matt said, "So where is she now?"

They looked from one to the other.

"Did any of you think to check her pulse?" Helen said.

Lydia shook her head. "She wasn't moving though."

"I stuck my finger under her nose when I pulled her from the water, but couldn't feel her breath," Mills said.

Helen sighed, turned back to Lydia. "What were you fighting about? Come on, Lydia, it's time you told us what is actually going on."

In a paper-thin voice, she started to tell them about her

relationship with Diana, how Diana had listened to her, understood her, *saw* her. Matt looked stricken as she talked, but said nothing.

She told them about the keys to the shop, how Diana was seemingly obsessed with Helen and her past. "She kept asking me about you, if I knew anything about your school friends, your childhood. I said I knew nothing, but she asked me to find out. I said I didn't want to get involved, wasn't interested, then she said you were having an affair behind my dad's back, had seen you with him, and that you deserved to be exposed for who you really are."

Matt looked sheepish. "I told her that. I saw him here."

Helen ignored Matt. "The genealogy project. That was a lie?" Helen said instead.

"Yes, I was just trying to find out more for Diana. Then I found the diaries. I didn't mean to, but I was looking through the boxes and I knocked one over, which pushed in the panel and the hiding place." Lydia took a shaky breath. "I couldn't see what was so important – with the diaries. I mean, yeah, it sounded like there was drugs, alcohol, that kind of stuff, but I couldn't work out what it had to do with Diana. Or what harm it would do to show her. So I did." The last three words were a whisper.

"Then what happened?" Helen pushed.

"She said she had some photos, of something that happened a long time ago. She said they showed what kind of person you really are – and how you were dangerous." Lydia reached down next to her and picked up a tightly wrapped plastic bag, laid it on the lounger in front of them.

Matt opened the bag and pulled out a pile of Polaroids. Helen knew immediately what they were, but she wasn't expecting the top photograph to be of her and Jason on the bench in the garden. She wanted to rip it from his hands, tear it into tiny shreds.

Matt flicked through them, confused, then tossed them aside uninterested. "I don't get it," he said.

Lydia continued. "She started saying all this stuff about Helen and how her best friend had vanished when they were at school, how it was Helen's fault. She said someone close to her had given her these photos, how they proved that Helen had murdered this girl because of the photos and the party."

"But how? Who?" Helen asked.

Lydia was crying again, her hands wringing in and around themselves. "Then she started telling me how it was only right that Helen paid for what she had done, that she didn't deserve all this money, this house, when others had suffered because of what happened. She said she had been using the photographs to blackmail Helen and would give me a cut of the money. She said she was so proud of me for helping her, that Matt and Mills were both weak, pathetic, unhelpful." She took a shuddering breath.

Matt scowled at the floor. "She did keep asking me about you, Helen, but I ignored it, was too busy trying to get her to like me. I thought it was because you are a writer or something, you know, like a minor celebrity – and then she lost interest in me, moved on to Lydia apparently." He spat the words at his feet.

"I'm sorry, Matt. I thought she loved me," Lydia whispered. "But as I listened to her today, I realised she was just using me. She wasn't interested in me, hadn't seen me at all. She's just as bad as everyone else."

She stopped talking, buried her face in her hands.

"So you lost your temper?" Helen nudged.

Lydia merely nodded.

Helen thought for a moment, working it all out. "But why drag your dad into it? He knew nothing about all of this."

"What do you mean?" Lydia asked in a shaky voice.

"Your dad. She has been blackmailing him for money, threatening to spread rumours about him and underage girls. The photo was a threat."

Lydia looked confused now. "I don't know about that. She told me it was all to find out the truth, to get justice for the missing girl."

"That bitch! He is upstairs now, despairing that his career is over! And for what?"

They all fell silent again. Matt got to his feet, started to pace.

Then Mills said quietly, "So what did happen, Mum? Who are these people? What is the truth?"

42

THEN

When I wake up, it is bright outside the window, the sun more cheerful than I feel. My chest feels like it is trapped beneath something heavy and my head is pounding in sympathy.

Tracey is still asleep, her face turned towards me, peaceful. I have a sudden thought that she is not breathing, so I stick my finger under her nose, relief flooding through me at the wisps of air against the tiny hairs on my knuckles. I lie, watching her, my eyes running over her face, her bottom lip thicker than her top lip, the way her nose slopes up at the very end and the bushy eyebrows that need to be shaped before they meet in the middle. I want to drink her in. This could be the last day we are friends because I know I have to tell her about the pills, the rumours, the photos. She won't want to have anything to do with me after today and I don't blame her.

I already know I will never speak to Eloise again or any of them. Brian, Jason, Steph, Emily – none of them took a stand. They all joined in, laughing, mocking, assaulting her.

The more I think about it, the angrier I get. They deserve to pay for what they did.

I turn to stare out of the small gap where the curtains have parted, the sunlight muscling its way into the room.

I feel Tracey move and I look over. She is lying with her eyes open, blinking. Those eyes, so beautiful, are dulled with tiredness.

"Hey," she says.

"Hey. How are you feeling?"

"Not great. You?"

"Same." I don't know what else to say, how to go about telling her. "I'll go get us some tea."

Martha is already up, bustling about in the kitchen as always. "Oh, you don't look too clever," she says as I shuffle in.

"I don't feel too clever."

"Tea?"

"Please. I'll take it upstairs if that's ok."

She fills the kettle, her back to me. "They made quite a mess of the pool house. I'll have to ask Arthur to come and sort it out, clean up."

I feel shame clinging to me. "I'm sorry. Things got out of hand."

"Well, these things happen sometimes. At least you had the good sense to call me before anything too bad happened. That was very responsible of you."

No, it wasn't. But I can't tell her that. I can't tell her what actually happened.

I take the tea back upstairs, some of it spilling over the

edge and scalding my shaking hands, dripping on the floor and leaving a trail behind me.

Tracey has opened the curtains fully now and is sitting up in the bed, pillows propped behind her, looking out at the water. I pass her the tea and climb back in the other side.

I have to tell her. She can't go into school tomorrow without knowing. It will be torturous anyway. I can guarantee that Eloise will have something planned. I can't send Tracey into it blind. She has to know.

"Tracey, I need to tell you something."

She sips on her tea, sits back against the pillows and exhales. "Oh god, is this when you tell me all the embarrassing things I did last night?"

"No, it's… it's my fault. I… so I've been taking these pills I found in my mother's bedroom. There's a few – I don't know… uppers, downers, sleeping pills, anti-depressants – you name it, she has it. Anyway, I gave some to El last night and she… put some in your drink. That's why you passed out and fell in the pool."

"Wait, I fell in the pool? I don't remember that. All I remember is sitting outside in the cold."

I tell her everything – the taunts that led me to going outside with Jason, coming back to find her slumped on the lounger, the photos, the touching. All of it.

She is silent for a while, her face pale, her eyes wide and scared. Then her eyes narrow. "Where are the photos?" Her voice is cold.

I hadn't thought about that. I hadn't given the Polaroids any thought at all.

And I don't know what I was expecting, but I wasn't

expecting the ice in her voice, the way she shrank away from me, like I was toxic.

"Wait, so you're not upset about the rumours about us?"

"I don't care if people think I'm gay. Rather that than a slut," she says pointedly.

I hang my head in shame.

"You're always so worried about the way people perceive you, the image you portray. I've spent my whole life looking different, feeling different. There are more important things in life, Helen. Like the fact that they assaulted me and took photos. There's evidence and I want it. Where are the photos, Helen?"

"I... I don't know. I came back up to the house with you and sent Martha to shut down the party. I left everything there. They may still be there."

"Or Eloise took them with her. You know she would. To humiliate me." She flings back the covers and gets up. "She could do anything with them. Pass them around. Copy them."

"I guess, but she wouldn't."

"Wouldn't she? She hates me, hates that we are friends, hates that I'm black. She wants to hurt me. Of course she'll pass them around. She will bring them to school tomorrow and—" She starts throwing on her clothes, anger seeping from every pore of her skin. "I need to get those photos. If I have them, she can't use them against me. Instead, I can use them against her, make a complaint, maybe go to the police."

This is now escalating into different territory altogether.

"She doesn't hate you because you're black."

"You are so fucking naive."

"I've heard her make comments, but that's more about finding something to pick on than anything else."

"You're really going to try and defend her, defend any of them? God, you're just as bad, if not worse because you can't even see it."

"No, I – I'm so sorry. I don't know what to say," I say.

"You don't know what to say? Did you think to stop her? Take the camera from her? When have you ever called her up for comments, the digs at me? Never. No, all you did was act just like her by shagging some random bloke and drinking more vodka, taking more pills, while I was being assaulted. None of it will get your parents' attention, you know! All of this. It's like you're determined to self-destruct. I get that you're hurting, but dragging me into the middle of you and Eloise isn't fair. And standing by and watching while they do this? I'll never forgive you."

She can't even look at me as she kicks her legs into her jeans.

I can feel the hot tears dripping from my chin. "I didn't know she was going to spike your drink or take the photos. I did try to stop her when I realised! But Steph, she grabbed me." It sounds lame – and she's right. I should've done more. I should've called them out for all the comments that were said before, all the little digs. "Please, Tracey, you have to believe me. You're the only real friend I have!" It feels like the ground under my feet has opened up and I am falling in.

"A friend? Really? Was I really your friend or just someone you wanted to toy with when your other friends were busy? Was it because I was exotic to you? Maybe you were in on it? How do I know you weren't?"

I can hear the past tense, refuse to accept that our friendship may be over.

I grab onto her arm, my fingers pressing into her skin, leaving rounds of pressure. "What can I do to make you believe me, to make it up to you? Please, I'll do anything!"

She glares at me. "You need to get those photos back. If they aren't in the pool house, call Eloise, tell her to come and meet you. Today. Tell her anything to get her to come here."

I nod. "Ok, yes, I'll call her straight away."

I pick up the phone, feeling sick to my stomach. Eloise's housekeeper answers as usual and I hold my breath as I wait for El to come on the line.

"Hels, what do you want?" No pleasantries from her either.

"El, I need you to come over today, let me explain about Tracey, about what's been going on."

"Why should I? I'm hungover and I want to stay in bed."

I swallow, inhale, think about what she would most want to hear. I turn away from Tracey, my voice low.

"The photos from last night. Where are they? Do you have them? I want to see them. I have an idea – I was wrong about Tracey. I should've had your back, not hers. So I've got something to tell you... about Tracey. A bit of gossip. And a plan I think you'll like, for revenge, but I need the photos first."

There is silence on the other end of the phone. I don't know if she is buying it or not. I hold my breath. Then she says, "Why should I believe you? Last night you were all over her."

"I wasn't – I slept with Jason! That must prove something?"

"It proves you're stupid. I got a lovely photo of that too. Might send that one to your dad." Her voice is vicious.

"Come on, El, it's always been me and you. Best friends forever, right?"

She is quiet again. "What does Tracey have over you?"

"Nothing! I don't even like her. Listen, this idea – for school tomorrow. To get back at her. Please, will you come over?"

I know the promise of gossip, combined with the thought of making someone's life miserable at school, will persuade her in the end.

"Fine, give me an hour."

"I'll meet you at the bottom gate. Bring the photos." I hang up. "She'll be here in an hour."

Tracey nods, then sits on the bed in silence.

"What can I do to make this up to you?" I repeat.

"You can get those photos from her, then leave me the hell alone. I don't want anything to do with you."

We head to the bottom of the garden. The grass outside the pool house is strewn with empty cups, bottles, paper plates and bits of food. Debris that tells a story of teenage debauchery and regrettable carnage, of reputations destroyed and friendships shattered.

I avert my eyes, don't want to see inside the pool house where Arthur is already using a long pool net to scoop cups from the water. I can feel his eyes on me as we walk past.

Judgement everywhere I turn – from Arthur, Tracey, even the house seems to be shaking its head at me, the windows in shadow as though it is looking away.

I open the gate and step out onto the path. The wind is strong, the clouds whipping across a bright blue sky, but there is a crispness to the weak sun. Winter around the corner. The wind picks up my hair and thrashes it against my cheeks. I let it. I deserve to be lashed, stung, pelted with rocks and showered in harsh truths.

Tracey is right. I'm trying to punish myself, self-destruct, give my parents a reason why they were right not to want me.

Tracey sits on the bench further along the path, but I wait by the gate, my eyes scanning the distance, watching for Eloise. Tracey hasn't said anything to me in about half an hour. She has just chewed on her fingernails, her face like a mask, her arms clasped tightly around herself.

Then Eloise is wheeling her bike through the gate, her hair tied in a low ponytail. She pulls up close to me, her cheeks flushed but there are shadows under her eyes, divulging her hangover. "What the fuck is she doing here?"

"She's... I..." I don't know what lie to tell now, but she doesn't wait for one. She drops her bike and stalks over to Tracey, her shoulders back, her mouth loaded.

"There's the lesbian slag herself. Not flashing your tits to everyone today? I have some lovely photos of you, by the way. Some very revealing stuff. I'm sure everyone at school will love to see them."

"Where are the photos?" Tracey's voice is a rumble, like the low growl of a big dog.

"They're safe, don't worry. I'm thinking of making a pretty collage ready for school tomorrow."

Tracey turns on me. "I thought you said she would bring them?"

I recoil from the acid in her words. "I asked her to!"

"What's the matter, Tracey? Worried your pathetic, uninspiring parents will see them? See what you've been getting up to with your girlfriend?"

Tracey launches at her and grabs her by the coat, spins her around. I have a horrible feeling she is going to hit Eloise. Her hands are fists, her teeth clenched. But she lets go of her.

"Do you know what, Eloise? You're not worth it. My parents love me. They know me and would never believe pathetic, childish little rumours from someone like you. You're the pitiful one, doing anything you can to be popular when in actual fact no one likes you. It's all for show. Even Helen, your so-called best friend, doesn't like you anymore. I'm done with both of you. I would hate to be like either of you. You deserve each other. I can still go to the police, make a complaint."

She turns to walk away, but Eloise's voice stops her in her tracks. A menacing rock of apprehension hits the bottom of my stomach. I want to tell them both to shut up, not to egg each other on, but I remain silent.

"And the police would believe you over me? Oh, please! I don't think you get it. It is *you* that should be pitied, not me. You with your constant smell of cow shit on your clothes and your pathetic, working class parents. You can't honestly think Hels wants to be friends with someone like you, do you? She's laughing behind your back along with the rest of us. You should hear some of the stuff she's said about you. You should go back to where you came from."

"No, I—" I start to say, but El talks over me.

"She told me last night that she's not interested in you, just wanted to humiliate you because you won't get the message that she doesn't want to spend time with you. She thinks you're pathetic, that your family are cheap and tragic. She's one of us, not one of you."

Eloise's lip is snarling, her face almost unrecognisable in its bitterness.

Tracey takes a step towards her, her back straight and her shoulders stiff.

But El isn't finished. "She told us about your brother. He's a *spastic*, isn't he? Can't look after himself? Simple in the head? A black spas? That's what Hels says anyway. We had a good laugh at that. Didn't we, Helen?"

"No, I never—"

But Tracey can't hear me over the growl that is coming from her. "You bitch!"

"What are you going to do, Tracey? Hit me? You don't have the balls," Eloise taunts.

Tracey is visibly shaking now. Then her face changes, a serenity seems to wash over it. She looks out to the sea, then back to Eloise and says clearly, "What is it you said to Tina the other day?"

"What?" Confusion flickers.

"The other day before you pushed Tina when the car was coming. You said something." She steps forward and says, "Tell your mother I saved your life."

Then she pushes Eloise hard in the chest. Eloise is propelled backwards towards the cliff edge, with the rocks below and the crashing sea waiting, its mouth open. Her arms pinwheel and I gasp, then reach out to grab her coat. At first there is nothing, just fresh air between us, then my fingers brush her zip and for a second I think I can grab onto her.

But the wind is carrying her over, the seagulls laughing as they watch.

There is a thud.

I step forwards, scared to look, but needing to.

The image of what is below will be forever seared into my mind.

Tracey is standing still, frozen in place, her face blank.

"What did you do?" I say in a tiny voice. "Tracey, what did you do?"

She turns away and walks to the bench, sits down, begins to tremble.

"Oh my god, oh my god," I say over and over again. My feet brush over the scuff marks in the dirt almost without me realising I am doing it.

"We have to do something. Before anyone sees. Before anyone comes." I'm trying to think, trying to scramble together my thoughts.

Her bike, I need to get rid of her bike. Did she tell her parents she was coming here? Would they think anything?

I grab her bike. The bell on the handlebars comes loose and falls to the ground, ringing once mournfully. I drag the bike to the edge and push it over. "Maybe someone will think she has fallen, skidded in the sand and gone over, a nasty accident maybe? Yes, that's what we'll say. No, wait, we won't say anything. We don't know what happened. We were never here. We never saw her. She didn't make it to the house. Tracey, are you listening to me?" I can tell she isn't. She looks vacant, like she has left her body altogether.

I rush up to her, slap her hard. "Tracey, listen to me. We

never saw her, she wasn't here. We stayed inside and you went home. Ok?"

She holds her hand up to her cheek, nods and I hope she is taking in what I'm saying.

"This is all my fault. This is all my fault. I will never tell anyone what happened here. This is all my fault. I promise you, I will never tell a soul," I say.

She nods again.

"This is our secret."

43

NOW

Helen walked over to the loungers, felt the chair shift as she lowered herself down next to Lydia. Then she picked up one of the photos. Tracey, her legs splayed, everything out for everyone to see, the smiling faces of the teenage boys with their big waves of hair and skinny bodies, the cruel girls staring down at her as she lay, passed out, her eyes closed, completely unaware of what they were doing.

"I tried to stop her, grab onto her as Tracey pushed her, but it was too little, too late," Helen said quietly. "But it wasn't me. Sure, I am partly to blame for not standing up for Tracey, the pills that they put in her drink, all of that. But I was seventeen, I made some bad choices."

"Yeah, we can see that." Matt was peering closely at another photo, then tossed it in front of Helen. The photo with Jason. Helen turned it over.

"Tracey, she—"

"Wait, Tracey? The woman who lives in the flat above the bookshop?" Mills asked.

"Yes. God, they hated each other. El was jealous of her, I guess, felt threatened, I don't know. And sure, there was probably a racial element to it – Seahaven was wall-to-wall white privilege. Thank god there were no smartphones then, no social media posts, no Snapchat. Everything could be erased as quickly as it took people to forget, to move onto the next drama. I hoped that was what would happen, but the photos. They were evidence – I had never seen them until recently."

"The plaque…" Mills said.

Helen nodded. "They never found her body."

"So why would Diana blame you?"

Helen shrugged. "I blame me too. It was my camera, my party, my best friend. I might not have pushed her myself, but everything else that led up to it was my fault."

No one said anything, but nor could they look Helen in the eye.

"What happened afterwards?"

"It was awful – the funeral, everything. It's all there in the diaries." Helen indicated the pile of notebooks still lying scattered across the lounger. "I stayed only as long as it took to finish out the school year, then I left. Tracey never really recovered from it. She was a walking ghost. The gossip around school was that she had got herself into drugs, the rumours of her being off her face at the party being the starting point, but I knew what it really was. Guilt, pure and simple. She lost control, a moment of rage. And when I came back to the village, she was still here, still lost. I approached her one day, felt dreadful because she had nothing. Her family had sold off most of the farmland and she was living in the dilapidated, rundown farmhouse, alone. I would see her in the village occasionally when she was buying groceries or visiting the charity shop. One day I started talking to her, a word here, a nod there, until I heard she was finally selling the farmhouse and had nowhere to go. So I offered her the flat above the bookshop. I guess my way of saying sorry for my part in all of this."

Then Matt said, "Ok, but there's something really important we are forgetting here."

They all looked at him.

"Diana. Where the hell is she?"

44

THEN

I expected my parents to return home from their trip early. Martha phoned them to tell them about the disappearance of Eloise March. I know she had to leave several messages before they eventually called back, because I was listening through the walls every time she did. Even so, the disappearance of their daughter's best friend wasn't enough of a draw card for them to cut short their trip.

The one-sided conversation I did hear was Martha promising she had it all under control and that I was doing ok considering (although I was pleased to hear Martha make the point that she thought I would appreciate hearing from them).

They never asked to speak to me. In the six weeks they were gone, they never once called to speak to me.

The police interviewed everyone at the party, but since Eloise had returned home after it and her mother saw her the next morning, albeit with a hangover, the events of that night were not linked to her disappearance. If anything,

Tina was questioned the most after the altercation in the school car park. She had obvious motive. But the other teenagers all clammed up, said nothing, closed ranks. The police had nothing.

The discovery a few days later of Eloise's bike on the rocks below the coastal path led to the assumption that she had fallen by accident while out cycling, possibly due to her hangover making her dizzy. They found the pill bottle in her room, which made it look even more like she was unsteady. The police surmised she may have been on her way to my house to talk about the party, but I told the police I never saw her that morning and had made no plans to. They assumed she never reached her destination.

Apart from some questions about the party, Tracey was not interviewed or asked if she saw El the day she disappeared.

And I have not told anyone.

Tracey has not looked at me since it happened. She keeps her distance, as though I am contagious.

School has been a strange place in the last couple of weeks. Sombre faces and silence for the first few days, our group looking lost where once we would've been the life and soul of the canteen. Now we are the subject of conjecture and rumour, whispers behind backs and sniggering as we walk past. Stories from the party have swirled around, growing bigger and wilder with every murmured word. Brian, Jason, Steph, Emily and I tried to remain together as a group initially, but without Eloise to glue us together, it seemed lacklustre, aimless, and we realised we didn't actually like each other after all. Not enough to stand up to the whispering tongues anyway.

Brian and Jason peeled off to cluster with other boys, probably adding their own versions of what happened to the folklore and bigging themselves up in the process, while Steph and Emily became more of a twosome, playing the grieving friends, wearing black and pushing for the sympathy vote until they had well and truly picked up the mantle of the popular girls in Eloise's absence, while throwing me under the bus in the process. Telling people I had turned on her before she died, that we weren't speaking.

But that's ok. It's no less than I deserve.

I want no part of any of it. I don't care what people are saying about me anymore. I remain alone, looking in, only raising my head when I hear Steph's grating laugh carry across the canteen, inappropriately loud and cheerful in my ears, her ponytail still tied with a black ribbon in solidarity. I sit with my face in a book and pushing a pile of chips aimlessly around the plate. The irony is I have lost my appetite, my weight dropping to where I would've been giddy with joy before.

Be careful what you wish for, right?

Tracey is still friends with Tina to a certain extent, but she is different. Where once she was neat, polite, studious, she now seems unravelled, like someone has pulled on a loose string in her mind. Her hair seems to be thinning in places, gaps now visible in the cloud of curls. Her eyes have lost their sparkle and she prefers to stare out of the classroom window rather than engage like before.

Everyone assumes it is grief.

My parents have returned home in a bustle of suitcases and

slamming car doors. Martha is busying herself with making tea and bringing out slices of homemade lemon drizzle cake while I hover in the hallway, not sure what to say to them.

Do I look different? So much has happened since they left that they must be able to see it on my face. But they don't seem to notice. My mother gives me a brief hug, tells me I am "looking fabulous – have you lost weight?" and my father merely nods and asks how school is going. We sit in the dining room, the cake growing stale on the plates in front of us while my mother chatters about the places they went to and the people they met. My father yawns, requests the newspaper and retires to the lounge. My mother says she needs a rest after the long journey and disappears to her room.

And it is just me again. I go up to the attic, but can't bring myself to write anything more than these diary entries. But my hand shakes uncontrollably as I go through the motions, see the words on the page that make it all true. My handwriting is almost illegible.

I still can't believe El is gone. I may not have liked everything she represented, but I have known her since I was four. It feels like she has left a gaping hole and I am standing on the edge of it, peering down, my toes over the precipice and my body aching to lean forward and fall in with her.

Without El and Tracey, I am completely alone. But that's fine.

I deserve to be.

The house is full as guests from the memorial service eat vol-au-vents and sip on brandy. There are bodies everywhere, sitting on the couch, knees touching; standing shoulder to shoulder in the hallway; handing coats to waiting staff and mingling politely. I have never seen so many people in Eloise's house.

I can see Steph and Emily on the other side of the lounge, both dressed head to toe in black once more for maximum sombre effect. I am also wearing black, but this morning on an impulse I added a cardigan in pink, El's favourite colour. Now my cardigan is standing out like an inappropriately bright neon sign and I regret wearing it.

El's mother is perched on the couch, not moving, staring into space. Her eyes are lifeless and I resist the urge to go and check to see if she is breathing. Then her trembling hand raises the crystal tumbler to her lips and I know she is still with us. People lean down to talk to her, offer their condolences, but she stares resolutely ahead. El's father is working the room, his voice gruff as he networks, thanking people, efficiently ordering the staff to bring more canapes, more tumblers.

I can hear my mother's shrill voice from across the room where she is regaling an acquaintance with tales of her holiday. I cringe as her voice carries. She has come home with renewed energy, all smiles and laughter with my father, but it won't last. He will return to London tomorrow and she will slowly descend into her usual spiral of paranoia, mistrust and chemically enhanced mood swings.

A tray of salmon blinis wafts in front of my nose and my stomach lurches and rolls over. I rush from the room to the downstairs loo, but it is occupied. I can feel vomit rising in my throat. I clamp a hand over my mouth and rush up the stairs to Eloise's room and her en suite bathroom.

I make it just in time before I collapse on my knees and throw up tea and not much else into the toilet. I remain on the cold tiles, breathing heavily, my eyes squeezing mascara drips onto my cheeks.

I have been sick for a couple of days now. Even the smell of toast is turning my stomach. I know what it means, but I can't bring myself to verbalise it yet.

I lift my head and find myself overwhelmed with sadness. The towels on the rail are monogrammed, pink letters on white cotton. Her bottles of expensive shampoo and conditioner line the edge of the bath. The smell of her soap, heady with notes of pear and ginger, rushes at me, mingling with the scent of her matching body lotion, as though she used it that morning and the smell of it is still fragrancing the room. Her hairbrush is balanced next to the basin, long strands of her dark hair clinging to the bristles, her leopard print scrunchy looped around the bright pink handle.

Everything is as she left it on the morning she came to meet me, the morning I tricked her into meeting Tracey. I get to my feet, my legs unstable. Through the door I can see a pile of clothes discarded on her bedroom floor. It is what she was wearing to the party. Flung off drunkenly and never to be worn again.

The bed is unmade, the duvet flung back, releasing her last dream into the air. The pillow is still indented.

My breath hitches into the silence, almost a sob but with no tears. I haven't been able to cry since it happened. It is like my emotions have shut down and I have dried up, like a husk. I walk to her desk, run my fingers over the photos of us pinned tightly to the board on the wall, different places and moments of time, but faces I no longer recognise.

I sit on the edge of the bed, hang my head.

I sense someone behind me and I turn to see Eloise's mother in the doorway. I shoot to my feet, feeling like an intruder. "Um, sorry, I..."

She smiles a little, says, "No, please, sit."

She comes to sit next to me. The air is still, the distant sounds of voices from below muted. Dust dances in the light and my stomach lurches again as it crosses my mind that those particles are little pieces of her, clinging to my hair and face, breathing into my lungs. But I can't move because her mother has reached out and taken my hand, is clasping it tightly, her fingers cold. I take a deep breath, focus on the pressure of her grip.

She says, "You were such a good friend to her. She loved you like a sister, would've done anything for you. You must be feeling so lost right now too." Then in a whisper, she adds, "I miss her so much, I can hardly breathe."

I don't know what to say in return. Everything seems too lame, too insubstantial.

She misinterprets my silence for grief, which it is, but a grief heavily weighed down with suffocating guilt. I want to tell her that it is all my fault, that El died because of me, but by doing that I would break my vow to Tracey and if there is one thing I can do to make amends out of all of this, it's to protect Tracey so that her life isn't ruined too. She doesn't deserve to be punished.

I do.

So I will live with this secret. I will carry the burden of blame.

She pats my hand, then releases it. The bed shifts and she is on her feet, moving out of the room like a ghost.

★

Voices shouting; lips pulled thin; tears falling dramatically. I remain in my seat, quiet, calm, patiently waiting for their histrionics to end. There has been an argument with Martha too. They are looking for someone to blame when really they need to take responsibility. Martha is dismissed unceremoniously, no loyalty to her but she doesn't seem surprised. She is not allowed to say goodbye to me.

My mother sniffs and sobs her way through a box of tissues while my father paces the room, wearing the carpet thin with his anger.

"You will have to get rid of it," my father says to me, his voice thunderous.

I rise to my feet. "I don't think so."

He glares at me. "That is not your decision to make."

"It is my body. It is my child. I want to keep it."

"While you are under this roof, young lady, you will do as you are told. You are not eighteen yet."

I glare back at him, not prepared to back down on this. I have thought about it long and hard since I peed on a stick and had my suspicions confirmed.

"No, you are not getting your way this time either."

My mother's head shoots up. "What do you mean?"

"I found your letters. I know." I raise a shaking finger, willing it to steady and point at him. "You never wanted me. You wanted her to have an abortion, but she didn't."

"Don't be ridiculous. You're acting like the child you are." But he can't look at me.

"That's why you've never taken any interest in me. Because you never wanted me in the first place. And you."

My finger turns its attention to my mother, now dangerously pale. "You have spent the last seventeen years wishing you'd chosen differently, haven't you? Because you made a choice between him and me, and you think you chose wrong, have done everything you can to make it up to him, but forgetting about me in the process."

"Now you sound like the spoilt little brat you are. We have given you everything – clothes, money, a top-notch education. Anything you need, we have provided and this is how you repay us," he says righteously.

"Everything except love and attention!" I can hear my voice rising, the scream building behind the words. "I didn't want all this stuff. I wanted your *love*."

"So you've gone and got yourself knocked up like a little tramp, just to get my attention? That just proves you are far too immature to raise a child." He stands in front of me, his hands on his hips, his eyes blazing. "Who was it?"

"Who was what?"

"The boy! Who was the boy?"

"I'm not telling you."

He steps closer to me, until he is so close I can smell the stale coffee on his breath, feel the heat of his anger sear my skin. "I will find out. It is not hard in a small village like this. Someone will know. And then I will make sure he is finished. Do you hear me? Or you can have the abortion, carry on with school and we will talk no more about it. Your choice. But if you keep it, you are out, today, without a penny. Do you understand? I don't want you here any longer. I can't bear to look at you."

I look at my mother, but she looks away.

She has chosen her side.

Cold steel against my skin. Searing pain. Scalding tears. Cramps that feel like I am tearing in two. Bright lights that remain, even after I have closed my eyes. The smell of disinfectant attaching itself to my hair, lingering for hours afterwards.

My mother sits beside me in the car, silent. She has said nothing to me, can't even meet my eyes. Even now when I am openly crying, when I need her to reach out and hold my hand or comfort me, she says nothing. She just stares out of the car window as Arthur drives us home. The sky is a dull grey, the rain splattering against the window. It is over now, but the pain will remain with me.

I will never tell Jason. He can never find out.

We pull up outside the house and wait as Arthur opens the gate. The house stares down at me, menacingly large, casting a shadow over the driveway. We drive into the gloom and I feel the house judging me, one more on the list of the disappointed.

A shiver runs through me as I stare up. My mother climbs from the car, but I don't want to get out, go inside, live there a second longer. I have to though, for now.

But when this school year is over, I will leave this place, happily turn my back on this poisoned house and never come back.

45

NOW

A loud crash ripped through the air.

Helen froze, then rushed out of the pool house. She halted on the grass, unsure what she was looking at initially. The long, stained glass window looked sunken in and it took her a moment to realise it was shattered. Beyond the jagged bits of glass she could make out shapes, bodies wrestling and fighting, male voices shouting.

"Hugh?"

Matt came up behind her. "Dad!"

They ran up to the house and burst through the kitchen doors. Helen could hear grunting and panting. At the top of the staircase, dancing across the shards of glass, were Hugh and Peter, throwing punches and kicking out at each other like children.

"Hugh! Peter! Stop!"

Peter stopped in mid-punch and turned his face to Helen, only for Hugh to land a slap across his cheek, then they started again. They were now halfway up the stairs and Helen shouted again, begging them to stop.

She turned to Matt. "Matt, get Lydia and Mills out of here. I'll sort this." Matt looked unsure, but for once did what he was told and shuffled them into the lounge, closing the door behind them.

The men paused in their assault, panting and sweating.

"Peter, why are you still here?" Helen said.

"He just came at me! I was about to leave, but he threw himself at me like an animal." Peter's voice was squeaking.

"Get out of my house! I've paid you enough," Hugh growled. "You're not getting another penny."

"You owe me – I've lost everything!"

"Leave my wife alone! She's mine!"

"I'll tell everyone about her!"

And they started again.

Helen was getting annoyed.

"Hugh, I am not yours! You do not own me! And Peter, get over yourself," Helen shouted. "Do you really think anyone will care? So I had an affair. Big deal! So has half this village! You've lost more than me. Your wife, your family, future jobs if this comes out. No one would believe your story about me sexually harassing you. Even Sally didn't! I bet I wasn't the first pathetic housewife you've picked up and I won't be the last."

"You're right. I should've been paying you, because you are just a little whore," he said bitterly.

Hugh roared in a fury Helen had never seen from him before. He stepped forward and pushed Peter away hard. Peter was knocked backwards off balance, his arms pinwheeling to remain upright, and Helen had a moment of complete déjà vu before he toppled backwards towards the broken window.

Then there was silence. Helen stared with disbelieving eyes at the sight of Peter impaled on a jagged shard of glass, blood seeping from his chest where it had pierced all the way through his chest, turning the glass from red to black. He had a look of utter disbelief on his face, shock draining the colour from his skin. For a moment he squirmed, his hands flailing loosely. He looked at his chest, then at Helen, then back to his chest as though it would magically correct itself.

His face was ghostly pale, depleted of all blood, which was now pooling and dripping onto the stairs.

Helen was the first to move. She rushed over to him, but didn't know what to do. She crouched in the blood, her hands held out uselessly.

She could see the life seeping out of him. His body slumped in on itself and she heard his last slow breath, like a sigh. He died with a look of astonishment on his face, as though he had spent his last moments wondering how his life had come to this.

Hugh sat heavily on the stairs and started to mutter into his hands.

"Dad?"

Matt stood at the foot of the stairs, looking up at the carnage.

"Matt, it was an accident. A horrible accident. Go and check on the girls. Now," Helen said.

"Dad!" Hugh ignored him. He turned his shocked face to Helen. "Helen? What should I do?"

"Matt, it's ok. I've got this. Go on."

He backed away, his eyes swivelling to the sight of the body impaled on the glass.

"Hugh, we need to think. Help me," Helen said with urgency. Here she was, covering over the marks in the dust once more. "We could say self-defence. He attacked you in your own home. You fought back. He fell. Help me get him down, so that it looks like we tried to help him at least."

Hugh was sitting and looking at his hands like Macbeth.

"HUGH!"

He jumped, looked at Helen vacantly, looked away again, still muttering unintelligible words.

"Hugh, think of Lydia! She is downstairs. Help me."

At the mention of Lydia, he got to his feet, swayed a little and Helen worried he would fall too, then he seemed to pull himself together enough to help Helen lift Peter and lay him on the carpet. There was so much blood and Helen could feel herself starting to lose her grip on reality.

Hugh inhaled a long, shuddering breath into his lungs. "Go and check on the kids, take them outside," he said, sounding a little more like himself. "I will take care of this."

Helen nodded, relieved that someone else could finally take over. She hesitated, then stepped over Peter's arm. For a second she had a sudden conviction that she would feel his fingers clamp onto her ankle. Like in the movies where the villain was never dead. But that didn't happen. He wouldn't be grabbing anyone ever again.

Helen pushed open the lounge door. Matt, Mills and Lydia sat together on the couch, their arms around each other, staring into space, no one talking. Clive was cowering in his bed in the corner. He always hid from loud noises. Fearless he was not.

"Helen, are you ok?" She was touched by Matt's concern. "Is Dad ok?"

"Erm, yes, your dad is sorting it out and calling the police."

"Let me go and help him," Matt insisted.

"No, Matt. Leave him."

He said nothing else, but his eyes fell on her hands and the red stains she hadn't wiped away. He started to weep quietly and she went to him, wrapped her arms around his broad back. He leaned into her, shuddering. Helen ignored the grunting and groaning sounds coming from the hallway, but she could imagine Hugh wrestling with the body.

What the hell was he doing?

"Mum, what's going on? Matt said Hugh and Peter were fighting?" Mills asked. She was trying to see over Helen's head.

Before Helen could answer, her phone pinged in her back pocket. The spell with Matt was broken and he pulled away, swiped at his eyes, went to sit in the far corner in embarrassment.

Helen looked at the message.

LET'S PLAY A GAME. COME AND FIND ME. HOT OR COLD.

Diana. Helen had forgotten about her. She shot to her feet.

"She's here. In the house. I want all of you to go outside. Now."

"But—"

"I mean it, Mills, go outside and wait for me there. Diana is in the house somewhere and I don't know how dangerous she is. Matt, please? Take them."

He nodded and shepherded them out of the lounge. Helen stepped into the hallway. Hugh was gone, a trail of slick blood signalling that he had dragged Peter into the basement. The basement door was still open. She stepped towards it, but her phone pinged.

COLD.

She turned back to where a dark red stain on the carpet was all there was to prove that Peter had been here, had died here, that it hadn't been a bad dream. She stepped over it and continued up the stairs.

At the foot of the next staircase, she listened closely, but there was only silence. Her phone chirped again.

GETTING WARMER.

She climbed up to the next floor and pushed open her bedroom door. The room was empty.

That left the attic.

She moved back into the hallway, saw the staircase was lowered.

She took a deep breath and climbed the stairs.

Diana sat in the one remaining bean bag, her legs crossed, a picture of relaxation. Tracey had sat in that very spot once. Helen felt like time had converged on her, the past and the present colliding irreversibly.

Blood had dried on Diana's forehead, but her hair was still wet, sticking to her cheek with either blood or water, or a combination of the two, and her mascara made a Halloween mask of her face.

"So you survived then?" Helen said.

"Disappointed?" Diana said. Her voice sounded slurred, like she had been drinking.

"Yes." Helen stayed where she was, just at the top of the stairs, wary. "So who told you about that day? Was it Eloise? Tracey?"

"You mean you still haven't worked it out?" Diana snorted. "This is all about you and how you don't see what is right in front of you, so I am not surprised. Someone who used to be close to you told me about the photographs a while ago."

Helen pulsed quickened. "But Eloise was dead. I saw her, lying on the rocks... She couldn't..."

"Not Eloise. You're right, she was dead where you left her."

"So who? Tracey?"

Diana started to laugh hysterically.

Helen waited patiently.

"Martha."

Helen recoiled, as though a hand had slapped her. "Martha?"

"Yes, Martha, my grandmother – who was unceremoniously fired when your parents found out what had happened while they were gone, about the party, the baby. She lost everything – her job, her home, you who she loved like a daughter – and all because she was loyal to you.

She covered it up, never told anyone that Eloise came to the house the next day."

"Martha knew? She saw her?" Helen's voice was tiny.

"Apparently Eloise knocked on the door and Martha let her in that day. She was looking for you, wanted to give you an envelope, asked Martha to give it to you after she had seen you. Martha couldn't understand why she didn't just give it to you herself, but she insisted, so Martha tucked them in the kitchen drawer. Then Eloise went to meet you and was never seen again. Martha never gave you the photos because when the police came to interview you, she opened the envelope and realised they gave you a motive for killing Eloise. It broke her heart, but she took the photos home and hid them so that they wouldn't be incriminating. All for you. A girl who wasn't even her own daughter."

Helen thought back to those dark days after it had happened, how she had locked herself away until her parents got back, how she assumed Martha would just think she was worried about Eloise. And Martha had kept her distance. Leaving food on a tray, not speaking to her much. It wasn't that she was giving her space; it was because she thought she was guilty.

"Then she was fired when your parents found out, lost her job, her income, everything, without so much as a thank you from you or your parents for all the years of service."

"Where is she now? Is she ok?"

Diana looked like she was about to cry. "She has dementia. Most days she doesn't know who I am, but she talks about you all the time. Calls me Helen more often than not. She thought I was you when she told me about the photos, told me how she had kept them a secret for you all this time, said it was time you had them. I've cared for her for the last few years when everyone else abandoned her and all she can talk about is *you*. Someone who probably hasn't thought about her in years. All she talks about is how your parents never loved you, but she did. How she wished you had been her real daughter."

"So why bring it up now? Why go to all of this trouble to torment me?"

"Because I can't care for her any longer. I have to move her into a home, but I can't afford it."

"So you what? Hoped to blackmail Hugh, then decided to try it with me?"

"Hugh wasn't supposed to be involved. I left the photo for you – I thought that was your office, not his. Then he was involved, so I made the best of it."

A thin trail of blood ran from her wound, past the corner of her eye, and she wiped at it, smudging it so that it left a smear.

"Hugh thought someone from his school was setting him up! He turned to online gambling to raise the money you asked for! He's a wreck, thought his career was over. Gave you all of his savings. That's on you!" Helen spat the words at her.

"Whatever, I don't care."

Helen's phone began to ring, but she ignored it.

"So it's about money after all, not the truth or the people involved. Just money."

"That might not mean much to you, since you have so

much of it, but it means a lot to me. And now that I have been left for dead by your precious stepdaughter, I will finish the lot of you off. You're all as toxic as each other, only caring about yourselves."

"Leave Lydia alone. She has done nothing to you."

"Oh, come on Helen, she tried to kill me."

Helen's phone rang again, then stopped. Then pinged. Helen finally looked at it. A text from Mills.

GET OUT OF THE HOUSE!

Helen frowned, then smelled the smoke wafting up through the stairwell. She had a fleeting moment to think, to realise she had a choice. She looked at the bitter, twisted human in front of her, slumped in a bean bag proudly smiling at her wickedness, blood snaking down her face, someone who had spent months torturing and manipulating her family, and she knew what she had to do.

"You know, Diana, I think you've brought this on yourself."

Helen felt surprisingly calm. She stepped backwards towards the stairs, muscle memory knowing exactly how far each step was, and was down the stairs and lifting the ladder up, securing it with the bolt on the outside before Diana could struggle out of the suffocating bean bag.

The smoke was stronger now, acrid. It curled in front of her eyes and around her hair. Helen heard thuds above as Diana stomped and pulled on the attic trapdoor. It was locked from the outside, She was going nowhere. She ran past her bedroom door. The air was thicker here, pungent, and she could feel her eyes smarting.

Someone was calling her name.

It was Hugh. The further along she went, the thicker the smoke became. She rushed towards Hugh's voice, pulling her shirt over her mouth, feeling the smoke steal her breath regardless. The heat was making her sweat. Hugh was standing at the foot of the stairs. She made it down and fell into him.

Flames licked up through the basement door and smoke obscured everything. The wallpaper around her was bubbling and curling, the house withering as it was engulfed. The old floors started to creak and groan, as if in pain.

The house was dying.

Hugh and Helen surged towards the kitchen and made it out onto the grass where Matt and Lydia were huddled together, their eyes wide, staring at the house.

"Where is Mills?" Helen screamed. "Where is she?"

She heard a loud but muffled thump behind her as something in the house exploded and flames started to lick at the ground floor curtains.

"I think she went in for Clive," Matt said.

Helen screamed and ran for the house, but Hugh held her back. "No, I'll go!"

Helen watched him run in. Her eyes were drawn to the attic window, to the face peering out. She looked away.

"Diana!" Lydia screamed and pointed. "Someone has to save her!"

Helen looked at Lydia, then said calmly, "Matt, stay here with Lydia. I'll go and save her." She ran back inside.

*

The air was impenetrable with toxic smoke and Helen struggled to breathe or see. She could hear barking coming from the family room. Tears streamed down her cheeks. The fire had now caught in the kitchen and the curtains were alight, tea towels, table cloth, anything flammable was now on fire. Everywhere she turned, there were flames flicking at her, teasing, taunting, grabbing onto her. She covered her mouth with her sleeve and pushed through the kitchen door into the hallway. The fire was spreading rapidly here too.

She had no intention of going up to the attic. But she did want to find Mills. She kicked the family room door open and found Clive quivering on the couch.

"There you are, big boy, come here." She reached down and hauled him into her arms, all 30kg of him, but to her he felt as light as a feather.

She battled back the way she had come and burst outside. Matt ran over and took Clive from her, grunting with the exertion.

Helen could see Hugh on the second floor, still searching for Mills. She ran back inside. The staircase was now almost completely engulfed, the ageing curtains and old carpet helping to fuel the raging flames. The house screamed in agony around her. Helen tried to fight her way up the stairs, screaming Mills' name as loud as she could, but she heard nothing in return other than the angry roar of the fire.

She couldn't breathe. It was like the walls were closing in on her, the house slowly engulfing her, consuming her, taking her with it. Even now, it wouldn't let her go, wouldn't loosen its grip on her. This was her penance, the price she was going to pay for all the lies, all the hurt.

She wanted to lie down, let it take her.
Finally, after all these years, the house had won.
She was so tired.

46

AFTER

Helen unlocked the door to the shop, but kept the lights off. She breathed in deeply, taking joy in the familiar smells, the thickness of the air, the reverent muffled silence that a room full of books brings. She had missed this place so much.

She made her way to the desk and sat on the stool.

The plastic hospital bracelet on her wrist rubbed against her skin.

She waited.

She knew she would come.

The door jangled as it opened, letting the night in for a moment.

Helen flicked on the lamp on the desk and weak light cut through the shadows.

Tracey pushed her hair from her face. She was thin, her skin no longer luminous and smooth, now sallow and lined. Her front tooth was missing, words a breathy lisp. Her arms were pinned to her waist, the sweatshirt she was wearing stained down the front. Ketchup maybe.

"Why am I here?"

"It's time for you to go."

"I don't understand."

"It's all over. The story is told. We are done."

Tracey released her arms. Her hands were sunken into the sleeves of the sweatshirt.

"Who knows?"

"No one. And that's how it will stay." She handed Tracey the bicycle bell, now mangled and charred. "You can stop now. Enough."

Tracey nodded once, then shuffled from the shop.

Helen closed the door on the police and exhaled. The last few months had been brutal, both physically and mentally, but she was ok. They were ok. She poured the remaining milk down the sink as she wiped away the tears that she had forced out – enough to make them believe her, but not so much that they were dubious.

Mills came into the kitchen. "So is that it? It's over?"

Helen turned and held out her arms to her and Mills folded into them. "I think so," Helen mumbled into her apple-scented hair.

Helen started to cough and turned away from Mills, her lungs burning.

"Ok?" Mills asked.

"Yeah, fine," she replied with a wan smile.

They sat at the breakfast bar in the tiny flat above the

bookshop. The streets below were quiet. No cheerful school activity; no rattling kegs being rolled into the pub; no rubbish trucks or car noise or clattering cups from the tea shop.

The town and the whole country had been in lockdown for the last few weeks because of the global pandemic and, if asked, Helen would say that it had come at just the right time.

It was only later that Helen learned how close she had come to losing Mills in the fire.

Hugh admitted to her that he had set the fire in the basement next to the cantankerous boiler, propping Peter's body up unceremoniously next to it.

Mills had run down to the pool house to gather up the notebooks and photos, conscious that they were left lying out in the open and aware that Diana could be anywhere. When she returned, the house was alight. She recognised the opportunity for what it was and had rushed into the house with the tote bag. She had thrown it into the basement where the flames were building rapidly, licking up the stairs already. She had wanted to destroy all of it, but then found herself trapped, eventually backed into a corner of the lounge by the smoke and flames. It was only Hugh's bravery that had saved her.

But it was Matt that had saved Helen.

There was a connection there after all.

When the fire was finally extinguished, the bodies of both Peter and Diana were discovered. The story that made its way to the ears of the police was that Peter had set the fire in a jealous rage to get back at Helen and had died when he was trying to escape. Diana was merely a victim, Matt's girlfriend in the wrong place at the wrong time, unable to escape in time.

Helen was in hospital for most of the investigation, recovering from burns to her legs and severe smoke inhalation.

The house was destroyed, but the insurance pay-out meant that Helen and Mills could rebuild it the way they wanted to and it would remain in the family for future generations. The pool house was all that was left after the inferno – and Helen had made sure it stayed with the new house design, but with the ivy stripped back so that it was a light and open space.

The local community rallied around Hugh and Helen in their hour of need, finding the family a place to stay, clothes, provisions, anything for such pillars of the community. Then, just as Helen was about to be discharged from hospital, rumours circulated of a lockdown coming. Hugh made the decision to move to Brighton so that Matt and Lydia could be closer to Francesca. His marriage to Helen was over anyway.

The night that Helen arrived home from the hospital, Tracey walked to the very spot where Eloise had fallen and threw herself over into the sea below. A dog walker found her body a few short hours later.

She had no dependents, no one to miss her, no life to leave behind.

The police had just called around to say there was no evidence of foul play. It would be ruled as suicide. "I'm sorry about Tracey," Mills said quietly. Clive nuzzled at her hand, demanding her attention.

Helen shrugged. "I don't know what to say or feel, to

be honest, other than what a waste of a life. All of it such a waste. She just couldn't live with herself any longer." She took a deep breath. "It's done now. It's over."

Mills nodded. Helen clicked on the kettle and the rumble of boiling water filled the silence.

"So, Zoom quiz with Hugh tomorrow night – have you got your questions ready?" Helen said.

Mills smiled. "Yes, I'm going to do a Noughties music round and one about Star Wars films."

Helen laughed. "You're mean! Hugh won't know anything!"

"He always does a really hard history round, so it serves him right. And Matt with his ridiculous art history questions – seriously!"

Helen peered in the fridge. "Agh, there's no milk. Could you pop out and get some, please? Thanks – wear a mask!"

Helen listened, then walked over to the window to make sure she was gone. Mills walked quickly over to the shop on the corner of the square, the mask obscuring her face.

Helen walked down the stairs and let herself into the shop. It was in darkness, but she knew where it was. She pulled open the bottom drawer of the desk and took out the locked cashbox. Hidden in plain sight. She quickly headed back upstairs to the flat. She fiddled with the numbers on the combination lock until they aligned correctly and the box opened.

Inside was one more notebook.

She flicked through it, reading the messy, slanted handwriting, nowhere near as neat and legible as her other fictional diaries, the ones she wanted everyone to find.

But this notebook wasn't meant for reading. It was

merely an exercise in therapy at the time, a need for Helen to get the truth out of her head and onto paper so that she could move on, function normally, not turn into a walking shadow like Tracey had.

Her eyes glossed over the sentences, how they detailed what really happened that day.

How it wasn't Tracey that had lost her cool.

It was Helen that had reacted to Eloise mocking Tracey's brother and her family, her constant racial slurs and taunting.

It was Helen that had said, *"Tell your mother I saved your life,"* before pushing Eloise backwards over the edge.

It was Helen that had felt a sense of relief as she watched the body plummet onto the sharp rocks below.

And it was Tracey that had kept quiet all this time out of gratitude and love, yet consumed by guilt at the same time.

Helen tossed the notebook into the sink, then grabbed some matches from the drawer.

She smiled to herself as the pages curled and turned to ash.

No one needed to know. Mills was happy – and that made Helen happy.

Except when she closed her eyes.

Because then, all she could see were two faces at the attic window.

Two bullies.

Eloise and Diana.

The faces she had never intended to save.

Acknowledgements

This book was written when the world was a strange place. Actually, I take that back. When isn't the world a strange place? But those oddities and eccentricities, weird stories on the news and international lockdowns plant story seeds that grow into books like this one.

This book was written more in isolation than any of the others and yet, despite being physically separated, I have had the absolute privilege of a team of people behind me, pushing me on, championing me, and supporting me all the way, so I have not felt alone.

Thank you to my agent Jo Bell as always – for the chats about not just the book and how far off deadline I am, but also about our common love of dogs and Peloton rides.

Thank you to my editor Thorne Ryan for picking this book up midway and running with it with enthusiasm, and to Hannah Smith for starting the journey with me.

Thank you to the team at Head of Zeus and Aria for the gifs, memes, posts and shares, enabling my little stories to spread far and wide.

Thank you to my readers, both new and old. I hope I have suspended reality for you for a little while and I appreciate you spending your precious time on my little stories.

Thank you to my family for the Zoom quizzes, laughs and endless cheerleading from afar.

And thank you most of all to Ted, Paige and Erin. My world. My muses. My inspiration.

About the Author

DAWN GOODWIN's career has spanned PR, advertising, publishing and healthcare, both in London and Johannesburg. A graduate of the Curtis Brown creative writing school, she loves to write about the personalities hiding behind the masks we wear every day, whether beautiful or ugly. What spare time she has is spent chasing good intentions, contemplating how to get away with murder, and immersing herself in fictitious worlds. She lives in London with her husband, two teenage daughters and British bulldogs Geoffrey and Luna.